OVERWORLD

C.A. Allen

Novels of Arborand by C.A. Allen:

A Dewdrop Away

Dewdrop Prequel Trilogy:
Flight
Fall
Overworld

Dedicated to you.

PROLOGUE

The running squirrel was going somewhere, there was no doubt about that.

Whether her tracks led her to fortune or something more grisly, the silent watcher did not yet know. Not that that bothered her. It was hard to know all in the beginning. She would have to slake her curiosity, at least until she caught the offending squirrel and made her answer a few of her more pressing questions.

The watcher had travelled for nights, and several days as well behind this squirrel, and she knew that wherever she was going, it must be somewhere worthwhile. She could think of no other explanation for the static, flailing steps of the other, for her incaution and for the sounds which sometimes emitted from the bundle she was carrying.

A child, the follower had at first surmised. But something made her doubt. The way the running squirrel held the bundle was strange; she always carried it held out at a distance from her body when she could help it, and the pursuer knew enough of children and how most favored them to think this odd. So much was strange about this, though. She could not be sure. And so she followed.

It had been three nights and three days, to be exact, and the running squirrel had done nothing but run. Soon she would fall, and when she did, her pursuer would be ready.

So she waited. The runner lasted much longer than she'd estimated she would. Sometimes she'd stop in some wooded area, turning about in the same spot and staring wide-eyed all around her—during these times, her pursuer had to stop and hide herself well enough not to be detected, though she needn't have worried. The squirrel she followed was so distracted, so, in a word, *mad* by now that it was unlikely she would have noticed a thing if the follower came out now and took what she wanted—not until it was too late, that was. So they ran, one after another, through thicket and thorn, across rock and stream.

It was on the fifth day that the runner fell, and on this day also that her hidden adversary came into the light.

CHAPTER I

"Oh, very good. Very *good.*"

The second time that Rin's body hit the ground, she felt her bones connect with the rock below her and instinctively rolled herself up in a tight ball, gasping.

It was the wrong thing to do in the presence of Yassar Krimpt. Sidling over to her, her stared down his nose at her prone form, his hot black eyes never swaying. The orange eye paint covering his face reminded her of the pounding now in her limbs, a hot black pain that would not let up.

"Rin of the seventh layer," Krimpt said, her name sounding like so much charcoal on his tongue, "Why do you fall?"

You pushed me, the young chipmunk was tempted to say; if she were a fool like her brother Morgil, she might have. But instead she maintained her silence, biting down on the rage that buckled inside of her. Every day it was the same. You would have thought that the elders would have found a better way of enforcing their will—those like Krimpt and several of the other Yassars were cruel enough to incite violence to the wrong ends in several of the less discerning chipmunks they trained. But then, maybe they were easier with their other charges. There were times, in the sweat between exercises, in the glimpses of inactivity, that she swore Krimpt regarded her with something like respect. This, in the end, was what kept her here, falling again and again at the mad Yassar's paws, barely restraining herself from jerking his whip from him, taking his power and meting out punishment on him for tangling with her. It was training, and only that.

Rin got up, spitting the grit from her mouth as she did so, and faced Krimpt.

"I fall because I am off guard," she said, around the taste of soil in her teeth and under her tongue. She waited, keeping her eyes level with the Yassar's burning black ones. Eventually, he looked away as she knew he would. They'd played this game before.

"And weak," the Yassar said. He waited, half-turned away from her. The room they occupied with its sound-proof dirt walls and its low, root-infested ceiling, swayed in Rin's vision for a second, but she kept control. She had to keep control. Krimpt was waiting.

"And weak," Rin agreed.

"Hmm," Krimpt breathed, as though in thought, but she was not fooled. When he turned again to attack, she ducked his paw and sank her teeth into his arm. Krimpt staggered back, flailing his whip at her unprofessionally. She ducked that, too, and rolled up against the wall, feeling her bones make contact with the rocks in the ground again. The pain felt sweeter now, like victory.

"Adequate," Krimpt conceded over the pounding of blood in her head. She realized with a pang that it was over, that he would not strike out at her again. Krimpt rolled his whip up into a thin coil, tucking it into the belt at his waist, eyes elsewhere already. He was panting slightly, where Rin's limbs ran liquid silver with the exertion.

"Time for you to be getting back to your level," Krimpt said slyly. She whipped around and stared at him, but his face remained noncommittal.

"It's only a drill," he said at length, staring at her condescendingly. "You must know that."

"I'm not stupid," Rin muttered, though sometimes she wondered. When the Yassar turned to leave, Rin remained in the spot she was, adrenaline slowly fading, running out from her limbs, her beating heart.

It was just a drill. Rin knew this, and yet she wished for it to be more. It was the most excitement she'd had in days, and if it was wrong to wish for violence, a heated fight to the death, well, she was very wrong indeed.

They would need her in time, though. They knew it. She knew it. It was the reason for the Yassar training her and the other Yassars training the thousands of other chipmunks they'd selected for this particular mission. They were preparing, already, for when the undying queen Somnia woke from her daze and told them, *go*. That would be all it took. Already they were preparing.

Rin remembered the day the flare was seen. There had been a disturbance at her door, and she had heard her father open it. She'd been playing taproot with Morgil, but both of them ceased at the sound of the stranger's voice panting, "We've been attacked! First level, there's a fire!"

Her father had gone immediately to see the truth of it, but when he returned and they clamored to ask him about it, he only said that it had been put out before he arrived.

"But it was there, no doubt about that. There was smoke flooding the corridor. I could hardly see." She remembered him, then, fixing her with a severe look. "Rin, the elders say they know who did it."

"Spearo the crazy? He should be locked up with Chamblis—"

Her father cut her off in a rush. He wasn't a fan of her blasphemy, especially where it might draw the queen's attention.

"No, Spearo did not do this. This is the fault of those above us."

Rin had only stared at him at first, unsure if he was kidding them. Those above, though everyone knew they existed, seemed more of a fiction than anything else to her mind then. She'd heard about the one who had come down into their land, about the strange power he was supposed to hold, and how he'd somehow gone to the queen's mad son Chamblis and survived. No one survived when Chamblis decided they needed to die, and no one could understand how he'd let someone from the upper world go.

The elders were alarmingly close-lipped about it. They would never hear from anyone in the overworld again, that was all the lead elder had shared with them, his mouth twitching oddly at one corner as though he doubted the words coming out of his own mouth. *He'd* seen the intruder from above. She remembered her jealousy upon realizing that; what did someone from above look like? She decided, later as she passed all of the bodies that had been injured or killed—in the case of two—by the flames, that whatever they looked like, they were nothing like her own. The Yassars were introduced shortly thereafter, and ever since, they'd gone from burrow to burrow asking to see all who lived inside. From her burrow, Rin was chosen. She remembered opening the door on Yassar Krimpt, a face that would become infinitely familiar to her in the next few days.

Krimpt had walked into the house, a slight swagger to his step, not bothering to ask her father for permission. Her father looked like he couldn't have cared less, but she thought, in retrospect that he must have been holding his breath. Krimpt reached out for her, and at first she flinched before steeling herself, ready to fight. He smiled.

"What is her name?"

"Rain," her father answered promptly. "Though we call her Rin." The other's skeptical brow lowered. "Her father...the one before me, that is...he was a little..."

"Yes, we are familiar with him," the Yassar said in a bored voice. He turned for the door, and then looked back at them. "I'll take her," he said, and swished his way out.

He left them all standing there, her father ecstatic, her in shock, but it took her a while to even register Morgil standing next to her, where he must have been all along.

"He didn't even look at me," Morgil said. They hadn't talked to each other once since then, but it wasn't through any fault of hers. Morgil was only jealous because she was the stronger, the faster, the braver. The fittest went to war, everyone knew it, and her brother was a damn fool.

Her mother had come back to the burrow a long time after the Yassar left, at which time her father did not waste his opportunity to detail her on what had happened on her absence. She'd glowed over at Rin, and Morgil had muttered something under his breath. Rin had to focus all of her will power on keeping from hitting him. She had bigger things to worry about.

In the days to come, the Yassar would drag her up to the room in which they would stage several mock battles in preparation for an attack, if their queen wished it. He would use the whip he carried, or a small knife, or even his teeth, switching the attacks up constantly so she wouldn't know what to expect. He was serious about it, too; if Rin slipped up, she was dead. In the beginning, her limbs froze and she kept thinking of what would happen if she made a mistake, but as time went on, she grew to ignore this line of thought, all lines of thought. One couldn't afford to think when doing battle. The rush of excitement on seeing the whip snake towards her, even in feeling it cut across her belly, as it had done once when she hadn't moved quick enough, excited the neurons in her body to terrifying heights.

Krimpt knew she was getting good; she could see it in the way he regarded her now, supercilious yet calculating. From each new hurt, she rose again and came at him, and twice she'd given him worse than she'd got from his attacks. He knew she was dangerous, and she was comforted by this: it meant she would be chosen when the time came. And come it would, for even if the queen didn't order them, tensions were high and there was no certainty that they wouldn't just go to war anyway...

It was a forbidden thought, of course. Mutiny. Still, she toyed with it like a harmless pet. It couldn't be all bad, could it? They deserved to get what they wanted, *all* of them, for once. And besides, wasn't what the Yassars were doing now a sort of mutiny? They were preparing, in silence, for something which no one had told them would happen.

Now, alone at the end of the last session with Krimpt, Rin considered these matters to get her mind off of the fading enthusiasm in her bones. Today the Yassar had looked at her differently before they started, he'd even made some comment that she couldn't quite remember. Something about starting or ending, or something. Something that made her think that the time to fight was soon. She'd discussed it only yesterday with her friend Kroner, who had also been chosen. Kroner wasn't the best of fighters, but he wanted sorely to see the world above. To him it was an object of wonder. She couldn't really understand his views, but they both agreed about the war: it had to happen, and soon. They couldn't let the world above get away with thinking it could set theirs on fire and not pay.

Though sometimes, Rin admitted to herself, she did wonder. She wondered what sort of mind ran so sharp on thoughts of fire and harm. She wondered what the face would look like that lived in the strange sun of the overworld, a face that showed no compassion. Such a mind, she guessed, would run in dark circuits of flame such as her own mind, even in thoughts of the purest violence, would never dream.

So Rin thought as she leaned against the rocky wall of the small cavernous room, staring into the brightness of the dim light all around her. Such a mind would be a terrible thing.

But beautiful, too.

CHAPTER II

Kinder woke up by falling out of his bed. He was sure there must be an interpretation for that, but now that he didn't have his dream book, he wasn't sure what it was. For a while, the fat fox squirrel stared at the lumps his feet made all tied up in the blankets, lying on the floor next to his bed. It was hopeless. He would have to assume that falling out of one's bed carried good connotations, even though he doubted it himself.

"It's difficult," he said to himself, "only because I haven't got any charms. Or maybe I only think it's difficult. There's no *reason* for it to mean anything. I mean, probability-wise there's probably a good probability that I would fall out of bed to begin with."

Telling himself this—and trying not to trip over all of his probablys— Kinder made up his bed and walked to the window. Pulling the curtains apart, he stared out into the predawn sky, only now fading to whites and pinks and reds. He wondered if Mariyen was up and if he should tell her what was on his mind.

What part of it? the mind in question reflexively asked. He felt a flush creep across his face.

The part where I need to get out of here, Kinder answered himself sternly.

Kinder had been staying with the flyers of Edgewood for the past few days, ever since he'd followed Zirreo, the white squirrel, here. Well, the white squirrel had disappeared—at first everyone waited for him to come back. He'd defeated the exiled seer gone bad, Absoulim, and yet they knew so little of the squirrel who had saved them. One of their number, Mariyen's mother Llewellyn, was also gone—Kinder had seen her jump out of the window of the observatory here, and she'd also never come back.

Afterwards, Kinder told Mariyen, a female flyer he'd been seeing in his dreams before he arrived, of what Zirreo had said to him when they first met. Absoulim had told him Zirreo was a messenger of Astrippa, sent from the goddess to the earth for some mysterious purpose. Zirreo had never really confirmed this as fact, though he had never denied it either. He'd said something about messing up time and how he had a purpose he'd left unfulfilled, which seemed to confirm the idea. Mariyen, in turn, had told Kinder her mother's story of the first time Zirreo came to Edgewood.

"And I don't think it's the last time he'll come," she'd said, sitting in the vacated meditation hall with him one afternoon, the steam from the tea she was holding spiraling up over their heads where it evaporated on contact with the high, slightly canted wood ceiling.

"What do you mean?"

Kinder, who had gotten his mind lost in other matters, turned to her and studied the way her face changed behind the steam. Her dark liquid eyes, wide and round, were staring into somewhere else, like there was something right between them he couldn't see.

"Kinder, do you know how I said I dreamed about him before he came here?"

"Yes...have you seen something?" he asked.

"Not really. It's just that, I *still* see him sometimes when I sleep. I think that when my mother told me about all that was between them—you know, how they had to destroy that child and everything—he became less guarded against me so that my dreams of him were less...clouded. I think we have a connection, but I think he's forgotten about it. I don't think he knows that I can see him."

"See him?" Kinder frowned at the ceiling. "How do you mean?"

Mariyen had shrugged, shaking herself a bit out of her intense posture. "I just see him. What I said. Whatever he's doing, wherever he's going, but I only see bits and pieces. It's only for a moment, too. Like last night, I saw him enter a tree. I don't know more than that, only that there were voices coming from the inside and that he was not alone. And he was apprehensive."

It was hard for Kinder to imagine Zirreo, with his calm façade and his air of mystery, being apprehensive. "Are you sure it was him?"

"What other white squirrel do you know of?" Mariyen said, raising her brow at him.

What a stupid question. Kinder wished he hadn't spoken, but Mariyen was already over it. She seemed deep in thought. "My mother could communicate with him, you know," she said. "In her dreams, she could talk to him and he would say things back. I don't quite have the courage to talk to him in mine, but I feel like he might hear me if I tried. Is that strange?"

It was, but so was so much else. He told her as much, and she grinned briefly, which made his stupid question from before fade into the pale at last.

"Usually when you see someone else in a dream," Kinder said, "It means that they're important to you." He remembered that one from his dream book at least, and he didn't realize the implications of what he'd said until he noticed her smiling at him like she was going to laugh.

"We knew he was important, didn't we?" Mariyen said, gently teasing, and Kinder had no better reply but to nod, his face hot. Why *Mariyen* had featured in his dreams and what she'd been saying to him in them was a mystery to him still, but there was something undeniably right in them coming together here, amid the steam from teacups and the ends of confrontations between those more powerful than them both.

"What I wonder," said Mariyen, "is whether I'm meant to find him. I saw you in my dreams, almost until the time I met you. So it stands to reason that maybe I'm supposed to meet him again. Maybe I'm supposed to follow him."

"But you don't know where he is," Kinder objected. A silence ensued then, in which he felt bad for reasons unknown. Chest cold, perhaps. Those could come from too much superstitious talk, especially around tea. He'd read that somewhere.

They hadn't talked about it since.

Kinder, unlike Mariyen, was not having dreams of any sort any longer. Well, that wasn't accurate; you always had dreams, he just wasn't remembering them any longer. He used to remember them *all*, too, back when he kept his dream book under his bed. It had made him feel weird to hear Mariyen talking about her dreams and not to know his own. He felt out of the loop, in a way. If Mariyen was meant to go after Zirreo, where did that leave him? He'd asked her, later on, whether she thought her dreams might mean Zirreo would come back here, to them. Mariyen had thought about it for a moment, then shook her head.

"No. I do think he'll come back to Edgewood. But I think it will be much later."

"Couldn't that still be what he's trying to tell you? That he'll come back later?"

"I mean *much* later. When we're dead," Mariyen said flatly. Kinder hadn't known what to say to that.

Mariyen worked here as a server, which meant she had to attend to the elder flyers when they needed her. She told Kinder she wasn't a seer, but she kept having all of these feelings he would only have described as premonitions. It didn't add up. Premonitions were very seer-like. Kinder had his intuition, which was a different sort of thing, because his intuition only told him about things that were already in the process of happening. Like if a loved one was in danger, or if he had to go to the bathroom, or even if he was hungry. The stomach was a form of intuition. No sooner had he had the thought, when his stomach voiced its opinion on the matter.

"Oh no," Kinder said to himself. It was still so early; no one was bound to be up, and he'd sworn to himself he wouldn't take from the kitchens again. He was shamed enough to have done it one or twelve times already during his stay here. The flyers just didn't eat very filling food, not to mention the size of the portions. It was probably why so many of the elders were so sour. Food made for lively spirits.

Thinking about it made Kinder unable to resist the siren song of his stomach any longer. He crept out into the passageway beyond his room, and turned for a moment in the direction of Mariyen's for a moment. No. She wouldn't be there. His intuition couldn't tell him if Mariyen was asleep, but, among other things, it told him that Mariyen was a seer. He had tried to tell her on more than one occasion, but she only got annoyed with him, or worse than that, sad. So he'd stopped trying. She said that if she were a seer she would have had a crystal ball waiting for her in the room with the crystal balls, which she'd checked, and she knew it wasn't there because she'd been through every one. He hadn't known what to say to that, except to lamely tell her again that he felt it. That was when she got annoyed. Her dreams were only dreams, she said, but Kinder had yet to know a squirrel who dreamed like Mariyen did.

Ah. He could smell the distinctive odor of acorn cake come to him down the hall. Was someone cooking this early? The idea filled him with joy and fear in equal parts: the last time he'd come down here and found someone else here, it was an extremely crotchety old flyer who tried to murder him with a ladle. Ladles were bad luck to begin with; Kinder didn't want another wielded at him today. He spotted the kitchen door and came over to put his ear against it, easing up against the rough wood and straining to listen. There it was, the sound of someone moving about, picking things up, putting them down with satisfying clinks. His stomach gave another rumble, and he clapped a paw over it; so immersed was he in trying to keep himself unobtrusive that he didn't notice the form bulleting towards him from down the hall. All of a sudden he was hit with such force that he was bowled over onto his side, ear still pressed up against the door, gathering splinters.

"Ouch!" he exclaimed, knowing whoever was in the kitchen could hear him. His chances at a discreet early breakfast were fast being carried away like leaves on the wind.

"Kinder!"

He straightened up. It was Mariyen.

She did not look like she was having much fun. Her fur was in disarray and she was panting hard, clutching at a stitch in her side, eyes wide and staring.

"W-where were you just now?" Kinder sputtered, trying to recover from the indignity of being spilled over on the floor. He decided he had better not try to get up right now; he wasn't sure he could do it in one go.

"Come here." Mariyen solved his problem by giving him a paw. He wisely took it, and they both ensued in the struggle to heave him off of the floor. She started back down the hall away from the kitchen, and Kinder cast a longing glance back before following her. They hadn't gone far before Mariyen pulled him into an empty room. She had barely shut the door when she spun around and faced him.

"The seer's body is gone," she said. Now he knew the look in her eyes for what it was: terror. His heart plummeted.

"Absoulim?"

"That's the one," she said. "They kept the observatory off limits for so long that I thought they wouldn't do anything about the body. They closed the place up after...everything happened there, and it was only after they found Horus that they decided they better do something about the seer's body too. I think they thought it was bad luck to touch it. If that's not a pack of ridiculous superstition...!"

Kinder flushed. It *was* bad luck to touch the bodies of the dead who had done you evil. Mariyen seemed to notice his consternation because she waved one paw as if to bat it aside.

"They don't know what killed Horus or when," Mariyen continued. "It could have been Absoulim. How did he survive, though? That's what I want to know. He had a knife right through his back."

Horus was the now former chief elder of the flyers at Edgewood. Kinder had never really known him. He knew only that in the minutes when Zirreo and Absoulim confronted one another, Horus had not been himself. Mariyen said that she suspected Absoulim had him under a spell. That to Kinder suggested that there were lots of possible explanations for Horus's death, Absoulim killing him only being one of them, albeit the most plausible.

"He did look dead to me," Kinder agreed, though he wasn't being entirely honest; he'd found it hard to look at the prone form of the seer the whole time he was in the observatory. On the other paw, the idea that he wasn't dead seemed ludicrous. He and Mariyen had spent some time in the observatory after everyone had left. The corpse hadn't moved. And that's what it was, a corpse.

The seer was dead. Kinder was sure of it. Or, he amended, at least he *had* been.

"He can't have been," Mariyen said, and for a moment Kinder thought she had heard him thinking and was refuting his very thoughts. "If he killed Horus, and I think he did, he must have still been alive. Maybe the knife didn't get his heart, or didn't go all the way through. Maybe he escaped. Scratch that, of course he escaped, once everyone was too frightened to enter that place again. It would have been easy for him."

Kinder thought about it. It still didn't sit right with him.

"How would he have gotten past everyone and back out again?" he asked.

Mariyen shrugged the question off. "He could easily have escaped at night," she said. "There are ways out of here that aren't so commonly known, you know."

He looked at her, startled.

"Kinder, I tried to run away once when I was young. It was stupid, and I wasn't prepared. I had only a few rolls from the kitchen and some water and no idea of where to sleep or how to get more food. I had no rengolds or any other form of currency. But I succeeded. I got out by a way only I knew and I walked for a long time, even slept out there. No one came to look for me. It's possible that, before I got scared and came back, no one had even noticed I was gone."

A silence ensued in which Mariyen stared fixedly at the wall behind Kinder, and he felt as though he'd unintentionally tapped against some old wound. But when she spoke again, her voice had none of the emotion he must have imagined from before.

"The council of elders had a meeting this morning," she said. "Bogus was the one to find out, and I guess he called the meeting. He's kind of the stand-in leader for them now when they can't decide. I think he should stay, though. Fairel will get the final vote though. The council likes her better. She's more conventional, and less likely to start any commotion. The last thing Edgewood wants is more commotion."

Her voice had a dark tinge to it.

"Mariyen," Kinder said hesitantly, "what are you going to do about it? If Absoulim escaped, he escaped. He could be anywhere now. I mean, it's lucky he's not here, at least. It's not like you can track him down and kill him for good."

Mariyen was silent for a moment, but Kinder had the feeling it was not a silence of indecision. Her face was set in solemnity, her mouth a grave slash.

"No," she said. "But I can follow Zirreo."

Kinder felt his heart sink even more towards the region of his feet than it had at the news of Absoulim's disappearance. They were back to this again.

"You don't know where he is, either," he said carefully.

"I'm sure I can find out," Mariyen said, though she looked less than sure. "Look, I'm sick of being here. I have no reason to stay, less so than when I was young. At least then I had the dream of being a seer. And make no mistake, this is a place for seers. All the disciplines they put you through, all of the meditation...for what? When they realize you're not going to become what they want, they try to shift you to one side in a discreet manner. Well, it hasn't fooled me. I used to have a mother to hang onto, a vision of someone nurturing. Well, she never existed and there's nothing anymore. There's nothing and I need answers. The fact alone that he's showing up in my dreams is a sign. I'm going to follow him."

Kinder sighed. His stomach rumbled at the same time, and he jumped: for once, he'd completely forgotten he was hungry. "Is there anything I can—"

"Do to convince me to stay?" Mariyen finished, eyeing him. "No. So don't waste your breath."

She turned toward the door, muttering something about getting something for one of the elders. Kinder's ears were buzzing.

"Wait."

She turned back, hesitant and quizzical at once.

"I'm going with you," Kinder said, cursing himself for a fool as soon as the words left his lips. He wanted nothing less than to find the white squirrel who had taken him away from his original quest and his first friend. He'd gotten enough of a taste of Zirreo to know he was a meddler and lacked something like a real conscience, and Kinder naturally wanted to stay as far away from the white squirrel as possible in future.

But Mariyen was going, and now he realized, so was he. She stared at him as though she wasn't sure he'd uttered the words that he'd heard come from his own mouth.

"Kinder," she said, and he could tell she was being careful about how she phrased the next thing she said, "You're needed here."

"I'm not. They think I am, but I'm not. Besides, they only get out of here once in a while; they just like the reassurance."

The elders had decreed that Kinder could stay with them as long as he accompanied them outside whenever they ventured there and told them whether the ground was safe to walk on. It had all been very well in the beginning, when Kinder assumed the ground really was still posing problems, but he hadn't felt the threat that he had felt when he was travelling with Lute for some time. If, as he hoped, Lute had managed to talk to the underground squirrels Zirreo had spoken of when they went to him, the results must have been good—either that or Kinder's intuition was failing him. He hoped that it was the former, that Lute had succeeded, and that right now he was aboveground somewhere else, enjoying his life in safety.

Mariyen was still looking at him as though waiting for him to say more.

"You need me more," he told her. That, at least, was true. On the off chance that the ground *was* still a danger, Mariyen would be walking on it much more in her quest to find Zirreo than any of the elders would be in twenty seasons.

She grinned at his determination. "They won't like it," she said, though not with disapproval.

"I know," he said, and shared the grin.

"Honestly, I'm glad if you really want to come. I saw you with me from the start. I just didn't want to force you."

Kinder blinked. "No."

Mariyen turned back to the door. "I really do have to be somewhere now," she said. "Got to behave at least up until tomorrow. Meet me at my room? Sunrise?"

Kinder nodded and watched her take her leave. Sunrise. That wouldn't be a problem, if the last few days were anything to go on.

The rest of the day went on like an exercise specifically designed to torment him. He couldn't get his mind off of the next morning, off of getting out of here, but he was nervous too. He had no charms anymore, no way of setting himself up against whatever obstacles they would meet. As he wandered the halls, flyers turning around to look at him openly every few paces, he hoped Mariyen was right about the secret passages no one knew about; it seemed to him it would be harder to get out of here than it was to keep his mother back home from chewing the walls. That was to say, impossible.

Kinder tried to trace his steps over the course of what would be a normal day, doing normal day things. He went to the kitchen a good eight times, where the cook was so resigned to him that she kept a bowl of extra food off to one side. He went outside with one of the elders, where the elder in question turned around in circles surveying the outside world and then said, "Where do you come from again?" He called this 'sightseeing.' A couple of younger flyers, in training to become seers, approached him to ask about his 'talent', and whether the ground would really eat them all at the end of the world like one of them had dreamed. Kinder didn't quite have the heart to tell this squirrel that it was probably the entire turnip pie she'd consumed before bed that was responsible for that dream. Finally, as day darkened to night, Kinder stole away to his room to prepare for the next day.

His eight trips to the kitchen weren't entirely without cause. He'd stuffed a bunch of extra food into his pockets each time he'd gone, and took it away to his old knapsack in his room, where it had slowly accumulated into what he felt was a pile of goodish size. Staring at it, he felt a trace of hunger coming back, and had to refrain from eating some on the spot. Wrapping his knapsack up good, he wished he had some sort of weapon, something to defend himself with. He'd never carried one before, but with Absoulim somewhere out there, he didn't feel quite as confident that they wouldn't run into any trouble.

Especially since Absoulim had tried to kill Zirreo during their confrontation. Kinder didn't fully understand his fixation on taking the white squirrel down, unless it was mere lust for power, but he bet that if Absoulim was alive, he and Mariyen wouldn't be the only ones on Zirreo's trail. Kinder did not want to risk crossing paths with the seer or any other enemies he was sure Zirreo might attract empty-pawed.

How he managed to fall asleep on that unpleasant note, he wasn't sure, but he was slipping into rest as surely as the sun had set, leaving the world beyond his window black and inviting, like an open-ended question. He dreamed hardly at all, except for the face that rose in his head in the first moments, before he truly lost consciousness. The face was Nadra's, the kindly squirrel who had cared for him as a child, cared for him more than his actual parents had even looked at him.

Her face was lit up by some source he could not see, and she beckoned him towards her. He came, unconsciously moving his legs on the bed in small twitches to correspond with his movements in the dream that was not a dream. She reached for his face, and stroked the side of his cheek gently. He could smell a pumpkin-pecan pie cooking. His favorite. He moved forward an inch, a decibel, and all dissolved into the question mark of darkness once again.

~~~

Mariyen dreamed as well, though this for her was not so unusual. In her dream was the usual set-up of the room of scrolls and crystal balls. She could see shelves beyond shelves, stretching for an impossible length. Indeed, Mariyen had been to this room so many times that she did not register the minor details that gave away its unreality: the way the shelves shimmered slightly, giving in to the clearness of air behind them in gentle flicks, the way when her paw got too close to anything, the thing in question disappeared.

She had one destination, but she knew full well she wasn't allowed to be in here, so she would have to hurry up. Hurry up before one of the elders caught her and questioned her, gave her the one answer to her ultimate question that she feared most of all.

She walked quickly along the shelves, slowing the slightest bit when she reached the shelves full of crystal balls, the beads of dew quivering in their ornate metal holders. They caught her prolonged attention in their mystic beauty, and she tore her eyes away impatiently. There was no time to be entranced.

Walking the route she knew by heart, up one aisle, searching the shelf on one side, and back down it, searching the other side, then around and into the next aisle: the aisle that read "INACTIVE" over the several spheres below on the shelf.

She had had the dream so many times, but something was different this time; she suddenly remembered that there was a place she'd never checked, a place that she was afraid to check. Skipping to the very last shelf, Mariyen rounded the corner to its far side, a point that marked the end of the room. She let her eyes wander, skimming over each row of balls, all undulating gently with swirling dewy liquid, completely impervious to her scrutiny.

There was one missing, on the third shelf down. This observation disrupted her search, even though she knew already what it was that used to fill that space. Still, she stared at the empty place, at the worn wood already covered with a thinner coat of dust where the holder of the missing ball used to stand. His, of course; she felt a quiver of revulsion on thinking of the seer Absoulim and the way he had used his crystal ball to draw the dead back to the form of shades, to have them attack Zirreo. It was gone now, melted away with the supposed death of its master.

Because she was compelled to, Mariyen looked to the left of the open space and at another crystal ball she knew well. The name read *Llewellyn*, a name she'd known well since childhood. She stared, held in sway by the light from this dewy orb, until suddenly the sphere broke, spilling water all over the sides of its holder and the shelf below, staining the dust with its mystic water. The holder, now empty, toppled to the ground with a striking clang that burrowed its way through her chest to her quickly beating heart.

No.

She took a step backward and raced for the door. "No, no, no," she whispered under her breath as she tugged at the handle, which wouldn't give way. Panicking more with each passing moment, she fell to pounding at the door, screaming the word over and over, the sound her fisted paws made sending echoes crashing back through her skull. *Bang, bang, bang,* And then the door gave way suddenly and she tumbled forward, caught unawares, forward and into—

A bed? Mariyen tussled with the sheets a while in an effort to sit up. Her head was heated and she felt sweat slide down her cheek as she sat up. The cold air from her open window hit her and almost caused a brain freeze, so that she took a while to understand what it was she was seeing.

Kinder was framed in the doorway, carrying a knapsack and smiling awkwardly at her.

"Kinder?"

"I just came in because the door wasn't open all the way and I didn't want anyone to see this," he gestured at the knapsack. "I-uh—you said dawn?"

Mariyen turned to the window again and started. It was full day. Getting out of bed, she went to the door and closed it behind him.

"Look, Kinder, I think we're going to have to leave tomorrow, possibly before dawn. I didn't mean to oversleep, and I didn't dream about Zirreo, either, so we don't have any fresh leads."

Kinder stood, taking it all in, his pack hanging forgotten in his paw.

"Did you dream about anything then?"

She had been hoping he wouldn't ask that.

"Yes, but I don't think it's important," she lied. Immediately, she felt bad for it. She had never really lied to Kinder before, she realized. Granted, they had only known each other for a short time, but she knew she could trust him. She knew there was no reason to lie, except her own fear of course.

"Have you had something to eat?" she said.

"No." She watched amusedly as Kinder tried to keep his face from lighting up over the prospect.

"Why don't you go and get it, then? You can keep your pack here, and I promise you I'll wake up next time. I'll find Zirreo," she said this last bit with less confidence than she hoped. "I'll come to you this time, okay?"

The last thing she wanted was for anything to point to Kinder instigating this whole thing if they were caught. It was the reason for her suggesting they keep everything in her room, too. If she were incriminated, the punishment would be severe, but she was a member of the Edgewood colony. Kinder was a stranger; they would show him no lenience, especially after their last encounter with a stranger.

She watched him turn and go out the door, heading for the kitchens for perhaps the last, or the fifth-to-last time. Opening the knapsack he'd left on the ground, she was surprised to find a bunch of well-wrapped food items inside. Well, she was impressed. Knowing Kinder, it had taken a lot of will power not to devour all of it. Thinking ahead, she thought, smiling fondly and stuffing the bag somewhere where it wouldn't be noticed on a quick examination of her room.

Alone now, Mariyen's thoughts turned more quickly and helplessly to the dream she'd had, though she thought 'nightmare' was more like it.

It's probably just my mind going weird on me, she thought. *It doesn't have to mean anything. Not all dreams mean something. Some mean nothing at all. It was just fear.*

But the more Mariyen tried to convince herself of this, the more forced and weak the words sounded. Maybe it was true for other squirrels, but when had her dreams ever meant nothing? When had they ever not been pointing to *something*, even if she didn't know what?

She turned away from her thoughts. No. Her mother was alive and fine somewhere, she was sure of it. Llewellyn wasn't one to lie down and die so easily. The dream was just a scare, and her mother was out there, living.

And even if she's not, she thought, allowing herself to go to that place, *even if she's not, why do I care? Why do I* still *care?*

CHAPTER III

Far to the west, in the region known to most as Beechwood, there lay the ruins of a mammoth redwood, once tall and mighty, now burnt to the ground, lying abandoned on a strange spit of beach-like land. The water to either side of this land made hungry slurping sounds at the shore which only registered to someone inside the tree as dull thumps, so rhythmic that they became a part of the background noise, a comforting sound to fall asleep to.

But there weren't many around to hear it, since everyone in the woods along the water knew to stay far away from the fallen tree. In the daytime, it seemed a dark menace, lying in wait for whoever was foolish enough to equate good lighting with safety, and in the night, its amorphous shape screamed danger to anyone passing nearby.

If any had bothered to get close enough to the fallen monster of a tree, they might have observed strange noises, like the muted beat of talking issuing from it; other times, there was dead silence. Some thought that the tree was haunted by the last inhabitants, who had died when it went up in flame and fell, and while this may or may not have been true, the fact was that someone did live there now, in the midmorning light of a day that seemed like any other.

"So soft," the old black squirrel cooed, staring down at her prize, "So young, still."

She cut off abruptly, squinting down the tunnel of darkness in front of and behind her. She thought she'd heard something, but now when she listened, all that came to her ears was the thumping of the water. It was making her feel sick. This place of all places, really! It was not what she would have chosen, but it did seem isolated enough. If she wanted to get her reward, she would go along with it.

Mercurie listened only a minute longer before deciding the noise didn't matter. He should be awake by now. What was taking him so long?

She studied her prize carefully. Days of tracking to find her, and then days of chasing her. Now the female flyer had no motion left in her, lying prone on the floor in front of her. Dead? Mercurie wasn't sure. Her chest wasn't moving, but sometimes the body fought for incredible lengths of time, the fight hidden under the surface. Mercurie wondered if she should make sure.

Not yet, not yet, her mind chastised her. *Remember the plan.*

Of course. How ironic that she, the greatest of sorceresses, was going on a *plan*. She would have laughed if it had been funny. Now she only stared down, her bright, cruel eyes narrowing.

"Where were you running so fast to, I wonder?" she asked the motionless form of her quarry. "Did you find it, I wonder? Are you merely insane? Hmm. Hmm indeed."

She leaned closer to the young flyer, and on sudden inspiration, reached out to touch her chest.

"Hhhhhssssshhh!" She jumped back quickly, as if she had been burned, and her eyes widened now to their full size and brightness. If the flyer woke up at this moment, what she would have seen looking down at her would have likely made her faint to unconsciousness again.

Mercurie, once her shock had subsided, felt a wave of glee and excitement come down over her. Oh, it was better than she thought! This was interesting! The power that she'd felt radiating from the young flyer was like none of the kind she'd felt before. Its nature though...she wasn't sure of that. Did she have time? It didn't matter, she had to know. As if he could stop her anyway!

Glancing around herself again, Mercurie bent over so that her face was parallel to her captive's. She had laid her paws on the other's chest, and was beginning to feel something move through her—yes, yes!—when she heard a definite sound behind her. Out of the dark from within the tree came the shadow of another squirrel, another flyer. Mercurie let her paws drop from the captive's chest with an effort, heart beating faster in spite of herself. *I'm not afraid*, she reassured herself. *It is surprise. He took me by surprise.*

"Witch," the voice that came out of the shadows was silent and rasping and not at all pleasant. Mercurie straightened up.

"Absoulim," she said.

CHAPTER IV

"Come on, slow down, will you?"

Rin eased her way through the cramped tunnel she was travelling—it was one of the older ones for sure, since all of their tunnels now were large and spacious, courtesy of the gorepedes, the worm-like creatures that they'd found and employed years and years ago.

She tried to ignore Kroner's voice behind her, but slowed just the tiniest bit. It wouldn't be good to have him faint going through this space— Kroner hated tight spaces.

"We're late for the assembly," she reminded him. "Do you want to miss hearing whether we're going to war or not?"

Kroner was too busy closing his eyes and muttering to himself as he squeezed himself through the tunnel she'd just parted from. She always forgot that he was a good deal larger than she. She cast a glance up the tunnel ahead, and resignedly lingered while Kroner pushed his way out of the smaller opening, breathing fast. He straightened up. She noticed that some sweat had made the blue paint on one side of his face smear.

"She'll be an advocate, don't you think?" he asked, all of a sudden much more present now that he'd gotten out of the tight space.

Rin shrugged. "Who knows what she'll do," she said darkly. Kroner had no response for that; they both knew the queen was a little eccentric. If the fact that she often let her insane son decide important issues for her wasn't proof enough of this, Rin didn't know what was.

They passed some other chipmunks in the tunnel, all heading in one direction. Kroner whispered something to her about not being the only ones late, which she ignored. When they got to a wider opening, a high arch built into the top of it, a small crowd of others had accumulated around them. Everyone started to slow upon reaching this door. Rin thought of pushing through to the front—they were going so slow—but she thought it would draw too much unwanted attention onto her. So she waited with the crowd as it surged forward bit by bit.

The inside of the chamber was something to behold: it was a gigantic dome-shaped cavern with one lone, thick root poking through the middle of the ceiling and travelling all the way down through the floor below. The floor was lopsided, however, so that it was closer to the ceiling on one side—the side closest to the door—and sloped down on the other, so that the place where the queen usually stood was downwind from them. There was no seating here, only a limited space to jostle with one's neighbors and attempt to bargain for a good view. Rin, who had been through this process so many times before, made her way to the root in the middle of the room, right across from where she was sure the queen would be when she made her appearance. Clutching the rough, grimy surface of the root with one paw, she surveyed the faces around her. Nowhere near all of the chipmunks from all nine levels had come for the assembly; it would have been impossible. Instead, as was traditional, one from each family had elected to come up to the first level to hear the verdict. After, they would carry the news back to their respective families.

Even considering this, it was a crowd of mammoth proportions. There was no free space to stand anywhere, and some of those who had come even later than she hadn't managed to get in the door. Kroner himself was still back at the entrance, his efforts to fight to a better spot having proved insufficient. He tried to catch Rin's eye, but she was too busy casting her eye over everyone else to pay him any mind. There must be at least a thousand here! Some of them were painted, while some were not; some chipmunks were laughing with a friend and some were paying rapt attention to the front of the room, waiting. But there was something in each one of their faces that confirmed what Rin knew. They were all hoping this was going to be their permission to go to war, and they were all scared that it wouldn't be. Even those who she knew would not have the strength or the motivation to fight were anxious; they still wanted justice at the paws of their brothers and sisters. Many of the younger ones were fool enough to think there was great honor in fighting. Rin was beyond that. Fighting was only blood and blood and more blood. And blood was the source of life. She put a paw on the blade at her side, feeling the solid roundness of the hilt. Few others in here were armed, and she doubted she'd need it, but she liked to come prepared.

A sound echoed from the front of the room to where she was standing, and Rin turned her head to the front again to observe the chipmunk making her way into the room, head held high.

The queen was an old chipmunk, but you wouldn't know it if you weren't told. If you weren't told, Rin thought, you'd think she was in her first twenty seasons unless you got closer, for then you would smell the stench of age hidden so well and see the one white, milky eye that stared out at all the crowd, never blinking. That eye was dead to the world, and so were the queen's sensibilities. Some called her mad, but only behind her back. To do so where she could see was asking for death, so they had dubbed her undying instead, a title she never tried to dissuade, never suspecting the resentment behind its creation.

Rin noticed Yassar Krimpt as well as a few of the other Yassars in the back of the room, leaning against the wall and frowning. They looked as though they did not have good hopes for this assembly, and Rin felt her insides give a twist.

The queen began to speak after taking her time to situate herself at the front of the room and surveying them all through her one good eye. She wore no paint on her face except for one white dot, on her throat: the symbol of absolute authority.

"Chipmunks!" she said, and her voice was strong, but Rin could hear the age in it, and the madness. "You are gathered here today because I was told by some perceptive scouts of mine that you wish to wage war on the overworld in response to the attack of flames from its inhabitants. Chipmunks, you do not even know what the inhabitants of the overworld are like, or what the dangers involved in going aboveground are. Have you not remembered the stories, or are you as empty-headed as the fools who made them possible?"

It was rhetorical, of course, a question to make them ashamed. Anyone who'd lived past a couple of seasons had heard all there was to be heard of the chipmunk who had gone up into the overworld, only to be burnt to death by a giant eye in an endless ceiling. There were others, too, but Rin took them with a grain of dirt. Legend, maybe; fabricated cautionary tales created to keep unruly children in line, more likely.

Some of the chipmunks around her were looking down now, or anywhere but at the queen, and she felt the sinking in her gut more acutely. They couldn't all have bought it! But the queen went on, and this time there was ice in her voice.

"I have heard that some of you do not see fit to wait for my answer; you are already training those you consider worthy of a battle." Her eye focused on the back of the room, and the sound of everyone craning around to look followed. Rin didn't need to. She knew that the Yassars had been discovered, and the thought was enough to make her feel nauseous. They had all underestimated the amount of spies and informants the queen placed among them to keep them in check, and now they would pay.

"I—with all due respect, your majesty, I don't know what you're talking about," one of the Yassars said, and Rin spun to look at him now. It was the Yassar to the left of Krimpt; she did not know his name. His face was pale beneath the paint, but there was a resolution to his eyes.

The queen's voice was like a purr. "Don't you?" she asked. "*Don't* you?"

It was the stupidest thing the Yassar had ever done, and everyone knew it. The Yassar in question seemed to realize his mistake; too late, he stepped back against the wall and shook his head.

"I-I'm sorry, your majesty. I am at fault," he said. "But we were only training them so they'd be ready! We weren't going to wage war without your say-so, of course not."

The queen stared at him, her milky eye somehow piercing in its deadness.

"Forgive me," she said, "of course not."

The Yassar missed the danger in her voice and leaned back in relief; Rin knew better. She watched as the queen's eye drifted discreetly towards the back entrance where a bunch of her own chipmunks were waiting behind her. Without a word, they stole off through the crowd toward the unfortunate Yassar, making small waves as others stepped back onto their neighbors to make room.

The Yassar was still at the back of the room, talking to someone to the left of him. Krimpt had noticed though; Rin saw his eyes travel the crowd and widen. Then they turned to meet hers and she knew all at once what he was thinking. It was only a matter of time before all the Yassars were imprisoned or killed as an example to them all. He was reading, in the rippling of the bodies moving toward him, his own doom.

"Now," the queen began again, "one of the results of war is drastic change. Our order will be disrupted so thoroughly that we may not be able to put it back together. If we lose, this change will not be good, and I suggest," her voice grew sharp, "that we will lose."

In the background, Rin heard the condemned Yassar cry out as the guards got to him. There was the sound of a scuffle somewhere behind her, but there was also a pounding in her ears that made it difficult for her to hear anything except the queen's next words.

"How can we win, after all, when we have never had experience with war? And they have, chipmunks. Those above often become crazed enough for blood that they fight one another just to satisfy their cravings. If we are to go out into that poisonous open sky, there is no telling what will happen, how the overworld will affect us. We might not only lose; we could turn on each other before we have the chance to lose."

"What about the fire?" one of the chipmunks up front bravely ventured to ask. "It nearly choked my sister to death!"

"The fire," the queen said with deadly calm, "is only a story. I'm not sure where this story is coming from, but it was evidently created to give us all a rise. I suggest you *remember* that."

"There was a creature from the overworld down here!" someone said. "I saw him."

The queen turned to him, and there was danger in the way she said, "Could you describe him for us?"

The chipmunk looked like he wished he'd never spoken. Now all heads were turned to him, and the small fellow looked around and gulped.

"He was gray and large and dirty. He was terrifying, probably the size of three of us put together! And elder Linnow told me that he had a mirror he claimed was magic!"

There was a murmur in the crowd at the word. Magic! They were hitting on all the rumors and stories today, weren't they? As if there was any such thing!

"So you see," the queen said, "Not only are these creatures larger than us and strange, they possess magic! I trust everyone at least knows what that is? It is only common sense to stay as far away from such folk as possible. They are not like you and I; they are not able to be understood like we are. They are able to make things behave as they shouldn't and they walk always under a burning eye. Are we really that foolish? Are we really that blind? Now," she drew herself up and stared around at them all, "There will be no war, and that is—"

The queen's eyes widened, until the milky one bulged comically from her face, her mouth still partially open like she was about to speak again. Putting one paw to the knife in her throat, she swayed unevenly and attempted to pull it out.

She could not. Rin had aimed right for the circle painted there, that target of authority, and it was a clean shot. After a time, the queen made one long gargling noise, and her eyes stared around wildly at the crowd before her as a bloody froth crept over her lips. She seemed to be mouthing something, but she fell to the ground before she could get it out. The sounds of her convulsions could be heard all the way to the far end of the chamber in the sudden absolute silence that had enveloped the room. They all heard as clearly as day the sounds of her gagging, choking, trying to speak until...there was silence to match that of everyone else, but deeper. The queen was dead.

Rin could hear everyone begin to turn in the shocked silence that followed, searching her out. She shouldered forward, not waiting for them to work it out. The chipmunks around her scattered as she trod on their paws. When she reached the front of the room, Rin knelt beside the body of the queen and pulled her knife from her throat, wiped it off on her jerkin, and sheathed it.

There was a period of silence that stretched on for what seemed like forever. All eyes in the crowd were on her, and she let them look. The whole time, however, she was thinking of the best route of escape if they should rush her. She kept her paw firmly on the hilt of her knife and waited. The silence lasted only a few more seconds before the crowd started to mutter, and to push towards her. The queen's chipmunks, now on the opposite side of the room, noticed her, and a shout went up.

"Murder! She murdered the queen! *Cursed*!"

Some of the others took up the chant. "Cursed, cursed, cursed, cursed!" The word echoed around her; the cavern now seemed much smaller than before. Rin wished she'd thought this through more, but in reality she hadn't even realized the knife had left her paw before she hit the queen, her reflexes had been so fast. She'd done an excellent job though. She stared down at her target, so cleanly executed, then looked back up at the chanting masses.

Grinning, she called out to them, "You think I'm cursed?"

The noise softened as some of the chipmunks were silenced, eager to know what she would say. Others just kept right on chanting and moving towards her, swarming her. She didn't pay them any mind. If they came too close, she would stick them, too. When the room quieted enough, she continued.

"Well, maybe I am and maybe I'm not. But if I am, your paws will surely burn if you touch me and you'll be cursed as well. And if I'm not, well, look at the favor I've just done you all."

Everyone looked. The queen was still lying where she was, no longer conscious of the world about her, blood flowing slowly from the fresh wound on her neck.

"Favor?" one of the chipmunks started to exclaim, but his neighbor reached over and clamped a paw on his mouth. "Don't talk to her!" she thought she heard him hiss.

"Chipmunks," Rin said, ignoring the murmurs going around the cavern, "Do you want war or don't you?"

No one spoke. Rin rolled her eyes. "Fine. Raise your paw if you want to fight."

There was more quiet before someone in the back, Rin thought it was Kroner, raised his paw tentatively. Then the paw next to him went up, and another nearby. One by one several paws started going up into the air until the whole cavern was filled with a forest of paws. She noticed that several of the queen's chipmunks had raised their paws as well. Of course, there were still several who would not budge. One of these called to her,

"You think you can just kill the queen and lead us to war?! There has to be proper punishment!"

"We're not prepared for war, anyhow!" someone else shouted.

Rin spotted the speaker, an older chipmunk stout of voice and body. She thought she recognized him from somewhere—maybe he was friends with her father? She leveled her eyes with his own, not sparing him her gaze.

"So you want all of us to suffer the insult of having fire dumped on our heads and do nothing about it? We can prepare for war. We have weapons. We have the gorepedes."

A muttering broke out afresh at this.

"They're not going to fight at our side!" someone snorted.

"We don't need them to," Rin said. "All we need is for them to begin feeding aboveground again."

Chipmunks began to exchange glances with each other, but they were in the minority. Most of those in the room, as she suspected, did not need much convincing. All they had needed was someone to tell them to do what they wanted to do. Someone strong.

"Go back to your families, you who will fight," she commanded. This must be what a queen felt like. What a dreary position. "You who won't fight, hide and wait until it is over if you want to. Just know that we will remember you and your families as those who did nothing."

There was some angry muttering at this, and one of the chipmunks yelled something at her, but the effectuality of the insult was lost in the hubbub. Everyone was moving for the door, and even those who wanted to stay and have a hostile word or two with her were having trouble maintaining their ground in the rush.

"Elder Linnow!" Rin called out, doubting she'd be heard. A sound came from beside her, though, and peering down from the platform the queen was so fond of preaching from, she saw a middle-aged, tired looking chipmunk with a series of blue spikes painted around his eyes. The chipmunk took a step toward her, then, seeming to notice her attention, stopped.

"I am Elder Linnow," he said, as the last vestiges of life aside from the both of them drained from the hall. The sound of voices was dimming away as everyone entered their respective tunnels, heading back to whatever level they were from.

Rin looked Linnow over; he was not what she expected. He seemed to know exactly what she was thinking, too, because he gave her a wan smile that she thought slightly condescending. She kept her paw on her knife hilt, and said, "You can speak to the gorepedes?"

Linnow nodded. His eyes were wary, but she saw that he had no weapon at his waist, so she wasn't too concerned with what he thought or did not think.

"You are going to go tell them that they can feed aboveground again," she said.

Linnow only looked at her for a while longer.

"Now," she said.

"Are you sure this is a good idea?"

She stared at him. She wasn't sure whether he meant the war or the gorepedes, but she answered anyway.

"Yes, I'm sure. Go tell them."

Linnow looked puzzled. "You don't need to come with me, child," he said.

She sucked in her breath. Child! She had half a mind to stick him with her knife right here and now and then see who would be calling who 'child'!

"Someone has to make sure you do what you say you're going to do," she said instead, once she'd calmed herself down inside.

Linnow gave her a funny look. He turned and headed for the back passage out of the cavern, the one through which the queen and her chipmunks had come.

She'd never been in the room beyond, a fancy little sitting room with a pleasant atmosphere. It was lit by several glowworm lanterns hanging from the thin vein-like roots criss-crossing the ceiling. When Linnow went over to close the door behind them, it became apparent why she'd never seen this room: there were at least five locks on the door.

Linnow saw her staring at it and said, "Her quarters start here. I'm surprised it's new to you. What with what just happened, I would have expected you to have cause to visit here before this."

She gave him a sharp look, but he only smiled disarmingly. Linnow made her uneasy. For one, he didn't seem to feel threatened by the fact that she was armed and he was not, and for another, he had a faint air about him that made her feel like she was missing something, an inside joke or a subtext that only he could read. It made her furious. She followed him across the sitting room area, noticing the roasted nuts in a bowl on the table and the aroma they were giving off as she passed. Taking one, she popped it into her mouth and let the flavor overtake her. These were *good*. She wondered where the queen got them; she'd never seen this type of nut anywhere before.

Linnow was waiting for her at the door, that infuriating expression on his face again. She ignored it; once she had what she wanted from him, she could show him exactly what she thought.

Rin kept track of the passages as they walked through them, making sure she knew the way. They went through a few more rooms that resembled the first in their finery and in the number of locks on the doors, before they entered common territory again. They went down a sudden, long sloping hallway, and Rin thought that they must be on the second level now. Her suspicions were confirmed when they passed the heavily guarded door that she knew housed

Chamblis, the late queen's insane son. From behind the door, she thought she could hear the sound of the fat lug singing to himself. He would die soon, she thought. She didn't think that anyone would bother to feed him now that the queen was dead; they hated and feared him almost as much as her.

She and Linnow turned one corner, then another, until they faced a long hallway, at the end of which lay a sturdy door carved from rock. Linnow turned back to her, to make sure she was following. She nodded at him, and he led her along the dim, lantern-lit passageway until they came to a dead stop at the door.

Linnow did not open it right away. He stood there with his head cocked, listening, so Rin, who was impatient to get inside, and get on with things, stopped too and listened. There was a soft, sinuous hissing coming from behind the door-directly behind it. Rin took a step back and checked that her weapon was still there, then she checked her fear. She had seen the gorepedes before, had crossed paths with them- there was *nothing* to be afraid of here. She turned to Linnow with her brow raised.

"Are you sure you want to go on with this?" he asked. His face was solemn, but Rin didn't know whether to feel incredulous or indignant. Did he really expect that she would listen to the sounds from behind the door and change her mind on the whole thing? He had a thing or two to learn about bravery and persistence. And even more to learn about her.

"Of course I'm doing this," she said. "Now get in there."

He stared at her for a while longer, and she thought that he would protest, but he must have seen something in her eyes he didn't like, because he only nodded at long last and turned to unlock the latches that held the door in place.

As the last lock was undid, the door moved slightly inward, and Rin jumped back, ready and aware. When she saw Linnow turn around and give her a laughing smile, she checked herself again and scowled. Linnow turned pleasantly around again as though he'd done nothing at all to denigrate her, and pushed through the door, leaving it open for her to follow.

The room she entered was large, and dipped into a gorge-like opening on one side; the side they'd entered on was level with the door and led up to a balcony looking out over the strange pit she'd observed. It was from this pit that the sounds were coming from.

Passing Linnow, Rin crept to the edge of the balcony-like projection and stared over its edge. There they were: all about as long as ten chipmunks down on all fours and as tall as two of them. Footless, and eyeless all except for two growths that looked oddly like plants or feelers of a sort, waving about in the air. They were a sight to behold.

They were perfect.

One of the gorepedes turned its eyeless head toward her, stopping its endless gliding circuit of the pit, and seemed to stare at her. Rin suddenly became conscious that there was nothing holding her back from falling into the pit with them, and stepped back from the edge, feeling slightly dizzy. It was then that she noticed the tunnels placed all around the area the gorepedes were circling, tunnels they could easily have entered to travel elsewhere. Except that the tunnels were blocked now, each held closed by a circular stone door similar to the one they had entered to get here.

"They're restless," Linnow said, and his voice was so unexpected that she jumped. For once he did not smile at her for it. "We feed them now by dropping things down there: worms, beetles, any other edible thing we can find.

But their time to feed up above was cut short, and they still crave it. They work in cycles, you know. When one cycle is disrupted...they don't like it."

She looked at his sideways profile sharply to see if he was still trying to make her scared, but he was staring off into the air above the pit, at the blank dirt wall beyond. He seemed in a partial daze, hardly caring for her presence.

"Tell them," she said, "that the cycle is continued where it broke off. Tell them they can feed on the overworld."

Linnow didn't respond immediately. He stared at the wall as though captivated by something on it, and then turned from it to the door behind them so quick that she could not see his face. She thought for a moment that he might try to make a run for it, in which case her dagger would be in his back quicker than those gorepedes could move...but he stopped just outside the door and called out to someone.

"Renner! Are you there? Open the doors!"

A voice from somewhere further up the tunnel yelled something indistinguishable back at him. There was a pause in which Linnow did not respond to whatever it was. Then, "Yes. I'm sure."

The sound of stone scraping over clay behind her made her turn around rapidly; the doors were opening again. The gorepedes seemed to notice what was happening, too. They all stopped their circuit and rose to lift their giant, eyeless heads, plant-like feelers waving in the direction of the sound. From behind her, Linnow spoke, only this time his voice was unrecognizable, the words he was saying not words at all but a series of low, muted clicks.

Some of the gorepedes shifted the heads towards him as he spoke in what Rin assumed was their language, while some remained facing the openings. After Linnow was done, however, all of the gorepedes began to move forward again, that hissing noise picking up as they made for the open doors. The sound they made as they crossed the threshold of each opening was slick and full of promised menace. Rin realized that the passages must all eventually lead up to the overworld. She turned back to Linnow, who was still watching the last of the gorepedes leave, his face set in the same troubled contemplation it had been earlier. She could leave now; she *should* leave now. She had other things to do, but a question had occurred to her.

"Will you be fighting with us, Elder Linnow?" she asked.

Without turning to her, he said, "No, I think not."

"It's a dishonor you do yourself," she started, but realized that her attempt would go wasted, and stopped. "Fine," she said. "Your job is done. I release you from your responsibility. I suppose you want to go scurrying back to your burrow now."

She left him standing there, feeling that every step she trod spoke victory to the empty room. She was almost to the door when she turned back again. Something had occurred to her, and now that she'd thought of it, it seemed she'd known it all along, from the moment she'd first addressed Linnow.

"You've seen one of them, haven't you?"

She didn't think he would answer, she thought she might have to force him, but Linnow spoke simply, with his back still turned. All of the gorepedes were gone now, so his eyes were resting on empty tunnels reaching up to the world above.

"Yes," he said.

She waited, but he did not offer anything more.

"They must be very wild," she said, digging for something, anything. "They must be fearfully uncouth. Savages. They must be nothing like you and me."

"No," Linnow said, after a long pause that made her think he would not speak again, "they are nothing like you."

She watched him intently but he gave no sign of turning, or continuing, so that at last she gave it up and left him. *So few words for such a wise elder*, she thought scathingly. Yet somehow those words lingered down the passages back home with her, and if somehow her footsteps lost some of their victory beat, she could not have explained why.

CHAPTER V

Mariyen was losing hope.

She had had no dreams, at least none she remembered on waking, for the last two days, and she'd had to tell Kinder they couldn't leave. She didn't understand: before she'd had them nearly every night. She'd see at the very least a flash of Zirreo doing something, going somewhere, but now there was nothing.

Now shouldn't be any different, she thought the night of Horus's funeral party as she tied a white ribbon round her tail. About to leave the room—she was sure Kinder was waiting for her—she looked out the window at the night framed with broken shards of glass. She could see lights down on the grass, the flames of torches carried by those who were waiting to bring Horus to his resting place. From here, they looked like the effects of a spell, and not like squirrels at all; a little line of lights marking the crossing into some magical territory. She blinked, and their negative imprints compounded themselves behind her eyes.

Got to go, can't be late, she reminded herself. She was in the oddest melancholy state tonight, and she did not think she could attribute it all to the memory of the late chief elder. It was almost as if she were in a dream herself, getting ready in slow, fluid motions, seeing everything as though it were draped in gauze and required suspension of disbelief to really see.

She was halfway to the open door when she went down.

All around her swum bright points of light in blackness like the afterimage of a million burning torches, and she tried to raise her head to blink them away, but to no avail. She was lying on the floor—that was the last thing she felt before she lost consciousness altogether.

The next thing she knew, Mariyen was immersed in a lighter, woodier darkness...soon she realized that the light was coming from lanterns and that the lanterns were lighting up the walls of whatever place she was in, creating that brown glow. There must be no windows in this tree, for it was too dark for their existence to be plausible. The air smelt of smoke and of food, and a dry, sour smell she did not like. Mariyen could not tell if she was on the floor, the ceiling, or just floating around somewhere here; her body was strangely absent. Normally, she would have tried to remove herself from such an alarming situation immediately, but something told her she was supposed to wait, so wait she did.

Soon, the sound of two voices talking came to her, along with the sound of a door slamming shut.

"...sure it's so close?" the first voice was saying. It was heavy and musky and she did not feel like she would trust the owner much; it made her shiver.

"Yes," the second voice said, firmly, and Mariyen felt a lurch in her stomach—or she would have if she had brought her stomach with her. It was Zirreo.

"The border of Oakwood is a straight shot from here. Even you know that, Vinson. Besides, I am used to taking my respite under the stars; I hope you won't mind terribly if I do."

There was a silence in which Mariyen realized the squirrel called Vinson was very angry, and apparently trying to hide it. He wasn't doing very well, she thought, for his voice was thick with hidden rage when he spoke next.

"So you just came by here to talk."

"Talking is nice, wouldn't you agree? It's a good way to pass the time."

Vinson didn't respond, and she could feel his anger building. Suddenly, Mariyen's field of vision made a strange turnaround and she was staring directly into Zirreo's face. He was standing next to a long bar in a room that had only one window, a slanted, shuttered thing shining only a couple of wisps of light down onto the bar table. The pieces of light landed exactly between Zirreo and Vinson, so that Mariyen not only saw Zirreo's face, she saw the half of Vinson that wasn't hidden in shadow behind the bar. He was a portly fellow with a stern face, but the anger in his voice had been more dangerous than his appearance now seemed to let on.

"Talking is not the best way to stay employed if you work somewhere like here," Vinson hissed. "And I hear you've been scaring those in the area, telling them...what was it? The ground is going to eat them up?"

"Not exactly the words I used," Zirreo said lightly, "but haven't you found that this was a problem for you before?"

"It hasn't happened in a few *days*," Vinson said, "But seeing a white squirrel around here is permission to be irrational for them. Everyone believes you, they think you've come back from the dead, or else you're the walking reincarnation of some god or other, Astrippa knows..."

"They say that?" Zirreo asked. His face was turned from Mariyen so that she could only see his profile, but his expression was very strange.

Vinson gave him a sort of double-take, then shook himself onward. "Yes, and it's not doing so well for me, if you must know the truth."

"Well, I'm sorry, but there's nothing I can do about who they say I am," Zirreo said. "I'm sure that as soon as I leave they will forget about me."

Mariyen felt something shaking her, pulling at her from somewhere far, far away. She tried to ignore it, and focused eagerly on the two squirrels at the bar.

"I'm going to make you a deal," Vinson was saying, but Zirreo cut him off, and for once, his voice was the one that carried invisible anger.

"No," he said, "I'm going to make *you* a deal. You let me go in peace, never speak of me or my destination to anyone here or any other travelers—and I will know if you do. If you do this, I will keep my peace on what I know you do to your customers."

"What?"

"Come on, Vinson. You want me to stay here the night, but you find I'm nothing but trouble for your...as you call it, business. Earlier today, the squirrel who left your guest rooms without her rengolds, weeping, what would you call that? Business?"

Vinson looked down at the table. "Times are hard—

"Spare me that. Do we have a deal?"

Vinson was looking resentful, like a scolded child. Zirreo turned, suddenly, as his companion picked at a spot on the table, and looked directly at Mariyen. Such a shock ran through her body—he could see her!—that when she felt the tugging sensation again, the air around her went dark and when next she opened her eyes it was to a well-lit room and to Kinder's very worried face.

"Mariyen!" he exclaimed when she turned her head to him.

"How long have I been...out?" Mariyen asked hesitantly. She felt like it must have been minutes on end. Kinder only shook his head.

"I don't know. I was coming to your room for, you know, the funeral, and then I saw you down here on the floor. I kept trying to wake you up, but you didn't seem to hear or feel anything. Your heart was beating very slow."

Mariyen tried to sit up, but she was taken by a wave of dizziness and had to lie back down again. She stared up at Kinder's face, which looked almost comically worried from this angle.

"I'm okay," she said. "Really, I'm okay." He did not look entirely convinced. That was when it came back to her, all she had experienced in her strange faint.

"Kinder."

"What? I mean, yes? I mean...whatever."

She stared at him, mystified for only a second before blurting it out.

"Kinder, I saw Zirreo!"

"What?! That's great! I mean, not that you passed out, but that you saw—"

"Yeah, I got it."

"What did he say?"

Mariyen shook her head. "He didn't say anything because I couldn't talk to him. Well, I didn't try, in any case. He was talking to this seedy bartender and then he looked at me, he looked *at* me and I had to go back, but—but—I know where he is, Kinder!"

Kinder beamed. "That's great! I mean, not the passing out, but—" He saw her look and stopped. "You know. Where is he?"

"Somehow he's all the way in the middle of Firwood somewhere. I know it's not specific, but he said something about the border of Oakwood, and Firwood is the only place that borders Oakwood, really..." She thought about it, and realized she actually couldn't be sure about that. "Well, even if he's not in Firwood, he's headed for the Oakwood border. He said as much to the bartender."

Kinder was looking a little less enthused than he had when she'd started talking.

"Er...Mariyen, Oakwood is a pretty far ways from here."

"Do we have any other choice?"

Her question hung in the air like an icicle poised before shattering, and a sudden burst of laughter from someone outside made them both jump a little.

"I guess not," Kinder said, after a time. "I need to find him. I can't let him go without...knowing."

Mariyen felt much the same. "Do you think he's running away?" she said suddenly. She didn't even know what she meant, really, but the memory of Zirreo's eyes when he looked her in the face, that dark pushing away at her that she'd felt and understood, stayed with her and commanded her to ask it.

Kinder seemed to understand.

"From what I know of him," he said, "it seems very likely."

The sound of someone saying something loudly and then another responding came drifting in from outside. The cold from the window suddenly became offensive to Mariyen, and she pulled a sheet from her bed around her and shivered, hoisting herself up to a standing position as she did so. Kinder watched her like he thought she would fall at any minute.

"How long have the funeral processions been going on?" she asked him.

"Oh, er, not long," Kinder said, looking like he'd expected her to ask him something completely different. "When you woke up, they were still getting organized. I know because I was standing with my back to the window to keep the cool air from entering, and I heard them talking."

Mariyen stared at him. "Why?"

"Why what?"

"Why were you trying to keep the air from coming in?"

"Ah, well." Kinder looked a little embarrassed. "A winter chill can cause a kill in someone who can't see," he chanted in a singsong voice, then promptly turned red.

Mariyen tried hard to keep from laughing. "Oh, uh...wow. Thanks, then, I guess." Then she dug under the bed for where she'd left their things. "Kinder, we have to go. This is the perfect time. No one is in Edgewood, and we've just heard from Zirreo!" She grabbed the bag of food and gave it to Kinder, before dragging out a long dagger tucked into its sheath and a slingshot. Kinder blinked at them.

"We have weapons now?" he asked. "Mariyen, where did you get these?"

"Edgewood would like to make believe it's the sort of place that doesn't even house weapons, let alone use them. That's a load of wash. We have to defend ourselves somehow, don't we?"

"You mean mind power's not enough?"

She looked over at him, puzzled, and then cracked up at the look on his face. "Good one. Now pick one, you. If we run into anyone, we can't just throw scones at them."

~~~

Kinder picked the slingshot, and now he was thinking better of it. He didn't even know how to use a slingshot, but he thought that it would be better than the dagger. He still remembered the image of Lute stabbing that gray squirrel and Llewellyn stabbing Absoulim, and he thought that for him, the less stabbing, the better was a good rule.

Mariyen started for the door, then had to catch herself from falling. Kinder, startled in the midst of his own worrying thoughts, made a move towards her, knowing it would be too late, but she didn't fall. She merely wobbled in place, looking a little sick.

"Felt like I was going to fall again," she said, laughing a little, and then under her breath, "I hope this isn't a new phenomenon."

Kinder hoped so too. He wondered if Zirreo was making this happen. He couldn't think *how* the white squirrel would do such a thing, especially from so far away, but he knew enough of Zirreo not to discard the idea.

When Mariyen was feeling more oriented, she began to lead him down the hall outside in the direction of the kitchen.

"Where are we going?" he hissed. He'd assumed they could just use the front door since no one was around.

"I wasn't lying when I told you I knew other ways out of this place," Mariyen responded. And then, as though she'd read his mind, she said, "There will no doubt be squirrels positioned somewhere near the entrance, just to make sure no one gets in, especially after the Absoulim incident. Some of them are half-expecting him to still be lurking around here."

"Oh," Kinder said. It made a lot of sense. He was glad to have Mariyen with him for this. Like Lute, she always seemed able to think ahead in any situation. Not that he couldn't when he put his mind to it, but half the time he was always being distracted by—his stomach rumbled—well, other things.

"Besides, everyone's at the front of the tree," Mariyen continued. "No one," she said with a mischievous grin, "is at the back."

They had come to a dead end. Kinder stopped behind Mariyen and peered around in the half-light. He couldn't see anything that looked like a hidden door, but decided to keep quiet. Mariyen was already down on the ground, searching for something...and sure enough, a few seconds later, she was pressing hard on a bit of the floor with a shallow knothole in it. The knothole began to sink in and Mariyen kept pushing on it until it fell inwards. Kinder heard a *thunk* as it hit the floor below, which must have been exceedingly close judging by how immediate the sound was. Mariyen motioned him forward and he began to move only to freeze again in terror.

"Mariyen!"

She was leaning over the trap door, oblivious to him. He heard the sound again, and knew he wasn't making it up, that it wasn't just a fabrication of fear. Someone was coming towards them down an adjoining hall. If his ears did not deceive him, whoever it was would come to an intersection very soon and see them. Kinder dug around in his knapsack, reaching for the very bottom where the food he'd packed days ago would be. Calling to Mariyen a second time would only give them away.

Sure enough, the sound of the footsteps got closer. Why wasn't this squirrel at the funeral? He fumbled with the slingshot, thinking as rapidly as his heart was pounding. *Which way do I hold it? Am I supposed to pull on* this? But at that moment, their unwanted guest rounded the corner.

"Hey!" a loud voice cried, and Mariyen jerked her head up, eyes widening. Facing them was a smaller flyer, with tiny, shifty eyes that were now shifting about so much at the sight of them that it made Kinder almost sick.

"Hey!" the flyer cried. "You're not supposed to be—*auuuuughhh!*"

The berry scone hit him in the face at record velocity—Kinder had never seen anything fly so fast. The flyer fell over and did not stir. Kinder began to get nervous—had he killed him? He started over to find out.

"Kinder! Get over here!" Mariyen hissed, just as the little flyer began to twitch and moan. Kinder ran.

He was expecting the fall to hurt, but he hit bottom quickly when he flung himself into the opening of the trap door, an opening he just barely cleared without getting stuck.

"Come on!" Mariyen urged him, pausing only to fix the piece of wood with the knothole back in place. "With any luck, he won't have seen where we're going!"

They clattered down the low-ceilinged hallway they found themselves in, which led only one way, both crouching down to keep their heads from being scraped too badly. When they reached the end, a surprisingly short ways away, Mariyen flung out a paw and said, "go carefully. It's a straight shot down from here."

Kinder didn't understand what she meant until Mariyen was out of the circular opening through which he could feel the cold air like a shockwave. Then he was able to look down, and able, simultaneously, to wish he hadn't.

It turned out that the hall they'd been traveling was merely a hollowed out branch, and that the opening he was now facing came out on the bottom of the branch.

Who would do that? he weakly asked himself, *Who would make a hole in the bottom rather than the top?*

Maybe it's only meant to be entered from the outside.

With that thought in mind, Kinder groped around for any purchase on the bark outside of the hole that he could find. Mariyen was already on the trunk, waiting for him, her expression anxious.

Thinking he heard a noise above him somewhere—did the squinty-eyed little flyer figure them out?—he made a mad gamble. Closing his eyes shut tight and clutching his bag in his mouth, Kinder swung out from the hole, clutching the rim tightly and trying not to think about how far below him the ground was. He let the bag go—he didn't need any extra weight for this—and attempted to swing himself parallel with the underside of the branch. On the third try, he got it, and began to scoot backwards to the trunk. When his back feet touched the trunk, he breathed out a rush of air he hadn't known he'd been holding in. His heart was pounding like crazy. Mariyen looked him over in the windswept night and opened her mouth, then just shook her head.

"All the stuff in that bag is probably squashed," she said.

He smiled back at her tremulously. "At least I put it to good use while it lasted."

She laughed out loud, then flung a paw over her mouth. Looking all around them once nervously, she smiled. "I take back my feelings on the usage of scones as deadly projectiles," she said solemnly. "But we really have to get out of here."

Kinder realized he could hear the sounds of the funeral going on around the other side of the tree from them. The murmur of voices with the occasional raised couple of words that he caught in full distinction carried to them on the wind. Behind them, the flyers were celebrating the end of the life of one of their own, and the beginning of whatever came next according to their beliefs—he'd never been sure what that might be. Perhaps he should ask Mariyen. But for now...

He looked in front of them, and saw nothing but dark, the quiet of a night that had yet to be disturbed by anyone's noise. That was where they were going, and to him the quiet suggested a path as yet unmade, a dimness in which anything could happen.

What came next for the two of them was just as much a mystery as any afterlife had to share.

CHAPTER VI

Rin had awaited the day when she would go aboveground for so long that after she'd commandeered the queen's meeting, she decided there was no time to waste. Getting the elders together—she looked for Elder Linnow at first, but he was conspicuously deciding to stay out of anything—she told them to spread the word and fetch anyone who would be fighting.

"Is there any...format to this, dare I ask?" Kroner said. Now that he was being put into the real test of action, he was afraid. It was so typical of him, though. She could remember when they were younger and played near the hottest part of level nine, where it was said that the god of life slumbered so close that one could catch a curse by being so near. Kroner had run away at the sound of a rock falling behind him, and for days after thought he was cursed and wouldn't go out of his burrow.

She looked Kroner up and down. Standing all alone in the queen's speech hall with her, he looked less like a warrior than a dung beetle. Oh, well. She doubted he would last that long in the heat of war, but they had to use all they had if they wanted to stand a chance against the strange beings above.

"No," she answered him, "there is no strategy. It's simple. We're going to go up there, using the old tunnels. The first overworld creature you find, you attack. Tell them any words you want to say before you stick their throat, if you want. Be creative."

She patted Kroner on the back and turned to face the influx of chipmunks swarming in through the doors, armed to the teeth and freshly painted in war colors, deep red and black. The mass of her fellows was staring at *her*, and she realized that she would have to give them some sort of speech. Rin, who had only applied two stripes of red beside each eye in the fancy of labeling herself a more silent menace, cast a gaze out over the crowd to quiet them. This worked remarkably well, and when she began to speak, every pair of eyes fastened on her greedily.

"Chipmunks," she began, in the way the queen typically did; she found this irony quite humorous, now. "The strange creatures of the world above us think it is right to set flame to a world that has never done theirs any harm. Do you or don't you want to get revenge?"

A loud rumble of 'aye' echoed through the cavern. It was good enough for her.

"Now, the only real question is, why are you still standing here, waiting for me to tell you more? Does more need to be said? I am not your queen; I refuse to be your queen. If we want to be effective, we must split our ways. The old tunnels are far and few. We must find them and send a good number up each one. For all there is of our world belowground, there is likely to be more of their world above us. We must not stop once we have killed the first, or the second of them; we must keep going on and on aboveground, taking every life in the overworld that we must."

"What about their magic?" someone asked. Rin looked around and could not locate him. It was probably better that way; what a horrible question. Too many here were fed on superstitions.

"Magic," she said calmly, "is not real."

"But your father," said Elder Cathos from behind her, and she stiffened. "Your father said that it was."

He did not speak loud enough for any except she and perhaps Kroner to hear, but she could feel her face heating into an angry scarlet all the same beneath her fur.

"I have no father other than the one standing in this crowd," Rin hissed at him, "and if you mention that again, I will stick *you* with my dagger."

The elder opened his mouth indignantly, then seemed to think better of it. He merely shook his head and turned away.

Though Rin's father was, in fact, somewhere in this churning crowd of battle-ready chipmunks, her mother and brother were not. Her brother, still stubborn and bitter about not being chosen by the Yassar—as if that mattered now—had refused to fight 'under her' as he put it, and her mother didn't want to leave him alone. They were left to the god of life's care, and perhaps the underworld would preserve them until she got back. If not—there was nothing she could do about it. They'd been given the choice. Rin felt impatience stir her bones and called the attention of everyone again.

"Chipmunks! Go! Spread out and fight! To the overworld!"

The crowd began to move immediately, as though all they'd been waiting for was some sign from her that they could go. Turning around, Rin expected to see Elder Cathos behind her—not that she wanted to, really, but he'd just been there moments before—but he was nowhere in sight. He must have gone off with a group of the other chipmunks. She looked at Kroner, who was still standing next to her, fingering his dagger in what was obviously a habit born of extreme nerves.

Once nearly everyone had cleared out—and it took minutes—she turned to him.

"Don't continue to feed me your doubts, Kroner. If you don't want to do this, don't do it. Go back to your burrow."

Kroner opened his mouth and closed it, several times. She thought he could not have looked less intelligent at the moment.

"If I do, you'll never talk to me again!" he managed to burst out.

"You're right," she shrugged. "I won't." She was too distracted by her urge for something, for some sort of action, contact at last with an unseen foe, to concentrate on anything else. Rin's heart was pumping too hard to really hear Kroner's response, but since he was still standing beside her, she guessed he'd decided to stay.

There was an old tunnel opening at the top of this cavern; she'd seen it many times before when everyone else was just glazing out on whatever lie the queen was feeding them at the time. Rin always paid attention, chiefly because it always paid off in the end, especially when no one else ever did.

"We have to get up there," she instructed, pointing to the pillar of a root that came down from ceiling to ground. The hole in question was right at its top, hidden in the darkness between the top of the root and some large stone. Rin could tell it was one of the old tunnels because of its size—it clearly wasn't large enough to be built by gorepedes— and the fact that no one would build a tunnel in the top of the speech hall; hence, the tunnel must have been built before the speech hall.

Kroner looked sick. "Rin, I can't...I can't climb," he protested.

Rin snorted. "Yes, you can. You're only afraid of heights. Big deal, so are we all. You'll only have to do it once."

At the time she hadn't realized what a lie that might turn out to be.

Clinging onto the root, she went first, levering herself up bit by bit, getting a firm grip with her back claws and pulling up with the front ones—it was really easy, once you pushed past the dizzying fear that came with the idea of being so far up. Her paws, built for digging, also turned out to be perfect for climbing. Not looking down to see if Kroner was following, she grabbed hold of the sides of the tunnel above, getting a firm grip on the rock beside the opening and levering herself up.

"Wait," Kroner panted, and Rin felt pained and obligated in one. He was one of her fighters, was he not? She supposed she had to at least make sure he made it above ground before leaving him to his own devices. It was hard, though. Her heart was pumping harder. She was more ready for this than she'd been for anything in her life. She could remember the feel of the Yassar's whip across her chest and the feeling that surged there, then, and she thought, *this, this is so much more than even that. This is what I was born for.*

Rin waited only as long as it took for Kroner to get ahold of the tunnel leading up before she was bolting through it. She went up for such a long time that she thought maybe she was mistaken and this path didn't lead anywhere when she felt something brush her face.

She stopped dead, paw hovering over her weapon, but she couldn't see anything in front of or behind her, except for Kroner, who came puffing around the corner and stopped when he realized she wasn't moving.

"Where are we?" he asked between puffs.

"Shhhh!" Rin put a paw to her mouth and waited. There it was again; something was definitely touching her face. It was almost a caress, but the source was invisible. Kroner must have felt it too, because he shivered and gave a little yelp of fright.

"Augggh! What is that?"

"I don't know, that's why I stopped," Rin said behind clenched teeth. She was really regretting her decision to let Kroner come with her.

"It feels like someone's breathing on my face, only it's really cold."

Ignoring him, Rin waited a few seconds more. When nothing else seemed to threaten, she continued forward carefully, turning a corner to find what looked like a bright circle staring down at her.

The eye!

She gasped, and drew back from it, running into Kroner, who made that little screaming sound again.

But the circle did not burn her where she stood, and she realized, after giving it another look, that it was the end of the tunnel. Above, that strange brightness that she saw, *that* was the overworld.

She didn't give herself time to think about it; this was her destination. Rin scrambled forward, bursting up out of the hole and staring around her.

She had no words for what she saw. Around her there was the dirt she was used to, but there were also large, shriveled looking things set in strange patterns, all a sort of dull orange color. She touched one of these and it crumbled in her paw with a crunching sound. What struck her most was the space. The space and the emptiness. She looked all around her, spinning about, and then up above her. The ceiling here was blue and looked like it went on and on forever, for an infinity that made her head spin. It was all around her, too, she noticed—like a dome was placed over her head, but a dome in which she could run all her life and never feel trapped. It was the sky, she remembered that from the stories, the only ones that were left by the First Ones, the ones who had gone aboveground, who knew the world here. The mammoth things shooting out of the ground and up towards the sky, all dark in color and sprouting strange protuberances that looked like roots—these were trees. There was one of them not twenty paces from where they stood, and Rin understood somehow that this tree was the source of the root down below, the one she had climbed to get here. She remembered the pictures from the old stories, the ones that used to frighten her as a child. The tree, rising so high, thrusting its fingers and tendons down so low as well, dividing the line of the ground drawn on the old parchment so thoroughly that it might not have been there. They had no limits, trees. They were unconquerable.

Rin raised her head to the sky once more, and immediately looked down with an involuntary cry. The eye! She hadn't had a chance to see it, but she felt it burn, a prickling in her eyes that made them water.

"It's the eye, isn't it?" Kroner asked. "It's here! The stories were all right!" When she said nothing he went on. "I don't see how we could have lived here, once, as well as underground. It's very...large. I don't like it."

Rin perked up. She'd just heard something and she didn't think she was making it up. She felt the invisible cold caress on her face, but now she remembered the name for it—in the records it was drawn as small blue squiggles, but that was just to give it form, she realized now—this was wind. It posed no threat to her.

"It's like...we could get lost easily and—"

"Shhh!"

Kroner looked annoyed. "Why are you always telling me to—"

"Someone is over there," she said, jerking her head in the direction of the tree.

No sooner had she said it, when she heard the noise again. It was a laugh, definitely a laugh, cool and clear and belonging to a female, she was sure. Without further ado, Rin began to inch towards the tree. She couldn't quite locate where the laugh was coming from, and she did not want its owner to spot her before she spotted them. When she reached the base of the trunk, she stopped and listened again. She heard nothing this time, but what she *saw* was a different matter. Staring up at the side of the tree, she noticed a hole, cut perfectly round, sitting just above a small branch. That was when the certainty hit her: whoever she was looking for was *inside* the tree, and this hole was a sort of entrance.

Rin cast a glance back at Kroner, who was spinning around, weapon forgotten on the ground beside him. She had no idea what he was doing, but from this distance, it could not have looked more idiotic. Or conspicuous. She didn't dare to call out so close to possible quarry, so she waited until Kroner's spin took his eyes to a place level with hers and motioned him over.

When he got to her, Kroner started to speak, but she was prepared, and clapped a paw over his mouth. Looking up the sheer length of the tree made her dizzy, so she only concentrated on putting one foot in front of the other, reaching for one hold and then the next, and began to climb. Kroner, for once staying blessedly silent, followed her.

The ascent wasn't too hard once she got past concentrating on the fact that she was so high above the ground that a fall would surely kill her. The tree felt rough under her paws, and actually offered plenty of holds that were previously unseen to her when she stood beneath it. Every so often she would risk looking above her to see how close she had come to her goal, but she never looked down. To look down would be a mistake.

Finally, Rin found herself level with the small branch she'd noticed earlier. If she'd gone any farther, she would have hit her head against it. Maneuvering herself up onto the branch was not so hard, and from there she found she could see straight into the hole she'd seen. Someone was indeed inside.

The creature she saw was large and gray and looked like a rather ugly, mutated form of chipmunk. It sat with its back to her in the middle of a small room with a few chairs and a table inside. The creature was leaning over something she could not see, and occasionally shaking with little gusts of sound—the laughter she'd heard, Rin realized. Kroner had just pulled himself up next to her, and she felt rather than saw him stare in at the creature. It was completely oblivious to the two visitors in its window.

"What is—" Kroner hissed in fright, and in that instant, the creature turned around, realizing it was being watched. Its face was startled at first, and then frightened, whether by the weapon Rin held, now gleaming unsheathed, or by the paint on their faces, it was hard to tell. Before Rin could do anything, make any move, the creature trapped in the hollow let out a scream so sudden and heavy in force that she flinched and almost fell backwards into Kroner. Recovering quickly, she started forward, but something was holding her back. She turned and saw Kroner holding her tail, mouthing, 'no.' She kicked out at him, and when that did not work—she saw out of the corner of her eye, the creature was making for a hidden set of stairs she hadn't noticed at the side of the room—she smacked the flat side of her blade hard against Kroner's skull. It made a sound she could almost see, and Rin pulled free in the few seconds remaining to her and propelled herself into the hollow. The creature was fumbling down the stairs, but Rin caught up to her quickly and raised her dagger. The other never saw it coming from behind and later Rin would shiver even as she smiled at the thought of failure so complete as that of her hapless victim. She could not turn, she could not defend herself; indeed, all that was left to do was to fall, in that silent, yielding way, until she was face down on the stairs, body still pointed where she no doubt intended to go, dagger sticking out of her back, looking for all the world like someone's misplaced wind-up toy.

Rin thought only once of leaving the body for the gorepedes down below, but rejected the idea. They needed to concentrate on the living now, more than ever. She recovered her dagger and walked out past Kroner, who was staring at her with wide eyes, rubbing his head. She was confident that it wouldn't be long before these creatures realized they were under assault and rose to meet the challenge.

"One down," she muttered, staring out at the land below her. When she pushed past the crippling dizziness, it was strangely pleasant to see how small everything was. "The world to go."

CHAPTER VII

The sound of someone screaming cut Mercurie's concentration, rudely shattering any bit of good mood she had in her today. She jerked her head up from where it was hovering just above the unconscious flyer she was watching so intently and stared around, listening for more. There was nothing. Muttering to herself, the old black squirrel went back to staring at her charge. He'd told her not to touch her, and that much alone made her angry. He had no right to make extra demands. They had a deal.

She remembered him coming to her that day, the day they made the deal. Absoulim. She scoffed at the name; it was such a typical flyer name. And this one: Llewellyn. Not much different. It was no secret that they thought they were better than everyone else, flyers. Able to give out orders at the drop of a leaf and *everyone* would follow them. It was superior, it was obnoxious, and it was naïve.

"What do you have there, witch?" It was the first question he'd asked once she'd brought this one back.

She'd stared at him with every indication of dislike.

"It's what you asked for," she said from behind clenched teeth. "You ask me to chase her and to bring her here, and I do. I want my part of the deal."

Absoulim stepped forward and examined the collapsed flyer. She watched him step around her in circles, watched the dim light coming through the cracks in the collapsed tree play on his tattered wings and the grotesque scar running across the top of his back horizontally. There was another identical to it on his chest. They were ugly, yes, but so were many things that should have been impossible. They were her work. The way he walked, kind of twitchy and uneven, with lots of stops and starts, that was not hers. The spell she'd done had never had the effect of nerve damage before, so she'd had to assume that was all his. He talked sort of like the way he moved, and he moved like the way he looked, with his gaunt, strange limbs and his pale eyes. There was just something...off about him. She did not like him, of course, but she could not imagine the other flyers liking him either. Strange, since she usually imagined them one large band of pretentious fools, sticking together by the sheer force of their pretentious foolery.

She watched Absoulim watch her captive through wary eyes. He leaned over her once, and she saw some strange charm or other glint as it fell forward from its place around his neck. It hovered between him and the other flyer as he lifted one long paw and ran it down her chest. The expression on his face was indecipherable. Suddenly, he looked up at her sharply.

"She's alive."

"Yes," Mercurie agreed. "Now I want--"

"Where is the child?"

Ah. So that was what she was carrying. Mercurie shrugged, though her mind raced with confusion. Now that she brought herself back to it, she remembered clearly that the female flyer had been holding something as she ran...holding something all the way until she fell, and when Mercurie got to her there was nothing.

That's not really accurate though, is it? she asked herself. *No, you lost her for a while, and then she was not carrying anything when you got her trail again. Admit it.*

To him? Never. "There was no child," she lied. Absoulim glowered at her. Let him glower.

"My part of the deal was to bring her," she gestured at the unconscious flyer, "and anything she carried. She carried nothing, so I brought her. I kept my part of the deal. You must keep yours. Breaking it would be...hard on you."

Absoulim stared at her sharply, then made some movement she guessed was a nod. "Of course. But *not*...now."

Mercurie, who had been leaning forward in anticipation, now frowned at him. "Why not?"

There was something wrong with this. Something suspicious.

Absoulim was somewhere in his own thoughts. His eyes flicked around, half staring at her, half at the wall or at the motionless flyer on the ground or off into space. Wherever. She hated those eyes.

"She's with the white squirrel, isn't she?" Absoulim said. Mercurie wasn't sure whether he was addressing her, or who this *she* was, but she didn't want to gratify him with a response in either case. He continued unperturbed. "She's with the white squirrel, I think." Suddenly his attention was all on Mercurie again.

"We need to wait until she wakes. We need information."

Mercurie stared at him, studying him. "And when you have the information you need? Then I can take her?"

Absoulim stared at the wall for a while, that charm still glinting on his chest. For an astonished second she actually thought he might refuse—and what a mistake that would be—but he merely rolled his eyes up to the ceiling, turning away before speaking. His paws, she saw, were shaking.

"Yes," he said into the silence, "Then you can take her."

She could not do it now, though, that was her trap. Absoulim wanted her to watch the unconscious flyer until he woke up.

That was the thing about what she did; they always got tired so easily. There was really no way around it: when you were brought back from the dead you were more exhausted than normal, your body needed more chances to refuel—at least in the beginning.

When Absoulim had employed her help, he hadn't asked her about side effects, and now, now when he was tired he blamed her. She recalled the image of him on the squiggly branch outside her door back on the border of Maplewood, which seemed such a far way away now. She hadn't lived too far from Edgewood, which she soon found was Absoulim's destination. She remembered being surprised, staring at the shivering flyer on her doorstep—he might not have been shivering, but at the time she didn't know about the way his nerves seemed wired strangely, so she'd merely thought him cold. It *was* getting colder then.

"You're not from Edgewood, then?" she could remember asking him, and he said something about it being a long story—a long story she would likely never hear, not that she cared. She knew he was an outcast, an exile, which, much as she hated to make any connection with her customers, led her to the strange and uncomfortable territory of sympathy. Who knew what he was cast out for; maybe, looking at him, she thought it was his oddness, that strange uneasiness she felt about him. Flyers especially might be intolerant of such vibes. She was exiled herself from her old colony of Oakwood, simply for having her abilities. In a group of black squirrels in which any type of magic was seen as gruesome and unfavorable, Mercurie was forced out before she knew exactly why what she had was so threatening.

She remembered doing it on a friend, back before she realized having friends never paid off. He'd fallen from a tree so high, that there was no way he could have survived if the medics had tried to heal him. On the way down, her friend had twisted his back, and she'd run to help him, knowing there was nothing she could do. Or thinking so, anyway. Mercurie had called for help, and then put her paws on his chest, trying to gauge his breathing. Her friend—Rictus was his name, she remembered even now—had grabbed her paws as she went to pull away to make room for the help that was on its way.

"No," he'd said, and she heard something of peaceful amazement in his voice. "Leave them there."

Bewildered, Mercurie kept her paws on Rictus's chest as he breathed shallow, final-sounding gasps of air. She remembered better than anything else that moment when she realized the gasps *weren't* so final anymore, that Rictus was starting to breathe easily, and then of course, that the others were starting to mutter, mutter and back away.

It was *her*. She was somehow, unbelievably, mending her friend at a point when he should have been far past mending. For a while, she had been so caught up in the jubilation of that thought that she didn't realize that the others weren't taking it so well. Even Rictus, now that he was breathing again, stared at her with a new thing in his eyes: fear. It was something she didn't like then, but she would learn to love it as time went on; it was mere adaptation. She had wasted so much time trying to get him to talk to her again, trying to plead with the elders of her colony when they discussed removing her. During that time, however, she had practiced her skill, on smaller things like insects, and she found that her power did have limits. The creature which she brought back to life could not be fully dead: that was one of them, and the most important one. They had to be holding on to some spark of life in order for her bid to not be in vain. She could not do it a lot, that was another. Her power seemed to have a tiring effect on her, so that, while she did not actually feel anything decreasing, she could not muster enough from within to revive two creatures at once, or even in the same day.

They banished her, eventually. She hadn't done anything worth banishing, and she knew it, but soon that fact would change. With nothing left to hold her to pretending normalcy, she began to experiment more freely, and then more illicitly, with her craft. At first, she'd thought to offer her services to others, perhaps as a healer, but everywhere she went to stay a night, everyone gave her the same look she'd experienced on the faces of those from her colony. That fear. Some of the more prosperous bars or inns actually refused her service. She had plenty of rengolds from her parents, who had shamefacedly thrust a sack of them on her before she left—they had remained quiet during the decision-making, as far as she knew, but they hadn't stood up for her either. For a while, this amount of currency was able to keep her living in a renegade's fashion, slipping from place to place. At one point, she did not know when exactly, she stopped hating the fear that crept over the faces of those she encountered when she told them what she could do. She began to feel a sense of importance instead; they were afraid because if she could do this, bring others back from near-death, what else could she do?

It was a fair question, and she began to consider it in the seasons that followed, before she finally settled down in Maplewood, where rumor of magic was more likely to slide by without creating a ruckus. She began to experiment in different ways. She took a lone, dying heart from the chest of a dying child and made it beat again, and then, turning herself inside out and hoping for the best, she made it stop. Bit by bit, she discovered new ways she could flirt with death, and she came to think: if I can flirt with the deaths of others, why not that of myself?

She'd done it once, when she could feel herself getting old and near her time. The first victim of her attempts did not work: a young male fox squirrel, healthy and vital. She'd tried to pull that life force she'd come to recognize towards herself, wanting it so badly, but it had not come. She'd killed him, then, lest he talk to others about it, and gone on her way. Two more were similar, a female black squirrel and a male flyer, the latter of whom seemed to possess some magical ability, like herself. Neither of them worked, and she grew close to despair, before she came upon her last hope.

The gray female was young and strong and playing in the woods terribly alone. That had been her last mistake, one her parents would surely mourn forever. When Mercurie closed in on her, took her easily and stilled her with the mystery of her aura, she did not have much hope that this one would work. But when her paw brushed the young gray's chest, and she jumped a little, she felt it, almost in time with the young one's flinch. She had magic too, though it was weak and Mercurie doubted she knew it. Those who had magic and knew how to use it had no cause for such fear. She'd prepared herself for failure, still, but when she and the young squirrel came together in the force of Mercurie's spell, she felt a curious sensation. That life force from the other, the sound of her beating pulse and even the fluttering of her eyelashes, was moving—*coursing* into her, and with it came that unnamable magic, whatever budded power the young one unknowingly possessed. Mercurie had it; she had it all. As the other body became limp and went still in her paws, she marveled at how *alive* she felt. She must be younger, at least by several seasons. She'd gone back to the elm tree she considered home and stared into the mirror there breathlessly, looking for what she had felt beyond a doubt. And it was there, though not as she expected.

She did not look any younger except around the eyes, and that, she supposed, was the limitation of this particular power. She could gain herself time, but she would never become truly young again. The young gray had worked, she had deduced, because she was both female and had latent magic abilities. The same, she thought, as the flyer lying next to her in the here and now.

When Absoulim came to her, her only question had been of how he knew about her, and in the end she decided not to ask; seers knew a lot of things no one was supposed to know. He'd told Mercurie, moving about her living room—she could see that twitchy strangeness in him then—that he had something to do, unfinished business with the flyers of Edgewood. He told her that he wanted her to follow him, staying behind and unseen, until he needed her. And he thought he would need her, that was the interesting part. In none of her other assignments had her commissioner stated so blankly that he or she thought they might die; but then it was rare that any of them knew the specifics of her power. It made her a little nervous to know that her secret might not be wholly secret anymore.

She refused, though, to be afraid of her customers. So it was that she followed him to Edgewood, watched as Absoulim entered the tree by a window up high, but did not move a muscle for the whole afternoon, and then the night, as she waited. She could feel his life-force up there, in that tree, and she felt the moment when it snapped and every bit started to drain out of him.

Except for one.

There was snow on the ground that night, and she had waited as long as she could afford to make sure everyone was gone from wherever he was. She had doubted at first that he would be alive now; indeed, she had considered forgetting the whole thing and leaving him for dead, but he intrigued her. For one, how was he staying alive, holding on to that one last little strand of life for so long?

By all rights, Absoulim should have been dead when Mercurie finally entered Edgewood under the cover of darkness. She had scaled the great tree, circling it until she could feel the pulse of that one little bit of life, somewhere close. There was a balcony-like projection on one side of the tree, a hollow with a spade-like lip, and she could sense that it was beyond this that Absoulim lay.

He'd been flat on his face when she reached him, and he did not appear to be breathing at all. She did not wonder whether she could have been mistaken; she was never mistaken. He was alive, as surely as she could bring him back. It would take a lot of energy though, and it did. He'd been stabbed through the back, right between the shoulder blades, and the dagger had gone straight through him. When he became conscious again, the first thing he said to her was "go after her." Mercurie had blinked at him, unable to believe the rudeness, the gall.

"It's a flyer," he started to say, "she's carrying something. I need what she's carrying."

Mercurie was silent. Then she said, stonily, "I've brought you back to life. Don't you think that's enough of a mission to be sending me on? I'm through."

Absoulim, to her surprise, did not show any alarm at this. He merely smiled—or did what passed for a smile for him, one side of his mouth jerking up a little. His face looked like a skull in the dark of the room.

"I think you'll want what *she* has," he told her.

Mercurie wanted to feel angry, but he'd hit upon the tugging need she'd begun to feel over the last season, the warning pullings of age on her frame. So it was that she had made up her mind to track this flyer, to see if it was really true, if she really did have some potential. If not, she told herself, she could show him exactly why it was no one messed around with Mercurie Blackwood.

But there was another, stranger thing he'd wanted her to do as well. She'd had to be careful for that one, since it involved sneaking into a highly guarded room deeper in Edgewood. When she came back with what he wanted, he'd stared at it hungrily, and then she remembered seeing that charm hanging about his neck for the first time.

"What are you going to do," she'd asked, "with a crystal ball?"

"I am going to travel," Absoulim had answered, and when she'd only given him an incredulous look, he gave a sort of impatient twitch. "*You* know. I register as spirit, do I not?"

Mercurie understood then, though she still could not believe her ears.

"That is a very complex spell," she said slowly, "If I were to...bind you to the crystal ball, especially since it is not your own, there's no guarantee that you'll survive it—"

"Are you saying you cannot do it, witch?"

Mercurie's blood ran cold with anger when she said, "Oh yes. I can do it."

And she did. For the time that she ran after Llewellyn, she carried the crystal ball with her in her pack. With the crystal ball was Absoulim. She had managed to make him become a part of the orb for the time being, but the time was limited. It was an ancient spell, and it took a lot from anyone involved in the casting. It was dangerous, and immediately she had wondered why she would agree to chance such a thing for an unsavory customer such as this flyer, but the pact between them was already made, and she realized that he'd introduced new terms. This spell was needed to get Absoulim anywhere; otherwise he would be too tired to make the journey, and they couldn't take the time to let their new objective, this runaway flyer, escape. Absoulim wanted whatever it was she had, and Mercurie, well, now she couldn't help wanting the squirrel who had it. She needed to find this squirrel she was tracking, and quickly, before both she and Absoulim died from the spell's expiration.

Well, now she was here, with the captive she'd managed to track until her collapsing, and she was still not sure she wouldn't have to show Absoulim what was what, *revoke* that little gift she'd so generously given him, so to speak.

He was aware. He was aware that she could end this for him, ruin all of his plans, whatever they were, as surely as sudden rain cured a drought. Yet still he kept quietly provoking her at times, complaining of how tired he was or of how roughly his healing was done. She would have thought, with his wings in the state they were in, he was used to rough healing. It wasn't as though the jagged, ugly scar down his front was marring an otherwise beautiful sight. Sometimes she thought that maybe he risked too much because he knew too much. With none of the seer ability herself, Mercurie could not tell what Absoulim was thinking, where he had been, anything of what his story was. But she felt that maybe he knew more about her than she was comfortable with anyone knowing. For this reason and many others, she was getting out of here as soon as she got what she wanted.

But oh, what a prize it was. The flyer lying on the ground beside her probably didn't have any clue as to the force of her power, but Mercurie could feel it even now, a steady pulse of prescience that filled her with hungry anticipation. With the last one, the young gray, she hadn't known the power that her victim possessed, so she could not make use of whatever power she had ingested. With this one, she was determined not to make the same mistake. There must be some way she could figure out what her power was, and how it worked. Was she a seer? She could find no answer to that question in the splaying of the younger squirrel's limbs or in the lines of her sleeping face. She would need to go deeper. But—she did not know if she had the time.

What will he do if he finds out?

Mercurie decided she didn't care. It wasn't as if she was taking the young squirrel right now; she only wanted to make the most of what she would be getting when she did.

Leaning forward until her face hovered, level, with the unconscious flyer's, she placed both of her paws gently on the sides of the other's face.

The jolt was so immediate that she almost let go; images flew through her mind in a blur of color and noise. Try as she might to hold on to one or two of them which showed with more clarity than the others, she found that they slipped right out of her fingers again. The whirring of images and sound did not seem to be coming to a stop, and Mercurie felt herself going dizzy, unconscious of the outside world with no way to steady herself. If she didn't get control of this soon, she could be harmed.

Speak, came a voice from somewhere—Mercurie couldn't discern whether it was the flyer's mind or her own, but she was no longer sure there was a difference. The voice seemed to be asking for her reason, for why she was here; it recognized her as something foreign, but it did not repel her. Her brain struggled for an image to grasp, some words, anything.

"The white squirrel," she blurted, without any idea why she should say that over anything else; she should have asked about the other's power, but she'd become disoriented. Absoulim had mentioned this white squirrel several times, as though he was at the crux of whatever the seer was trying to do, but Mercurie had never been terribly interested. As soon as she spoke, however, the whirring stopped and she was looking, as through another's eyes, at the blurry image of a conference room of sorts. An elderly flyer was standing at the head of the room, addressing the squirrels to either side of her, and she realized that she was one of their number.

"The white squirrel," the elder was saying, "Is a danger to us all. We do not know the reason for his elongated stay, but we can tell you right now for sure that it is nothing good."

Mercurie did not feel herself turn, as she seemed to have no control over her own body, but her vision suddenly shifted to the back of the room, where she saw, to her considerable shock, someone who was unmistakably recognizable as Absoulim, leaning up against the wall. He was standing a considerable ways apart from the other flyers, all sitting down, and he looked much younger, more awkward than creepy, all except for those unsettling eyes, which at this moment were staring right into her own. Her vision shifted again to the front of the room; the old flyer was giving them all a very stern look.

"I warn you, if your training is important to you, if you want to keep to the hope of becoming a seer, than you will steer clear of him for the time while he is here. Leave the elders to deal with him, to figure out what he wants. This is your only warning..."

The scene shifted and Mercurie was in a small hallway now, with nothing but a few firefly lanterns ranged along the wall for light.

"So you think I'm dangerous, now?"

The white squirrel was standing right in front of her, his face set in a roguish grin.

Her eyes went up to meet his, which persisted in staying in the shadows at this angle.

"Don't be stupid, Zirreo" she heard a voice say which was not her own, though the vibrations came from the body she was in. "I wouldn't have come to see you if that were the case. But...they say you have powers that are best left alone. Is that true?"

One of the firefly lanterns guttered out as the creature within died and there was a noise behind her as of feet racing away. Mercurie's host turned so quickly that she felt dizzy. There was a long while in which she watched the hall behind them.

"Llewellyn," the white squirrel called Zirreo finally said, and Mercurie's eyes were back on him as Llewellyn turned.

"I thought I heard something."

"Afraid of us being alone now?"

"No!" But she realized he was teasing, so she subsided. Mercurie could feel that she was angry, though. "What is it that you have? Why do you keep avoiding that question? If I mean anything—"

Zirreo put a paw up to her mouth and beckoned her forward. He was clasping his paws together now and at first Mercurie couldn't see anything. Then, slowly, his paws became filled with a strange light, flickering but modestly strong. It was bright as the light thrown off from five candles, but there were no candles in sight. Holding the light in his palms, he walked towards Llewellyn a few steps before holding them out to her.

"Touch," he said.

Mercurie watched as Llewellyn reached a paw out, tentatively.

"Will it hurt?"

Zirreo didn't answer. The light looked very much like that of a candle's flame, and Mercurie knew what her own answer to the command would be, but a second later, Llewellyn's paws came down, connecting with Zirreo's. She gasped a little, and he took both of her paws and put them together between his own. The light flared up again for an instant, then it was gone.

"That is what I have," Zirreo said quietly.

"*All* you have?" Llewellyn asked, but her voice sounded groggy. She pressed her face up against Zirreo's chest, and Mercurie only saw blackness.

"Yes," came Zirreo's voice from above her.

It was apparently enough.

The next time the scene changed, it was to a busy hallway filled with the daylight from one long window set in the end of it. Several flyers passed her, all looking under twenty seasons, all talking animatedly to one another.

"So I guess I'm mating Genhaw," Llewellyn said, swerving around a cluster of squirrels who had stopped to chat. "Get out of the way!" she called back to them in a mock-scary voice. Someone shouted something back but Mercurie couldn't hear what it was. "I don't want anyone to get suspicious, or anything," she continued.

"Who else would it be?"

Mercurie thought she recognized the voice even before Llewellyn turned and Absoulim was in her sight once more. Those unnerving eyes were looking right at her, and the squirrels walking past on the other side of

Absoulim gave him occasional stares which he didn't seem to register. Many of them gave him a wider berth than was necessary to get by.

Llewellyn started to say something when one of the doors up ahead of them opened, and out came Zirreo, pushing his way through the crowd away from them in what Mercurie thought was a rather anxious manner. From the door he'd just vacated came two wizened looking flyers, both of whom stared after Zirreo before starting forward after him.

"Move out of the way, go on! You'll move for him, but not for your elders! Shame on you all!"

As the elders cut their way through the excitable crowd, Llewellyn turned back to Absoulim. For a split second, the expression on his face was unguarded, though Mercurie perceived that Llewellyn didn't register the emotion there.

"I don't think that white squirrel is that powerful," Absoulim said.

"He is," Llewellyn said, much too quickly. Absoulim stared at her.

"I mean, you don't need to talk to him to know," she said awkwardly, "It's just his aura."

"He seems weak to me."

"You don't need to do horrible things to be powerful," Llewellyn said, and there was danger to her voice. "I think we should talk to him, though. About our powers. He might know something that will help us bring them out. Probably knows more than the elders anyway. And the elders would freak out." There was a definite grin in her voice as she turned to Absoulim, who looked less than enthused.

"I already know my power," he said. Those eyes were so weird, half looking at Llewellyn, half elsewhere.

Mercurie noticed he was holding a scroll of some sort in his paws; it did not speak to her of standard issue reading material. As she watched the scroll began to shake, and she had to wonder whether his tremors were all as random as she'd assumed.

"That's the thing, though," Llewellyn was saying, and this time her tone took a dip towards troubled, "everyone else is getting the hang of theirs. Genhaw, that obnoxious twat, knows his, Admira and Thilen know theirs, even you—"

"Even?" But at that moment, Absoulim stumbled over something on the ground; there was a shout of laughter from somewhere nearby, and as Llewellyn started to speak, to move forward, the scene changed...

She was in a room, a long room filled with curious shelves on which large beads of dew glistened atop ornate, metallic frames. These crystal balls filled the room with a light so eerie that Mercurie wouldn't have been sure she was in the same tree anymore if she didn't recognize the room from her own ventures. The white squirrel was here again, and he was standing with his paw against one of the shelves, looking down at her.

"That's all?" Llewellyn asked, but it sounded forced. There was a deep joy in her voice that Zirreo seemed to pick up on.

"Yes," he said, smiling. "Just remember that if you get discouraged. You're in here, so you're in the plans."

"What plans?"

He only smiled again. "It's just a figure of speech."

There was a period of silence in which each squirrel looked somewhere different, pretending at observing the room casually. Then: "Can you show me?" she asked.

"What could I show you?"

"You *know*. My power. I feel it, sometimes, I think. But...I'm afraid of it."

"Well, that's no good. You need to be open." There was a long pause, and Zirreo seemed to be thinking. "I can...teach you, if you want."

Llewellyn turned back to him so fast that Mercurie became dizzy again. The black squirrel was holding her breath now, hoping against hope...

But something was happening. The air around her was getting thinner, and though Mercurie saw Zirreo open his mouth to speak, the words that came from his mouth seemed immediately sucked away from her on a wind she could not see. The air began to brighten, then the room started to spin around her. She was being dislodged from Llewellyn, she realized, and tried desperately to will herself back to her unwitting host.

"Your power," she said this time, "show me your power," but her own voice seemed lost to her on the current of whatever change was taking place.

Suddenly she felt herself shoved backwards, as though an unseen paw had actually *pushed* her forcefully away, and she felt solid ground under her body.

She was back beside the unconscious flyer, in the damp rotting darkness of the burnt out log, and all was silent except for the ringing in her ears, the ringing left over from the memories she'd managed to intrude upon. Her own head was aching something fierce, and when the world stopped spinning around her, she attempted to sit up and felt a shooting pain go through her head, barreling at the speed of merciless light.

"Ah!" she gasped, and raised herself more slowly this time, glancing about herself to make sure she was really alone still. Yes, Absoulim was nowhere in sight, which she took as a sign that the seer must still be resting. If he'd been here to see what she'd done...well, so what? She held the cards, after all. She should not have to keep reminding herself of this. She held the cards, and she was alone.

Not quite, she realized, as she looked over at Llewellyn, the flyer she finally had a name for. Her eyelids were fluttering and she was moaning something, some indistinguishable mix of words, deep in her throat. Suddenly, she understood why she was thrust from the flyer's mind so violently.

Llewellyn was waking up.

CHAPTER VIII

Kinder was surprising himself with his own skill as a pathfinder. Really, it was his memory doing all the work; he'd come with Zirreo by all the landmarks he led Mariyen past now, the only difference being that then everything wasn't covered with a thin layer of snow like it was now. The appropriate fall weather of today had made the snow begin to melt into the cover of leaves beneath it, however, and the world wasn't too unrecognizable to him. He knew he could take them to Firwood, the last place Mariyen had seen Zirreo, but how they would find the border between Firwood and Oakwood was a mystery to him—a mystery he tried not to think too long and hard about. No one, in all the tales of travels and adventures he remembered from his youth, came two thirds of the way to their destination before becoming hopelessly lost. It just didn't happen.

Mariyen walked slightly behind him as the day turned slowly to dark. He would have to find somewhere for them to stay soon. Kinder started measuring up the trees and all of the places on the ground around them.

"We're going to have to stop soon," he told Mariyen, voicing his thoughts. He wondered again if going after Zirreo was worth it, and decided again that it was. The white squirrel had been less than a joy to travel with, and he had undeniably used Kinder to his own ends, bringing him to Edgewood as a diversion and then leaving him there as he went about whatever mission he was on now, but he was interesting, there was no denying that.

And he knew it. Wasn't that how he had survived so long among so many who were unlike him or distrusted him? Kinder remembered too well how Zirreo himself had admitted to not getting along with the other white squirrels. His own kind! They had imprisoned him for being troublesome. And he had survived that, too. There came a point where you had to wonder...

"*Can* he die?"

"What?" Mariyen had broken out of her own reverie of thoughts.

"Nothing," Kinder said, feeling his face heat. He was not ready to share that one with her yet. Saying it out loud made him realize how ridiculous it was. Besides, hadn't they both seen Zirreo near death when Absoulim threw that spell at him in the observatory at Edgewood? He didn't think a seer like Absoulim would set out to kill someone they knew could not die—and seers knew everything. Or a good deal, in any case.

Mariyen was still looking at him, brow raised.

"You look troubled."

"I just want to find a spot to stay before the night comes again."

It was a solid reason, he thought, though he didn't think Mariyen was entirely convinced. They *had* been travelling for a night and a day already without rest, and neither of them was going to argue with the good sense of what he'd said.

"Kinder, do you think Zirreo knows?"

"Knows what?" Kinder took a piece of oat bread from his pack and began to eat it, hoping Mariyen would be too distracted to say anything. They'd eaten an hour ago, and Mariyen had threatened to carry the pack herself if he kept depleting their rations.

"I wonder if he knows..." She turned, and Kinder jumped, thinking she would mention the bread, but she only gave him a contemplative look. "...that we're following him?"

The thought made Kinder uncomfortable. He quickly swallowed his last mouthful of bread. "What makes you think he would know?" he asked, unsure whether he wanted so much of an in on her visions, if that was what this was about.

"When I fainted...or whatever happened to me back there—Zirreo looked at me. It was how I ended up waking up. It was like he...propelled me out of the dream or something. Like he knew I was there and he was telling me to go."

"Maybe it just looked like he knew you were there," Kinder suggested. Mariyen didn't look convinced. "I mean, if he knew you were watching him, he wouldn't have mentioned where he was going, would he?"

"Maybe he didn't know then," Mariyen argued, but she looked comforted by the idea.

Kinder stopped by a good-sized maple tree and began to circle its trunk. He came back around the other side and gave Mariyen the thumbs-up. She followed him to where he was standing and stared down at the spacious shelter made by four or five of the mutant, raised roots of the tree. She flashed him a grin, nodding, and crawled into the shelter, sitting down and leaning her back up against one of the roots that served as a skeletal wall.

"It's perfect, Kinder!" she said, leaning back and appearing to relax. Kinder shoved his pack in and then leaned over and stuck his head in after it. He *had* done a good job. Maybe there was hope for their ragged team of two after all. Pulling the rest of his body under the shelter, he was pleased to notice that he didn't get stuck on the way through, though once inside, he found that he became extremely conscious of what close quarters they held. He was about to say something to dispel his own awkwardness when Mariyen spoke again.

"What do you think he's doing, Kinder?"

Kinder turned his attention from the rapidly darkening sky. He could see patches of it through the branches of the other trees around them, and if one only concentrated on a single patch, it looked like as much like the portal to another world as it did a harmless patch of sky. He was glad Mariyen had spoken. Even if she was talking about Zirreo again. Even if Zirreo was not the best subject to relieve his nerves.

Where Zirreo was going, though...he had honestly never thought of it. With the type of squirrel Zirreo was, he had always just assumed that he had some business to do elsewhere, some covert operation befitting someone with his rumored skill. Kinder didn't doubt that skill. He'd travelled with the white squirrel before, and though it may have seemed coincidence then that no serious trouble befell them, that the journey went swiftly and running into other squirrels was a rarity, he sincerely doubted that dumb luck was all to blame. But there was another option, another explanation of why Zirreo might have left.

"He's trying to hide himself, I think," Kinder mused.

Mariyen seemed to think about that, before nodding. "You know, you're probably right. He told the innkeeper that no one would remember him within a few days, though I don't know how that's possible! A white squirrel coming through any area has got to create quite a stir!"

Kinder thought he knew, and he told her as much, told her about the strange luck of his journey with Zirreo. What Mariyen said just confirmed his idea that Zirreo wanted to get as far as possible from anyone who knew him, leaving the trouble he'd caused for others to clean up. He probably wanted to build a home in some abandoned tree, put up wards around the place, and call it home, just as he had been doing when he and Lute found him. Kinder felt his eyelids drifting shut toward one another, the queer magnetism of extreme fatigue.

"Why," he heard Mariyen say, through ears that seemed to mute everything he heard, "would Zirreo be going to an exact location like the border between Firwood and Oakwood if he only wanted to hide himself? And why would he tell anyone?"

"Perhaps he was lying," Kinder said, not truly thinking about it. Mariyen went silent at that, or he thought she did. He was almost completely in the land of slumber now, and neither Mariyen's voice nor the possibility that they were going on a luckless chase of a squirrel who could be headed in the opposite direction for all they knew, could shake him from the warm swelling of sleep coming up to snatch him away.

The sound of Mariyen screaming did.

It felt only a few seconds later that Kinder jerked himself up from the prone position he'd settled into, hitting his head soundly on one of the roots above him. At first it seemed that the panicked thudding of his own heart was what had woken him; then he remembered, as the second scream pierced the night and he stared out, trying to locate whatever it was with his own eyes. As he did so, he realized that there was another part to his unease: the nauseating, edgy feeling he used to get from the ground at times was back, and it was strong, much stronger than he'd ever felt it before.

It was then that he heard the rushing, sucking sound coming from somewhere beneath him, and the dread increased tenfold. Kinder tried to move, but he felt paralyzed to the spot, the roots that had once formed a shelter seeming more a cage to him now. He managed to throw himself to the ground and began to crawl for an exit, not sure which way was the right way to be going. Where was Mariyen?

Suddenly, the explosive sound of ground breaking, rocks falling, and roots snapping assaulted his ears, and Kinder felt the ground beneath his back feet slide away under him. As frightening as that was, the feeling he was getting on his tail, the feeling of something hot, too much like breath, was far worse. Something whipped across his back, soft and pliant and cold to the touch. Frantically, he clawed himself forward, forward, until he was out of their shelter, or what remained of it anyway.

Kinder turned to look back once, for as long as he dared, and what he saw behind him was enough to put the chill in any bedtime story. The thing was long and huge and of some opaque white color in the night. It had come up through the ground like a monster of an earthworm, and in its hunger, plunged its body straight through the top of Kinder's root shelter. It was possibly the only reason he did not die, he realized; the beast was momentarily stuck in the coil of roots, but it was a problem that it was quickly remedying, he noticed. Two tentacle-like protrusions on the front of the thing waved about desperately as it tried to free itself, a project that was soon to come to an end. Sure enough, the roots began to crack under the weight of its flailing, and its giant, eyeless head turned toward Kinder.

He ran, tearing over the ground in a heady race for safety, knowing that however likely he was to escape, he was hundreds of times more likely to be caught by the creature and eaten from the inside. Images flashed through his mind of the other victims of these creatures that he and Lute had stumbled upon, flattened empty husks of the squirrels they once were, eyes empty, insides completely gone. That sucking sound was nearing him—he thought, in his panic, that he felt the hot breath of something on his back and he dove forward, feeling himself collide with something else.

"Ow!" Mariyen said, and Kinder jumped up immediately and began pulling her in the direction he was going.

"Mariyen, we have to get out, we have to—"

"Not that way!" she screamed, "there's more of them!"

More? Kinder's stomach felt like it had been turned inside out and set to a temperature of freezing. He felt Mariyen pull him in another direction and heard the sucking noise again, this time right behind him for certain.

"Run!"

Without another thought or another look back, Kinder did just that, taking off in the direction Mariyen was going and hoping to Astrippa that another of the beasts wouldn't come up from the ground right in front of them and end their flight for good.

Kinder saw a tree rise up out of the darkness in front of them, and when Mariyen got to it, she immediately leaped for the trunk, Kinder not far behind. The moment he felt his feet hit and grip onto the rough, comforting bark, he tore up the tree without thought of what he might encounter above. It surely couldn't be worse than what they were running from below.

He followed Mariyen blindly as she plunged into a hollow that opened up before them like a trick of magic; he hadn't seen it there before, but he dove into it as though it were his only salvation, and, not daring to look beyond the lip of wood in front of him, he huddled on the ground, panting hard.

The two squirrels waited in silence for a while, listening. Kinder was sure he heard the hissing of something right below them—or was it coming up the tree at this very moment?

"Can they climb, do you think?" he whispered to Mariyen, noticing as he did so that his own voice was trembling so much it was barely recognizable.

She shrugged, but didn't say anything. He understood that she probably didn't have the breath or the voice to speak, something he also felt himself experiencing as the moments ticked by.

At long last, Mariyen raised her head from where she, too, was crouched on the floor, and said, "I think they're gone."

"Er," Kinder began, also rising to a sitting position, but quickly falling into a slump against the wall. "We're not going to go outside and check, are we?"

Mariyen stared at him, then burst out laughing. In the hollow, the sound seemed a most welcome, most unearthly thing of beauty, and it drove Kinder to laughter as well. Sides aching, he slumped further down on the wall and sighed. The sleep was almost coming back to him, but he still felt so weird, so like he'd just avoided death that it was hard to relax enough even now after he'd let the laughter go in waves of stress and fear.

"What were those things?" Mariyen asked him at long last. Kinder knew she'd refrained for as long as possible, as the topic would surely drive all salvaged levity from the room. And sure enough, no sooner had she mentioned the beasts below when Kinder remembered the thing that had brought him to this place, sitting in a hollow with a flyer he really hardly knew, so far from the place he'd once called home.

"They're monsters," he said baldly. "The—Zirreo told me about them. Well, me and Lute, when we were trying to find out what was wrong with the ground."

He thought of Nadra, the elderly squirrel who had treated him like her own son back at home in Pinewood; she'd been killed this way. She'd run at one point and tripped, but unlike him, she hadn't managed to get up in time, hadn't managed to save herself. Instead of a warm hollow in wait for her, there was only the road back to where she'd come from, where her mate Skellan suddenly felt the forebodings of bad news and set down the pie he'd been trying to keep warm for her arrival, letting it go cold.

"My—I knew someone who died because of them. She was one of the best squirrels I ever knew."

"She?"

"She was like a mother to me," he said, and Mariyen seemed to soften her posture against the wall.

"Is that why you're here, then? The elders...that was what they wanted guarding against?"

Kinder nodded.

"Well, for once I can't say I blame them," she said, looking down. Then, "It's happened before, you know."

"Yeah?" Kinder looked up again. He could sense that she was trying to keep him from his more destructive thoughts, and he appreciated it, not being alone right now.

"Yeah. I saw their records, right before I moved into my room. I was checking it out, and I knew I wasn't supposed to, because the elders don't like for anyone to see anything important without their permission. Horus found me...they were records of recent deaths, all seemingly resulting from the ground, as though it just reached up and swallowed them whole. Some of them were older than others. This phenomenon, I guess, has gone on before. It feels weird not to have known about it."

"Well, it didn't directly affect them enough," Kinder said, then hoped he wasn't taken the wrong way. Mariyen only nodded.

"I could feel it, you know," Kinder supplied. "Before. I just thought that the ground was releasing, well...bad vibes or something. I had a lot of, um, charms then. I just used them to comfort myself, I think." He wasn't entirely convinced of this, but he was surprised to find some truth pocketed away in those words once he voiced them aloud. "It's just—it's the first time I've ever seen one of *them*."

"They're horrible," Mariyen shuddered. "I wonder why they went away for a while?"

"Zirreo told us that they were being controlled by something, or someone," Kinder told her. "These sort of underground squirrels."

"Underground squirrels?" Mariyen couldn't seem to hide her disbelief, and Kinder had to agree. It was ridiculous. To imagine a whole colony of squirrels living underground made him dizzy.

"Well," he said, "It was the white squirrel. I don't know how he can know anyway."

"I'm beginning to think he really knows everything," Mariyen said. "It's really started to creep me out. If he knows so much, why isn't he doing anything to stop it?"

Kinder shrugged. There were really only two possible answers to that, and they both knew it.

Either he couldn't, or he wouldn't.

They both knew which one they wanted least.

~~~

That night, Mariyen dreamt, and in her dream was a heavy ridge of fire, a thousand jeering eyes in the dark, and the wormlike creatures coming closer, closer to her where she stood on a rise on some unidentified part of the land.

She felt that she wanted to run, but knew she couldn't anymore, even though there was nothing but the open air behind her, teasing at her back and tail. She stood there, and those things in the dark moved as one, coming ever closer. The dark, too, was moving with them, and as its tendrils climbed over the sky in front of her, she began to feel sick. She sensed that something was in her paws, but she could not look down to see what it was.

I can't do this, she thought, over and over in rapid gut-aching repetition, though she could not have said what it was she couldn't do. There was a sentient part of her that suddenly realized, *this is a dream,* and this made her no less frightened because as it pulled at her, beckoning her back to the land of the waking, the dark and the eyes and the beasts got closer, and her conscious self began to flicker on the edge of extinction.

Finally, she turned from herself, gave herself up for a lost cause, and it surprised her that she could turn away from herself in a dream—she was oddly not stuck in her own body, it seemed. The Mariyen on the hill looked sick to her stomach, but Mariyen found she could detach herself from the intensity of that feeling by turning away. She could not get rid of the sickly unease that continued to run through her veins as she proceeded to ignore herself, though.

"Something's wrong," she said, seemingly to no one, but moments later she realized this was not so: of course.

The white squirrel was sitting in a wicker chair on the side of an adjoining slope, looking for all the world like he'd appeared out of nowhere.

Okay, Mariyen told herself, *it's only a dream. I'll just go with it.* She could feel herself too much in the mind of dream-Mariyen, where fear still raged uncontrollable, and she needed to pull herself out in order to maintain herself.

"Of course something is wrong," Zirreo said, not seeming bothered by the pronouncement. "Something is always wrong, when you think about it."

"What do you want?" she said, then hoped that she hadn't sounded too impertinent. What if he refused to speak to her?

Zirreo raised his brow. "What do I want?" he asked. "I could ask the same to you. I am going to have to ask, unfortunately, that you do not follow me any longer."

Mariyen took a step back. "I—we want to know—"

"You cannot," Zirreo said.

"Absoulim!" she cried desperately, for she could feel herself being pulled out of the dream, as if Zirreo were doing it himself and she could buy herself more time if she only thought quick. "Absoulim is still alive!"

The persistent tugging continued, but Zirreo stared at her now with something that resembled surprise. He opened his mouth, and she hoped with all of her being—

"You need to go back," he said, though his face was not entirely composed and she couldn't shake the notion that she'd said something to him that he hadn't known, hadn't anticipated.

"I know where you are," Mariyen continued, because the pulling she felt lessened the slightest bit when she talked to Zirreo. "I know where you're going, too. I heard in the—"

"Do you?" Zirreo interrupted, and she felt something clamp down inside her head, making her thoughts seem fuzzy and overlarge. She struggled to remember what they were talking about, to find some words to say, but before she could formulate a single phrase, she felt herself repelled almost violently, pushed from the picture again in the way she could remember from the other dream, or vision, or whatever it had been.

Mariyen woke up on the cold wood floor of someone's hollow—not her own—and for a moment she couldn't remember where she was. Turning over and raising herself up on one paw, she saw the heavy snoring lump that was Kinder, and it all came back to her.

Those creatures...she'd wandered away from their shelter just to think without disturbing Kinder, to take a walk so that she didn't fall asleep. She was afraid of sleeping for the dreams it brought lately, but her efforts had obviously gone out the window. She needed to sleep, and sleep she would, sooner or later. After those beasts, the way that eyeless head had reared up, breaking through where seconds before there had only been solid ground—well, after them, the thought of dreaming wasn't so terrifying.

The beasts had followed her to the dream though, she remembered that. She strained to remember the rest, but it was slipping from her as she thought.

Zirreo. He was there. She found it harder to remember what she'd seen as dream-Mariyen, on the hill in the middle of nowhere, but she remembered Zirreo.

He didn't want them to follow, that was no longer up for debate. And he knew they were following, there was another thing she and Kinder would never have to wonder about again. But they would follow anyway, whether Zirreo liked it or not. They needed to find him, they needed answers.

She knew it wasn't a good idea. What would a white squirrel who reputedly knew a long dead sort of magic do if he knew they were following him against his will? She doubted he could do much from wherever he was now, but what about when they caught up to him at...

At where? Greater than any jolt she'd received in the dream was the one that came along with realizing she didn't know where Zirreo was headed.

She had once, though, she was sure of it. They wouldn't be going on this chase if she hadn't known.

It's okay, she tried to calm herself, *he's going...he's obviously going...he's going...*

But she couldn't remember. She thought then of Zirreo and of his firm words, and of that last sensation, that blurry clamp on her mind, and felt a sinking sensation spread through the pit of her.

The first light of dawn tinged the inside of the hollow with a warm glow, and after minutes of lying in it, Mariyen began to feel warmer. She looked over at Kinder when he shifted in his sleep, muttering something about soup, and a thought occurred to her: was it possible? She didn't dare to hope too much.

Finally, when the sun was almost high in the sky, Kinder began to stretch and stir into wakefulness.

"Mmmmm," he murmured to himself, still apparently caught in the throes of some wonderful dream, "yes, and some of that tart, if you don't mind..."

Mariyen felt a bit jealous; why couldn't her dreams be about tasty treats instead of dangerous forebodings?

"Kinder," she hissed, when his stirrings turned out only to be attempts to flip himself over, a task that seemed arduous in nature. "Kinder, wake up!"

When he didn't stir, she reached over and pinched his nose shut. It took only a few seconds this time.

"Aghhhh!" Kinder shot up and stared around him frantically. "Where is it? Where's the pie?"

When he'd looked around the hollow twice, Mariyen could see the realization registering on his face, and then the embarrassment as all he saw was the rising sun and her grinning at him.

"Was there a feast of some sort?"

"Um."

"Kinder, I have to ask you something," she remembered, coming back to her original purpose so suddenly that he blinked, still trying to disengage the sleep from his eyes.

"Where are we going?" she asked.

Kinder stared at her. "Huh?"

She tried to hold onto her patience, but panic was beginning to grip her. "Please tell me you remember. *Where are we going?*"

Kinder seemed to register her alarm, and said, "Well, the white squirrel, right? We're going to see him." He stared at her in confusion.

"Where is he though?"

"Well, we don't know," said Kinder, giving her a bit of a look, like she'd hit her head in the night, "but you told me it was between Oakwood and Firwood. You know, the border. So...we're going there."

He stared at her apprehensively. "Are you all right?"

But Mariyen was more than all right. She relaxed, realizing how tense she'd become in questioning him.

She was one step ahead of Zirreo, it seemed. Her mother used to have a dream link with him, and somehow—Mariyen, remembering the dream of the crystal ball, tried not to dwell on *how* too long—that link had been dissolved and she was left with it instead. But what she'd momentarily forgotten was that Kinder had no such link with the white squirrel. Kinder couldn't possibly know what Zirreo was doing, but that also meant that Zirreo couldn't possibly know what Kinder was doing. When she'd seen Zirreo in her dreams, she had the sensation that he knew she was following him. Now she not only knew that was true, but Zirreo had attempted to erase the memory of his destination—what *must* be his true destination—from her mind. He assumed that without knowledge of where he was going, Mariyen would have no choice but to quit following him, to give up her chase.

What he didn't know was Mariyen's secret weapon. Zirreo didn't know that anyone else was with her. He didn't know about Kinder, and that was their strength.

You have less control than you think, she told Zirreo's face as it cropped up again in her mind, still incredulous, still superior. *I'm*—we're—*going to find you, and there's nothing—for once—that you can do about it.*

Zirreo's face only continued to raise its brows back at her.

She supposed he had nothing to say.

CHAPTER IX

Rin stared up above her, through the leaves of one of the trees. The sky was divided into small triangular factions of blue and silver-rimmed white. There were a few berries left dangling on the tree above, and they looked ripe and juicy, though she refrained from eating the fallen ones on the ground all around her, just in case they were not as they appeared.

Nothing here was as it appeared; this was one of the more important lessons she had to learn. The world looked so deceptively beautiful, but when the eye in the sky found her, her neck prickled with heat and her eyes burned. The creatures here spoke a language she understood and looked almost like her from a distance, but they were large and ugly and crude up close. The berries here, too, she suspected, though so perfect on the surface, would be rotten at the core. It was only logical.

The eye in the sky was beginning to disappear, to hide itself, though Rin knew from previous nights that another eye appeared, this one duller and safer to look at, but its beams still seemed strikes of violence against her eyes, unused to anything but the light of glowworms. She flipped over on her side, and got up from the ground, dusting herself off. She couldn't believe she'd been lying around for so long! She mentally berated herself for all the time she'd lost. Earlier in the day, she had tried to sleep, but the light made it difficult for her. Even when she closed her eyes, she could see it pounding in bright red behind her eyelids, demanding entrance: it was infuriating.

Her original plan had been to search out her enemies during the night, when most of them seemed to be asleep, but she didn't know if she could keep up with it if she couldn't get any sleep under the light of the eye. It had worked wonderfully the night before, though; after taking the female to the god of life below, she had stumbled upon a tree with four inhabitants, all asleep. It had been rather easy to take them by surprise, and then by emotional force—two of them were children.

"Kroner!" Rin called into the surrounding brush. Part of her wanted to leave without her reluctant companion: the night before, he'd froze up, completely useless as she executed all of the deeds. He'd have to pull his weight if he wanted to continue to fight. She looked around her and then anxiously at the sky. Where was he? The clearing was empty. And then, sure enough, the rustle of leaves sounded and she felt her spirits rise and plummet simultaneously. Kroner walked into the clearing, shaking a leaf off of his head and awkwardly reaching down to straighten the dagger at his side.

"Have you tasted those berries?" he asked her, before she could begin to tell him her thoughts.

"No," Rin said shortly. "They're probably poisonous."

It wiped the grin off of his face. "Poison? How many do you think it would take to kill me? I had five."

He stared at her, waiting desperately for an answer.

"Kroner, we have to get going."

His face sunk, if that were possible, and he began to pick at a patch of dirt that had become caught in his fur.

"Rin," he said, and she could read caution in every angle of his face and every gradient of his tone. She was not looking forward to this, but she couldn't say she hadn't seen it coming.

"I'm thinking," Kroner continued when he noticed she wasn't stopping him, "that maybe—I mean, I know the squirrels are bad, but—"

"Squirrels?" Rin raised an eyebrow.

"Yeah." He looked surprised at her question. "That's what they call themselves. Didn't you hear, the other night, how that old one—"

"I guess I must have been busy. You know, doing things we were *supposed* to do."

"I held that kid for you," he said, and she couldn't tell whether he was sulky over the fact itself or her lack of recognition for it.

For a moment they were both quiet, and Rin wondered if Kroner would forget about what he was going to say. She turned and started out of the small clearing they'd found to sleep in, pushing the short, thorny branches out of her way and letting them snap back in front of him as he followed. It was a silent warning, though she doubted he got it: stop there.

"Look!" Kroner exclaimed, nearly the moment they emerged from the bushes.

"Shhhhh!" She was beginning to think that the element of surprise would never be on her side so long as Kroner was with her.

"Come *on*," she hissed. When they'd both been training under the Yassars, she had taken him for someone with much more of a head on his shoulders. Kroner did not come on, though. He was standing back where the bushes let out into the rest of the field she was travelling across now, gesturing towards something frantically. When she turned in the direction he was pointing, she saw it: a bit of movement at the far end of the field, the opposite of where she was going. Someone was moving on the border, very slowly, starting then stopping as though they were stalking something. Rin put her paw on her dagger and started forward, unsure. There was something about the way the creature walked...

"It's Grinton! Rin, it's Grinton!"

The figure stopped at the sound of his voice, looking up and over at them. Rin relaxed her paw on her dagger; Kroner was right.

The plump chipmunk began to move towards them out of the distance, and his features came into focus just as he began to speak to them.

"Kroner? Rin?"

"That's us!" Kroner said, still too loud. He grinned and slapped their fellow chipmunk on the shoulder in greeting when he reached them.

"I've been looking for someone else for a really long time," Grinton confessed. "I was about ready to give up."

"Where are all the others?" Rin asked, fearing the worst. A moment later, her suspicions were confirmed.

"Most of 'em," Grinton began, "wanted to stick together. They were afraid, see, that when they hit surface, the enemy might not only be ready for them, but they would outnumber them."

"What are you saying?" Rin hissed.

"Just that all of them headed for the first tunnel. You know, the one they all know about, the one that's only in the case of emergency, the one that your fath—"

"Yes," Rin cut him off. "I'm familiar with it."

"That's where they all went to get out, I think. I thought maybe someone else would do what I did and try to strike out on their own, but you're the first I've found." He looked around him like he might find someone there now to contradict him. "These berries, though, they're great!"

Kroner turned and looked at Rin, who ignored him. Her mind was elsewhere, on what Grinton had just revealed. The others had gone out the first tunnel. The first tunnel was leagues north of here, and to catch up with them, she would need to travel fast.

"We need to get to them," she muttered. "Should have stayed in a group..." She hated to admit it, but the others had the right idea. In a group, they would attract attention, but they would also attract battle. All of them, as Kroner proved, would not work well as silent assassins. They needed obvious, angry targets, and that was what travelling in a group would inevitably provide. She needed to catch up to the group; she wanted to be there when the fighting began. When she turned to Kroner and Grinton, however, she noticed that they were sitting down on the grass, in the shade of the bushes and Grinton was talking.

"...saw one too. They're very different from what I expected."

"What?" Rin asked, sitting down beside them.

"The creatures here," Grinton said.

"Squirrels," Kroner supplied. "They're called squirrels."

Grinton tried his mouth on the word. "Squirrels. That's a strange one. Well, I came across a tree that had a few of them living inside one morning. I thought I would sneak attack them, but one of them spotted me out the window." He had the dignity to look shamefaced for a moment before continuing.

"It was a couple of—of—squirrels, just sitting down for breakfast or summat. The one who saw me called me something like a chickaree. She looked really freaked out, but the other one said I wasn't a red thief, whatever that is. He came outside and just kind of stood there. We watched each other for a long time, and it was sort of creepy, I guess, but that's not how he meant it. He looked curious more than anything. After a while, he asked me what I was, and I told him. He asked me what I was doing here, and I was going to tell him, that was going to be my moment, see. I would tell him I was here for revenge, and I would drive right in at them. I was pretty confident I could take them—they were unarmed and everything, unless you count a fork as being armed, heh heh. But then the one inside—the scared one—asked me if I wanted to come in and eat with them. She wanted to know about me, she said, and I didn't know what to say. I--I ran away."

He lowered his head, and there was a moment in which none of the three gathered chipmunks said anything. Then Rin said, "So you didn't take them?"

Grinton looked up at her. "I really couldn't, Rin. You weren't there. I know they've done something awful, but I didn't get the sense that these squirrels even knew about it. Maybe they weren't the ones what did it. Maybe they were innocent."

Rin stared at Grinton, noticing with horror that his face paint was smeared.

"No squirrel is an innocent squirrel," she said firmly.

Kroner was staring at Grinton too, only he was beginning to smile.

"That's how I felt, too!" he said, his thoughts from earlier spilling out in a rush now that he had a companion to back him up. "I thought—we went to a family, and they had children and everything, and they were crying and I kept thinking, this is wrong, they don't know anything, they don't—"

"We have to go," Rin said, standing up. Grinton and Kroner both turned to look at her, Kroner's eyes impossibly wide.

"Rin, didn't you feel it?" he asked, like they had just uncovered some wonderful secret and she was being daft. "Did you feel how—"

"We need to go," Rin said again, and Grinton stood up at her words.

"Kroner, she's right. We have to go to warn the others. I don't know who set the upper level on fire, and I'm not excusing it, but I don't think most of them were in on it. We've got to tell the others before they cause any lasting harm. We have to—"

Rin felt like she was having déjà vu. Things seemed to go extra slow as Grinton ceased talking and noticed the knife sticking out of his midriff. He opened his mouth again in surprise to speak, his eyes connecting with Rin's, but the blade had gone too deep and he could not say a thing. Grinton remained standing for only a second more before he fell to the ground heavily, mouth still working in shock.

"Rin!"

She turned to Kroner, who kept staring with those giant eyes at Grinton, then at her, then back at Grinton. "Rin," he moaned, "what have you done?"

Rin walked over to Grinton, who was still twitching on the ground, and took her dagger from him smoothly. "What do you mean, Kroner?" she asked. "I haven't done anything to him. It must have been the berries."

She watched as Kroner's expression grew more panicked. So this was the end of the road. He'd never shut up after this.

"Rin! You—you—"

Her dagger found him before he finished his sentence, and he dropped to the ground with a little scream. Rin stalked towards him and buried the blade deeper, silencing him for good before pulling it out again.

"I forgot," she said, though Kroner had already gone. "You ate them too."

Sheathing her dagger, Rin looked dispiritedly about her. It was a shame that she had to dispose of two of her own, but they were turning against their own cause right before her eyes. She needed to take some action.

This is what the squirrels can do, she thought. *They separate us by turning us against one another.*

Her hopes for the rest of the chipmunks were greater; they were in a group somewhere, and would remember what they came for. All that was left to her now was to find them. She gathered up Kroner and Grinton's daggers and made room for them on her own belt; you could never be too prepared. With a look back at the field, she began to make for the forest on the other side, then changed her direction. North. She was going north now. The two prone chipmunks she left behind her became great lumps and then small spots in her line of vision as she distanced herself from them. The gorepedes would have them for lunch, she expected. Their only loyalty was to the living.

~~~

Yassar Krimpt was one of the few in charge of the pursuit forward, a job he liked less and less as time went on. The journey to the first tunnel was uneventful, but once everyone reached the top of that tunnel, they became harder to keep in line. You either had chipmunks who wanted to experiment with everything—the flowers, the leaves, the fruit—or you had the ones who jumped at everything, over-suspicious and wary. To keep a group together and focused towards a common goal was a harder job than he'd thought, or honestly, given the head Yassar credit for. Not that that any of that would be coming out of his lips until he was dead or worse, Krimpt thought, looking over at the Head Yassar, who marched only a few feet from him. As expected, there were no signs of what he could be thinking on his face.

Head Yassar Vogt was difficult to read in the best of times. A stoic-faced chipmunk of few words, Krimpt had only seen him about occasionally before Vogt crafted the idea of having Yassars, or war trainers. The fact that Vogt knew everyone well enough to know who to pick and who not to pick for that rather covert operation right under the many eyes of the queen was astounding in itself, and made Krimpt think Vogt must have eyes everywhere as well. He resented the silent constancy of Vogt, resented it even more because Vogt himself didn't appear to resent much of anything.

"Stop MARCH!" yelled Yassar Grumble, at a look from Vogt. Krimpt was sure that Grumble was chosen only because he was the loudest chipmunk anyone had ever had the misfortune of meeting.

The whole group behind him shifted, making loud shuffling and clanking noises as they fanned out for inspection. Yassar Krimpt set out with Yassar Pelf down the ranks of chipmunks, looking them over cursorily.

"Dander, drop that flower, it's not edible. Pernal, if you keep falling asleep you're going to fall behind and stay behind. Do I need to convince you?"

Krimpt stroked his whip to get his point across. It was one of his favorite parts about being in charge, that sting of authority he knew his voice—and his whip—carried.

"Where are we going, though?" the tired voice of Pernal whined. Immediately, at least twenty heads snapped around towards him. Pelf stared at Krimpt over the heads of their troop from where he stood on the other side. It wasn't the first time Pernal had asked this, or the second, or even the third. Krimpt sighed and flicked his whip up into his paws. Pernal seemed suddenly wide-awake at the sight of it. He flinched prematurely, but when he realized nothing had happened, straightened up with a foolish grin on his face. That was when the whip cut across the air in front of him again, too fast for him to react. It left a thin red cut on the side of his face. Everyone watched as a single drop of blood ran over the yellow zigzag symbol drawn on one of his cheeks, the paint mixing with the blood in a rust-colored trail.

Pernal was still closing his eyes, expecting more, but Krimpt ignored him now, turning to the masses gathered around him.

"Does anyone else have a question like Pernal's?" he asked. Someone raised their paw, but another next to him yanked it down fast.

"I've already told you all we know for now. We're marching north from where we come up. We have sent scouts ahead."

"But why—" asked a chipmunk in back of Pernal, "why haven't we seen any of them yet?"

Krimpt knew exactly who she meant by 'them', and he also knew he had no satisfactory answer to the question.

"They obviously know we're here, in their territory, so either they are biding their time, or our threat is too large for them to handle. Any other questions?"

Krimpt's look told them all quite clearly that more questions were about as welcome as Pernal falling asleep and slowing them up again. Satisfied that no one would start up again, he turned around, not before giving a look to Pelf, that said quite clearly, *let's get on with this*. Pelf nodded and they started for the front of the crowd once more. Chipmunks shifted left and right to let them through. Yassar Leader Vogt waited until he was in front again to give Grumble the signal to shout again. The leader never involved himself in the disciplinary tasks: that was mainly for Krimpt and occasionally Pelf. The leader was the mind of this organism of theirs that had somehow become so powerful.

"Start MARCH!" hollered Grumble, sounding for all his volume like he was standing right behind Krimpt. The crowd lurched forward once more, leaving Krimpt to his thoughts for the time being.

It had been his idea to march forward in a group, to come up through the first tunnel, which was known in legend as the first tunnel any chipmunk was supposed to have dug to flee below the earth so long ago. His idea had been based on the idea that the descendents of their enemies of that time long past might still be in the area. Perhaps these squirrels would see them and remember their own stories of old, and cower in fear under the might of the Yassars and their massive army.

One of their number was noticeably absent, and already she was a legend among this group. Rin. The one he'd offered to train because no one else wanted to become involved with that family. Rin's family's reputation had been in shambles ever since her true father had ventured above into this cruel land and found it wonderful; he'd brought back tales and memories and even talked to the creatures above, as he so foolishly broadcast. He was put to death for this and no one was allowed to speak his name for seasons afterward, until no one, not even his old wife, enraged by what he had done, remembered it.

This daughter was as different as could be from her foolish father; she went through the fighting like she'd been born for it. The drills to test her seemed to tap into some rage, some burning dangerous *thing*, and he'd been glad to think of using her for his army, until the assassination of the queen. That troubled him. It wasn't as though there were not several among them who would have done the same, but they would have done it smoothly and in private and after much planning. There was just something wrong, something off about Rin that made him nervous. He'd sensed it in their lessons, and though he'd hidden it well, sometimes he had been afraid to push too far for fear of what he might disturb. It wasn't what he saw in her eyes that frightened him— it was what was missing from them.

Are you running from your own student? Krimpt asked himself, and recoiled inwardly at the thought, turning his mind to other matters. He was honestly very happy with his replies to the questions he'd been asked by the troops. In truth, he'd wondered the same things himself, but it was a foolish thing indeed to let anyone know you were in doubt or wondering about anything when you were in charge of leading them. Certainty was the order of the day, though the last chipmunk's question still echoed in his brain.

"Why *have* we not seen them?" Krimpt muttered to himself, clutching his whip tighter as he did so. He was sure the answer would not be good.

At first, the flecks on the horizon seemed like rocks or bushes or some sort of landmark—they were marching through a bit of field, after all—but as his vision sharpened, he realized that not only were they moving toward the flecks, but the flecks were moving towards them. Were they what he thought they were? Were his words and his secret thoughts enough to summon the presence of the strange creatures who had been lacking from this land?

Krimpt wondered if he should call out—he had one paw tensed to throw out in front of the others, and was on the edge of shouting when he recognized one of the shapes loping towards them and relaxed his body. It was only Mica and Sherk, their scouts. He hailed them as they came in closer, and Mica threw him and Vogt a salute before closing the distance to the front of the ranks.

"Mica! Sherk! What have you to report?" Krimpt asked, and Vogt caught his eye and gave Grumble the signal once more.

"Stop MARCH!" Grumble shouted, enjoying himself far more than his job description entailed. Everyone ground to a halt again and a whisper began to trail its way back through the ranks at the sight of the two scouts returned from duty. Heads craned around and over other heads and bodies as all tried to get a good look without stepping out of form.

"We have—" Sherk began excitedly, then stopped, looking between them. "To whom do I speak?"

"Me, if you like, Sherk," Vogt said, and Krimpt closed the distance between himself and Vogt in order to hear.

"Well, we've found what looks like a large group—a colony, maybe—of the creatures."

Krimpt started. He hadn't expected this. "How large?" he asked without thinking. Vogt didn't seem to mind; he already looked in the depths of his own thoughts.

Mica's eyes were wide and honest as he answered, "Yassars, sirs, it was the largest group of anything I've ever seen all in one place."

Vogt frowned. "Larger than us, do you think?"

Mica seemed to think about it for a while. "No," he said after a time. "They're not that large."

Vogt looked around at everyone behind him and then said at long last, "All right. We'll go for them."

"Full attack?" Krimpt asked, feeling his own eyes go wide against his will to remain cool.

"No," Vogt said, and despite his anxiety of a few seconds ago, Krimpt felt slightly put out. Whether Vogt knew his thoughts, he found hard to discern. The leader only turned to him and said, "We will proceed with caution and negotiate first."

Krimpt might have argued with this in another situation, but he could see the strange way Vogt's eyes were lit and he sensed that his leader wasn't being straightforward, exactly. When a Yassar said they would negotiate, they rarely meant only with words.

~~~

Spy-guard Camphor removed himself carefully from his station behind the clump of bushes he was using as cover. The resourceful black squirrel had heard enough of what the intruders' purpose was to write a book—if not that, he thought with a silent chuckle, to report back to Deepfen with. Ritorren would be interested in hearing about this. With one last glance over the mass of 'chipmunks'—for that was what he'd heard them call themselves—he scurried out from behind the bushes and away to the north, hiding himself every few feet or so either by the landmarks or by the natural camouflage techniques he knew so well.

The group of these creatures was massive! The way they marched, as though they were going to war, made the whole of them ripple until every single body only appeared to be one small part of some large form, some natural disaster sweeping across the landscape. How many of them were there? Camphor privately thought that the chipmunk leader he'd overheard was right; they were far outnumbered. No matter, he tried to convince himself, staring at the sea of grotesquely painted faces stomping past him. He would beat them to it and they could have their own troops prepare in quicker timing. He had heard the chipmunk leader say he wanted to negotiate; Camphor prayed to Astrippa that that was true.

Running up ahead of the chipmunks without being seen was not easy; Camphor continually had to hide himself and slow things up, but once he got to the forest beyond the field they were traversing, he knew he'd gained plenty of time on them. From the way the first of the chipmunks moved as they hit the trees, Camphor could tell that these creatures, wherever they were from, were not accustomed to the forest at all.

It made him wonder: where *were* they from? Camphor had never been to the southernmost regions of Arborand, it was true, but he could not imagine that it was so different from Firwood or Oakwood. He could not imagine a place with no trees: the thought of it made his head spin!

Camphor had to slow when he reached a certain point in the forest; he had entered gray territory, and some of the grays living here were downright crazy. He had no desire to be caught, as he had some time ago, by that insane group of greys who thought they needed to sacrifice him. It was a funny memory, if he ignored the part where he nearly didn't escape.

Their own commune, placed exactly on the border of Firwood and Oakwood, was made up of a strange mixture of grays and blacks. It was a precocious alignment, but an unstable one at best. Each group still silently competed with one another, and leadership was a tenuous thing. They were capable of holding up a strong front, but only if they united completely, and considering that the grays and the blacks had only recently settled their disputes and shared the line Deepfen straddled between their respective lands, Camphor had to wonder whether this attack was coming too soon for them to take.

With the sounds of the army of chipmunks marching none-too-quietly through the crisp, fallen leaves behind him, the spy-guard scaled a tree and began to leap through the branches in a line of energy-engendered heat that would bring him where he needed to be faster than that whole group of chipmunks could make it past three standing trees and a fallen one. He'd never been very modest when the awesome truth was staring him in the face.

Minutes that seemed only seconds later, Camphor was bulleting into the richly carved front doors of Deepfen, set high as they were on the tallest branch of the great oak. The two other guards on duty at the door, a gray and a black, shook themselves from what seemed near-sleep and one of them held a paw up in objection.

"Hey—"

Camphor only sped past them and up a short length of spiral stairs until he came to the double-locked, solid door that he knew marked both the very top room of Deepfen and Ritorren's chambers. He knocked boldly and then stood back and waited for a count of five. Still their leader did not appear. Where was he? Ever since Ritorren had acquired his own room, he liked to take his time answering requests and letting others enter. It was getting very old. Camphor raised his paw to knock again, louder this time, but stopped when he heard the bolts churning behind the door. He waited for a count of three clicks, and then he heard a grinding that signified one of the three doors to Ritorren's chambers had opened. He waited through a second repeat of this sequence, and then the third, in which the doors finally parted to show him the exasperated face of Lord Ritorren.

From what Camphor could gather, Ritorren had been holding some type of meeting. Gerien and Venul, two of his closest advisors—and friends, before he became lord by popular vote— were standing behind him, at the back of the room. They were both staring out at Camphor as well. By their postures and expressions, Camphor could tell he'd interrupted something important, some thread that perhaps they would never pick up again once he left.

Well, what he had to say was important too, and he refused to believe that it wasn't more so than whatever they had been discussing!

"May I come in, Lord Ritorren?" he asked, obeying the courtesies Ritorren had had installed, an uncomfortable fact of his sudden leadership. Ritorren was younger than Camphor by a good many seasons, and he remembered the days when his mother had to keep paws all over him at all times to keep him from eating bark.

Camphor had to hide a smile at that thought. It was a humorous image to conjure up, that of the adult, immaculately groomed and well-dressed Ritorren, stuffing bark into his cheeks.

Ritorren must have seen some portion of this levity on his face, for he frowned before standing back.

"Enter if you must," he said, reaching up in a self-conscious gesture to smooth the sleek gray fur on his head down even further.

Camphor wasted no time in following the command. He stood and gave a short bow once he'd entered the room, then turned to face his leader directly.

"I have very good reason to believe," he said, getting straight to the point, "that we are to be attacked within the day."

Ritorren's paw drifted from his head to his side again and he stared at Camphor, eyes slightly narrowed. Behind him, Gerien's eyes widened and Venul shifted a bit. Camphor plunged into telling them what he'd seen and overheard. When he was done, Ritorren walked to the one window in the room. Like the doors, it was normally equipped with double bolts, but now it was flung open wide, and Ritorren turned his face into the cold sunlight coming through. Camphor very much doubted he was thinking so much as admiring the idea of how his noble contemplation must appear to everyone else in the room. Still, he was hesitant to speak lest he anger his unpredictable leader.

"What are these chipmunks?" Venul asked challengingly. Camphor eyed the other black squirrel squarely.

"I have no more idea than you," he said, "But they look like some type of squirrel. Like a chickaree, with stripes. They look—" he hesitated to say the word, "savage."

"I think I've heard of them," Gerien said suddenly, and Venul and Camphor both turned to him abruptly. The gray looked abashed, but quickly overcame it.

"My family used to tell me stories when I was younger, stories about the old world. You know, when the white squirrels were everywhere and the chipmunks," he said, "were above ground." Gerien paused and realized that everyone was looking at him now; even Ritorren had turned from his feigned contemplation to listen. He swallowed and went on.

"I don't remember what it was exactly...magic! Yes, it was magic. The chipmunks never had magic at all. Most squirrels didn't either, of course, but it cropped up in us now and then just like it does with us now. And the white squirrels, they *all* had magic. Anyway, no chipmunk was ever known to have magic, and they were angry about it. We—that is, all squirrels, really—got into a dispute with them. They didn't live in the trees, either. They were always below, in the shrubs and rocks and logs. Many of them had burrows in the ground, for they were good at digging. Well, at the end of their dispute with us, they decided to create a society away from ours, one without any magic, without any white squirrels, and one where they could travel everywhere, know it entirely. So they moved underground."

"How come we've never heard of this before?" Venul asked, eyes narrowed.

Gerien shrugged. "I didn't think it was true! It seemed too farfetched, and my family always did like to fool with me," he grinned, but the grin quickly faded. "If what Camphor says is right, which I don't doubt, we're in a lot of trouble."

There was a moment of silence; Camphor was getting very antsy. He turned to Ritorren and found that the leader was staring right back at him.

"If they're close," he said, "there's nothing we can do but to ready everyone for war. Gerien, Venul, tell everyone to gather anything they can find from the armory. Then tell the best archers—Dakul's— to get to the highest branches and wait. The rest of us will wait for their approach and then spread out in the surrounding trees. Make as much of a circle as possible; we want to have them surrounded as soon as they get here. Wait until we see the first hint of them to assume your positions; if it took Camphor hours to get all the way back, it's going to take a troop of that size a day to get here, at least. We'll post sentries in the night." He finally turned to Gerien and Venul, looking them in the eyes. "I don't need to tell you how important this is. Call a meeting. Go."

"But what about our—" Venul started to speak, but Ritorren gave him a very menacing look, and after a time, the black squirrel left resentfully, closing the door a bit harder than was necessary.

Though he was less than fond of the other's bluster and freshly accumulated superiority complex, Camphor had to admire the way Ritorren could direct a group, the way he was rarely discomposed and always had a plan at hand. Really, he had all the qualities necessary for a good leader, but then again, he had *only* the necessary qualities. Perhaps that was the problem, Camphor thought.

"Camphor," Ritorren said suddenly, aimlessly smoothing the fur on his chest.

"Yes, Lord?"

"Go back and find them again. Keep an eye on them. When they get close, come back and tell me."

Camphor nodded and made to leave his leader's chambers.

"Oh, and one more thing," Ritorren said. Camphor turned again, hoping he wasn't about to get some speech or other, but Ritorren merely took something from behind his chair, a solid thing of plain oak. It took a while for Camphor to realize that what Ritorren retrieved was actually a dagger, and a fine one too. His leader threw the dagger to him, and Camphor deftly caught it by the hilt.

"For if they catch you," Ritorren said to him, and they both knew what he meant. Camphor nodded, trying to put a damper over the fast beating of his heart. He sheathed the dagger by his side, silently praying he would never have to use it, and walked out the door.

CHAPTER X

Shadows drifted back and forth, back and forth, like the great lurking forms of nightmare beasts, tearing around behind her eyelids. For a while, Llewellyn could not remember her own name. Those shadows kept darting around, growing deeper and darker, the light around them getting brighter. She tried to tear open her eyelids and found that she could only open them a crack. What she saw when she did made her come to faster than she might have under any other conditions.

Where am I? Llewellyn thought. The deep, dank wood above her gave her no answer. She'd meant the words to come out of her mouth, but her mouth didn't seem to be working properly. Trying the next best thing, Llewellyn tried for some movement. She felt her back legs twitch, and tried to heave herself into a sitting position. Immediately, she felt nauseous and extremely tired. Her eyes started to drift shut again, and the shapes closed in once more.

"No!" Llewellyn screamed out, and was surprised when she found that her voice didn't only sound in her head anymore. She flinched at the sound of it, and tried to turn herself over, so that she could see whatever it was she was trapped in, for it felt like a trap. This room was too warm, too close around her, and it smelled so heavily of rot that—

Llewellyn almost cried out again, but a paw clamped over her mouth before she could gather the breath. She'd turned to the side, and in doing so, found herself staring into the dark, malicious eyes of an equally dark form.

At first it seemed to her that it was one of the dark shadows behind her eyelids, come to life to grab her and pull her under the unknowable edge of life, and she pulled away. Then the figure spoke and she realized it was indeed just another squirrel, though her coat was black as night and she stared down at Llewellyn through deeply cold, deeply intelligent eyes; she had withdrawn her paw from Llewellyn's face, though, which Llewellyn was immensely glad for. Still, she couldn't shake the feeling that she was about to be killed. Her eyes had finished adjusting to the light, enough to know just how little light there was in here, though where 'here' was, she had no idea. She couldn't think much in any direction with the black squirrel staring at her. There was something wrong with that face. It was an older face, but there was a touch of creepy vitality to it; she would not have called it youth, but something even older than actual old age, a deep and musty cunning—and very little moral qualms.

You're making it up, Llewellyn told herself, as the face still watched her in silence. *You had too much mint tea and fell asleep on your bed and now you're having weird dreams. You'll wake up soon, Horus will knock on your door and you'll try to seem annoyed with him but you'll be relieved in truth and you're making this up. Above anything else, you're making this up.*

Llewellyn shut her eyes tight, but even then she felt the burn of the other's gaze—perhaps it was this gaze alone that had created those dark forms drifting behind her closed eyes. How long had this squirrel been staring at her, she wondered?

"Where..." she struggled to speak, her voice sounding rusty and underused, like she'd been lying here for fifty seasons.

But I haven't. I'm sure I haven't. This is still some dream. I'll wake up.

Llewellyn tried to summon her voice to speak again, though her tongue was paralyzed in part by the other's stare. When she finally got the beginnings of a word out, no more than a hoarse bleat, the other squirrel raised a paw and put it to her lips, then smiled. The smile was a horrid thing and made her want to throw up.

"Ssshhhh," the black squirrel bid, the sound of her voice at last after all this silence making Llewellyn jump. She tried again to sit up, and felt an aching pain jolt all through her body, moving like lightning to every extremity. She lay back down with a sigh, keeping her eyes on the other squirrel the whole time. She tried to speak for a third, valiant time and this time the words came to her.

"Where am...I?" she asked the squirrel beside her, and she watched the thing's eyes go even darker with excitement, seemingly just at the sound of her voice. However, the black squirrel only raised a paw to her lips again, turning briefly from her at last to peer behind them into the never-ending darkness. Llewellyn was quite sure she didn't want to know what the other was looking at—or for.

"Ssshh," the black squirrel told her again, smiling almost like this was some game they were playing. "You're here, at my home away from home."

Llewellyn didn't understand. By the way the black squirrel was still smiling at her, she had to wonder whether she wasn't just trying to play some trick on her.

"Who are *you*, then?" Llewellyn said, and, still clinging to the idea that she would wake up any moment, she risked raising herself to a sitting position. All of her muscles and joints screamed at her in a cacophony of aches. She kept her voice to a whisper, just so the other squirrel wouldn't tell her to be quiet again. Again, the black squirrel looked behind her rather excitedly; Llewellyn peered into the dark where she was staring, but still couldn't see anything. There was an echo in here of water dripping, and she guessed she must be in a log of some sort, or a fallen tree. If she was, though, she saw no sign of any light on either end of it; it was this endlessness that gave the dripping such an eerie sound.

The black squirrel hadn't answered her question. After a time of staring at Llewellyn exultantly, she said, "I saved you."

"You what?" Llewellyn forgot to keep her voice as low this time. When had she needed saving? She tried again to think back to what she was doing before she woke here, and again she could not. A twinge occurred at the back of her brain, and she realized that her whole head hurt something awful. It felt as though someone had pried into her head while she was asleep and moved parts of her brain around, performing surgery on anything in sight. She groaned, and the black squirrel looked at her curiously.

"You don't remember anything, do you?"

Llewellyn looked at the other squirrel in some alarm. Had something really gone on that she didn't know about? To consider that would be to admit that she wasn't in a dream, that the squirrel in front of her was real, and she wasn't ready for that.

"All I can remember is falling asleep," Llewellyn lied, and she was terrified at the grin that flitted ever so briefly across the black squirrel's face.

"You really don't remember," she breathed. "This is wonderful."

"*What?*"

"Nothing. Never you mind. You were...how shall I put it? You were in grave danger, unconscious in the middle of a forest, close to the water and oh so alone! I did wonder, then, what sort of quest you might have been on, where you might have been going. I rushed you in here; it's getting cold out, and you would have died if it had decided to snow. You're lucky I was there," she said with a solemn nod.

Llewellyn could only stare in confusion. She was afraid now, more so than she'd been before, because she sensed that, as much as she distrusted this squirrel on instinct, part of what she was saying was in fact the truth. But when she couldn't remember even the last thing she'd done, how could she determine which part? Would she have to trust this squirrel? She couldn't bring herself to do it, but it might well be that mistrust would be just as dangerous to her now.

"Where am I?" Llewellyn asked again, this time aiming for the specifics, and the black squirrel seemed to know what she meant.

"You are in the far southwest of Arborand," she said promptly, a smile playing about her lips again as she said it, "Beechwood, to be exact."

Llewellyn felt her gut lurch. Beechwood? Beechwood was nowhere near Maplewood, where Edgewood, her home, stood. How did it come to be that she was all the way across Arborand being watched over by a strange malevolent squirrel?

"I...I don't understand," she managed to say. "I don't live anywhere near Beechwood. There has to be a—"

"Mistake?" The black squirrel rolled her eyes to the ceiling in false sympathy. "No, there's no mistake," she said, flashing Llewellyn another sickening smile. "You, my dear, are exactly where you're supposed to be...Llewellyn."

Llewellyn froze, her tongue stuck to the roof of her mouth, whatever question she'd been about to ask stuck with it. *No. You heard wrong. No.*

The black squirrel smiled, seeing her confusion or, more likely, her fear.

"You can call me Mercurie," she said, "I feel that we're on first name terms by now."

Llewellyn briefly experienced the sensation of sinking, falling so dizzily through a mire of unfamiliarity that she had to blink several times and shake her head from side to side to clear it.

I need to run. I need to jump up, take her by surprise, and leave this place.

Even as she had the thought, Llewellyn knew it was useless. She didn't even know where the door to this place was, if there even *was* a door. She couldn't hope to escape through mad dashing. Any getting out of this situation would require her to think, and most of all, to remain calm while she was doing so.

"Why are we keeping our voices so low, Mercurie?" she asked the black squirrel, applying first name terms as per her sinister companion's request. The name felt raw and horrible in her mouth. It went too well with the figure by her side.

Mercurie hesitated, and the gleam went out of her eyes for a split second. At that moment, there was a movement somewhere in the dark behind them, a distinctive shifting sound.

"What was that?" Llewellyn asked, forgetting to keep her voice low in her fear.

"You'll see in a moment," Mercurie said darkly. She didn't sound too excited about the idea, which made Llewellyn wonder if the black squirrel was completely in charge here. The thought didn't comfort her at all.

"I believe," Mercurie continued, "that you know him."

Llewellyn turned, confused, to watch the shape of the mysterious third squirrel come out into her range of vision.

It was the way he moved that gave him away long before Llewellyn even saw him up close—that strange twitching fluidity—and then she thought *it can't be.* Suddenly, her memory seemed to spill back to her, out of some hidden crevice in her mind. Some invisible blockage was taken away at the sight of him, and she knew; she remembered. She'd seen him *die*—by rot, she'd been the one to drive the dagger into his back! It couldn't be.

And yet somehow, it was.

As Absoulim came nearer to her, dragging his tattered wings, she had to fight the urge not to back up. There was a gigantic, twisted scar across his chest, a white, furless mass of tissue that seemed to shake with every slight tremor of its owner's. Absoulim's pale, distracted looking eyes gazed at her at the same time as they seemed to be looking off elsewhere, at Mercurie or at one of the walls. Llewellyn's mouth was dry; she could not speak. A horrid thought was beginning to rise in her, as the images in her mind filed themselves into order.

"Llewellyn," Absoulim said, the ghost of a smile playing around his mouth. "It hasn't been too long, has it?"

"What happened to Mariyen? What did you do to her?" Llewellyn blurted. If Absoulim were still alive, what was the fate of all those she'd left behind in Edgewood?

Absoulim gave a shrug that looked more like a gigantic twitch. "It's—she's fine, as far as I know. I would not kill her so needlessly. Did you think otherwise?"

Llewellyn just stared past him into the blackness, that endless dark from which her memories and her fears had so recently emerged.

"I *know* otherwise," she said. "I need proof. Where's the proof that she's alive and well?"

"I don't know where she is," Absoulim snapped, but she ploughed on, heedless of his anger.

"What did you do to them? Is everyone okay? Where's Horus? Where's Zirreo?"

Absoulim, whose face was darkening at every word, gave a brief, ugly smile at Zirreo's name.

"The white squirrel," he said, "yes. I know where he is, as it happens." He moved forward so that he was standing between her and Mercurie, who was staring up at him with an expression of impatience and disdain rolled into one. Llewellyn noticed that Absoulim was wearing something around his neck, a shining, dangling memento of some sort attached to a string.

"How can you—" Llewellyn began to ask, but she stopped. There was too much here that was impossible. "How can you be *alive*?" she said, leaning forward defiantly.

"Magic," Absoulim answered, tracing a long, lightly trembling paw over the scar on his chest. Mercurie shifted, and Llewellyn caught the look of resentment on her face when Absoulim did not elaborate. So the black squirrel was involved, somehow. Llewellyn couldn't think on that particular notion for long because already she needed to know the other thing, the other question she'd been baited with, the one she knew he wanted her to ask more than any other. She shouldn't let him have his satisfaction, but she needed to know. Still, even after she'd professed in her heart not to care, she needed to know.

"How do you know where Z-the white squirrel is?" she asked, trying her best to ignore the smug expression that came over Absoulim's face when she asked.

"Magic," he answered again, simply, and turning to a place just beyond him in the dark, he pulled something towards him. Llewellyn could not see it until he held it up, and when he did, she heard herself let out a sound like she was sick.

"How—where did you get that?" she gasped, standing up so quickly that she felt all the blood rushing from her head at once and almost fell back down again. Her paw shot out and she was surprised to find the wall closer than she'd imagined. She stood there, disoriented, reeling, staring at the object in Absoulim's paws in abject horror.

It was a crystal ball, and somehow Absoulim was holding it without its stand in his paws, something that ought to have been impossible. The bead of quivering dew stared up at her in the ensuing silence, and even though she had no name tag to reference, no way to know, she knew all the same.

It was hers.

"You didn't," she breathed, her breath coming hot and full of emotion. "You can be cursed for that, forever."

Absoulim only laughed, a sound that was discordant and horrible in the near darkness, like the sound of someone being strangled. He spread his arms and pushed out his narrow chest so that his wings and his scar were impossible to ignore.

"Because I've been lucky up until now?" he asked, and she conceded the point by letting her eyes drop momentarily. She felt like she was going to throw up all over again. The memory was back to her in full, the memory of leaving Edgewood, of jumping from somewhere high, feeling the wind rush about her, hitting a prematurely snowy ground. The sound of Zirreo's voice echoing in her head, calling her name over and over, his voice strained against the wilderness she ran into. Where was she running though, and why? This she could not remember, and now, standing in this darkness with this horrible specter of her past, she felt things unravel beneath her and thought that whatever the reason, it could not have been reason enough. She had made things so much worse, and the feeling of having woken from a year-long nap, sick and groggy and unsure, came over her. She needed to sleep again—she needed to sleep so badly.

"You had a dream link with him, I see," Absoulim said.

She was not afraid; she would not be afraid of someone she'd known since she'd trained to be a seer. It was hard for her to believe that he was her age, looking at him now, at the gaunt planes of his face in the dark—she could not imagine how he would look in the light. She steeled herself and nodded to his question; there was really no point in pretending she didn't know what he was talking about. If only she had a dagger here, if only she'd held on to the one she had before. She swore if she did she wouldn't hesitate to run it into him again, through that repulsive scar all over again. Only this time she would hold it there; this time there would be no rush, she would twist it from side to side. She would make sure.

I'm so sorry, Mariyen. What did I leave you with? What did I do? Most of all, why?

"I have been able to use that dream link while you were on the edge of death," Absoulim explained, his voice silent, even more weak and raspy than she remembered. "So much of you is contained in this, you know."

Llewellyn stared at the crystal bead, held in Absoulim's paws, and wanted to snatch it away. She was horrified. Every seer's crystal ball was their own unique property. It was not supposed to be touched or marred by another. She felt as though her thoughts had been raided, made dirty and turned inside out, molested by Absoulim's probing.

"You should not have done that," she said, hearing the rage in her own voice, only half the intensity of what she really felt. "You should *not* have done that."

"Tell me where it is," he said, unphased by her rage or by the fact that it had been she who'd tried to kill him to begin with. "Tell me where it is, and you can have it back."

"Where *what* is?" She paused, confused. The strangeness of the situation came over her again. How had she gone from running away from Edgewood to here, and why was she with Absoulim and this black squirrel now? She looked at the black squirrel now, and the other's eyes were wide and eager. "What do you want from me?" she raged, staring between them.

"The child," Absoulim said simply, and Llewellyn could not remember for only a second more. It seemed as soon as someone mentioned anything to her, it set off the flood of a memory, and now she understood more fully. *I had to go. We were going to kill it and we couldn't, so I had to go. The prophecy...*

She stared balefully at her crystal ball, still clutched in Absoulim's paws.

"I don't know where it is," she said, and admitting so gave the dormant panic within her life.

"You have to know," Mercurie spat out, suddenly rising into a standing position. Her eyes were wider now and appeared possessed.

"I really don't!" Llewellyn protested, unsure why she was fighting over this. The truth was the truth. "I don't remember going as far as Beechwood, I can tell you that too. What would *you* want with a child, anyhow?" she shot at Absoulim.

The question lit his pale eyes up with a strange flame.

"That child," Absoulim said in his broken voice, "is the most powerful squirrel in Arborand."

Llewellyn found herself unsurprised. Had she always known it to be true? Had she felt something when holding her—the child was female, she could tell, even though she had tried so hard not to assign a name or gender—that told her something of the potential she possessed? Was it something in her weight, the way she cried, or was it merely a given considering her parentage?

"It's with the white squirrel, isn't it?" Absoulim said, seeming to read her thoughts.

"I. Don't. Know," Llewellyn said tensely, stretching the words out to coat the expanse of her anger. "I don't know. Why don't you just believe me already?"

Absoulim made some miniscule twitchy movement and Mercurie came towards her. Llewellyn felt she should run, but before she could make any moves, she felt the light prick of something small and extremely sharp enter her skin. She tried to swat it away, but her paw felt heavy, and suddenly she was too lethargic to keep her eyes open. As she fell back slowly to the ground from which she had awoke, she heard Mercurie and Absoulim speaking, but their voices were muffled and soon enough she could not hear them at all.

The world was dark for Llewellyn once more, and completely vacant of dreams.

~~~

"It works well, that stuff," Absoulim commented, reaching awkwardly to take one of Llewellyn's paws from beside her and lay it on her chest.

Mercurie frowned.

"Remember our deal," she hissed, and Absoulim whipped to face her.

"I haven't forgotten, witch, but if you speak of it one more time—"

"Our deal is now," Mercurie went on, ignoring him. "You said you needed information, well, you got it. When she wakes, she should be mine."

Absoulim's face looked like it had caught a bit of his tremors when he looked at her then. She knew he was angry, but she knew she was right.

"I didn't get anything out of that," he said, putting the crystal ball back in its place as he turned from her, trying to get himself under control.

"You never mentioned anything about—"

"I am going to find the white squirrel," Absoulim snapped, "And then, once I have the child, you can have her, damn you."

"What happens," Mercurie persisted, following him back into the deeper reaches of the fallen tree, "if the child isn't with him? She says she doesn't know, but—"

"She doesn't," Absoulim answered. "The white squirrel is renowned for his trickery. He could have easily taken the child from her by some magical ploy, without her knowing, and wiped her memory." He paused, panting, and clutched his chest. "Why am I tired again, witch?!"

"You know why," Mercurie snapped. She was getting tired of this. "The length you can go without resting will grow as time goes on." She veered back into their previous conversation, unwilling to give it up without an agreement. "I'm not waiting for you to kill the white squirrel; that is so far from our deal it is laughable."

Absoulim glowered at her but she wasn't bothered in the least. She held the power here, after all. She might have made him give her the flyer Llewellyn now, except she had grown curious over this white squirrel. Something told her that perhaps waiting a while longer would not be a bad idea.

"You go find the white squirrel," she said, "I assume you're thinking of binding yourself to the ball again?" His lack of answer gave her what she needed. "Well, then, I'm finding him. And once I do, and you are free to do what you will with him, I take the girl."

He stared at her, his face twitching slightly. The tremors, she realized, got worse as he became more tired.

"Fine," he said at last, and turned to leave her.

"One last thing," she called after him, grinning in the dark. "You need to tell me where the girl and I are going. Where is this white squirrel?"

"He's in Firwood now," Absoulim said, "but he is...headed for the border with Oakwood. There is a colony of squirrels there. Mixed. Interesting." A weird little grin jerked across his face. Mercurie backed up against the wall unconsciously.

"Are you sure of it?"

"Of course I'm sure of it. I have seen it."

"The border?" she breathed. "How...interesting indeed."

Without knowing it, Mercurie had signed herself off to travel to the place she hadn't been in seasons upon seasons, had purposefully avoided for the majority of her life. Oakwood. The place of her birth.

The place of her exile.

Perhaps, she thought, smiling wide this time, it would not be such a bad idea at all to give them a visit.

CHAPTER XI

Kinder reached the base of the elm tree and stalked out as far as he would dare into the open area beyond. It was too far to the nearest set of trees, a towering group of slender maples that he thought he remembered from somewhere. Frowning, Kinder darted back to the lower trunk of the elm where Mariyen was waiting. When his paws touched the rough, comforting bark he immediately felt better, until Mariyen asked him the question that had become routine with them ever since the gorepedes had attacked their campsite at night.

"How soon?"

Kinder shook his head. "We're going to have to walk for a while. We can go really fast, though, until we reach..." he trailed off, the horrible realization coming on him all at once. "Oh no."

Mariyen just looked at him, waiting for him to explain, her eyes tinting darker with worry.

"I recognize those trees up ahead of us. Zirreo and I went through them on our way here, and he said that they were chickaree territory. When we went through, he told me not to climb any of the trees under any circumstances-- there's a path running straight through the middle somewhere, which we'll have to find. We didn't see any chickarees when we went through, but Zirreo was good at not running into things he didn't want to."

Kinder was not at all certain they'd have the same luck this time around.

"Can we go around them?" Mariyen asked. There was no real hope in her eyes. They both saw how far in either direction the trees ran; if they were to go around them, they might lose their sense of direction altogether.

"I don't know how to avoid it," Kinder said helplessly, and they both stared into the trees opposite them for a time without saying anything. The trees were close-crowded and misty, and when a slight gust of wind picked up a few leaves and blew them in front of Kinder, he jumped. Mariyen felt him flinch, to his own consternation, and she looked over at him, trying to smile.

"Stay armed, I guess," she said, paw going to her dagger, "and run."

Kinder touched his slingshot nervously; he felt a lot less confident about using the thing when he was surrounded by a group of squirrels.

"We can't run, either," he told her, wishing he didn't have to say such a thing. "The chickarees lay out traps. That's what Zirreo told me, anyway."

Thinking back to that time, Kinder could remember how many knots his stomach had been in when Zirreo had urged him to walk the path between these trees. Then, he'd still been carrying all his charms, and, after Zirreo had taunted him for them, he'd ended up dumping them on the ground for the chickarees, as an offering. He'd given them all he had, and he had nothing they would be interested in now, nothing to divert their attention from the two travelers who would soon be making their wary way through these trees.

Kinder detached himself from the trunk of the elm, hopping down to solid, near-frozen ground: the morning had been unnaturally cold. It seemed deadly appropriate now. Trying not to think too much about what might be waiting for them amid the maple forest, he reached out a paw to Mariyen, and felt foolish when he realized she'd already jumped to the ground.

"Do you think we should keep them hidden," Mariyen whispered, gesturing to their weapons, "unless we're attacked?"

He liked the notion of attack being uncertain, and he nodded to her as they set off across the cold, cracked ground. Some more sparse leaves swirled about them in another gust as they neared the forest. For once Kinder was not thinking of the gorepedes or the danger they posed. He was not imagining them coming up through the ground, monstrous with their eyeless faces and thick green bodies. It was still a possibility, and he was still scared of them, but the new fear of the unknown, of the added dangers that would arise when they walked into the maple forest, had swept in and taken first priority in terrorizing his mind.

"Concentrate on not tripping anything up," he whispered to Mariyen as they neared the entrance to the trail. He knew she didn't need the reminder, but he needed to speak something out loud before they entered and couldn't speak at all. Mariyen, who had her paw on what he was sure was the hilt of her dagger, nodded twice quickly, eyes unfocused. He knew then that her feelings were very similar to his own in the moment. He caught her eye again and nodded a second time, and with that nod, they both slipped into the maple forest.

It was dark: that was the first thing Kinder noticed about the forest. It was no doubt due to how closely grown so many of the trees were, he thought as he surveyed the gloominess to the beat of his own heart in his ears. Some of the trees had grown so close that they melded into one another unnaturally at the strangest points before breaking away and growing on their own again. He wondered why they did not spread out to grow rather than grouping so close that they became mutants, for trees always chose what was best for themselves when it came to growth. The way they were grouped made him feel like they were hiding something among them.

That was when Kinder began to feel like he was being watched. He kept having to urge himself to look at the ground to make sure he wasn't tripping on anything, but he felt the burning of someone's eyes on his back and his profile whenever he looked down. Every time he looked up, however, he could see nothing and no one in evidence and it was beginning to make him feel foolish—or it would have, if beside him Mariyen weren't doing the same thing. Their eyes connected once, when both of their heads shot up at a sound like a twig breaking far off to the left of them, and they both tried to smile, but Kinder felt strained, like he could smell his own fear. He felt a tugging on his mind to look left, and when he did, he could have sworn he saw a shadow dart out of his range of vision just in time. He peered, heart drumming in his ears, into the woods where the sound had come from, and this time he saw, quite distinctly, some type of other darkness move behind the mist and the close-grown trees. A tingling in his ears— always a bad sign—told him to look behind him, and when he did, he saw more of the same shadows, all grouped together in the tops of the trees. He had to focus a long time to bring them into clarity, and when he did he saw they were unmistakably the shapes of squirrels. Kinder looked back in the direction they'd come, and found that he couldn't even see where the path opened up into fresh air anymore—the way was closed off with the same cold mist he could see creeping among the trees to either side of them. They were thoroughly trapped at the mercy of whoever was watching from the trees.

Kinder felt Mariyen nudge his side and when he looked around at her she beckoned him forward. He came, feeling the mist creeping in behind him and closing off any passage back the way he'd come. He tried not to look to either side as he went, but it was hard with that feeling always on him and the road in front of him always so long.

A second later, Mariyen, walking slightly ahead of him, threw out a paw in front of him. Kinder stopped, looking around before he realized that Mariyen was pointing to something with the paw she'd thrown in front of him. He stared at the spot she was indicating, and at first he didn't see anything and looked up at her with questioning eyes. She stabbed her paw again towards the same spot on the earth, and Kinder saw it when he leaned forward this time: so dark that it blended almost perfectly with the ground, a small, thin wire mounted between two rocks over a small dip in the land.

Kinder whipped his head back around to Mariyen, sweat dotting his brow. He had almost stepped on the thing. Another twig snapped, closer this time and from the right, and this one was without a doubt not a part of his imagination.

They're all around us, he mouthed to Mariyen. She stared at him for a frightened second and he wondered whether she'd understood. Then she nodded, once. *Yes.*

As though this were the signal, several forms dropped out of the overhanging branches and more still materialized out of the mist between trees. Mariyen's eyes widened and she clutched the hilt of her dagger until her paw went white. Kinder backed up, straight into the trip wire. He twisted around, trying to steady himself, but his flailing got him nowhere: he ended up bowled over, pack falling behind him with a crash as he hit the ground. He could have sworn that some of the approaching figures snickered at him, and he realized, panicked and trying to rise to his feet again, that he had not been wrong. The squirrels in front of him wore eager leers and nasty smirks alike on their faces, and were edging in on he and Mariyen, closing them off in a circle they couldn't hope to escape from.

"So!" one of the chickarees screamed, "Thought yew'd come into our territory!"

"This is chickaree woods, it is!" another added, stepping forward and thrusting a wicked-looking albeit rusty knife into their faces. One of the squirrels behind him pushed him.

"Lemme see, lemme see!"

A tussle promptly ensued, and the crowd shifted as more chickarees either moved aside or joined the fray. Kinder again tried his luck with getting up from the shallow dip in the ground. Someone behind him screamed out with shrill laughter.

"The fat one's stuck! Lookit this, the fat one's stuck in the trip hole! Ehehehehee!"

More laughter followed this—as well as more tussles, breaking out all around him for no discernible reason. Kinder's cheeks burned, and Mariyen, daring to take her paw off her dagger, turned around and helped him up.

"Where's your leader?!" she shouted, turning around to face the chickarees nearest her. Kinder could see her paw shaking on her dagger. "Where is your organization?" This last, she mumbled to herself rather than spoke aloud, but someone nearby heard her.

"We en't got org'nization!" the chickaree in question howled. Another came up behind her, trying to push for a better view of the intruders, and she took an absentminded swipe at him with her knife. "Our leader—I wouldn't be wanting her to come if I were yew," she snickered.

Mariyen looked like she was going to respond, but the breath of the chickaree had overwhelmed her for a second too long and before she could get any words out, the chickaree had turned around and begun to battle in earnest with the red behind her.

"Calm, calm! Calm down, yew louts!" shouted one of the most earsplitting voices Kinder had ever heard. A larger chickaree was pushing his way through the crowd, stopping to bite or stab at his fellows at leisure. He had a couple of gold rings in both of his ears and one stuck through his nose. Kinder reached up and touched his own nose gingerly at the sight, and the larger chickaree sneered at him as though he'd noticed the movement and was proud of the effect he had.

"Silence all if yew want some treasure!" he called, turning back to the masses and waving a curved dagger in the air. His voice was so loud that no one could be faulted with not hearing it, and slowly, the chickarees began to die down again. Kinder had the uncomfortable sensation of burning again as forty or more sets of eyes latched onto him. The mass of chickarees became silent and the large chickaree seemed pleased with himself, with the knowledge that he was in charge for the moment.

"Yew don't want me to tell Saecka about this, do yew?" he asked the assembled group.

"No!" one of them yelled out, and a chorus of agreement sprang up among the others.

"We found 'em first!"

"She's gonna want first pick!"

"She *always* gets first pick!"

Kinder felt a jolt at the name Saecka. It felt familiar to him, like he'd heard it somewhere before. But where? The answer came to him in the form of a sinking feeling in his chest just as a ripple was created in the mass of chickarees standing around them: someone else was coming through, and no one wanted to stand in the way of whoever it was this time.

Kinder thought he had a pretty good idea who it was, and sure enough, as the group parted, he saw her as he remembered her, when he and Lute had stumbled upon her and her band, picking for treasure in the pockets of a dead squirrel on the borders of Firwood.

Saecka was no bigger than the other chickarees, though she was older than most ever lived to be and she exuded an air of having matured into savagery in some indefinable way that the others, mere rogues and thieves, had not. There was a cunning to her fierce black eyes that made even those on her side step back as she approached—chickarees were never really on anyone's side, and a safe distance from their unpredictable leader, as they had learned through trial and error, was an essential step in living another season. A few larger chickarees followed Saecka close behind, guarding against any attack on their leader; there was no great love in their role, merely the knowledge that they would have first dibs on whatever treasure she discarded. Saecka frequently had to replace the guards, whenever one of them decided they were sick of second choice and wanted to dispatch her. It happened every now and then, and always the offender ended up on the ground with a cut throat and the others digging in his pockets. If they hadn't learned by now, they deserved to die: Saecka was always ready.

Now Saecka came forward to stand in front of the captives. She was interested to hear what they were doing here, and even more interested to know what they had with them: few came through the chickarees' woods without very good reason, and often those with very good reason were carrying something of very high value. There was that or the possibility that they were just extremely stupid, and Saecka didn't deal well with stupidity. She already had to deal with so much of it on a daily basis. They would be killed, in that case. Or, she thought darkly, in either case.

Kinder watched the leader of the chickarees come towards he and Mariyen. He heard the *tick-tick-tick* of the antiquated looking watch Saecka wore on a long silver chain around her neck. Staring at the thing for too long made him dizzy, as it rocked to and fro with its owner's steps. He wondered if she would recognize him, and decided it didn't matter. Recognition wouldn't matter for much with this crowd, he was assuming. He wished fervently that he had at least some of his charms back. The only good-luck counter he could think of when facing this situation was to spit on the ground and turn around thrice, and after being laughed at for falling on the trip-wire, Kinder wasn't so sure he wanted to risk that move.

"I would take your paw off your blade if I were you," the one called Saecka commented, and Kinder thought at first she was speaking to him, before he caught Mariyen's movement from the corner of his eye. She slowly lowered her paw from her dagger, staring all the time at the leader of the chickarees, or possibly the clock about her neck. Kinder knew she was thinking the same as he was: they were officially rotted. There was no way they could take on this group. There was only one thing left to them, and even that did not look too promising considering their audience: negotiation.

"You've come so far into our woods and you've nothing to say to us?" Saecka asked, heaving a little fake sigh. Kinder noticed that her voice, unlike those of the other chickarees, was deeper, less shrill, and she used perfect grammar when she spoke, leveling her sharp eyes on them all of the time, a smile growing on her lips.

"I guess," she said, "that we will just have to find out a little bit about you for ourselves."

"Can we take their things?" one impatient chickaree shouted from somewhere further back in the crowd. Kinder felt a paw on his arm, and he tried to jerk away but the chickaree clutching him only gripped him tighter.

"Let me jist see what they have," he hissed excitedly, jostling Kinder uncomfortably and reaching for his pack.

It happened faster than Kinder could even see. Saecka grabbed a dagger from the impressive assortment at her waist and threw it in a motion so quick that Kinder couldn't follow it with his eyes. All he knew was one moment the chickaree was breathing his rank breath in his face and going for his belongings, and the next there was an extra weight on his pack as the chickaree, still clutching it, fell to the ground, gurgling and moaning.

"Someone may finish him off," Saecka said to the crowd, and as if they'd been waiting for the call, at least five arrows thudded into the squirrel next to Kinder, who released his hold on his pack in death. Kinder felt paralyzed. He felt that he should speak, but he couldn't get his body to move or his tongue to form any words.

Mariyen suddenly spoke. "What is your purpose? We might give you a deal."

Saecka's smile told them both that she knew very well they were in no position to give out deals to anyone. Mariyen, who seemed to know this, went ahead unsteadily. They really had no other option.

"If we give you everything we have," she said, "will you let us go?"

"That depends," Saecka said, her smile widening, "on what you have. Lute!"

Kinder jumped at the name and looked up from where he was fixated on the ground. It couldn't be. The crowd was rippling again, and squirrels were making grunts and hisses of distaste as they were shoved aside or moved apart. The squirrel that moved into the center to stand next to Saecka was a dark blackish-gray in color, messy-furred and scrawny. He held some wicked looking knives with intricately carved wooden hilts in his loose-fitting belt, and when he came to focus on Kinder and Mariyen, his face froze.

~~~

Lute had been enjoying a day off from stress and from the decidedly enjoyable but tiresome fights in the Branching Bar when the news came to him.

"Three," he said, skipping his chessnut over six adjacent circles on the chessnut board, taking two of Jinning's chessnuts in the process. He stuck one into his mouth and grinned at Jinning's scowl. "Two rengolds, then," he said, adding to a tally that no one needed to write down. It was fastened too intently in their minds.

"That's not in the rules!" Jinning protested, trying to do the math in his head. "Three an' six, they 'ent the same!"

"Two threes is a six," Lute said calmly. "And it's in the rules. Yer turn, yellow-head."

Jinning glared up at him. "Yew gotta gimme the knife, yeah? Gimme one of yer knives, that was our trade."

Lute just shook his head, leaning back in his seat and smirking at the other's frustration. Chessnuts was the favorite game of chickarees everywhere. It was also the oldest. Created by a conniving chickaree hundreds of seasons back, the first set of tenuous rules came into being long ago: so long ago, in fact, that no one remembered any of them, which arguably made it the most pointless game as well.

"Yew didn't get three of my chessnuts in a row," he said, throwing out a fake yawn to display how disappointing the game was to him. "Yer not getting anywhere fast. How very sad for brave two-tailed Jinning."

A shower of chessnuts hit Lute in the face and fell off of his shoulders as Jinning flipped the board over and got to his feet in a shot. Impressive, Lute thought with sarcastic humor, flipping out his best knife and grinning. The two squirrels squared up against one another on the tree branch they'd chosen as their playing area. Lute saw Jinning come at him, his own, much less impressive knife aimed straight for Lute's chest. He waited until Jinning was almost upon him before diving to the right, slipping around to the bottom side of the branch and coming up around behind the enraged chickaree. Adrenaline rushed through his veins as he positioned himself again, aiming his knife—

"Lute!"

He looked up, expecting the worst, and getting it. The only time Cinno delivered a message was when he was held at knife point or when Saecka persuaded him to. The plump chickaree raised his brows at them like he did not engage in treetop fights most every day of the season.

"*What*, Cinno?" Lute narrowed his eyes, pocketing his knife, and waited for the explanation.

"Intruders," Cinno said, and a grin made its way ever so slowly to his face. "Saecka's on her way to meet 'em and yew know how she always likes yew to perform the duties," he growled this last, giving the larger squirrel a disgusted look of barely concealed jealousy.

Lute perked up a little. Intruders were a rare thing indeed in this neck of the woods. In all his time here as a young squirrel, those who had wandered into the woods had been far and few. On the one paw, this was a source of great pride for Saecka. On the other, it meant less treasure for the rest of them, which was the reason the band took marauding missions every so often, infringing on the unofficial territories of other reds for the thrill of competition. He passed Cinno on the branch, and as he did, the plump squirrel muttered something low under his breath.

"What's that?" Lute asked, spinning to face him, paw travelling into the territory of his belt.

"I said, I can't see why yew git all the privileges, comin' back all proper and all of that. Yew smell like gray."

Cinno ducked preemptively, but Lute was faster even than he was prepared for. At first he straightened up, smirking in the belief that he'd evaded Lute's knife, before the gash on his stomach dispelled his organs onto the branch below him. Staring down at them, dumbfounded, the hefty chickaree toppled off of the branch into the brush below, taking his intestines with him. Swallowing the inadvertent gag reflex that threatened to come up, Lute licked his blade, a sign of unapologetic domination, and sheathed it once more.

"Who's proper now," he muttered, turning to go see what the fuss was out on the road. Jinning followed him, cowed and keeping his distance.

Lute spotted them up the road, a cluster of chickarees pressed in around one single point, a point where he could only assume the luckless travelers had been stopped.

"Lute!" he heard the unmistakable voice of Saecka rise over the throng and pressed towards it, wondering vaguely what sort of possessions the witless victims had brought with them into such an unsafe area. Little could he predict that he was about to get the largest shock of his life.

Lute slammed into a few chickarees, pushed a particularly menacing female out of his way, and arrived next to Saecka. It was to the sound of the watch Saecka wore around her neck, constantly ticking, that Lute turned to face the travelers, and it was to the sound of that ticking that he stared, unmoving, unbelieving, at the face of Kinder, very real, and very much alive.

~~~

Kinder had thought he'd lost Lute forever after Zirreo kidnapped Kinder for his own purposes, leaving Lute to complete the original purpose they'd set out to complete: to keep the things in the ground from causing any more havoc and killing any more innocents. Though he'd assumed Lute had managed to survive—he couldn't imagine someone like Lute *not* surviving—he'd never thought he'd run into him again. He wanted to call out to him, to ask his friend so many questions, but he was keenly aware that to do so would be to lose whatever chance of escape he had.

"See what they've got on them, Lute," Saecka said, and Kinder averted his eyes from his old companion. He didn't want to give any sign that he knew Lute. Even when he turned away, he felt Lute's eyes on him. Still not looking, he heard his friend step forward across the ground towards them. He felt a paw clamp, none-too-gently once again, on his arm, and then a tearing sound as Lute ripped his pack from him. The contents scattered across the ground, and now Kinder looked up, alarmed, at all of their food discarded in an untidy pile, and his slingshot, lying ludicrously in the middle of it all.

One of the chickarees in the surrounding group gave a short laugh, but several of the others edged inwards, scanning the pile, grabbing at it with their eyes.

"He doesn't have any gold!" one of them shrieked, and there was an answering hiss of disapproval.

"Pockets now, Lute," Saecka said lazily.

"Turn out yer pockets!" Lute ordered, and Kinder was momentarily immobilized by his voice, proof alone above all else that this was indeed Lute standing before him. When Kinder hesitated, Lute took a knife from his belt and he jumped, turning his pockets out. There was nothing in them except a small rock, a piece of string, and a stale bit of cheese that he'd pocketed earlier when Mariyen turned around and nearly caught him eating from their pack. He held these things out to Lute, who took them, sifted through them, and discarded them. As he moved on to Mariyen, his eyes briefly met Kinder's, so briefly that Kinder couldn't read what was in them, if anything.

Mariyen had her paw clamped over her right pocket, the one that Kinder knew contained their scanty supply of rengolds. Lute faced her and nodded toward her pocket, knife still at the ready. Mariyen put a paw on her own dagger, and Kinder thought, *no. This can't be happening.* He tried to get Mariyen's attention but she was too fixated on Lute, on whatever move he would make next.

"Drop yer weapon," Lute said slowly, warningly, and when she didn't comply, he rushed up to her so fast that she had no time to react and grabbed both of her paws, forcing them behind her back.

"I wouldn't struggle if I were yew," Lute said, voice low and full of the effort of containing her as he stripped her of her belt, threw it into the pile at Kinder's feet, and then reached into her pocket and turned it inside out. Fifteen rengolds, all of their expenses, fell into his waiting paw. Kinder felt anger rising in him as he watched Lute. He remembered the other squirrel telling him that he had been raised by this group of chickarees, but the way Lute had told it, Kinder truly believed he was done with that life. Had Lute been lying to him, or had he been recaptured and trapped by the one called Saecka? When last they'd run into her, she had asked Lute to join her again. Perhaps once he was alone, after Zirreo took Kinder, she'd come back with the band and overpowered him. It was certainly possible, and it was what Kinder wanted to believe, because the alternative...

"Fifteen rengolds and naught else," Lute said, turning to Saecka. He didn't show any recognition to Kinder, running his eyes over he and Mariyen without really looking at them.

"It's scanty," complained a chickaree, possibly the same one who had cried out before.

"Think yer gettin' any of it?" another challenged, pushing him. A fight broke out where they stood, but Saecka was not distracted by it; Kinder was beginning to suppose she was used to such things occurring. The tussle grew to include a couple more chickarees and a guard chickaree, who evidently felt he deserved something of the aforementioned money. Chickarees, as Kinder's mother was so fond of telling him between bites of the wall, didn't even use money due to their penchant for outright thievery: they merely attached worth to how shiny it was. He wondered once more how his mother seemed to have so much to say about chickarees, but his aimless wondering was diverted and brought painfully back to the reality of the situation when he heard Saecka speak.

"I say take them to be held," she said, grinning unpleasantly at Kinder and Mariyen. They're obviously going somewhere, and if that somewhere is a location we can reach that holds a lot more than *this*," she gestured disdainfully at the pile of rengolds in Lute's palm, "Then we can use them to lead us there."

"And then kill 'em?" A chickaree asked from the back of the crowd. Saecka smiled grimly.

"Who said anything about killing?" she said, and there was an appreciative snicker throughout the crowd which she silenced with a cold look.

"Come," Saecka said, "Ginfer, Arbond, Sigel, take them."

The chickarees she called came forward. They were larger than most, and when one of them grabbed Mariyen's arm she cried out, so tight was the grip. Kinder breathed in sharply as one of them took him. He tried to wriggle around for some sense of comfort, but his captor was unyielding and he only ended up tiring himself out, panting hard. The third guard chickaree stood between the both of them and their captors, prodding them with a stick and snickering.

"Cut that out," Saecka snapped at him, "We want them in good shape."

"Good luck with that," the chickaree holding Kinder muttered, once she and her entourage were out of earshot. "This one's not gonna be any time soon!"

He and his comrade shared an unpleasant laugh over this before starting off in the direction of the trees to the side of the path. As they went, Kinder looked over his shoulder. The other chickarees had all cleared away in a flurry of movement, and so, it seemed, had Lute. He noticed they were going off to the other side of the narrow road, and it made him wonder where they were headed. All he could see behind him was the forlorn pile of their food, still sitting in the roadway. Their weapons had been carried away—and likely fought for—by some overly eager chickarees.

As he and Mariyen entered the misty confines of the woods, Kinder had an idea.

"You know," he said, addressing the chickaree ahead of him, the one with no captive at hand. "You know, I left you a good deal of treasure last time I came through here. I was the one who left all the charms." He wished he'd remembered this when he stood in front of Saecka. It was possible neither of these squirrels knew what he was talking about, but he persisted when the chickaree he had addressed turned to look at him. "That's a lot of treasure. Surely it's enough that you don't need any more. You know Astrippa doesn't honor the greedy."

Kinder knew he was going out on a limb with that last statement, but he wasn't quite prepared for how hilarious the chickarees apparently found it.

"Astrippa!" one of them hooted, as another exploded into a fit of snickering so loud and excitable that Kinder thought he might hurt himself in the process. "Astrippa! That's a good one! Yer a natural joker, fat one, heeeheeeheeeheeee..."

He wheezed to a stop abruptly and said, "Saecka already knows all that about yew and yer charms. She says she wants yew captured and that's why, see. She wants to know where yer goin'. If the first time yew got charms, you gotta git somethin' different this time, eh? Maybe somethin'...better?" His eyes were alight with a creepily intense greed. Kinder flinched away from him.

He knew. Or rather, he corrected himself, Saecka knew. He could remember the first time he walked down this path behind Zirreo reluctantly, and he could remember that same feeling of being watched, of having eyes on his back at all times.

Apparently, it hadn't only been his imagination.

"How come you didn't ambush us?" Kinder asked, genuinely curious now. He winced as he was dragged over a protruding root in the ground then went to looking inquisitively towards the chickaree ahead of him. He'd assumed they'd got lucky, that the eyes on his back were mere figments of his imagination, or that Zirreo had somehow managed to make it so they weren't seen.

"Yer kidden', right?" the chickaree asked him. He played distractedly with one of the silver hoops in his over-pierced left ear, then leaned over close to Kinder. "Cuz there was a white with yew, that's why."

"The white squirrel?" Mariyen asked, and the chickaree holding her shook her in a way that made Kinder want to shake *him* a few times.

"Shh!" the chickaree who'd spoke to Kinder hissed. "Not so loud, yew stupid flyer. Yew can't talk that way about the white squirrels, yew never know if they can hear yew." He looked up at the branches above him and all around as though he expected a white squirrel to jump out at him. "Madgicked, they are," he said, apparently satisfied for the moment that they weren't about to be struck dead. "The white squirrels is madgicked, and yew know it." He squinted hard at Kinder. "Yew were with him." He looked a little nervous at this thought, and Kinder had a tentative idea.

"What if I told you I had magic too?"

For a moment, the chickarees froze, seeming to consider this, and then the two holding Mariyen started laughing and everyone followed suit. Kinder gritted his teeth at the sound of their laughter and hoped that wherever they were going, these squirrels would not be staying with them.

No sooner had he had this thought when the chickarees stopped walking, coming to a stop before a tree that Kinder figured must be their destination.

It was a grotesque sight. About an estimate of ten trees had grown together, each dissolving into the others and reaching out wildly with its branches at the same time, as though flailing for escape. They were birches, and the white amorphous mass that their grown-togetherness created was what the chickarees headed for.

There was a door set into the tumor-like mass of tree, and they headed for this. When Mariyen's captors reached the door, they knocked twice, sharply. Only a second later, as though he'd been waiting behind the door for this moment, another squirrel, small even for a chickaree, opened it and stared out at them.

"Captives?" he leered at Mariyen and Kinder. The chickaree in front of Kinder, who until now had been occupying himself with poking him and Mariyen every so often, dropped the stick he was carrying.

"Yeah," he said, "but you can't touch 'em until Saecka's seen 'em."

"How much treasure do they git?" the chickaree said, still leering at them like he thought they might taste good.

"Nothin' fer yew," one of the chickarees holding Kinder sneered, and they pressed forward to scale the tree—or trees, rather— the small distance up to the bulbous point of their joining. One of the chickarees holding Kinder suddenly pushed him, and he fell to the floor beyond the threshold, past the smaller chickaree, who sniggered appreciatively. A second later, Mariyen fell hard next to him. They had only one moment to look at each other before they were shut into complete darkness. The voices of the small chickaree and the others were obscured completely.

"We're alone," Mariyen whispered to him, confirming what he hadn't dared to hope. At least there was that. If Kinder was locked in a dark place like this, he would rather not share it with a chickaree or two. He listened hard but still couldn't hear anything outside.

"Where did they go?" he asked, mostly talking to himself. It was how he dealt with sudden darkness falling, the sign of the unknown settling in. He hadn't even gotten that one from his dream-interpretation book either.

When Kinder's eyes failed to adjust to the dark, he began to feel dizzy, or imagine that he felt dizzy. Didn't squirrels go insane in pitch blackness? He heard Mariyen move off to the right—or was it the left?—of him, and scuttled backward...and into something hard and full of angles, strangely furry to the touch. He jerked back at the same time as the faint smell hit his nose. Panicked, he ran in the opposite direction, anything to get away from what he was sure he'd felt in the darkness.

"What is it?" Mariyen asked when he tripped over her. Kinder couldn't answer her.

"I say we just stay on this side of the room for now," he said, pressing himself up against the wall he found at his back.

He could feel Mariyen's quizzical look even if he couldn't see it, but he couldn't bring himself to explain. They sat in the same place for what felt like an hour, and Kinder became so claustrophobic, so nerved up that he noticed everything. The number of seconds ticking by, the curves in the walls, which he imagined he could see only momentarily (and wasn't sure if he could really see at all), that horrible faint smell, how close he and Mariyen sat, the cadence of her breath, the fact that when she breathed her side nearly touched his own...

"What's that smell?" Mariyen asked suddenly, but Kinder was saved from answering as the door creaked open at that moment. Kinder could hear the sound of the wind coming through the trees, slight as it was in this misty forest, and he turned eagerly to look. As soon as he did, however, the door closed again and they were surrounded in blackness once again. It was almost as if the wind itself had opened the door, but Kinder knew that was impossible. A door that acted as such a sound barrier would be impervious to such minor threats as wind.

Mariyen shifted beside him, her discomfort tangible; Kinder himself was not feeling overly calm or safe. The door had opened—even though he felt as though his mind was deteriorating in the darkness, he knew he hadn't made that up. Mariyen had heard it too. There was an imperceptible shift in the close air here, even though they couldn't sense any movement or hear anything aside from the sound of their own breath and hearts beating. But something was different. If they'd been in doubt about it before, now there was no avoiding what they both knew in their private thoughts, too afraid to voice aloud.

They were no longer alone.

CHAPTER XII

Every time Llewellyn woke, she felt worse, and this was no exception. She no longer believed—if she ever had—that the black squirrel wasn't drugging her.

"I'm not thirsty," she said automatically when Mercurie inevitably noticed her conscious state and hurried over. The black squirrel gave her charge an impatient look.

"You're feeling better then, are you?" she asked, her eyes slightly alight despite her apparent aggravation.

"Yes..." Llewellyn hesitantly answered. She'd been getting questions like this for a couple days now, and she had the idea that they were waiting for her to 'feel good' for some unexplained reason. What could they have planned that required her being in full health? What were they doing that required *her*, period? Llewellyn didn't want to find out, but today was the day she would have to. As little as she wanted to confront whatever situation she'd gotten herself into, the idea of keeping up living the way she had been was even worse. She'd been pretending to be asleep most of the time. In the beginning, she really had been tired, but later it became only an attempt to avoid Absoulim when he was awake, a technique Absoulim was growing impatient with, as she gathered from his hushed conversations with Mercurie as she lay with her eyes tight shut, listening.

They were planning something, and she hadn't the barest slip of an idea what it was.

Mercurie didn't fix her a drink for once this morning, something she was exceedingly glad for. She suspected that Mercurie might be catching on to her pretend sleep and wanted to make sure Llewellyn really did rest when she and Absoulim talked. She stared at Llewellyn instead with excited eyes—a frightening sight on the old sorceress—and exclaimed, "Then you are ready!"

confirming Llewellyn's suspicions in a painfully straightforward way.

"Ready for what?" she dared to ask, but Mercurie had scooted off into the dark recesses of the log behind her to make something to eat, she assumed. Feeding Llewellyn was on par with giving her things to drink: not for one second did she believe that any of it was done out of concern for her well-being.

"We're going to go on a journey, my dear," Mercurie said, voice sounding muffled in the recesses of the log. When she returned, she had a small wooden bowl clasped in her paws, with a sort of soup inside of it. Llewellyn had no desire to taste the stuff; she'd had enough of what Mercurie called her 'cooking' to last a lifetime.

"A journey," Llewellyn repeated. She was gearing up for what she knew she needed to do. This 'journey', this dedicated preparing, it all stank of something awful—more awful than the soup she was now warming her paws on. If there was one thing she'd heard consistently from the whispered tones of Mercurie and Absoulim, it was talk of the 'white squirrel'. The phrase came up in nearly every conversation, and even though Llewellyn could feel herself becoming drugged before she could hear the rest of the talk more often than not, those three words were consistent.

This had something to do with Zirreo. She would have liked to be surprised, but nothing was further from the truth. Ever since Zirreo had come into her life so many seasons ago when she was young and impressionable—or, she thought wryly, simply stupid—he had influenced her. He'd held a sway over her life—and her private thoughts— that she could never shake off, even as she grew to want to. Why should it be any different for anyone else? She remembered well how hung up the other flyers were on Zirreo the whole time he stayed with them long ago. They were all so interested in him, and the ones who weren't were afraid of him, but most were some mix of the two. And Absoulim...well...

"I need to talk with Absoulim," Llewellyn said, sliding off of the makeshift bed that Mercurie had set down for her. Mercurie scowled.

"What for?" she asked, looking suspiciously at her, and if Llewellyn had doubted whether Mercurie trusted Absoulim or not before, her doubts were fully confirmed. First there were their constant whispered arguments, and then there was the way Mercurie watched Absoulim when he was awake, like she expected him to put one over on her and she was readying herself in aggression.

"I think I have the right to find out what he's planning, and I want to hear it from him," she said.

Mercurie looked behind them nervously, then turned to her. "Fine," she snapped with less grace than a pricker bush. "But I could tell you the same as he will."

Llewellyn doubted it. She didn't really mean to ask Absoulim much about his plans; her real purpose was something much more dubious, something she did not feel comfortable asking of Mercurie. Mercurie, who eyed her like she was a chunk of hazelnut flan in periods when she didn't think Mariyen was looking; Mercurie, who liked to act nice to her, not for the sake of being nice, but with that secretive gleam like she was getting something out of it.

Llewellyn stood up and, following the direction of all of Mercurie's glares and nervous glances, started to the right along the length of the fallen tree, her eyes adjusting as she went. The insides of the tree, she could see as she went, appeared as though they'd been blackened in some places and left their original color in others. *A fire,* she thought as she passed what might have been a table and the remains of an old bed, pushed up against a wall and blackened just like the walls. This tree must have been fallen for many seasons, judging from its rotted quality, but it still made her insides bunch up and chill to pass the belongings of someone—or a bunch of someones—who no longer lived.

She came to a place where there was a collapsed set of stairs and something that looked like a wall but she knew was a ceiling, and searched around for the hole at the top—or the bottom—of the stairs, where she could go through. She had no idea whether she was going up or down in this uprooted relic of a house, and it made her feel uneasy. Squeezing through the rotted wood where she found the hole, she was greeted by another place that must have been a bedroom at some point. There were a couple of pictures smashed on the floor, glass everywhere in glittering shards promising hurt, there was a chair pushed into a corner, obviously moved since the house fell, and several firefly lanterns set up about the room, giving it a glow that only enhanced rather than alleviated the creepy atmosphere.

Absoulim sat on an overturned bed, watching her. She knew he'd seen her from the moment she peered inside; otherwise, she would have contemplated running, giving up on her idea. But it was a cold rotting day before Llewellyn would run in fear from Absoulim, especially when he could see, so she stayed. His pale eyes watched her intently as she entered the room.

"We need to talk," she said.

Absoulim raised a brow at her. "I wasn't aware of that," he said. She thought for a second she sensed something like discomfort in his tone, and was surprised out of continuing for a second. Maybe what she wanted would work after all. Absoulim's eyes drifted over to the chair in the far corner, and she saw what she had missed before: her crystal ball was sitting there, vibrating to the hidden pulses it seemed to pick up from the air. She thought of running over and snatching it, but she was afraid, and for more than one reason. The last time she'd held her own crystal ball, it had not been a pleasant experience.

"Listen," Llewellyn said, trying to avoid looking at the scrying ball. It seemed to know her name and was calling to her in the language of non-words. She blocked it out and turned to Absoulim. "What do you want with me?"

"You haven't guessed?" Absoulim asked, and she stared at him for a long while, at those unusual awkward features that had gotten him so alienated among the flyers. Absoulim had always been a little...off, but that hadn't excused what they'd done to him, something she liked to wipe from her mind under the rationale that some squirrels were born for evil. She remembered how it felt to be the only one who talked to him. She'd ignored all the disturbing signs then, and not because she didn't see them but because it was taboo to hang out with Absoulim, and the young Llewellyn would do anything that seemed risky or frowned upon by convention. Did that make her any better than most of those she'd disliked, like boring Genhaw, who she'd been forced to mate? She'd befriended Absoulim for selfish reasons, not the least of them being curiosity. What was it to the strange squirrel the other young ones in her learning group disliked, the one they once locked in that spare room until the elders found out about it? The elders hadn't punished anyone too much for that, either, and she could see that they felt the same even as they pretended to reprimand. There seemed a trace of fear in their dislike, and that had intrigued her.

Yet she'd shut the window like everyone else when they tore his wings, and that proved beyond a doubt that she was just like the rest of them, possibly worse. She could not tell herself she'd never cared for Absoulim, but now was different. He'd killed, not one, not two, but a bunch of other innocents with the black art of self-fulfilling prophecy. She didn't know what to feel over any of it, but she couldn't help feeling that one of those feelings should not be guilt.

"This is about Zirreo," she spoke aloud, and, noticing how he scowled at the name from her lips, said, "I know you wanted to mate me."

In the silence that came after, Llewellyn could not believe she'd uttered those words.

"Wanted," Absoulim said at long last, and another space of silence ensued.

"I don't love Zirreo, you know," she said, and wondered why she felt like that wasn't completely true. Absoulim just regarded her quietly.

"Is that what you think this is about?" he asked her after a time, his rasping voice slightly incredulous. "You must think yourself very powerful, to hold such sway."

Llewellyn didn't know whether to feel relieved or frustrated. "Then what?" she demanded.

Absoulim got up and went over to the chair across the room. He picked up the crystal ball and held it, head turned down in supposed contemplation. When he looked up at her again, he met her eyes full-on for the first time since she'd entered the room.

"Power," he said.

When she didn't speak, he went on. "The white squirrel has a great deal of power, as I'm sure you know. The very fact that he has lived so long and hasn't...weathered, in quite the same way as the rest of us, proves it. The child...*your* child was the only one who had more."

"Then you want to get it from them?" she asked. It was her turn for incredulity. "You must know, surely, that you just can't *do* that."

Absoulim stared at her. "Of course not," he said, "I intend for them to teach me."

Llewellyn blinked at him. "The child is not with him. I don't know where she is, I promise, but she's not with him," she said, hoping against hope it would do something to change his mind, to keep him away from Zirreo. It was not for any feelings she had for him, she told herself, but merely because no one deserved to have a squirrel like Absoulim come attempt to 'learn' from them.

Absoulim wasn't convinced, as she know he wouldn't be. "If the child isn't around, than the child is dead," he said, voice crawling over the words like a disease. "And in that case, the white squirrel is the most powerful, once again."

"What if he can't teach you?" she asked loudly, desperately.

"I think he will. Absoulim's smile made her sickened and anxious at once. He studied the crystal ball in his paws before lowering it again to its chair and turning away.

Llewellyn, without thinking too much about what she was doing, reached out for his paw and took it, trying to fight down the revulsion she felt at the cold bony touch.

"Absoulim," she said, and her voice commanded him to look at her. "I knew you. I would never have considered you a friend if all I'd seen was this quest for power. It's mad. You're more than that."

"You've made mistakes before," Absoulim sneered, though she thought he hesitated before pulling away.

"Don't you ever just want to go back to Edgewood how it was and forget the whole thing?" Llewellyn said, desperately searching for something to stop the mad rushing in her ears.

Absoulim laughed, the strangling sound full and unpleasant in her ears.

"Back to Edgewood...because it was so much *fun* there."

She realized how stupid it'd been in retrospect.

"What do you need me for?" she asked again, changing her tack. "You have a soul, Absoulim. Why don't you prove it and let me go?"

Absoulim smiled again, and her heart sank.

"I would like to, but I can't. You see, you're going to be the one who allows me to get close to the white squirrel. I'm not fool enough after all to go over there without having some...leverage."

Llewellyn backed away, towards the dark opening of the door she'd come through. "No," she heard herself say. She had to leave. Whatever he was planning, she wouldn't be a part of it. She wouldn't lead Zirreo to his destruction that way, no matter how she felt he'd slighted her. "No!" she broke into a run and fell out the opening, through a mess of splintered, rotting wood. Getting to her feet immediately, she made to run off. If she was quick she might get away without anyone even noticing. She backed away from the opening, turned to run, and found herself facing Mercurie. The black squirrel had a strange smile on her face.

"Where are you off to in such a rush?" Mercurie hissed. By the way she kept her voice low, Llewellyn knew she'd been listening in on their whole conversation and didn't want Absoulim to know.

"I'm going," Llewellyn snapped, and attempted to pull out of Mercurie's hold, but the old black squirrel was stronger than she had any right to be, and kept Llewellyn where she was.

"I think," she said, "It's time for you to take a nap again."

Llewellyn knew what was coming. She tried to fight it, but the liquid Mercurie seemingly produced from nowhere and forced down her throat tasted of fire and dirt, and made her choke. Llewellyn coughed and struggled, struggled and coughed until she found her eyelids getting heavy against her will and her struggles became weaker and weaker, her coughs subsiding into the long, steady breaths of sleep.

Mercurie dragged Llewellyn back to where the flyer had been lying only a little while ago and stared exultantly down at her. Things were shaping up better than she had thought they would. She had been concerned about Absoulim. The way he acted around the flyer made her think he might retract his promise of giving her Llewellyn's life when he was done. Her suspicions had been confirmed in part by the conversation she'd overheard, but her doubts were blown away. Llewellyn was hers.

"Whether you want it or not, my dear, you're in the game," she said softly, watching the now oblivious Llewellyn's sides rise and fall as she dreamed things that were no doubt better than her present waking life. They were going north, and they were going very soon. She thought tomorrow morning would be a perfect time for the ritual, and this time, she didn't think Absoulim would disagree.

CHAPTER XIII

"Hello?" Mariyen called. Kinder heard her reach out in the blackness and nearly fall back against the wall behind them. Whoever was sharing their prison with them was choosing to remain silent, and the deadly stillness was making the fur on his neck rise.

The sound of something tinkling, like glass, reached Kinder's ears, and he pressed himself to the wall just as a dim light flared up somewhere in front of them and then quickly flickered out.

"Rot it all."

The sound of the muttered curse was familiar to Kinder, but he dared not hope...then the light flared up again, this time stronger, and they both saw, silhouetted against the darkness, a face that was undoubtedly not that of a chickaree.

"Lute!" Kinder cried. He heard Mariyen exhale in relief next to him and knew she understood. He'd told her about Lute in his recounting of his last adventure and knowing her, she may well have recognized him earlier on, when they were surrounded.

Lute responded to his cry of welcome by putting a paw up to his mouth.

"Shhh!" he muttered. "I've taken care of yer guards, ninnys that they are, but I can't promise yew no one's going to come looking for me or yew in a while, so yer gonna have to contain yer enthusiasm for once."

Kinder kept quiet, but it was extremely hard with all the things he wanted to ask Lute. Lute broke the silence anyway, speaking in a whisper.

"How're yew alive?" he asked. Kinder wasn't expecting that, but then he remembered: the last time Lute had seen him, after all, he'd been falling from the edge of a precarious cliff to the ground below—where, unbeknownst to his friend, he'd been abducted by a certain white squirrel with a lot of nerve in the arena of interference in the lives of others.

"Zirreo took me," Kinder said, but he was met with a blank stare. "The white squirrel."

"Ah." Lute was looking uncomfortable. "I...I'm glad yer alive." His voice sounded odd, and Kinder realized with a shock that it sounded like he might cry. To save Lute some face, because it was obvious the other squirrel would be mortified at such a display, he began to talk about what Zirreo had taken him for and what happened when Absoulim caught up to them.

"Zirreo didn't come back, though," he finished, "We're hunting him for answers, I guess you could say. No one could find Absoulim's body back at Edgewood and the ground is still a dangerous place. I *saw* them, Lute. I saw the gorepedes."

"Wha...?"

"I saw them. Well, Mariyen and I both saw them."

"They were horrible," Mariyen said, shuddering at the memory.

"Lute...they had this green skin and these...feelers, I guess you'd call them and..."

"No eyes," Lute finished. Kinder stared at his partially illuminated face in no small surprise.

"Have...have you seen them too, then?" he asked, hardly daring to believe it.

"Kinder, I went underground," Lute said. "Did yew think I just quit on the mission and went here?"

Kinder didn't know what to say. That was, in all truthfulness, what he'd assumed Lute had done, but he didn't want to admit it.

"You went—underground, with...with *those* things? How did you survive?"

"Well," said Lute, "Yew remember how whatsisname...Zirreo was telling us about underground squirrels?"

"...Yes." He did remember, now that he was told again. "*Were* there underground squirrels, then?" He leaned forward, eager to hear about this. Zirreo had told them that their only hope was to bargain with the underground squirrels. Evidently, if Lute had tried, he had failed, but how was it then that he was standing in front of them now, whole and breathing?

"I ended up in the middle of them as soon as I hit the end of that tunnel yer *Zirreo* so wisely told us to go through," the sarcasm in his voice was thick when he spoke of the white squirrel. "They wanted to kill me, even handed me to their local insane guy so he could make the decision. I had to make up something fast, so I made up this story about the mirror I had then, pretending I was some king from up above to freak him out. Well, it worked for the insane guy, and because he decided not to kill me, no one else could kill me—some justice system—so me and the leader bargained over it. He took me to where they keep those things, so I got a nice look at them all, all sliding around down there like freak worms. He told me they went aboveground every few years to feed but he could make an exception and order them not to feed aboveground if I didn't tell anyone above about them. And I didn't. But it looks like they've broken their promise anyway, if yer story's anything to go by."

Lute fell into silence, and Kinder could sense the anger seeping from the last thing he'd said and knew that it was true: Lute had actually seen and spoken to these squirrels.

"Why would they release the gorepedes if they knew you could tell everyone about them?" he asked, and then, he had a worse idea. "I've told Edgewood about the underground squirrels. Not everyone there knows about them, but I've definitely mentioned what Zirreo said to more than a few of them. Do you think it's possible that they know I've said something?"

Lute studied him for a moment, then shrugged. "I don't know. I guess anything's possible with them. It was just—it seemed like such a real thing, yew know, when we had the agreement. It was like, I got where they were coming from. They have some sort of insane queen who makes all their decisions for them. Well, sometimes her insane son, the one I was thrown in with, makes the decisions, and she reinforces them, but they seemed kind of sad and trapped. I thought we'd understood each other..." he paused. "It just doesn't make sense either. If they were going to break their promise, why didn't they just kill me? That leader could have let the insane one have me, or he could have pushed me into the gorepedes and let them finish me. Then he would have known for sure I wouldn't tell anyone about them. Unless he was still afraid of me, but I don't think that was the case. He seemed so...honest about it. I know he saw through my story."

There was a silence in which Kinder thought he heard something outside of their enclosure and flinched, but it turned out to only be the sound of rain hitting the branches outside and the ground all around. That roaring sound, coming in place of the dead silence, actually made him feel less afraid, though he couldn't have said why.

We're going to get out of this okay, he told himself, and didn't argue the point in his mind. He decided he'd hold on to that little piece of positivity until he was proven wrong.

"What if," Mariyen said, breaking the silence and punctuating the continuous patter of the rain, "what if it was someone else who let the gorepedes go? The leader might have been honest with you, but what if someone else in their group wasn't so honest? I mean, with a mad queen in charge, there's got to be some dissent among them."

Lute turned to her. "Yew know, yer pretty smart," he said, "and pretty, if the dark isn't deceiving" he added, with a type of wink. Kinder turned to stare at him and he began to laugh. "Hey, sorry," he said. "Just an observation."

He sobered up and went into what appeared to be deep thought again.

"If, like yew say, one of them chipmunks—chipmunks, that's what they call themselves—if one of them went a little crazy and decided to loose all the gorepedes, maybe it isn't such a problem. I hope yer right, Mariyen? Mariyen. Because if it's really this leader who thinks I've betrayed them, he sounded pretty serious about coming after me, after *us*, and doing some damage."

He lapsed into silence for a while and then swung his firefly lamp about to get the creatures inside stirred up again. The area around his face lit up again.

"Hey Kinder," Lute said suddenly, "where's all yer charms? Did Saecka take 'em or something? Isn't there bound to be some sort of catastrophe coming up? Yew know, where yew'll need a long-life medallion or whatever the rot yew were wearing?"

Kinder flushed at the teasing, but spoke matter-of-factly. "Zirreo thought they were ridiculous too. Last time I came through this place with him, he made me leave them for the chickarees. So now they have them." He glared at Lute. "Or you have them, rather, since it seems you're a part of them now."

"No way," Lute breathed, ignoring the heated tone of his voice, "so that's why Saecka's so into yew. Usually she'll just kill yew if yew haven't got anything, but she thinks yer associated with the white squirrel."

"So we heard from your friends," Kinder said scathingly. He hadn't meant to get angry, but now that he was onto the subject of Lute's allegiance, he found he couldn't stop it from coming.

"This is good," Lute said, ignoring his anger. "Yew'd probably be dead if it weren't for that white squirrel. Yew should've found an alternate route, Kinder. Really, yew can't get past here." Kinder couldn't ignore the fact that there was a touch of pride in Lute's voice when he said it.

"Oh, and if they decided to kill me, can I assume you'd be helping them?"

Lute finally faced him and gave him a look that made him ashamed in spite of himself.

"What do yew think I'm here for?" he asked. "Honestly, Kinder. I'm getting yew out. Though I've got to tell yew, if yew come through here again, there may not be much I can do for yew."

Kinder started to speak, but Mariyen, perhaps preemptively realizing what he was going to say, cut across him.

"How *do* we get out of here?" she asked.

Lute looked grave. "Carefully," he said. Kinder thought his face seemed a little white, but it could have only been the effects of the lamplight.

The rain pounded around them and Lute put a paw to his mouth and led them across the floor to the door. As they went, they passed the place where Kinder had tripped and run in fright and the lamp briefly shed light on the area. Kinder cried out.

"Kinder, what—?" Mariyen began, but then her eyes followed his and she fell silent, horrified. Lute turned around to face them. He did not look terrified in the least; he even appeared slightly annoyed with them.

"It's a prison," Lute said, "Yew think they're going to bother to clean it out?"

He passed the light more fully over the body lying on the floor beside them. Kinder couldn't tell what type of squirrel it was anymore; though it still had some of its fur, it was so degraded into the ground that he couldn't really make a definitive call. Beyond that squirrel's body, there appeared to be others, all in the process of becoming one with the ground again. It looked like the last time this prison had been used was a long time ago. He tried to ease his blood out of freezing when Lute started forward again. It wasn't only the sight of the unfortunate squirrels that was giving him anxiety, but the idea that he and Mariyen would join them if they were caught trying to escape.

Lute wouldn't let that happen, he thought, but already there was uncertainty to it. Honestly, Lute was a bit of a closed book to him. He'd thought he had known the scruffy squirrel well enough when they'd travelled together, even though so much of his past seemed obscured, but this new, more dispassionate side of his former friend was nothing he'd seen before. Or maybe he'd just overlooked it. He saw for the first time, as he hadn't been able to see at the eager and naïve time he'd met Lute, that the other squirrel, whatever else he might be, was dangerous. He wondered if Lute really would have stabbed him all that time ago, when they'd first met. Kinder, naturally friendly and believing the best, had merely thought of him as reticent and grumpy, and had forced his way into Lute's life with no thoughts for negative consequences. He wondered now, staring at the back of Lute's head lit up by the glow of the lantern as he made his way up to the door, just how much of his friend he'd never thought to question.

Lute paused by the door, sliding his ear up against it and listening intently. Kinder had to wonder why when the door was clearly soundproof. He voiced that thought in a whisper now. Lute looked at him incredulously.

"This door isn't soundproof," he said.

"We couldn't hear anyone after we were shut in here, even though they were right outside the door," Mariyen explained.

"Ah, well," Lute said, "that would be about the time I silenced them."

"Silenced them?"

"For crying out loud, Kinder, what do yew think it means when I say I took care of the guards? That I gave them a warm dinner and a swamp bath? Yeah, I followed yew two and Ginfer and the others. They left Sigel and Arbond to guard and I guess Ginfer didn't leave 'em the key after locking yew up. In any case, they didn't have it, so I had to pick all the locks. It took a very long time, so thank yer lucky stars or yer goddess or what have yew that I wasn't caught."

Kinder was impressed, despite his doubts about the journey they were about to embark upon. He hadn't heard a thing when Lute went through all those locks, and he hoped that that stealth could be lent in part to him in order for he and Mariyen to get out of here.

After a while more of listening at the door, Lute seemed satisfied that no one was on the other side, and turned to them.

"We're going to mainly travel out of here through the tops of trees, okay? They're close enough together so we'll never have to go down. The important thing is, if one of the others sees us, which they will, yew have to stay quiet and look scared. I'm going to head in the direction of Saecka's quarters for a while, pretend like I'm taking yew there. Actually getting too close to Saecka's quarters, mind, is something we don't want to do, so we're going to veer off when we get close enough, then run, and say our prayers."

Any ease Kinder had been beginning to feel was wiped from his mind at this plan.

"Isn't there any, uhm, more foolproof way to do it?"

Lute stared at him, a weird half-smile on his face. "Well. Kinder without his charms is afraid to do everything, isn't he?"

He didn't give Kinder a chance to respond, but opened the door and pulled himself out, holding it for them to come behind. Mariyen smiled back at Kinder encouragingly, and Kinder felt the burning desire to prove that he wasn't cowardly. He took a bold step out, but forgot the top step and tripped. Mariyen tried not to laugh, shushing him with a paw to her mouth, a humored light glinting in her dark eyes. When Kinder got over the top step and dragged himself, flushing, to where they stood, Lute also turned and put a paw to his mouth. His face was grave and reminded Kinder that now was not the time for rash actions. He found himself really missing his day by day book, the book written by Humphrey the Lunatic every new season with tips for each day. Though the others would scoff, he was sure he could face this whole scenario with more confidence if he had some idea of how to act in order to avoid trouble. One day at home he'd managed to find a piece of cheese under the couch by being extra cautious and checking all surroundings before entering a situation, as the book suggested. He guessed such behavior would work for this situation too, but he missed the certainty.

"Close the door," Lute whispered to Kinder, who started out of his daze and slapped the door shut without thinking. He received a sharp glare from both Lute and Mariyen for his efforts.

"Do yew want 'em to hear us?" Lute hissed.

"Sorry," Kinder mumbled, wishing for his book more than anything, except perhaps his pack. The anxiety was making him hungry.

Trying not to look at the two shapes of the obviously deceased guards at the entrance to the place they'd just vacated, Kinder followed Mariyen, who followed Lute up the nearest tree.

"Shouldn't we do something about them?" Mariyen asked, indicating the guards.

Lute shrugged. "Nah. It's normal enough. They could have just refused me entry. Which they did. So I won't even be lying. Remember, I'm taking yew somewhere important."

Mariyen went quiet and Kinder wondered if she was also thinking about the connotations of such violence being commonplace. If it was an everyday event for these squirrels to kill one another with wild abandon, he couldn't help thinking that they'd be stabbed in the back before Lute could explain anything to anyone.

He expressed this concern to Lute, and Lute, instead of making him feel better, nodded. "Yeah, that's a distinct possibility. Which is why yew got to be ready to fight 'em back."

"Fight..."

"But we don't have our weapons anymore!" Mariyen said. "We've got nothing to defend ourselves."

Lute grinned grimly and pulled a knife from among the many hanging on his waist.

"Yers," he said, flicking it toward Mariyen. Kinder saw the panicked look on her face before she managed to catch it, and hoped he wasn't about to receive the same test.

Instead, Lute climbed higher in the tree until he got to a fork and rummaged around somewhere out of Kinder's range of vision. When he turned back to them, he was carrying their pack, and it looked moderately full.

"This has got yers inside, Kinder," he said, "but I can't let yew have it; it's too noticeable." He rummaged in his belt and brought out one of his own knives, selecting it through some process unknown to Kinder. "Here," he said, throwing it to him. Kinder missed, but by some stroke of luck, it landed on the branch below him. "I'll carry this," Lute said, indicating the bag, "and yew two: keep yer weapons hidden and only attack as a last resort. Yer to let me handle it unless it's too much to handle, in which case, I'll signal yew. No sense blowing our cover over a minor confrontation. Got it?"

They both nodded. Satisfied, Lute turned his back on them and scampered up the tree with their pack in tow. Mariyen and Kinder followed.

When they reached the top of the tree and broke out from the mist, Kinder looked down and was amazed at what he saw. He'd found this place just plain unsettling and creepy when he'd come, and he never expected to see anything that could convince him of any other opinion, but the view he found himself looking down on was captivating in a unique way.

The mist was below him, just floating amid the trees, stopping abruptly much of the way up so that it looked to him like the tree he was on was poking up through a cloud and he could see below him a floor of white with some very strange, short plants—the tops of the trees—sticking out from it. The rain was harder up here, with no branches to buffer its fall, but as little as he, or any other squirrel for that matter, liked to be wet, Kinder found himself thinking it might be worth the view.

"It gives us an advantage to travel up here," Lute explained. Those below us aren't going to pay us much attention, and there are few of 'em who hang out up here, especially when it's raining like this. Good day to be doing this, at least," he smiled wryly.

Lute was right in that there hardly seemed to be anybody up here; it was like a different world to Kinder, and he actually had to remind himself that it was still red territory. Lute was also right in that the tops of the trees were all close enough so that they could always travel on this level and wouldn't have to worry about dipping into the mist again.

They'd been travelling without event for a couple of minutes before Kinder heard the sounds of talking.

"We're near Saecka's quarters," Lute whispered, and Kinder noticed that even he looked apprehensive. "If we can't avoid being seen, we need to keep silent."

Kinder swallowed, hard, and looked toward the horizon. He thought he could see the edge of sunlight beyond the stretch of mist and wet, but the voices were between it and them, and soon Kinder found the source of them through the constant blur of rain.

Two chickarees sat up in the limbs of a particularly tall elm, sopping wet and looking unhappy about it, muttering amongst themselves. The way they were just sitting up here in the rain made Kinder nervous. It seemed unlikely to him that there was no purpose to their stillness, and sure enough, when they noticed Lute, Mariyen and Kinder, they stopped talking and one of them got up.

"Fancy seein' yew here, Lute," he said; his voice sounded too unsurprised for comfort, and Kinder saw Lute rest his paw surreptitiously close to his set of knives. The chickaree took no notice.

"Saecka said she expected yew might do something like this," he said.

This time, Lute couldn't contain his surprise. "How?" he asked.

"She don't forgit anythin'," the other chickaree said, "and she remembers the fat one. Says yew were with him once. Says in non-reds, that creates loyalty." He put emphasis on the word 'non-reds', and Lute scowled.

"So what're yew here for then?" Lute said, drawing one of his knives. Neither of them appeared to notice the subtle movement. "My welcome committee? The group who tells me, I told yew so? Yew must feel so *fulfilled*."

One of the chickarees scowled. "Look here, Lute," he said, "We got only to alert Saecka, and she'll come and put these two back where they belong."

"Yer bright," Lute said, still clutching the knife, "but we're already goin' to Saecka, aren't we?"

He turned back on Kinder and Mariyen so fast that Kinder didn't even need to fake his flinch.

Both of the chickarees frowned, put off for a moment.

"Nah," one of them said, finally, though he sounded uncertain. The other smiled like he'd just hatched the cleverest plan in the world.

"If yer goin' to Saecka," he said, "go to Saecka. I'll follow yew."

"Yew won't," Lute said, and for the first time they noticed the knife he was holding.

"SAECKA!" screamed one of the chickarees just before Lute lunged for him. "SAECKA, THEY'RE ESC—"

Lute knocked the wind out of him. The momentum he carried as he leaped to the branch holding the unfortunate red caused the chickaree to topple over and fall straight for the ground with a hopeless shriek. The second of the chickarees was creeping up behind Lute, with the obvious intention of taking him by surprise while he stared down at the other's descent. What he didn't count on was that Lute was only pretending to be distracted. When he got close enough and raised his own weapon, a crudely fashioned club, Lute spun around and sunk his knife into his chest. The chickaree made a gurgling sound that sounded a lot like shock and the club dropped from his paw. Lute pushed him from the branch to fall after his fellow, pulling his knife back and sheathing it as he did so, and motioned to Mariyen and Kinder.

"Hurry!" he hissed. Kinder shook himself from the daze he'd entered when he realized how fast the attack was happening and ran after Lute without any second bidding, only looking around to make sure Mariyen was keeping pace. She was doing better than him, he found, when he looked behind him and panicked because he couldn't find her. Looking ahead, he realized she was almost level with Lute and sped up, breathing hard. The rain that came pelting down on them made the treetops more treacherous, and twice he nearly slipped, pulling himself back up again before he could go falling down to join the two chickarees they'd tangled with. He was beginning to taste bile in the back of his throat when they reached the edge of the forest and Lute stopped, wrapping one paw casually about one of the branches at the border and shooting a brief grin back to them.

"Yer out," he said, and for a moment they only stared out at the land beyond them, blinking back the water from their eyes. The sun was attempting to shine despite the rain, creating a dull, golden glow that seeped across the soggy valley below them and brushed the branches of the more friendly looking group of trees across the way with a yellow tint. Kinder had never seen a drearier day look more welcome.

Lute smacked him with the pack and he came out of his daze shakily, turning to his friend with a questioning look.

"Yew guys have to get going," he said, passing the offending pack to Kinder. "They'll be looking for yew if Randin hasn't died from that fall. Yew've got to make it over to that group of trees before they catch sight of yew, so, yew know, yer whereabouts are in doubt and all that. They'll think twice about goin' in there."

Mariyen turned to Lute. "You're not coming with us?" she asked, and Kinder understood her concern. If the fallen chickaree were still alive, Lute might be in trouble. He turned to his friend.

"You should come," he said.

Lute looked down for a moment, then back up at them.

"Nah, I can't," he said. "I'm done with that, just...all that." He made a face. "I belong here."

Kinder couldn't find it in himself to agree with that last statement; he wanted, in fact, to argue it to the death, but something kept him from doing so. He thought maybe, in some way, he understood.

"Thanks, then," he said hesitantly. "If you're sure."

Lute cast a glance behind him. "I'm sure," he said, "for crying out loud, Kinder, it's been great and everything, but yew need to *leave*."

The rain had stopped; Kinder hadn't noticed it happen, but now that he did, he felt the world grow freer around him in accordance with that certain liberation. He turned to Lute again. It seemed such a waste to let him stay here. It seemed like resigning him to something he was above, but again he kept quiet, looking away when Lute met his eyes.

"Are you going to be okay? You know, for saving us?" he heard Mariyen ask as he turned his back reluctantly and started down the tree. He turned just in time to see Lute give a crooked smile.

"Yew wouldn't know it, pretty, but I always am," he said. "And Kinder...good luck."

Kinder flushed. He could have sworn that in that moment he didn't know whether Lute was looking at the road ahead of them or at Mariyen. He decided it didn't matter. When Kinder made it down the tree, he knew that the woods beyond, those yellow-brushed strong oaks, each growing solitary and all its own, were his safety. He set his sight on them and, as Lute advised, made speed. He heard Mariyen behind him, then saw her at his side, then grinned privately to himself as she passed him once more in their pursuit of the forest. For once—what was actually the first time in his life, though Kinder couldn't know it—he didn't look back.

~~~

Lute sensed her behind him even before he turned around. If he was apprehensive, he did not outwardly show it, but it was true he hadn't planned this meeting and he wasn't sure what to expect.

Saecka smiled at him when he faced her; it was a cold thing.

"I guess I have underestimated you," she drawled, tracing a paw along the clock around her neck. Its ticking was like an endless metronome heralding the dawn of unplanned action. He didn't know whether he should turn away or be on guard, and he cursed that his day had come to such a turn.

"I told you you were never a hero. It appears that you are. I admit to being a little...disappointed. Your absence has changed you."

"They had nothing yew would want," Lute said.

Saecka drew her weapon so quick that even to Lute, who was always prepared, it was an unexpected blur. He found himself pressed up against the thin upper body of the tree he'd climbed to the very top. Saecka breathed into his face as her long, serrated dagger came up to stroke his cheek.

"There are no heroes among thieves," she hissed.

The bark of the tree was digging into Lute. He squirmed to the side ever so slightly, freeing up his arm to go for his belt; Saecka didn't seem to notice. The world seemed much more large now, under his consideration of his actions. The strangers he had no problem drawing his knife on were many, those who appeared enemies and even some who didn't. All of these chickarees, who lived like he had, who had taught him to live this way, often fell victim to his blade, under an understanding that such was normal. But Saecka...she was in all he could remember of a childhood, teaching him to steal small trinkets and chasing the others off his tail until he could face them alone.

His paw wavered, and Saecka went in for a stab at him. In the moment when she'd stepped briefly back from him, he slipped free of his position and spun around to face her. His knives came up, two of them into his two empty paws, and Saecka seemed almost to bare her chest at him invitingly as she turned around to look him in the eye. He wanted to run but he understood that that was no longer an option; and anyway, Lute had never run from a fight before. He might as well be consistent.

"I don't want to do this," he said, at the same time readying himself for a strike. Saecka dived for him again, clock ticking wildly, and he lashed out with one of his knives.

Saecka straightened up. The knife hadn't cut very deep; a thin line of red trailed down her midsection, passing the clock and its relentless ticking on the way down. She put back her head and laughed at him.

"Is that all?" she called. "Lute. *Lute*. I thought I raised you better."

Lute felt his paws tremble and his anger rose, but he sheathed his knives and turned from her.

"That's all," he confirmed.

The dagger entering his back felt slightly different than he had always assumed it might. It was a cold that so quickly turned to heat as it forced its way through him. He closed his eyes on the warmth, because he felt like it and because he could not keep them open anymore. Rarely had fate so aligned with his wishes. That burning and that last, sarcastic thought were the last sensations Lute would ever have.

It was a perfect hit.

Saecka pulled her dagger from Lute's limp body with some effort and watched him fall from the highest branch, down, down, down. She would find him later, if only for his knives: she was damned if she was going to let some mangy chickaree take those carved masterpieces off of him before he even went cold.

She stared off into the woods to which she knew his friends had gone. She wouldn't go after them. They were out of her territory and her reputation was no longer at stake with Lute, the offender, dead.

She stared into the horizon. That dim skyline held many places she'd been to before, to steal and to kill and to hurry back here, already on to coveting the next thing. One thing she ought to have told him, if she could have predicted how he'd be taken from her, was that that horizon was not such a safe place; the world beyond could mess you up if you stayed too long, until everything became confusion, every thought an unsure gray.

"Oh, Lute-boy," she said in a whisper that only she could hear. "You should never have left."

CHAPTER XIV

Rin stalked along the border of the forest she'd come upon, flinching every time she heard a noise. She was in a vicious mood, even more so than usual. She hated the overworld. The terrain was sometimes hard to travel, the food was hard to find, and recently, that endless ceiling had thrown heaps of water at her, an event that had caused her to raise her head and snarl at the sky.

The eye had been dimmer then: that was the only good thing she could parse out of the thorough wetting she'd gotten, and now that it was over, the eye was right back to its usual blinding intensity and she was back to being sour, a state she'd never completely left.

There were less of those so-called 'squirrels' around, too. The last few days, she'd been able to find a large number of them and had given them the silent revenge she hungered for, but it was harder to seek them out now. Usually, there were plenty of trees in attendance, and where there were trees, there were squirrels, or so she was learning. It was easy, once she found the home of a family of squirrels, to calculate when and how she should strike. She felt herself becoming a natural.

Just the other night Rin had hidden in the nick of time in an old elm and overheard the story of the random killings spreading across Arborand. She had nearly burst with pride to know that she was responsible for creating such a rumor and instilling such fear, and took it as a sign as well that the other chipmunks were doing well. She'd taken a detour and begun to move east, not wanting to move in a predictable line, but so far today, she hadn't found any more squirrels or likely looking trees. True, there was a forest to one side of her, had been for quite some time, but she'd also heard—from the same source from which she'd heard of her miraculous killings—that there were something called 'chickarees' in those woods. Rin didn't know what a chickaree was, but as long as it wasn't a squirrel, she didn't want to risk tangling with it. Those woods gave her a bad feeling anyhow, all misty and dense, so that she couldn't see even a foot into them to what lay within. She'd walked along their border for several days now, and only just now, when she was beginning to feel she should start in another direction, did she find another forest, this one almost deceptively friendly looking. This other forest would require for her to begin going north, but Rin was fine with that. She had no real direction to her travels, and took pride in her newfound ability to take things as they came.

Rin crept up to this new set of trees and had begun to peer into its depths when she saw a flash of movement out of the corner of her eye.

She froze. It felt like so long since she'd encountered another creature that she was desperately hungry for a meeting, even if it meant danger, but she had to exude caution. It was one of the skills she'd learned with the Yassar, and she didn't want to just throw it to the dust, so she waited, and watched some more. Soon she realized exultantly that the spot she was staring so intently at was not completely still after all: a thin, low-hanging branch on one of the trees was swaying ever so slightly back and forth, exactly as though it had been nudged by someone or something moving incautiously past.

Rin frowned; it looked as though the squirrel was traveling the ground. From what Rin knew of squirrels, this type of behavior was unheard of unless the trees posed a threat. This forest might not be as friendly as it appeared.

It was hard to find her quarry at first, and she wondered how far ahead of her he or she had managed to get, when she nearly burst in on not one, but two squirrels having a bite to eat in a particularly sparse clearing.

Rin frantically backed up into the bushes.

"Did you hear something?" asked one of the squirrels, the smaller, silvery colored one with the strange flaps of what looked like skin between her arms and legs.

The other squirrel, a fat russet colored one with tufted ears, was too busy tucking into whatever they were eating to speak at first. He looked up and scanned the area around them with a worried look on his face.

"No, I didn't," he said. "Do you think they followed us?"

The winged squirrel shrugged, but began to put the various bits of food spread out around them back into a large sack lying to one side. Rin had to grit her teeth to keep from jumping out at them right then and there. The sight of all that food made her stomach tighten and gurgle in protest. Sometimes Rin had been fortunate enough to salvage some food from the homes of the squirrels she'd finished, and however rotten these squirrels were, their food was really something else.

The fat squirrel was getting up, collecting bits of food as he went. For every one he saved for the bag, he put another into his mouth, and Rin saw the winged squirrel give him a stern look. She didn't know why she didn't come out right then and there. She could have easily taken them unawares, and finished them as she had the others. They appeared to have weapons, but she wasn't too concerned about that: Rin had great faith in her own abilities to wield a dagger. Perhaps it was simply the fact that these were the first squirrels she'd ever stumbled upon who weren't in their homes keeping out of the cold. She did not know whether the overworld was always this cold, but regardless, from the pack they were carrying between them and their weapons, she knew they weren't planning on home.

These squirrels were going somewhere, and even though she was positive it wouldn't matter where, her curiosity got the best of her. She wanted to find out more about her victims before she made her move.

And so, Rin waited. And with every break her oblivious companions took, she sharpened her blades.

~~~

Mariyen and Kinder were in dire need of sleep.

They had both agreed (Kinder with some persuasion) that they should travel all through the first night in order to put distance between themselves and whatever persistent chickarees might have followed them into the woods. Mariyen was still a bit shaken due to the sound she'd heard earlier. She knew she hadn't made it up, though she supposed it could only be one of the squirrels who lived in the area, checking to see that they were no threat. The first time they settled down for sleep, even though it had been a night and a day, and every rational part of her knew that any chickaree would likely not have followed them doggedly for this long, she still felt curiously watched. She had to keep herself from mentioning it to Kinder, for every time Mariyen brought up the idea that they were being followed, Kinder got twitchy and did things like standing with his back to whatever direction the wind was blowing for luck for minutes at a time until she told him she'd probably made it up. She didn't want to create any more false alarm, and the fact that nothing had happened to them as of yet made her doubt herself.

She knew what chief elder Horus would have said to that. *Never doubt your deepest-rooted feelings,* he had told her group of young flyers on the journey to becoming seers. *Self-doubt is the first long stride on the way to disaster.*

She acknowledged this wisdom as such, but still...when they were out here, under the cold night sky with its piercing stars, nearly out in the open, it seemed ludicrous that someone would still be following them. It seemed even more futile to worry. Tonight was a night for sleep, and so, to the discordant music of Kinder's snores, she stretched out beside the scantily sheltering brush they were staying under, and let her eyelids droop.

She'd known he would be there. Almost as soon as she slipped into sleep, Mariyen opened her eyes again to find herself standing—or floating, perhaps—beside a tree of massive proportions. Its surrounding neighbors were no less gargantuan or impressive, and she was struck with awe at the beauty of the structure, so full of life and festooned with windows and doors, bare though it was of leaves. A squirrel marched up to one of these doors, and even before she went for a closer look—her vision obliged her by zooming in as though she'd magnified everything underneath a very large dewdrop—she knew who it was.

"Zirreo," she said, and the white squirrel paused at the sound of his name. For a moment, his face registered something like shock, and then fear; but as quickly as it appeared there, it was gone. Zirreo continued his march to the door and raised his paw to knock. But suddenly they were not alone. Mariyen raised her eyes to the branches above them and saw the lights of dozens of eyes in dozens of faces, gray and black alike. They weren't staring at her in anger, nor was it a friendly gaze she found herself under. In fact, she wasn't sure if they could see her at all. After all, in the other dreams, no one was ever able to see her except for Zirreo. It was a very similar scene to the one her mother had described to her where Zirreo had first showed up at Edgewood, and it made her apprehensive for the squirrels up above. Did they know what they were welcoming to their home?

But at that moment, her eyes were torn from the squirrels above and plunged downwards, to the bottom of the trees, to the horizon where she found what seemed thousands more eyes all coming towards her, all fiercely concentrated on one destination.

"We're being attacked!" someone screamed, and she tried to direct her attention to where the shout was coming from but she felt the by now familiar sensation of being dispelled from the dream. This time she did not fight it; she had no desire to stay.

When she awoke in the cold night, the first thing she saw was a face staring right into her own.

"Arghh!" she shouted, thrashing about frantically to free herself from the imposter's hold. The shadow of the other jumped back and landed in the dirt beside her with an anti-climactic *thunk*. Immediately, she was filled with embarrassment.

"Kinder?"

"Yeah," came the muffled reply.

"Sorry."

"I shouldn't have been so close, I guess," he was quick to say, "but you were screaming something about an attack, and, well..."

Mariyen felt her face heat up. She could hear Kinder pick himself up and saw his form move about their campsite. She knew that he was about to go put his back to the wind or something, so she tried to explain quickly before he got too worked up.

"I just had a dream," she said.

Kinder stopped his pacing. "With Zirreo?" he asked. Mariyen nodded in confirmation, and he slowly lowered himself to the ground again, casting glances about him as he did so.

"He was going to some place with black and gray squirrels both living together under the same branches, or that's what it looked like. He didn't talk to me. There was a group of squirrels, huge, coming for us in that tree. I couldn't see them well from that far away—"

"A group of huge squirrels?" Kinder looked sick.

"No. I think they may have been small, actually, sort of like the chickarees. The *group* was huge. I would have estimated it to contain at least hundreds. They were all coming to this tree, towards the tree and this group of gray and black squirrels. I don't know what it means at all."

Kinder had regained his composure. "Do you think this means he's reached his destination?"

Mariyen thought about it. Zirreo's destination was supposedly the border between Oakwood and Firwood. Oakwood was chiefly populated by black squirrels, while Firwood was run by grays. It was entirely possible, and if so, it would explain the look of ultimate horror on Zirreo's face when he realized she was still on his trail: now she'd seen his destination, there was nothing he could do about it.

Mariyen nodded. "I do, and I think he still doesn't know about you," she told him. "He thinks I'm more powerful than I really am, probably, if I'm able to keep tabs on him even after he tried to erase my memory."

Kinder sat in silence for a moment, then grinned. "We can let him keep thinking that, can't we?"

She smiled back. "Oh, absolutely." After another moment of quiet she couldn't help but say what was on her mind. "If the place he's going is really being attacked, should we risk it?"

Kinder thought about it, then looked at her and shrugged in utter helplessness. "Do we have a choice now?"

She realized how true that was. They'd come through the chickarees, and she would rather die than have that be for nothing. Especially since Kinder's friend had helped them...

As though he were reading her mind, Kinder said, "Do you think Lute's okay?"

She turned around fast and found him staring at the knife he held in his paws. It was the knife Lute had given him out of his own belt to defend himself with just in case, Mariyen realized. It was more than a knife, though; it was a work of art. Carvings of twisting vines and lazy bumblebees adorned it, and she couldn't help but wonder at where Lute had gotten it. She had never seen such a thing in any shop or armory. Kinder saw her looking at him and held it up, smiling sheepishly.

"I forgot to give him back his knife," he said unnecessarily.

"I'm sure he wouldn't mind," she said, though she wasn't so sure of it at all. "He seemed to have a lot of others with him."

"What did you think of him?" Kinder said after a time. She looked over at him, but he was determinedly not looking at her. She smiled.

"He was a bit on the wild side," she said with a laugh. "He might have been handsome if he weren't so unkempt."

"He was always pretty vulgar, too," Kinder said, after a moment of silence in which she had begun to worry. She had to keep herself from laughing out loud.

"Why do you ask?" she said, trying desperately to keep from grinning.

"No reason," Kinder was quick to reply, and it didn't have to be daytime for her to know he was flushing. She could always tell from his voice.

"Well, if there's no reason," she said, laying herself down on the ground again and rolling over. "I think we should get more sleep. If Zirreo is really where he seems to be, we may need to go another long while without resting."

She heard Kinder turn over after a moment, and waited. It took longer than usual, but he began to snore soon enough. *Well,* she thought, trying to comfort her other fear, the one she still hadn't managed to quash. *If we were being followed, that great honk of a whistle would have alerted anyone within a three mile radius before now.*

Rin stretched out in her uncomfortable position between two bushes a mere yard or so away from where the two squirrels lay. One of them was definitely asleep now, she was guessing the fat one, and his snores promised a lack of the same for her.

She didn't care much, though. She was in an unusually good mood. It seemed she'd been right to leave the squirrels unmolested for now; their last conversation had been very interesting indeed. The squirrel with the wings was talking about dreaming of an attack somewhere. The winged squirrel was beginning to make Rin uneasy with her knowledge, so like magic, that dreaded tool of the overworld. All the same, Rin felt the news fall on her like deliverance.

It seemed these two squirrels were following someone, some white squirrel, who was going to some borderland. Rin had already inferred this from earlier in her experience of stalking them, and did not consider it particularly enticing news. She did not care for any white squirrels unless she could wreak revenge on their heads, such as was her wish for every other cursed squirrel on the surface. She had begun to think that she should have just attacked the squirrels and moved on. But now...

The news of the attack, by others that the winged squirrel described as *small*, made Rin tingle with recognition. The winged squirrel hadn't been able to describe the attackers properly—perhaps they had been obscured in her dream—but Rin would have bet a whole basket of edible beetles *and* all three of her daggers that she knew who they were.

The other chipmunks had arrived, and these squirrels were travelling towards them. Rin planned to move with them. Once they got where they were going, Rin would not only be able to join up with the rest of her colony, but she could exact her wishes on the winged squirrel and the fat one. Once she no longer needed them, she'd be able to give them what she'd planned from the beginning.

Better yet, from observing them together, she thought she already knew a bit of their weaknesses.

~~~

Far across Arborand, someone else was making their way across the expanse of land on the invisible path towards the Oakwood and Firwood border.

Llewellyn traipsed along beside and slightly behind Mercurie as they marched towards what the old black squirrel kept referring to only as their 'goal.' The morning after she'd been knocked out—or a few days after, Llewellyn could not be sure anymore—she'd awoke to find Mercurie at the end of her makeshift bed.

"It's time to leave," the black squirrel had said to her. Llewellyn, trying to remain polite for the sake of survival, had asked her where they were going, but Mercurie hadn't given her a clear answer. 'Where we need to go,' had been her ambiguous reply, though now that they were on the road, Llewellyn thought of the trip as the last thing she needed.

The strangest thing was the lack of Absoulim. She'd asked Mercurie where he was, but Mercurie had been elusive once more, telling her only that Absoulim would be 'coming along', and that he would 'catch up with them.' She had never thought that the *lack* of Absoulim's presence would make her worried, but she guessed there was a first time for everything. After the talk she'd had with him, and his disclosed motives, she was sure they were going to wherever Zirreo was. It didn't make sense that he wouldn't be there with them. Sometimes she found herself thinking that it had something to do with the crystal ball, though she couldn't think how that made sense, and tossed it off to her growing obsession.

Many a time Llewellyn caught herself staring longingly at the crystal ball Mercurie held as they traveled. She knew she should not touch it, but she longed to hold what was hers more and more as the miles rolled out before them. She knew it would be dangerous for her to do so, especially since Absoulim had tampered with it. She didn't know how much he had fooled with it, but if it was enough for him to have seen where Zirreo was, something that had been personally reserved for Llewellyn not so long ago, there could be very extreme consequences if she were to get desirous enough to touch it. Every now and then, Mercurie would catch her looking at the crystal ball and would shake her head at her, or worse, stick it further down in her bag, hiding it from Llewellyn's view altogether.

If she could get to it, she thought in her madder moments, she could find Zirreo as Absoulim had and warn him. But she knew somehow that she would not be able to find him again; all of the other times she'd talked to him, it had been through a dream connection, and finding that connection in the crystal ball would not bring it back to her for good. Somehow, when she'd nearly died, she'd lost it, and she didn't think anything, no matter how powerful or magical, could bring that back.

Do I want it back? Really?

She wished she could answer with a resounding no, but she was unsure. As she followed Mercurie across the miles, she repeated these same patterns in her head, questioning and finding no answers.

At least, she thought, watching the sun rise in front of her after a long sleepless night, *I know he needs to be warned. That's all I want the link back for. Please, when I sleep tonight, or whenever I sleep next, let me dream. Let me dream and let me find him.*

One last time.

CHAPTER XV

"No ranks," Venul pressed, knowing all the while that his objections were falling on deaf ears.

Ritorren turned a page in the book he was reading, something about fortifications or modern power method. Though Venul couldn't quite read the cover from where he was sitting, he knew it would be one of these or else something equally off-topic.

"I like the idea," said Ritorren, not dropping that lock-jawed composure for once as he spoke.

"Ritorren," Venul said, moving to the edge of his seat in hopes that he would somehow register higher on the pompous squirrel lord's radar. "This is a tenuous society to begin with. If we employ ranks, everyone will hate us."

"You and Gerien are ranked."

"We're your best friends!"

Ritorren looked up at him for a split second. Venul had thought that blunt was the best way to go, and he didn't think he was wrong. He just could not be as blunt as he would have liked. Venul was still very young. Ritorren was young, too, only a few seasons older than himself, but he used the fact that Venul was still technically a child against him whenever he could. He sensed that it would be coming to that now.

"Venul, I was advised against picking you as an advisor, did you know that?"

Venul kept silent. They'd been through this several times—whenever they got into an argument where Venul had a valid point, as a matter of fact.

"I was told that your family's reputation is not very good."

"You knew that already," he had to point out. He hated it when Ritorren got so into being king that he purposefully pretended like he knew nothing about anything he thought a king wouldn't.

"That doesn't change the fact that you come from an unstable past," Ritorren said, his voice rising this time. Venul was glad. At least he'd been able to get some sort of reaction out of him.

The unstable past that Ritorren was mentioning was actually not so bad as it sounded, he thought resentfully. His great great grandmother had been a sorceress and had practiced magic back when the blacks were one colony in Oakwood and magic had scared everyone away. Now that sort of thing wouldn't make anyone bat an eye. The only other case was that of his father, who'd gone insane shortly after the premature but natural death of his mother. Many had suggested that he'd already been insane before her death, but no one knew for sure. All that was widely known was that he'd taken to singing to the sky and insisted that he was a mayfly to random passersby. In a late autumn not too long past, he had fallen from the very top branch of one of the trees neighboring his home. Several had speculated that it was suicide, though one of the closest witnesses said he'd just forgotten he could climb.

"That's besides the point and you know it," Venul said, losing all of his patience. He sprang from his chair and was about to give Ritorren a clear, unadulterated part of his mind for the first time since his former friend had become king, when the door to Ritorren's chambers flung open and an old gray squirrel stood panting and wheezing for breath against the doorframe.

Ritorren got up and rushed over. Venul noted sourly that he hadn't said a thing about how the older squirrel had not knocked for entry. This elder's presence was valued because he had come in at the opportune time; if it had been one second later, Ritorren would have been screaming at him, but as it stood, he served as the perfect distraction. Ritorren would drop the conversation for good now; it was likely that Venul would never get the opportunity to get to this place with him again. When Ritorren didn't want to talk to you, he was excellent at avoiding you, as he, Gerien, and several members of the spy-guard undoubtedly had come to know.

"Whoa there, Jakin, out of breath, are we?" Ritorren said, bustling over and motioning for the old squirrel to come in.

"An excellent observation," Venul said. Ritorren shot him a look that bordered on crazed. If there was one thing the young lord hated, it was being embarrassed in front of anyone, especially a neutral third party who was supposed to blindly adore him. Venul knew it wasn't wise to rile Ritorren too much in one sitting, so he shut up for good and turned for the door. He noticed as he passed, with a surge of curiosity, that the old squirrel was armed, and with a dagger no less. They'd all heard of the ensuing attack, and though Venul, like most others, wished it were somehow a false alarm, this sight took him aback. They would never expect a squirrel of this one's years to fight, much less with a dagger. He'd been about to leave, but he decided he would stay to listen this one out.

"Yes, thank you," Jakin panted as Ritorren offered him a seat in Venul's vacated chair. Venul pressed his back to the wall as if doing so would enable him to keep any unwise remarks to himself. As Jakin was getting settled, Ritorren's eyes flashed over Venul, and Venul took it to be a warning. He gave no response, however, and he saw Ritorren hesitate, eyes moving back to him. Venul gave him a brief nod this time, but he could not have felt more triumphant.

So. There was an opening.

Jakin had gained his breath and was now staring up at Ritorren in wide-eyed fervor.

"My lord," he said, and Ritorren's attention was claimed away from all else at once, caught up in the title. Venul thought he could have imagined, even, the look he'd been given so recently, the one that reminded him not of a lord, but of his young, scared friend, the one who used to eat the bark from trees and race from dawn till nightfall.

"My lord, I've been told to tell you that our attackers are nearly on our doorstep!" Jakin went on. He had just retrieved all of his breath back and Venul thought that delivering the news might make him begin to hyperventilate again. He didn't think the old squirrel could take another such rush of excitement. Perhaps Ritorren was having similar thoughts, because he interceded before Jakin could say anymore.

"Are they?" he asked, peering closely at Jakin. "And how did you find out about this?"

The question was unexpected. Venul could feel Jakin frown; was Ritorren really going to go into placement issues right now?

"Well...you will forgive me, lord, but I was on the border with Vivendi and Polo and some of the other guards. I know I shouldn't have been, but Polo is my son and I needed to give him something he forgot."

He paused and bit his lip. Well, the border venture explained the dagger—the old squirrel was probably thinking he might get attacked at any moment out there, something he couldn't be faulted for. Venul could tell that he was wondering whether he had been wise to mention his son—would Polo be in trouble now too if Ritorren decided to take offense?

Ritorren, however, seemed to see this as another opportunity to play the magnanimous lord. Waving one paw as though to clear cobwebs out of the air, he said, "These times are dangerous and it's understandable, I suppose, to lose sight of wisely placed rules every now and then. Don't we all know the feeling of the father's worry for the son?"

Venul nearly choked on his own tongue. Ritorren decided not to acknowledge him this time, and he was thankful for the lord's decision, because he didn't think he could keep his first word from coming out a strangled hoot of laughter if he were pressed to speak.

"However," Ritorren said, and Jakin straightened up at the word, fear rushing back to him already. "*However*, you must realize that rules are in place for a reason. I truly care for all within my rule, and while I am your friend, I am also your king." He shot Venul a full-on look when he said, "You must be careful to remember that, because the consequences would be poor if you didn't."

Venul had had enough, however. Jakin's first news might not have gotten through to Ritorren, but he for one cared a whole lot more about whether invaders were on the cusp of attacking them whilst they stood unprepared than he did about Ritorren's reasons for installing rules.

"You say that the attackers are on our doorstep?" he asked, stepping forwards from the wall. Ritorren looked up at him, a muscle twitching slowly somewhere near his mouth. "Wouldn't that make them within our gates now?"

Jakin looked from Venul to his lord and back, evidently aware of the tension and unsure how to answer, or who to answer to. Finally, he looked to Ritorren, and said, "They're very close to us. They may be—within sight now. We need to get prepared, get armed—"

"I will be the judge of that," Ritorren said, walking over to the single window with its many bolts and locks and staring out at the scrubby land that was Firwood to the south. Venul came up behind him and was alarmed to find that what he originally had mistook for the wind blowing dust about was actually a disturbance on the horizon. He turned to Ritorren and there was no mistake that the young lord had seen it too. He spun about and left Venul by the window, tracing his way back to Jakin.

"Your fears are well founded, my friend," he said. Venul, still staring intently at the cloud of rising dust, could only imagine what was going through the poor old squirrel's head right now. Namely, *who is this lord and why is he still talking to me?* He was sure Jakin could remember the days when Ritorren wasn't king, when he was lorded by whoever headed the grays back in Firwood, and Venul could only assume that whoever that was had his acorns more in order.

"Should we not get the troops prepared? Send up the signal?" Venul asked through gritted teeth. He didn't even turn to meet the look Ritorren was sinking into his back. He wondered when the king would learn that politics was indeed a double-edged sword.

"Yes, Venul, why don't you go do that? After all, you seem very eager and oh so very sure that you can get the job done how it should be."

Venul was to the door already by the time the pointed comment had finished crossing Ritorren's lips.

"Yes, I do. Thank you very much for noticing, *my lord.*"

He left before Ritorren could respond. Hopefully, by the time he was back, the young king would have forgotten the remark. He knew it wasn't wise of him, and that in order to band together, no matter how insufferable Ritorren became, he would have to keep himself more under control. He always had Gerien to release his tensions to. The older gray had been Ritorren's friend for a shorter length of time outside of his reign as lord, which Venul often accepted as the reason Gerien was able to remain so calm under the brunt of Ritorren's arrogant words and harsh flourishes, but he knew that was a load of rot. Gerien was simply more mature, less impulsive than his younger counterpart, and could keep himself cool-tempered much easier than it had ever come to Venul. He had a way of putting things so reasonably and without any signs of personal interest, that he'd even been able to make Ritorren reconsider a move or two on the rare occasion. Venul felt himself sorely in need of a talk with Gerien, if only to convince himself that sanity still existed within the walls of the great tree.

Halfway down the winding staircase from Ritorren's chambers, Venul ran into spy-guard Camphor and a couple others. One of them, a black, looked familiar to him if only for his odd appearance. He was chewing on a small stone, Venul realized, and kept flicking it around his mouth even as he merely stood in place. It was Vivendi, he later realized, and the other unknown must be Polo. Of course they would have followed Polo's father here to wait for the verdict of their lord. The one he guessed to be Polo looked especially nervous.

"What did he say?" the young squirrel blurted, as soon as he recognized Venul as one of Ritorren's two special advisors (advisor, he thought, was a bit strong of a word. It sounded almost like a joke after what Venul had just experienced in the lord's chambers).

"Your father's okay," he reassured Polo, whose posture loosened immediately. Vivendi elbowed him excitedly.

"What did I tell you, eh?" he said around his stone. Polo smiled wanly.

Venul turned to Camphor, and the sturdy black squirrel snapped to attention.

"Spy-guard Camphor, I need you to give the signal for all of our troops to get into position. We need everyone ready to attack, hidden and up front, far and near. Remember the strategy. Go, now!"

Camphor needed no other bidding; he was off like a shot and down the winding passageways to the very bottom of the tree, the place near the roots that currently served as the barracks. Polo and Vivendi followed, the latter still sucking his stone vigorously.

Venul was turning to follow them down the wooden stairs when he heard a tapping coming from behind a door to his left.

Was someone knocking to get in? At a time like this? Sure, they had stations on the boundaries and one of them might be hurt and needing to come in, but this, the door closest to the lord's chambers, was the last door any of the troops was supposed to come through. It was always locked for extra precautions, so anyone who knocked here must have extremely valuable information, or they would not risk a disruption. Venul glanced up the short flight of stairs up to Ritorren's room. Well. If it was an enemy, he would be prepared. Undoing the many bolts on the inside of the great door, he inched it open bit by bit.

Venul nearly slammed the door shut again when he saw the squirrel standing outside, but something beyond his telling, beyond his willing, compelled him to keep the door open. The stranger's gaze was serene but intense. It was almost tangible, the inexplicable desire forming to speak to this creature, but Venul's tongue took a full few seconds to un-attach itself from the roof of his mouth. When he did manage to speak, he sounded every bit the dunce and knew it.

"H-hello. Are you lost?"

Lost? his mind shouted at him, *Is that any way to talk to him?*

He had no idea who *him* was, he realized, but the white squirrel at the door only smiled at him as though he were used to this sort of reaction wherever he went. Perhaps he was, Venul thought. Perhaps, again, he should shut the door before his strange guest could get in. The second the white squirrel took a step forward, however, all of these notions vanished from his mind and the only movement he made was to step back to allow him access.

"Thank you," the white squirrel said, speaking for the first time. His voice was like his gaze, cool and composed yet not at all unfriendly. Venul stood on the landing inside with this new visitor, awkwardly wondering what to do now.

"Allow me to explain myself a little," the white squirrel said. "I've come as a sort of...visitor, you could say. I know you are in bad times, so perhaps I can help."

Venul was still trying to remember whether any white squirrels were supposed to still exist. He'd heard about their magic powers, or those they were rumored to have, and it sounded from this one's declared intentions like those rumors might be true.

He realized the white squirrel was giving him that politely curious look, waiting for him to say something.

"...Oh?" Venul choked out. He felt like throwing himself out the nearest window immediately. It seemed he couldn't even form coherent sentences in front of this squirrel, and he wondered whether he was practicing his magic on him even now. The thought made him ashamed as soon as he looked back up into the white squirrel's kind eyes. He had always imagined all of the white squirrels in the legends as being older and therefore, he supposed, 'wiser', and though he knew this was a tired cliché, he couldn't help his surprise at how young this white squirrel appeared. He was much older than Venul, but this wasn't saying much as Venul had crested his seventeenth season not long ago.

"I'm sorry if I've frightened you," the white squirrel said, and Venul had a mortifying notion: the white squirrel no doubt saw him as nothing more than a child, one who had perhaps been told to guard the door by his higher-ups. He felt his face grow hot, which added to his embarrassment; since when did he blush like a young squirrel?

"You didn't...it's okay," he managed to choke out. The white squirrel smiled at him again, and somehow he couldn't quite manage to feel condescended. Thoughts of the attack, even, seemed to have flown his mind with the appearance of this strange figure.

The white squirrel seemed to recognize his helplessness in the face of his aura. "I'm sorry, I forgot to introduce myself," he said, again in the sort of tone where Venul could not decide whether he was being condescending or merely kind. "My name is Zirreo."

Venul waited for a surname but it didn't come. "Venul Blackwood," he said, reaching out to take Zirreo's proffered paw. At the white squirrel's touch, much of the unexplained tension he felt slipped away. This was just another squirrel he was facing, after all. Venul imagined Zirreo must be sick of being singled out as a white squirrel, a magic-bringer, by now. The hidden message in those kind eyes, he was convinced now, was *please take me for even less than I appear.* A humble request, and Venul intended to follow it through.

"Venul," Zirreo said thoughtfully, trying out his name, "yes."

Venul wasn't sure what he was on about, but he stood and waited, stifling the returning anxiousness.

"Do you have a leader here, Venul?" Zirreo asked.

Venul flinched, feeling his mood immediately sour. He'd known it would come to this, but he was hoping not so soon. A selfish part of him wanted this mysterious visitor to himself for a while.

All the same, he nodded and gestured to the stairway behind him.

"Ritorren," he said, by way of explanation. Then, fearing Zirreo might start away immediately, added, "he might not be too happy to receive a guest at the moment, but I wish you better luck with him than I've ever had."

Zirreo paused in what indeed appeared to be the beginning of a walk up this second flight of stairs, his foot on the first step. He studied Venul more carefully, looking him over with that strange intensity of his. Then he nodded.

"I see," he said, "so the crown sits unevenly on the ruler's head?"

Venul shrugged, not sure what Zirreo meant and not wanting to admit so. "You could say that," he said, "He calls himself a king, anyway. We made him leader. Honorary, you know. He's forgotten that."

Venul blinked as soon as the words had exited his mouth. Had he really just said all of that? If Zirreo did go to Ritorren, it would be over for him faster than he could repeat the offending words a second time. Zirreo only smiled faintly.

"You're his friend?"

Venul shrugged again. He didn't want to talk about it anymore. "Sort of," he said, turning from the white squirrel's study of him. Zirreo thankfully did not press any further, but gestured down the stairs to the other side of Venul.

"If you have a bit of time, would you mind showing me around?" he asked.

Venul looked incredulously between the older squirrel and the stairs and back again. They were being attacked imminently, and the white squirrel wanted a tour?

"You're in danger, I know," Zirreo said as though he'd read his mind. "But have you guessed what sort?"

Venul, trying to keep up with the change in subjects, could only shake his head. Zirreo nodded and ducked out of the door once again, disappearing into the wintry air.

"Hey!" Venul cried, thinking the white squirrel had just decided to run off on him. "Hey!"

He darted out onto the branch leading away from the door, nearly forgetting in his haste to close it again. He doubled back and shut it, turning around in place to try and locate the white squirrel.

"There's no need to get so upset," the familiar voice said, and Venul found his attention jerked downwards to a limb below him. Zirreo was sitting there as though he'd been standing in place all along.

Venul breathed a sigh of relief and went to join the strange squirrel, but Zirreo was off again as soon as he stepped onto the white squirrel's branch.

"Hey," he said, running to keep up with Zirreo's mad and seemingly random dash. "Would you mind telling me just what it is you're doing? I am second in command here, if you didn't know, and I could easily have the guards evict you—"

Zirreo halted in front of him, so suddenly that he had to curb his own speed to keep from running straight into him. At first he thought it was his words that had caused Zirreo to stop, but the white squirrel was peering off into the distance beyond their grove of trees.

"Your attackers are arriving," Zirreo said.

"I know," Venul began, but when he followed Zirreo's eyes he noticed what the white squirrel meant.

The first squirrels were cresting the last rise over the land in front of them, and now Venul could see them as individual specks, moving fast across the ground toward them. Quickly, they turned into the larger, more real shapes of squirrels, or chipmunks, as Camphor had said they referred to themselves as. Were they truly a different species? Venul squinted across the land and hoped sincerely that this was not so. Squirrels were bad enough. Another species would be so... unpredictable.

"What is your plan, Venul Blackwood?" Zirreo asked, turning to him as though he were actually curious.

Venul watched the dust kicked up by the approaching horde rise into the air.

"We plan to negotiate," he said. Spoken out loud, it sounded like the dumbest plan ever, but he met Zirreo's eyes all the same. He tired of looking down.

"Venul!" Gerien's voice echoed slightly, and Venul looked down to see him on the end of their branch, waving a paw. If Gerien took any notice of Zirreo standing there, he didn't say anything. "Venul! You're wanted on the balcony! We have to go quick!"

Venul turned once to look at Zirreo again.

"Good luck with this one, son," the white squirrel said, still staring out at the approaching storm, face completely unreadable. Venul opened his mouth to speak, then closed it and turned against his better judgment. There was so much he still wanted to ask the white squirrel, and he should not leave a guest no one else knew about here alone—he could be a plant, Venul thought, then pushed the thought aside with a fervor—no. Gerien waved to him again, this time more forcefully, and Venul came running.

As Gerien led him along the twisting branches that led in a covert sort of passageway to the balcony tree, he couldn't shake the imprint of Zirreo's words from his mind: *good luck with this one, son.* His first instinct was to brush it aside with a snarl—this intruder was not his father, and he couldn't see why it should matter so much to an outsider whether they won or lost the confrontation in front of them now. But...Venul knew very well that any extra support they might have was a good thing, and still, implicitly, he trusted the white squirrel for reasons he could not name. And his father was dead, and before that insane. He could not think back to a time when he'd been spoken to with that twinkle of the eye, that curve of the lip.

It probably meant nothing. He shook traitorous thoughts from his head and wondered if all of his good sense had up and left him with the arrival of the white squirrel.

"Who was that with you?" Gerien asked, and Venul's insides clenched; so he had noticed.

"Someone I know," he muttered. He might have told Gerien more, but they were coming up on the balcony and Venul could see Ritorren standing there with a few of his best guards and archers. Gerien noticed them too, looked between Venul and Ritorren for a second, and then thankfully did not press the point. He clambered up onto the balcony, a flat, strangely plate-like protrusion coming off of the lip of a large hollow in its respective tree. There was a railing encircling the balcony for safety reasons, crafted of the sturdiest oak, and it was this railing Gerien clutched onto as he pulled himself up and over onto the balcony. Venul followed, and with as little exuberance as he could muster, faced the lord of the borderlands for the second time that day.

Ritorren beamed at him. Venul hadn't thought the young lord's bravado could get any more out of control, and sincerely hoped that he was just covering up his fear.

Gerien made it over to Ritorren and whispered something in his ear. Venul froze. What if it had to do with the white squirrel? From the way Ritorren continued to beam, he guessed it was nothing of the sort, however, and inwardly thanked Gerien for being just as wise as ever and keeping his mouth shut.

"Venul," Ritorren said, grabbing his paw and shaking it as though they'd just met at a tea party. "I'm glad that you could make it."

Venul looked at him incredulously, but Ritorren had turned to his guards and whispered a command to them. The stoic head guard, an upright gray with a scar across one eye, nodded curtly to whatever he was saying and disappeared into the hollow behind them, where Venul saw several other squirrels, huddled out of sight and waiting for their signal. Most of them carried bows, though a few had daggers and similar weapons. Several were whispering amongst themselves, and as Venul caught snatches of it he realized that it was conversation for the sake of conversation, the sort employed to keep one's worst fears at bay.

Gerien had turned and was now standing at the very end of the balcony, leaning over the rail to get a better look at their attackers. Venul joined him under the guise of doing the same, when really he kept looking to the sides, scanning the border of the trees, trying to find some hint of where Zirreo had gotten to. He spotted the branch where he and Zirreo had been sitting moments before, watching the same horizon. Had the white squirrel left? Or was he still watching from somewhere more hidden?

He could hear the sounds of the chipmunks walking over the ground below now, and Gerien nudged him. He realized with embarrassment that he had been staring at the same place in the woods for a full minute. Gerien had to have noticed, but the gray squirrel was too soaked up in the scene unfolding below them. Venul followed his gaze, and immediately all of his thoughts of the white squirrel's whereabouts were chased from his mind.

"There are so many of them," he hissed to Gerien. The gray squirrel nodded, his jaw tightening. Behind them, Ritorren was saying something to the archers, only part of which Venul could catch. "Never fear!" the leader was saying, "They're only small and we have the element of surprise!"

Easy for him to say, back there not planning to take any personal risks, Venul thought scathingly. The chipmunks were indeed small, even moreso than chickarees, perhaps, and the markings on their backs told Venul quite clearly that chickarees in disguise they were not. No chickaree marched like that, anyway. Whoever these squirrel-things were, they were impeccably organized. They had a purpose and they intended to serve it; nothing said that clearer than the way they moved, slow and clean and vigilant. Far off in the distance, the last few chipmunks crested the rise he'd seen the first ones come over minutes ago. Even then, he could not tell if it was truly the last of them, or if they merely had to stop because the lead chipmunks had reached their very gates. There was a great settling sound, a collective shifting accompanied by the clanking of weapons as the troupe below them stopped all at once. A silence collected, and not a comfortable one; it was the sort of silence born to be shattered, and both Venul and Gerien leaned forward on the balcony, watching the collection of striped backs and heads and waiting for the inevitable stirring that would break the hush.

Surprisingly enough, it came from behind them. Pushing through his own guards, Ritorren was making his way to the railing. Venul cast a glance at Gerien, who shrugged in earnest. When Ritorren reached them, he waved them aside. Venul stepped off to the left, feeling as though he may have entered a very bad dream; when Ritorren spoke, it did nothing to dispel this notion.

"Welcome, chipmunks, for we hear that is what you call yourselves!" Ritorren called out. Only the front of the ranks below would be able to hear him, but he didn't seem to care. Some of those in the front raised their heads to stare up at them. Venul suddenly felt many eyes on him and struggled to hold his poise. He could see Gerien to the right of him, beyond where Ritorren stood, trying to do the same.

"It has reached my ears that you plan to attack us!" Ritorren went on, and Venul thought he heard those down below shift in answer, the ominous clink of weaponry resounding into a vibration beneath his feet.

"I must warn you," Ritorren went on, ignoring the movement, "that no squirrel who knows what he is doing is willing to attack the squirrels of the borderlands!" He left an ominous pause here. Venul had to give him some grudging respect on his skill as a speaker. Most of the chipmunks below seemed to be listening attentively, and they hadn't yet had a thing thrown at them.

"So I must know what it is you want," Ritorren said, raising his voice even further. "What must you want to have come so far from wherever you call home? And why now? Perhaps we can work something out so it does not have to come to war. For though we are adept at killing, we do not enjoy it."

There was a silence after this grand speech, and again the horde below shifted around. Ritorren gave it a moment before he spoke again.

"Come, do you have a leader? Have him speak now!"

For a while, there was no response to even this challenge, and then one of the chipmunks up front stepped forward. His voice was harder to hear because the wind kept snatching it away, but the squirrels above all cupped their ears to listen.

"We accept your offer of negotiation, if you allow one of ours to come up and talk with you face to face. Civilized, like," he added.

It was Ritorren's turn to go silent. Venul knew he was weighing the idea of letting one of the chipmunks into their trees versus denying negotiation. It really wasn't a hard decision.

"Unarmed," he shouted down at them, and the chipmunk who'd spoken before appeared to nod.

"Yes, unarmed. Naturally. Are we agreed?"

"We are," Ritorren responded, and a ripple spread through the crowd below; one of the chipmunks was forcing his or her way through the crowd. The squirrels above all waited tensely, trying to get a good look at their soon-to-be visitor.

"Go open the lower doors," Ritorren ordered some of the guards standing behind Venul. Venul's stomach did a flip-flop at the command. Not, for once, because he thought Ritorren had made the wrong decision, but because he knew they couldn't go back on it.

In a moment's time, the sound of the lower doors grinding open filled his ears.

CHAPTER XVI

"Kinder," Mariyen said for the second time in a row, and Kinder turned sheepishly, brought back from the daze he'd drifted into. They'd travelled for so long without stopping that he felt his feet had become an infirm presence beneath him. And they'd come here. He wasn't sure exactly where here was, and that was what he was trying to figure out. Staring up into the naked branches of leafless trees or feeling the cool wind blow through his tail in a sensation that was half pleasant and half unnerving, wouldn't tell him what he needed to know. It was somehow familiar here, but no doubt to Mariyen it was just another bunch of trees.

When Mariyen realized she'd at last gotten Kinder's attention, she didn't waste any time.

"Kinder, I don't want to interrupt, but you know the feeling I told you about where we're being watched?"

"Yes."

Kinder remembered it vividly, because every time previous to this that she'd shared the sensation with him, he ended up being laughed at for his attempts to protect them. His heart sunk.

"Don't tell me you're feeling it again."

Mariyen nodded. "I'm afraid so. But it's not just how it used to be, Kinder. It's stronger. A lot stronger. It was easier to ignore before we walked into these woods, but now that we're here, Kinder...I feel like we're in the center of a crowd, being watched like test subjects."

Kinder was a bit startled by this observation. He realized that he didn't feel much different, standing in the middle of all these trees. These hauntingly silent woods, this feeling of being watched...hadn't he experienced this before?

"We're going in the wrong direction anyway," Mariyen told him, "We need to start heading west. I think we've hit the border, so we must be close, anyhow."

Kinder turned about in the woods, raising his head to stare at the lifeless branches above him again, contrasting dully with the gray sky. Mariyen's words took a while to hit him, but when they did it was with a solid impact he could not escape.

Of course.

They'd hit the border. The last time Kinder had been on the Firwood border, he was with Lute. And some other unwelcome companions.

"You're right," Kinder said hurriedly. "We should leave."

He turned to do just that and found himself facing the last face he wanted to see at this place and time.

"Engelwaithe!"

The name came out of nowhere, smashing its way out of Kinder's subconscious memory. The face in front of him did not respond to the name, however, and Kinder wondered if he was mistaken, until he saw the truth.

The face he had mistaken for Engelwaithe, the fanatical gray squirrel who had captured he and Lute with plans to sacrifice them for a crime as simple as trespassing, was indeed Engelwaithe. But he was no longer alive.

Kinder remembered well the wraiths that Lute had seen within the cells. A wraith was an unnatural occurrence, the result of an untimely death or an unhappy life or both. They had been created, in the case of the gray squirrel colony, out of the victims the grays had sacrificed to their underground god. This so-called god, Lute and Kinder had later found out, was only a bunch of gigantic worms, something the gray squirrels had feared enough to slap the title of divinity on. They had sacrificed any 'intruders' to the ground, chaining them to trees so they could not escape and waiting from the safety of their own great tree for the gorepedes to take them. Now it appeared that Kinder had stumbled into the cursed territory; he suspected that the great tree could not be far off, but it was hard to do much thinking with Engelwaithe staring him in the face, silent and expressionless.

Kinder swallowed and backed up a step. The wraith did not appear to move and yet Kinder found he and it were the same distance apart that they had started from. The wraith's eyes were nearly blank, but Kinder thought he saw a snatch of desperation in them. He tried to speak, but his throat was too dry. The constant stare of the wraith was undoing him. He tried to turn to the side, to look for Mariyen, and at first his head wouldn't move away from Engelwaithe. When he was finally able to turn from the wraith's unwavering stare, he saw Mariyen staring at him in open terror. Somehow, that look was enough to shake his paralysis.

"It's okay, I think," he managed to say. In the silence of the woods around them, his voice seemed too large, and much, much too confident.

"What...is...he?" Mariyen gasped, unable to take her eyes from Engelwaithe's silent form.

"He's a wraith," Kinder told her. "They're...from what Lute and I know, they won't do anything to you if you didn't do anything to them." He realized how unconvinced his own voice sounded and tried to lighten the mood. "Honestly, I like him better this way." He cast his eyes nervously to the side, hoping the wraith wouldn't decide to take offense.

"He's someone you know?" Mariyen asked, seemingly unsure whether to direct her question at Kinder or at the wraith at his side.

"Well. Knew. In a way," Kinder amended, feeling highly uncomfortable with Engelwaithe breathing down his neck. Did wraiths breathe? He didn't particularly care to know. "He was...the leader of the colony living here when Lute and I crossed the border from Pinewood." He paused, wondering if he dared to say more. He took another sideways glance at Engelwaithe, who seemed not to be listening, and plunged on.

"They took us captive once, and there were these wraiths--I didn't see them, but Lute did—in the room where we were being kept. They're typically squirrels who are unhappy or have unfinished business here and can't yet pass to the dark forest. That's what I've heard at least..." He passed a look back to Engelwaithe, but the gray squirrel's wraith, though he was staring at them, appeared not to take an interest in their conversation. "The wraiths Lute saw last time we were here were the ghosts of those the grays here had sacrificed. I don't quite understand why—" He looked off at Engelwaithe again and shrugged. "I guess we should be on our way."

"And just leave him here?"

Mariyen didn't say it out of any love for the wraith, but Kinder could tell she was thinking along the same road as he was. Why was Engelwaithe a wraith? Was it an illusion cast by the real Engelwaithe to draw him in? He didn't think so. For all his self-importance, Kinder doubted the gray, or any of his followers, had been gifted in the art of magic. If they had, they would surely not have followed some false god under the ground, falling under a cloud of superstition that a magic-wielder would have been able to see through. So the question became, why was Engelwaithe here and why had he chosen to appear to them? He turned to look at the wraith, which was still staring at them both, not moving from its spot and definitely not giving him any hints.

"Yeah, I guess we should leave him here," he said aloud. Silence greeted this proclamation. He didn't know what he expected—for Engelwaithe to object? He knew wraiths couldn't speak. Kinder gave a shrug; he and Mariyen turned as one and began to move out of the woods, tracing west now to the Oakwood-Firwood border.

It should not have surprised him as much as it did when the wraith appeared in front of them again, cutting off their route and nearly making Kinder walk into it with its sudden apparition. Kinder turned to the side and attempted to walk in a different direction, but the wraith appeared there too. He then tried to walk through the wraith as he had almost done before, and abandoned that experiment early when he felt a burning sensation all over his skin and jumped back so fast he fell over. At first he didn't even notice Mariyen's paw, outstretched to help him up, because he felt as though his insides had turned to ice, ceasing to function. He opened his mouth to breathe and found he couldn't suck the air in towards him.

"Help...cold..." he managed to get out, and Mariyen looked around helplessly before crouching beside him and draping her tail over his body in an attempt to warm him up. He felt her fur tickle his face as the air slowly come back to him, and with it came a tingling in his paws, evidence of heat restoring itself. There was also, he found, an unnaturally great tingling in his cheeks, and he rolled over as soon as he could before Mariyen could see it. He sat up to see her looking at him with an expression of deep concern. Engelwaithe was just behind her, also gazing at him, expressionless, just as before. Apparently being walked into was not even enough to get the wraith perturbed. He just stared with those haunted eyes at Kinder, and then at Mariyen when she turned, realizing what he was looking at.

"Why don't you go?" she said to the wraith, her voice near as cold as the chill that had gripped Kinder moments before.

The wraith did something that neither of them expected then. It turned and began to sort of glide off— Kinder couldn't have explained the way it moved. It was a drifting, smooth movement that made it look as though the wraith wasn't moving at all, but was merely being pushed by some invisible being behind it.

Kinder looked at Mariyen, whose expression was still cold and angry. She watched the wraith move for a second, and then turned.

"Come on," she said, "We should probably be going. If Zirreo's already there..."

But Kinder couldn't move. He didn't know whether it was the aftereffects of nearly walking through the wraith, but he felt frozen in place, just watching the shade that used to be Engelwaithe disappear off into the woods.

"We should follow him."

The words were out of his mouth before he could truly consider them, and when he looked at Mariyen again he found her gaping at him.

"What? But...why? Kinder, have you lost your mind? It's leaving us alone!"

"Aren't you the least bit curious?" Kinder said, beginning to walk as he realized they were losing sight of the wraith completely. It had tried to block them from leaving, but it hadn't shown them any malevolence. He didn't know how to interpret that. Perhaps wraiths just couldn't show many of the typical emotions most squirrels were able to, and he was leading himself and Mariyen into a trap. However, he had begun to sense a strong desperation coming from the wraith, and silly though it was, he knew he would feel bad if he were just to leave without knowing for sure what it was the wraith wanted of him, for he was sure now that it wanted something.

The only question was the price.

Mariyen was following him now; he could hear her behind him, bounding over the leaves and keeping up pace as well as she ever did, though she did not say anything to him. He wondered if she was angry with him, and shrugged helplessly to himself. He would be angry with himself too, if he were Mariyen, but the thought made him upset all the same, so he kept Engelwaithe's departing back in his sight and tried not to focus on anything other than the wraith as they moved deeper into the trees. Every once in a while, Kinder felt Mariyen looking at him and had to resist the urge to turn around and look back at her for fear of her judgment.

The wraith led them both deeper and deeper into the border forest, until Kinder guessed they weren't so far from Pinewood, the land where he'd grown up. The thought made him nostalgic and made him want to turn and run in the opposite direction at once. There were too many conflicting emotions to deal with at the thought of the place, and the memories, though they really weren't so long ago, made him feel as though it were a place removed from this time, and he was a different squirrel than the Kinder in the memories. He supposed that he was, maybe.

The wraith brought them to a clearing in the woods and then seemed to disappear. Immediately, they were put on the defensive—or Mariyen was. Kinder was with her at first, spinning around and reaching for his slingshot, knowing it would do little good. Then he recognized where they were and his paw dropped to his side with no small relief.

The tree before them was larger around its base than twenty squirrels and went soaring, smooth and strangely barkless, up to touch the sky and back down again in a dizzying drop so that it appeared to be growing into the ground once more, a detail that Kinder hadn't forgotten, but which made the scene spread out before him now even more chilling.

There were wraiths all over the tree, swarming up over its twisted branches to stare with haunted eyes in the direction of the two travelers.

Mariyen saw them and slowly lowered her dagger, shooting an uneasy look sideways at Kinder, which he didn't miss.

"I don't think—" Kinder began, but then one of the wraiths, Engelwaithe, began to float towards them over the ground once more and his words died on his lips. He had been about to reassure Mariyen that the wraiths wouldn't hurt them, but in that moment, he wasn't so sure anymore.

Engelwaithe lifted a paw so suddenly that Kinder flinched before it, and beckoned to them. He turned to Mariyen, who only shrugged, looking a bit ill but well-composed; Kinder had a feeling he probably looked a lot worse right now, and the thought helped encourage him to always look forward to where the wraiths were rather than sideways at Mariyen. He put one foot in front of him, then began to walk faster, on the trail of the wraith, who led them, without pause, up to the very roots of the great tree. Engelwaithe then turned to them and merely stared, just as the other wraiths were doing.

"What do you want?" Kinder said, after a time, talking into the silence the wraiths refused to, or couldn't, break.

Engelwaithe and the others just stared back at him. Looking around at them all, Kinder noticed something: all of the wraiths appeared to be gray squirrels. A vague suspicion started to loom over him, and he moved into its shadow and examined it more closely. It made sense.

Back when he and Lute had been imprisoned here, the wraiths had been all kinds of squirrels, captured by the grays and imprisoned before being sacrificed to the gorepedes. They had hung around because of their unusually terrible deaths and their burning want for vengeance. Something had died unsatisfied in them, and a shell of who they once were had come back to try and remedy it.

Those wraiths, as far as Kinder knew, had been satisfied in aiding Lute and he to escape. But there was more to the story, he remembered. When Lute spoke to the grays from a hidden hole in the floor, making them believe he was their angry god, he had told them that sacrificing members of their own group would be the only way to sate his appetite.

Lute had obviously done this out of spite, and probably hadn't given it that much thought afterwards, and neither had Kinder. He'd only vaguely realized at the time that it was an unfair idea, but now...

Lute, what did we do? he thought, looking around at the wraiths. He was sure of it now. Engelwaithe and the others had truly believed in a fierce underworldly god and had gone along with the solution of sacrificing one another...gone along until there were no more of them to sacrifice. Guilt began to creep up in inside of him, and he did nothing to push it aside. He had been a part of this too, and he knew better than many what strong belief in something, however ridiculous, could do someone.

At the time, he'd battled away his doubts by reminding himself that they needed to get out alive, a fact that could not be contested. He'd never expected to see the results of what they had wrought upon this colony. It was clear to him now exactly what lay beyond the haunted faces of the wraiths watching him from their former home. They had died, and whatever they found beyond the grave, Kinder had a good idea that it wasn't the raging inferno of some underground god. How much of a nightmare must these wraiths be living, caught between life and death, with no one to blame but themselves and a monster they could not see. It seemed there was no vengeance to be had, nothing they could do to set themselves free.

Perhaps, Kinder thought, their vengeance needed to be cast upon his own head for duping them and escaping their grasp. He knew now that Engelwaithe had to know who he was, for the eyes always seemed to look directly at him, as though Mariyen did not exist.

"What is it?" Mariyen whispered to him, as though the thought of her name had summoned her voice.

Kinder's mind was aswirl with thoughts spiraling to an inevitable conclusion. He turned to her.

"I know what they want."

The wraiths, as always, paid no attention to their whispering, but sat as though they were in constant waiting. Kinder believed they were.

"Er...Engelwaithe," he addressed the wraith who had led him here, and Engelwaithe's eyes continued to watch him with such an intensity that it was hard for him to speak. "You might remember me and my friend coming by here not so long ago. I don't know what's happened since then, but I assume you have...erm...sacrificed yourselves to the ground."

Engelwaithe made no move, either to indicate he'd heard or to attack Kinder, and he continued on uncertain ground. "As you've probably figured out, we played a trick on you to save our lives." He couldn't help but look up again after saying this, searching for their reaction. He thought that maybe Engelwaithe had moved a little closer to him, but he couldn't tell, and forced himself to look the wraith in the eyes when he said the rest of what he needed to say.

"I don't know if you know what it was that was killing your own squirrels and those you caught who came through your territory." He thought briefly of Cainus, the black squirrel he and Lute had talked to while in the prisons here, the squirrel they'd witnessed die at the paws of these squirrels, and a bit of his guilt edged away in favor of anger. "It was no god that killed any of you or your victims." *It was yourselves.* But he refrained from saying it. He noticed that Engelwaithe was indeed getting closer to him, and he stepped back involuntarily, rushing to say what he needed to say.

"It was an underground creature, controlled by the squirrels who live underground. Chipmunks, they call themselves."

Engelwaithe had stopped his approach, but Kinder noticed that the other wraiths had all started to edge forward. Engelwaithe cast a look back at them and they halted their soundless approach. He turned back to Kinder, who swallowed before continuing. Mariyen was watching the wraiths as he spoke, paw on her dagger.

"I take it you came to me to be released. You need vengeance."

Please prove me wrong.

But the wraiths nodded, suddenly, almost as one, and once more began to edge towards him. Mariyen's paw tightened on her dagger and she began to back away.

"I'd like to help you," Kinder said desperately, trying not to think of what might be running through the wraiths' minds right now. "But I don't know how—"

They began to close in more rapidly and Kinder knew what it was they had in mind, he could feel it radiating off of them in cold waves. A wraith couldn't attack in the traditional sense, but he remembered all too well the feeling of Engelwaithe, that deep, bone coldness that had shot through him, paralyzing him. If all of the wraiths were to go through him at once—he remembered suddenly the spell the seer Absoulim had performed on Zirreo back at Edgewood. Even the powerful white squirrel had been brought to the edge of death by the vengeful wraiths Absoulim had sent through him. He and Mariyen were cornered and they could do nothing, not even fight for their lives. He knew what would happen if the wraiths should choose to flow forward at them. They had to do something, and they had to do it fast.

"I know!" Kinder shouted as one of the wraiths reached for him. The wraith didn't stop, and Kinder shut his eyes and waited for the coldness.

Nothing came.

Kinder cracked his eyes open again and found Mariyen standing with her paws outstretched.

"He knows how to end your suffering!" she yelled to the wraiths swarming them, who had started to back off in gliding, fluid motions. "He's the only one who knows! If you kill him, your chances will be gone with his dying breath!"

Kinder didn't like to think about his dying breath, but it appeared that Mariyen's words were working.

Engelwaithe settled backwards, and all the remaining wraiths who still circled him followed suit. Kinder straightened up and tried not to panic. He had no idea what he would say, but Mariyen gave him a prompting look and he knew he had to say something.

"The creatures under the ground I was telling you about," he began, and an idea suddenly sparked in his mind. "I know when they're coming. I'm able to tell when they will surface. These are the things that have killed off your numbers one by one. If getting revenge on them is what you seek, then I could lead you to them."

He looked up at Engelwaithe and the others, aware that it was a stretch. The wraiths were silent for a long moment, and Kinder began to feel less confident under their constant stares. Then Engelwaithe nodded, once. The other wraiths took up the gesture, and Kinder's ability to breathe returned to him slowly.

Engelwaithe glided up to him to stare him in the face, and Kinder forced himself not to look away. He knew what this was; it was Engelwaithe's way of warning him that trickery would not be tolerated. He nodded to the wraith with a calm he did not feel and Engelwaithe drifted off, still keeping eye contact with him. When the smoky gray eyes of the wraith had receded a generous distance from his face, Kinder asked the group a key question.

"Can you all, uhm...disappear? If you're whole when we travel, we'll all be spotted easily."

But as if they had anticipated this, the wraiths were already fading. The swirling substance in their sheer forms was draining out of them, appearing to sift into some other dimension. Soon, he and Mariyen found themselves alone once more, standing in the clearing with the great tree. Kinder didn't need to look at Mariyen to confirm that she still felt them too. The wraiths were all around them, as before, only now they couldn't be seen.

This is going to be a very uncomfortable journey, Kinder thought. He longed to say what he thought aloud to Mariyen, but they could no longer voice their thoughts to one another without the specters of the dead listening. He wanted to discuss his plans, or rather, his lack of them, but that would be catastrophic in the circumstances, so he only stood next to her for an instant before speaking resignedly.

"I guess we should get going."

Mariyen nodded, searching him. They began to backtrack through the woods the way they had come, until they got to where they would turn west and head along the border. Kinder was still getting used to the idea that forty or so dead gray squirrels were following him. He didn't know whether to address them or not, and in the end decided not to because he couldn't figure what to say. Once he felt a cold touch on his shoulder and jerked away, but it did not happen again.

As he and Mariyen started away they were both thinking along the same lines. For once, they were wishing that Kinder would feel the telltale pullings that signified the coming of the gorepedes. To Kinder, however, the ground, frozen by the premature frost of nighttime falling, had never felt more still.

~~~

Rin followed behind her targets, keeping as great a distance as she could without losing them altogether. She had watched, disbelieving, from behind one of the trees on the border as the winged squirrel and the fat squirrel followed the ghost into the woods, and she'd followed them to the clearing where they met yet more of the terrible beings.

The ghosts shocked her to her core. She felt herself recoil at the thought of them. She had denied the existence of such things for so long that when the first ghost met the winged squirrel and the fat squirrel, she passed it off as a trick of the light. But she couldn't ignore for long how strange this third squirrel looked, how intangible...

At one point when the two squirrels were talking to their ghost friend, the undead one had been looking over the fat one's shoulder and Rin could have sworn that he was staring right at her. She'd disguised herself more fully after that, of course, burying herself further in the surrounding thicket. However far she'd gone into hiding again, she could not shake the feeling that the ghost squirrel had seen her. Perhaps he could even see her now, as she followed at a distance that should have been safe for anyone. Ghosts played by different rules than everyone else in the stories she'd heard; they could not be cut down by any paw with blood still running through it. It was why she hated them so much.

But something interesting had happened, something that made her wonder if these ghosts were really as dangerous as the tales said. The two squirrels had made a bargain with them, a bargain Rin could not hear from where she'd been hiding, but it proved to her that they could be reasoned with. Manipulated, as she was sure the squirrels had succeeded in doing.

In any case, there was one way that the presence of the invisible horde of ghosts behind the two squirrels, was working to Rin's advantage: the more that the winged one became distracted by the wraiths, the less she spoke about being watched and the more her eyes stayed only on the trail ahead.

So it was that every day Rin was getting ever closer to her goal. She knew that when she arrived, it would be worth everything she'd seen here, ghosts and all.

They would all get what was coming to them before her job here was done.

CHAPTER XVII

Yassar Krimpt shouldered his way through the crowd, only absently noting the chipmunks up ahead of him, who tried to scurry out of the way before they were pushed aside by the temperamental Yassar. He normally would have taken pride in the level of their haste and fear, but his focus was on one thing only: the huge iron-studded door opening before him only yards away. To think, just yesterday they'd been marching for this place, the cursed 'borderlands' as the squirrels liked to call it. And today...well, today he was going inside the very fortress they had set up to attack.

At the edge of the crowd, a paw shot out and caught him just as he was starting for the door. Yassar Krimpt turned around like a snapping bough, ready to unleash his anger at whoever had dared to touch him. His paw flew to his whip, but instead of some unlucky insurgent, he came face to face with Leader Vogt.

"Remember," Vogt said, "Don't do anything rash."

"I do remember," said Krimpt, "of course."

Vogt gave him a looking-over, eyes still expressionless as unmarked coins. Finally, he let go with a curt nod.

"Do not disappoint."

"That," Yassar Krimpt said, already starting forward again. "Is not something I make a habit of doing."

Privately, Krimpt was flattered that their leader had picked him to confront the squirrels, though he never would have admitted it aloud. His paw went to his whip again, but now it was for a different reason. He'd reached where the door opened up, set almost at ground level in the great tree. He sent a prayer to the god of life and to any foul gods of war there were, and was now eyeing the squirrels at the door, sizing them up. Though they came forward to meet him, they appeared afraid. It was an impression the Yassar, with his considerable girth and elaborate war paint, liked to encourage.

"You must get rid of your weapons," one of the squirrels in this lackluster welcome party informed him. He considered refusing, but looked back to where Vogt was standing watching him at the head of their group, and decided against it. Unhitching the whip from where it hung coiled at his waist, he went to place the thing on the ground and hesitated.

"I will have this returned to me?" he asked, voice gruff. It was not really a question, and the squirrels seemed to understand that. They shot one another looks, but the one that appeared to be in charge, a black squirrel with a scarred face, nodded.

"Of course. In fact, you can leave it right out here," the scarred squirrel said. These squirrels all wore some sort of weapon, mostly daggers, about their waists, but Krimpt suspected that this toughened guard and his cronies weren't the squirrels he'd be talking to. He placed his whip on the ground just outside of the doorway where he knew none of his chipmunks would dare touch it, and crossed the threshold into the home of his enemy. The door closed behind Krimpt with the force of finality, and he strode after the guard squirrels, who formed themselves in an organized cluster around him. Though he tensed up at their closeness, he understood that their formation was only a precaution to keep him from being hurt by their own kind.

Once inside, Krimpt found himself looking on a well-lit hall so spacious and well-aired that it resembled a courtyard of sorts. The Yassar found himself looking up at the ceiling just to make sure it existed. How strange it would be to live in such a place; it was not much different than living out in the open air of the overworld, but these creatures obviously reveled in it. The entrance hall was empty of squirrels for the most part, which made Krimpt, always looking out for anything out of the ordinary, suspicious. In ordinary circumstances, he knew, there would be squirrels hiding in the corners of the hall, staring out at him with wide, and—he allowed himself the privilege —frightened, eyes.

They climbed a set of wide, wooden steps, kissed by the dim, cold light of near-winter, and commenced to the end of a hallway, this one a bit dimmer and less drafty, lit mainly by lanterns. It too was devoid of the presence of other squirrels, except for one, who passed them walking quickly; if she'd looked at Krimpt, she'd done so so fast that he had missed it. Yes, there was something off here. If there were so little squirrels here, they must have been ordered to be somewhere else. Which left him to draw one conclusion.

The squirrels knew they were being attacked, and had prepared.

The hallway Krimpt was being led down turned into another hallway at its bend, and this one rose up slightly as he walked it. With a twinge of nervousness he could not suppress, he wondered how high they were going. Surely it was not all the way to the top, though now he thought about it, the very top seemed a likely place to house the leader.

"Where are we going?" he asked the weathered guard beside him, the one who had told him to discard his whip. His voice filled up the hall, a violent perturbation of the already unnerving silence. The scarred black squirrel turned to him, with something like a half-smile quivering on his lips, eyes cold and watchful.

"This one, Camphor?" one of the other guards asked. The scarred guard looked away from Krimpt, over at the door his fellow was indicating, the last on the right, and nodded. They pushed open into a new room, this one small and windowless, yet still too bright for the Yassar's liking. Getting through this meeting without his paws itching for his whip every few minutes might be hard, he was beginning to realize.

This new room included a long table with a bowl of something Krimpt guessed was edible in the middle of it. There were chairs placed around this table and Camphor indicated that he should sit in one of them.

Krimpt looked around at the guards, so much taller than he was already.

"I would prefer to remain standing for now," he said stiffly.

Camphor shrugged, though some of the other guards exchanged looks with one another. A grinding sound of wood on wood echoed from the other end of the room, and Krimpt whipped his head around to stare at an opening that hadn't been there before. Emerging through the opening was a young, stern looking gray squirrel with a crown seated atop his head and fancy robes that appeared anything but functional. Behind this squirrel trailed another one, walking with a cadence that was less cocky and more assured than the other; this squirrel was pure white in color, and appeared older than the crowned one.

The crowned squirrel nodded to the Yassar before taking a seat at the head of the table and motioning for the guards to leave. Then he glanced up at Krimpt, clearly suggesting that he sit as well. Sighing to himself, Krimpt settled uncomfortably into the seat on the opposite end, keeping poised and watchful on the edge of his chair.

"You're the king, I take it?" he asked the crowned squirrel, jumping straight into things. "Or is it you?" he directed his hot stare at the white one. The crowned one flinched back against his will at first, and the Yassar smiled to himself. He didn't need to know the answer to the question he'd asked for real; the crowned squirrel's getup told him everything he needed to know. What he did need to know was the sort of king he was dealing with, and he was happy with the answer he was getting so far.

"Yes, I am the king," the gray said, clearly annoyed with the implication of doubt. Krimpt saw him pass a look to the white squirrel beside him as though blaming him for the mix-up. The white squirrel only smiled slightly, eyes never wavering from where they rested on Krimpt.

"I was told I would only be talking to the king," the Yassar said, trying to scrape away the white squirrel's stare with the force of his words. "I was not told there would be anyone else here."

The white squirrel only smiled at him wider, and he turned away before his face betrayed the extent of his anger.

"This is my guest," the king said offhandedly, indicating the white squirrel. "I promise you he is only here to listen and not to talk." He gave the white squirrel another look when he said this. Krimpt was getting the idea that the gray hadn't told the white squirrel to do anything. He was getting the feeling that he couldn't.

"More to the point," the king said, rushed as if he were reading Krimpt's mind and didn't like what he saw, "You have come here to attack us without provocation. Can you explain your motives in this?"

Krimpt was truly surprised now, and he felt the flush of anger heating his face. Was the king really going to stoop this low, to travel *this* route so early in the game?

"You of the overworld," he told the king and his mysterious crony. "You have attacked us with the method of fire, and now you would deny it in front of me?"

The king truly did look confused, but it gave the Yassar pause only for a moment.

"We drove a fair bargain with you—one that was more than fair—not to let our gorepedes feed above ground if your messenger did not tell anyone of our existence." He spread his paws wide. "You have erred, gray king, for your squirrels waged deliberate attack on us."

"I don't control all of the squirrels in Arborand!" the king protested, sliding forward in his chair. A thin line of sweat stamped his brow, betrayed by the darker fur there. Krimpt smirked.

"You are suggesting that this messenger went down onto our level without any direction whatsoever? He was speaking for all of the squirrels above, and so all of the squirrels above are responsible for what he did afterwards. He was told not to tell of us, and he did. We made another promise down there, or haven't you heard? We promised your messenger that if he did tell anyone in the overworld of our world, we would see him again, and the meeting would not be to his liking. Well, we're just keeping that promise. You can't fault us for that, can you? If your messenger hadn't—"

"He didn't tell," said a softer voice, before the king could speak again. Yassar Krimpt spun on the white squirrel.

"Who did, then?" he asked, sarcasm edging his voice. "I very much doubt that you knew of us all along." The white squirrel's mouth quirked upwards at that, but Krimpt ignored it. "It was too many years ago that we mixed. And we agreed, then, in the legends of old, to keep our worlds separate."

"Now you have joined them," the white squirrel said. "It only stands what you intend to do with that fact."

Krimpt stared at him for a long while before spinning to face the king.

"You said that he wouldn't talk!"

The king turned accusingly to face the offending white squirrel, but he seemed only half-hearted. He, too, had been momentarily held sway by the white squirrel's simple statements. Was the white squirrel here to practice the magic the overworld was despised for? Was he even now putting a spell upon both he and the king?

"Please," the king said, though his tone suggested he was not making a request. "What is it you would like to negotiate? I have heard nothing but complaints and tales of our supposed wrong-doings from you, chipmunk. What would you have us do, and what will you do in return, to quench this fighting before it starts? I warn you, if it does come to a war, you will find us more than a match for you."

The Yassar found himself impressed in spite of himself. He never would have expected such a powerful speech from such a young, over-confident and blundering squirrel. *I see why you're king now, fool, but it will not save you.*

"Your words are big, king of squirrels, but they are not big enough. They are not big enough to cover up your wrongs of the past, or to abdicate your responsibility for those of your kind. And they are not big enough to face what reality will become if you do not take heed and follow our wishes."

The king sat rigid in his chair as the Yassar spoke, and when he was finished, his body relaxed, but there was a gleam in his eye that didn't fade, and Krimpt knew it for what it was.

Fear.

"You ask what I would like in terms of negotiation. I will tell you. I would like for us to be able to go back underground as we were before, and not to have you bother us. I would also like for the gorepedes to be able to feed once again. You have negated your right to have them kept away from you. I am sure with your magic and with your trees, you will have no problem keeping away from them if you are careful. You must pay, and you will pay in what they take from you. Aside from that, we will leave you be."

"What are the gorepedes? Is this some creature you've made up to distract me?" the king asked, and it was Krimpt's turn to be bemused. How could he not know? He quickly decided that the king must be bluffing, but decided to go along with it.

"They are worms, of a sort, who live underground and feed above it, by sucking out one's entire life force. Sound familiar?" he asked, for the king had paled.

"That explains...those deaths, only a while ago, all of those squirrels..." The king looked at the white squirrel briefly, as if searching for support in his calm façade.

"What do you say to my bargain, then, king of the squirrels?"

The king of the grays blinked at him, his cheeks beginning to color now.

"That is not a fair trade."

Krimpt shrugged. "It is what it is." He was coming to the end of any enjoyment he'd taken in this talk and a pent-up frustration and need to be out of this room, to collect his whip once more, ruled him. "So what will it be?"

The king squirrel drew breath but hesitated to speak. The white squirrel turned to him and the two made eye contact for an uncomfortable pause. Krimpt wondered if the white squirrel was doing some kind of hypnosis on the young king, but the king turned back looking very much awake; awake and decided.

"We will not agree to your trade," he said. "Even if these gorepedes don't threaten us too much, they will threaten some other innocent squirrels—because make no mistake, that is what we are. I don't know who set fire to your tunnels, but it was no one here, and we won't condemn Arborand to the fear of randomized death for a crime we didn't commit."

The Yassar stood, again amused by the way the young king spoke, and again holding his amusement in. Without warning, he struck the bowl of what he now recognized as nuts from the table. It shattered on the ground, the sound of a million pieces being forced apart, a music wildly out of tune. Nuts and glass scattered everywhere under the table. Pushing his chair back roughly, the Yassar turned for the door, and found the same troupe of guards who had brought him here awaiting him. He turned back to the king and the white squirrel before they could take him away.

"You have a war on your paws, king of the squirrels," he snarled, "I pray you will give us at least a bit of a challenge."

Krimpt felt paws clench over his arms and let himself be dragged from the room. He'd said all he needed to say, and as he was pulled backwards through the hall, he never let his eyes waver from those of the king.

When the guards shoved him out the front door and shut it, Krimpt hardly felt the hard ground as it rose up to meet him. He got to his feet unsteadily, gaining back his orientation when he noticed the throng of chipmunks standing before him, Vogt at its head. They were waiting. Yassar Krimpt let them wait a while longer as he searched for his whip. Collecting it from the ground, he straightened and stared around at them all, last of all at Vogt, who stood unimpressed, waiting.

"The king of the squirrels refuses to negotiate with us. He will not accept our terms," Krimpt declared, staring into Vogt as he said so, silently begging his leader to see the same conclusion he'd come to. He didn't think he could wait now for his whip to meet the flesh of his offenders.

Vogt's eyes, expressionless as always, swept over the crowd of chipmunks behind him. There was a silence in the air that felt even heavier for the sheer number of them, for every mouth present that wasn't making a sound.

"We attack, then," he said at last, turning back to Krimpt and curving the side of his mouth up in a strange, thin smile the likes of which the Yassar had never seen on the stoic leader's face before. A giant cheer, made of the sounds of screaming and whooping, and shouted threats, began to well up in an increasing murmur until it broke out like a giant tidal wave over the heads of those in front of the group. Krimpt felt the noise thrum through his ears like the sweetest of melodies. It was the sort of ovation that their mad queen would have demanded, and so would have received, from her followers after a rousing speech. But unlike the queen, who was literally miles away now, unseeing and long deaf to any more such cries, the Yassar and Vogt hadn't had to force the emotion from those they led.

It was real, and it was all the more beautiful for it. All the more beautiful, and dangerous. So sweet was his revelry that the Yassar couldn't understand why it was, as he let the cheers wash over him, that he couldn't quite get the image of the young king's face and his confusion at the mention of the gorepedes out of his head.

It didn't matter. It couldn't matter. Krimpt propelled the image away with a deep breath and a roar to rival that of any standing near him. Through the noise and confusion, he could not hear his own voice, only the vibrations it made as it left his throat, climbed up through the ears of others and into the empty, endless sky of the overworld.

~~~

Ritorren heard the shouts from where he stood just sheltered beyond the balcony, out of sight of the eyes of any chipmunk who chanced to look up. The young king pulled his robes close about him and turned to Zirreo, where he stood in the darkness beyond the awning. The white squirrel was staring out into the distance, as though he could see the crowd from where he stood. Ritorren only dared to look at him when he knew the white squirrel wasn't looking. He couldn't determine if he liked what he saw. The white squirrel made him nervous, that was for sure, though he would die before admitting it. He didn't seem too old, yet he had the air of knowing much, much more than was advisable for anyone. He'd met Ritorren coming down from the balcony just before his meeting with Krimpt. "Please," he'd said then, "I am a visitor and I never had a chance to speak with you. I apologize for the rudeness, but I think I can help."

The next part of it was curiously blank for Ritorren. He thought he remembered the white squirrel showing him something, but the memory was blurred and hazy, as though he'd been asleep for part of their meeting. All he knew now was that he'd agreed to it, and there must have been a good reason, for normally all of his senses would have been screaming out against such a reckless course. The white squirrel had given him confidence, he had to admit. The chipmunk they'd talked with, though small, was stout and well-muscled and his eyes were black and very, very wicked. He'd been glad to have Zirreo with him; for all his brave words, he didn't know how he would have held together against the warlike visitor without some buffer. Every other minute, though, Ritorren found himself alarmingly aware of how little he knew the white squirrel at his side.

"You cannot blame yourself for how the meeting went," Zirreo said, breaking into his thoughts almost as though he'd been following them silently up until this point. The crowd below the balcony was still making a racket, and the din surrounded the two hidden squirrels like a buffer for their conversation.

"I don't blame myself," Ritorren said harshly, wondering even as he said it if his words were entirely truthful. A silence fell between them in which Ritorren began to feel the weight of all his previous questions pressing in on him. He turned to Zirreo, and was unsurprised to find that the white squirrel was not looking at him.

"Who are you?" he asked suddenly, sharply, and Zirreo almost looked his way. Almost.

"I have told you who I am," he answered, but Ritorren wouldn't take let go that easily.

"I don't mean that. I know your name. That's all. What is your purpose? Why are you here?"

Still calm, though with a hint of danger, Zirreo replied, "You know all you need to know. My name is Zirreo, and I am here to aid you."

"If you're here to aid us, go get a bow. By the sounds of the ruffians down there, it won't be long before we're attacked."

Zirreo ignored him, and Ritorren reached for his crown, adjusting it. Finally, he spoke again, unable to keep his thoughts inside. "We don't have any other way of knowing you're not spying for them, do we?"

He did not expect Zirreo's reaction. The white squirrel snapped his head around as though he was viewing Ritorren for the first time. His pink-tinged eyes burned angry imprints into Ritorren's own. The squirrel leader tried to keep his own open and staring levelly back, but the effort stung him, along with something else: shame. The feeling crept through his body, washing him with guilt over the accusation.

"I didn't mean—" he started to say, the closest that proud Ritorren would come to an apology in many years. He broke off; Zirreo was smiling now. Somehow the smile made him more uncomfortable than the scathing look he'd been given moments before.

"I can help you in other ways, that do not concern the bow," the white squirrel told him.

Ritorren turned his full attention on the white squirrel. He hadn't been expecting that.

"Other ways?" he asked. "Like what?"

~~~

Yassar Krimpt walked along the lines of chipmunks gathered before him, paw ever ready on his whip, sharp black eyes watching for any little kink that needed fixing. He twitched the whip threateningly when he caught one of his soldiers examining a piece of grass, and the offending chipmunk snapped to attention at the sound, paling and dropping the offending distraction. Krimpt nodded curtly and moved on, all the way to the end of the line, where he turned once more to face Yassar Pelf, who stood at the other end of the first wave of chipmunks. He tipped the other Yassar a salute, and Pelf nodded. Krimpt watched as he began to talk to Vogt up front, before turning back to Krimpt and giving him the signal. Together with Yassar Grumble—who hated to be left out of anything that involved spirited shouting—they screamed, "ATTACK ON!"

Without further hesitation, the chipmunks began to stream for the trees rising up in front of them on the horizon. Those who had bows reached for them as they went, and those with daggers ducked among the others, attempting to keep a low profile until they got into a prime position.

Krimpt watched the trees, looking for any sign of life moving among them. He couldn't see anything from such a distance, but that didn't tell him anything, of course. The squirrels were crafty, more clever than he wanted to admit, and if they weren't already fully prepared for an attack as he had suspected when inside of their great tree, they had had time to be when they heard the sounds of Vogt's troops rejoicing.

Krimpt's suspicions were confirmed when he saw the first chipmunk go down, falling among his fellows, who parted to avoid him but did not stop for a second to help: he had trained them well. Seconds later, another went down close to the first, and then another and another, this one one of the number who'd almost made the trees. Krimpt was impressed, and he openly admitted it to himself. Of course, being an archer from a higher position gave one much more advantage, but he was yet to actually see one of the squirrels appear on the scene. Part of him longed to go running off and join the group of attacking chipmunks, but his duty was to remain here with those that had fallen behind to wait for the next wave. He would get his chance.

Some of the chipmunks had managed to get a hold on the trees at the perimeter of the forest now and, unsteadily but surely, began to scale the heights. At one point, the Yassar could have sworn he saw something fall from one of the trees, and though he was far away and could easily have misjudged, he didn't doubt his perception once.

It was a squirrel, bow in paw and fighting days clearly over.

Krimpt grinned. Anyone around to observe him would not have found it a welcoming sight, and some of the chipmunks massed around behind him stirred, but Krimpt was too lost in his thoughts and did not reprimand them. The squirrels may have the upper paw for now, but their numbers were far fewer than that of the chipmunks, and they would only have the upper paw for as long as they could weather the attacks, which Krimpt was guessing wouldn't be for long.

He could not believe that only earlier today he had been entertaining doubts about their decision to breach the surface—for he had been, and it was only now in his confidence and his rapture, that he could admit it.

No longer, Krimpt thought, seeing another squirrel felled from the treetops. *We're here, and we mean business. Business which we're not leaving until we've completed.*

He thought of Rin then, and the look on her face sometimes when he whipped her in training, the look that she had when she pulled her knife from Somnia, the dead queen. Maybe she had known something the rest of them hadn't. He was grateful for it now, at the same time as he was grateful Rin wasn't here with them.

Where is she, then? he wondered. Young though she was, the Yassar found that he couldn't imagine his former pupil dead. No, wherever she was, she was living.

And wherever she was, there was no doubt that those around her were aware of her presence.

CHAPTER XVIII

They weren't at all aware of her presence, Rin thought gloatingly. Even with all the opportunities most chipmunks would have had to be caught, she'd managed to remain hidden. Of course, she wasn't used to the need to remain hidden, and the urge to burst out from obscurity and cause some real damage was a fight she constantly had to wage with herself.

Rin stretched out as comfortably as she would dare on one of the lower branches of the trees surrounding the campsite. The glow of a flickering flame dashed in rapid heat patterns against her eyes, patterns that made her feel sick and overly hot. She knew the need for the fire was due to the cold; nights in the overworld were freezing to a barbaric degree. Underground, there had never been such problems. The soil was insulating, and the farther down one got, the warmer it got. Even the upper layers were never this cold. It was symbolic, she thought, of the hell she was in, following these squirrels to what she could only hope was a reunion with her kind. Rin's eyes drifted shut as she concentrated on the flames, the edges of the shadows moving about before her, the forms of the two squirrels talking becoming blurry and indistinct. For a moment, she didn't understand what was happening to her, then she snapped her eyes open again, feeling as though she had to exert too much force to do so.

Rin hadn't slept for three days. *At least*, she amended to herself. She wasn't even sure how long it had been in truth, only that she had hardly slept at all since she'd begun to follow the two squirrels, the fat one and the winged one. She watched them talking now, trying to figure out what they were saying, and unable to because of the new distance she had to assume from them. If she got any closer than she was now, Rin would impede on the edges of the clearing they had settled into for the night, and she was afraid she would run into a ghost. She hated to admit that it was a fear, reminding herself that it was necessary to enact caution when facing an invisible threat. And so she maintained her place on the tree branch, catching her eyes every time they drifted into seeing nothing but darkness, and trying to make out the words of the two squirrels. She could hear none of it after a time, the cadence of speech dissolving into rivulets of sound, trickling into one ear and out the other, in with one breath and out with the exhale...

Rin did not know it, but she had finally surrendered to sleep.

~~~

"I've never asked you anything about where you come from," Mariyen mused, stretching out in front of the meager fire she and Kinder had managed to light up. They had just gotten through her telling him more in detail about how she'd been raised in the Edgewood colony and of the disciplines and the focus centered around becoming a seer. Of how she'd been demoted despite her dreams. It was something she thought about more often lately, that strange lisp of fate that had ultimately caused her to be flung into the middle of all of this, whatever *this* was. She wondered about Kinder's story, too; whether he felt similar.

"It's not really important," Kinder said. He looked away but Mariyen refused to be deterred and held him under her gaze. She could sense him fidget. "I mean, you know the basics. Nadra died and Lute and I went to figure out why the ground was unsafe, then we ran into Zirreo..."

Mariyen laughed. "No, before that," she said, but she got no answering smile from Kinder.

He sighed after a moment of looking off into the forest around them. At first she thought that he wouldn't answer, that maybe she was being too nosy, but then he shrugged and she felt the tension diffuse a little.

"I was naïve and incredibly superstitious. Those rituals, like some of what you see me do now," he said with an apologetic smile, "I did them all the time. They took up my day. It was like if I did them enough, things would get fixed. My father would come back, my mother would get her mind back. I don't even know if she's alive anymore."

Mariyen wanted to say that she understood, but she knew that in some ways she couldn't. She thought of her estranged mother and her complete lack of parental figures growing up. At least for a flyer in Edgewood, such things were normal, almost procedural.

"I'm afraid to go back there," Kinder said at long last, and the crackling of the flames could not disguise the break in his voice.

"Look—" Mariyen began, heart beating rapidly, chest burning oddly, only vaguely knowing what it was she wanted to say. It was then that something stirred right beside her, and she leapt into the air with a little shriek, only to find out it was one of the wraiths, materialized out of thin air.

"They have got to stop doing that," Kinder said. He had snapped out of his introspection at the materialization of the wraith, and switched into staring at it apprehensively.

Engelwaithe ignored Kinder's last comment, and merely pointed at them. Mariyen didn't understand.

"Us?" she asked. "Are we being too loud?" Did wraiths even sleep? She somehow doubted it.

Engelwaithe only shook his head. He pointed to them both again and then, apparently on sudden inspiration, held up three ghostly claws. Mariyen looked sideways at Kinder, but he looked as lost as she was. Three? Engelwaithe repeated the motion, pointing to Kinder and Mariyen and then raising three claws.

"I don't understand," Kinder confessed. "Us, and then three? Three of us?"

Engelwaithe nodded.

Kinder looked at Mariyen uneasily. She didn't understand what Engelwaithe was getting at either, but he wasn't making sense, and something in the way he attempted to communicate, all silent and staring, was starting to really creep her out.

Suddenly the wraith turned around and then looked back over his shoulder for a moment before gliding off to the perimeter of their campsite, keeping his pace slow.

"He wants us to follow," Mariyen realized, and Kinder nodded at the suggestion, already on his feet. She was more hesitant: following Engelwaithe into the woods unguarded, surrounded by a bunch of invisible, ever-watching wraiths did not seem to her like a smart move. Still, she figured that Kinder knew more about the motives of the wraiths than she did; though his steps were tentative as he started out behind Engelwaithe, she saw none of the foreboding or deep misgivings she had mirrored on his face, so she calmed the pace of her thudding heart and got up to follow, keeping caution by her side in the form of a paw on her dagger.

Engelwaithe moved soundlessly over the ground, turning around only once to put a paw to his lips. Suddenly, Mariyen was filled with a deeper fear. If Engelwaithe wanted them to be quiet, that meant that whatever he wanted to show them must be alive, alive and with ears to hear them approach. Was it allied with the wraiths? She had to make an effort to block out her concerns as she went forward, the thick black of tree trunks rising up before and around her and the slight crunching of dry leaves and needles under her feet.

They hadn't gone far when the wraith stopped abruptly and stood in place for a moment. Mariyen waited for his intentions to become clear, paw still clasping the hilt of her dagger, though she knew it would do nothing for her if the danger took the form of more wraiths. She felt the air move around her, and something cold brush against the back of her neck, sending a shiver down the length of her body. They were around, that was for sure.

Engelwaithe motioned for she and Kinder to step closer, and pointed at what looked like just another tree, a low elm with few leaves left to its name, a dark silhouette in the night.

Kinder shrugged, voicing her opinion exactly in the movement. Engelwaithe remained, pointing to the tree. His expression hadn't changed, but Mariyen thought she could sense impatience rolling off of him in waves. He was trying to tell them something about this particular tree. She glanced at Kinder, who nodded, and they started forward past Engelwaithe, who still stood with his arm outstretched. As Mariyen went, she felt the cold of the invisible wraiths behind her, closing the space behind her with their chill as she moved.

Following us, she thought, *But for what purpose?* Mariyen peered at the spot Engelwaithe was pointing to; at first she saw nothing, and she almost spoke, but Kinder clapped a paw to her arm lightly and made her turn. He pointed this time, and in the line of his paw, she finally saw what it was the wraith had been trying to tell them.

Asleep on one on the tree's branches, faced purposefully toward the firelight still visible winking through the trees at them, lay another squirrel, fast asleep.

At first Mariyen thought it was a chickaree, that one of Lute's band must have followed them all this way, just as she'd suspected. Her old feelings of being watched flew into recall and her grip on her weapon tightened, but as she looked closer, she found something even more puzzling than the idea of a single chickaree tracking them over so much ground for the simple hope of treasure.

The squirrel they were looking at possessed the most unusual markings: stripes of black and white ran side by side over the flanks of its gently rising and falling body.

Mariyen looked to Engelwaithe, her stare in the form of a question, but the wraith was looking at Kinder now in a similar way.

Instead of being discomfited by Engelwaithe's stare, as Mariyen half expected, Kinder pointed to the small squirrel sleeping on the branch and then to Engelwaithe, and swept his paw around in a gesture that Mariyen could only assume was meant to encompass all of the other wraiths in the area. Engelwaithe seemed to understand, for after staring a long moment at Kinder, he nodded, and put a paw to his mouth again. It was Kinder's turn to nod. He took Mariyen by the arm and motioned that they should move off back the way they had come. She understood then what must have come to pass, and her paw relaxed for the first time since they'd entered the woods, falling away from its firm, half-unconscious grip on her dagger.

"They're keeping watch for us," Kinder whispered to her needlessly when they reached the safety of their self-made fire, which was sputtering weakly now, on the verge of guttering out.

Mariyen nodded, and stretched out in the dying heat of the remaining embers. She'd figured as much; the wraiths would not let their follower escape come morning without a good explanation.

She only hoped they would wait for one.

~~~

Rin opened her eyes to the dawn light and the comfortable sensation of having slept semi-well for the first time in days. She had had a dream, and it was a good one, so innately good that she wanted to merge back into it again. She'd been underground again, it was warm, she was reading a book of some sort...

Something coursed through her at the thought. Sleep...no, she was not allowed to sleep! It all came back to her then, everything, and she cursed the same dream she'd been longing for moments ago; it had taken her from her duty, her most important duty!

She shot up, falling from the tree she was resting on and onto the hard ground below, her fall only cushioned by a few dry leaves, which crunched and disintegrated at her back. Twisting around, sensing movement on one side of her, she was up in a flash, daggers in her paws and breath coming easy, turning around in slow circles to catch the enemy off guard if it wasn't too late. And she knew there was an enemy; she could feel them watching her, even if she couldn't see them.

"Show yourself," Rin called, voice bold and devoid of even a shred of natural fear, the voice that had frightened many of her fellow chipmunks. "Show yourself, and this might go easy."

All around her, forms started to swim out of the forest, and she knew that she was doomed to lose this fight even before they finished revealing themselves.

Rin had forgotten the ghosts.

The air around her, already carrying the chill of impending winter, went a lower shade of cold, chilling her insides. Beside her, something began to take form, and she jumped away, a look of horror and disgust rolled into one on her face as she watched one of the ghosts, a misty form with vague features, solidify and turn into the shade of the squirrel it had once been. Rin was no longer calm, but her voice continued to come out cool and expressionless as always.

"What do you want with me?" she asked the one she identified as the leader shade. She had seen the winged squirrel and the fat squirrel talking to this one, and she attempted to suppress her shudder as she addressed it now.

The shade did not speak, and nor did its fellows. There must be at least thirty of them, Rin thought, staring around. She wet her lips to say something more, and a small, hard something hurtled out of nowhere, smacking one of her daggers free of her paw and sending it soaring away amidst the crowd of wraiths. She reached in her belt for her third dagger and quickly snapped into position again, looking for whoever had attacked her.

The wraiths still stood in the same formation, and she noticed that not one of them had weapons; all the same, she thought it a bad idea to attempt to walk through them—they obviously had some other, hidden advantage. She'd seen the fat squirrel fall backwards when he tried to walk dismissively through a wraith, and Rin was no squirrel. She thought out every action calculatingly, for every action counted.

Or that was what she liked to think. Any who had known Rin might have disagreed, might have labeled her unpredictable, and when the fat squirrel parted the ranks of wraiths, who all floated aside for him, she felt a glimmer of what it would be like to stand on the opposite side of an unpredictable force.

The fat squirrel was putting away something in his bag as he walked—a slingshot, she realized. She watched as the winged squirrel came not close behind, both treading their way through the wraiths with not so much as a bead of sweat dotting their foreheads.

"I didn't realize I could do so well," the fat squirrel was saying to the winged one, who was looking impressed. "Only my second shot and all."

"And what was the meaning of your attack?" Rin pushed in, leaving no time for the two squirrels to attempt to get the upper paw on her with intimidation. "Why hit a stranger you hardly know with rocks?"

"We know you've been following us," the winged squirrel said.

"It was a carrot," said the fat one, at the same time.

Rin looked between these two new enemies. They both appeared to be armed. Normally, she would have had no problem attacking them, but there were still the wraiths to consider. If she were to attack their masters, the wraiths would no doubt attack her with whatever strange magic they possessed. The thought of magic made her shiver, and the winged squirrel looked at her closely, suspicion darting behind her large liquid eyes.

"Look," she said, "I know you're cold. But you've been following us for a while now and I want an answer. Why?

Rin's eyes darted between the two squirrels. She understood when she was outnumbered, and she knew there was nothing she could do about the fact now. Without warning, Rin raised one of her remaining two daggers and flung it violently at the two squirrels. Her eyes fixed on an opening she'd found some time ago, she sped off, beyond the two squirrels and the wraiths, out of the forest, past the campsite, and over the nearest rise in the land, until neither Kinder nor Mariyen could see her any longer.

Both squirrels blinked. The dagger had flown right for Mariyen's face, and she'd ducked out of the way just in time. With everyone distracted by the deadly attack, the strange, small squirrel had been able to slip off, and now, recovering from the fright of having certain death miss her by an inch, Mariyen cursed.

"Should we go after her?" Kinder asked. Engelwaithe's blank eyes were fixed on them both, seeming to ask the same question of them.

Mariyen shrugged. "She was running like insanity. She's probably miles from us now." She was more uncomfortable with the idea of letting their strange follower go than she let on.

Kinder's eyes, meanwhile, went wide in the middle of some thought.

"That was a chipmunk," he said.

"What?"

But Kinder didn't answer. His mind had gone into overdrive and he didn't want to speak until he knew he had something intelligent to say. An idea, a trace of a suspicion was forming in his mind, blooming, turning itself outwards to reveal its inner workings.

"We might as well keep going. We're going in the same direction after all. If we catch up with our follower, then we can make sure she gives us a better answer the second time around."

Mariyen nodded. She sheathed her dagger and began to walk in the direction they'd been going before they needed to set up camp the night before. When Kinder didn't turn to follow immediately, she waited for him, a frown furrowing her brow. She wanted to ask him what he was thinking, but decided against it. She had enough to think about herself. The wraiths, for one, were getting restless, and she hoped that they would be fortunate enough to find a way to shake them off before they turned on them. She was also having dreams of her mother again, but she hadn't wanted to share that bit. They were all the same dream after all, the one of running down the long room of crystal balls and scrolls, of finding her mother's crystal ball, and of watching it melt into nothing.

She would rather have dreamt about Zirreo, but she couldn't locate him. Her sleeping mind drew a blank when it brought his image up; she felt as though a barrier had been erected to keep her out.

And that concerned her as well.

She looked at Kinder a couple of times as they readied themselves to leave, wondering if she should mention any of this to him, and decided for the second time against it.

They were almost where they wanted to be, and when they were, they would have no space for doubt, or for fear.

Still, it was easier said than done to leave it behind.

~~~

Rin ran across the uneven terrain, up one rise and then the other. Her tiredness was coming back to her, despite the night she'd been able to spend asleep, but she was determined not to stop; she'd been running half a day, for the sun was dipping below the horizon, but she could not stop. It was crucial to her success that she did not stop. She expected the wraiths to be full on her heels, to overtake her even as she was thinking about them, but nothing happened. Several times she looked behind her, even though she realized that if they were following, she wouldn't be able to see them. They were invisible, those cursed ghosts, and they could be anywhere—but she did not feel the cold around her as she had when she'd found herself trapped in the middle of them, or when she'd weaved her way through the gap in their circle for freedom. Rin slowed as she considered this, a grim smile coming over her face before she ran straight into something...or someone.

"Ugh!" Rin was knocked off her feet by the impact. She was sure she knew who this was—it was the fat one, or the winged one, with their wraiths not far behind. She hoped only that she could get a kill or two in before the wraiths took her, and her paw scrambled around for her dagger even as the wind went out of her.

The face that hovered over her own was not that of either of the two squirrels she'd followed, or of their wraiths. It was that of a black squirrel, a black squirrel that was currently holding Rin's dagger in one outstretched paw, a wild gleam in her dark eyes.

Rin lost her breath at the sight of her weapon in another's paws—her only weapon. She struggled to sit up and glared at the black squirrel, noticing as she did so that the offender was not alone. Behind her stood the winged one.

"How did you get here?" Rin snarled, directing her anger at the winged squirrel. The questioned party only stared at Rin wild mild interest, and the chipmunk saw the truth in her eyes: she did not know her. This was clearly another winged squirrel, though this one looked so like the other one that it was hard for her to accept.

"Llewellyn, come here," the black squirrel directed, and the winged one moved forward to stand only slightly behind her companion now, her interest in Rin already seeming to fade. She commenced to stare at the pack the black squirrel carried like it was entrancing her and she could not look away.

"Llewellyn, remember what I said," the black squirrel said through gritted teeth, and the look that Llewellyn fixed on the black squirrel then was one of resignation and disgust, which struck Rin as odd. Weren't they travelling together? Weren't they both squirrels, and therefore kindred? Underground, all chipmunks worked as one in most instances. Were the squirrels of the overworld really so barbaric that they would turn on their own kind?

"We have a guest, Llewellyn," the black squirrel was saying, "A *chipmunk* if I'm not mistaken. And I rarely am."

Rin felt as though someone had thrown a cold dose of that water from the endless ceiling above over her. She wasn't sure what sensation it was that she was experiencing, or why it was that she could not simply break free of her paralyzed state and attack the black squirrel with force. She would have done it under normal circumstances, just as she had done on several instances when she'd first arrived aboveground. If the one called Llewellyn were alone, perhaps she could have done it to her, but the black one exerted some sort of force over her that she could not fight. She remained, staring wide-eyed and feeling more stupid as the seconds passed, up at the old squirrel.

"You think me old?"

Rin jumped. The black squirrel had just read her mind!

"Quit playing your magic tricks with me, squirrel!" she burst out, knowing it was unwise but unable to stop herself. "And give me back my dagger, or else."

The black squirrel looked startled by her outburst, even impressed. Slowly, she brought Rin's dagger to her side and stuck it into her own belt.

"I don't think so. Not right now. Tell me one thing, though, chipmunk, before you unleash your"—she stopped to give a sharp, cold laugh—"*wrath* on us. How do you happen to be up here, running about upper Firwood with no escort, so far from your home below us?"

"Wouldn't you like to know," Rin snarled, but no sooner had the words fallen from her mouth then she found her own dagger thrust up against her throat. Again she felt the binding sensation, and could not move. "What do you want?" she managed to croak, feeling the blade cut into her neck even as she spoke. A warm trickle made its way down her chest, and Rin smiled, sharply and genuinely, for the first time in a long time.

Rin's captor's facial expression quirked from a confident sneer into something like incredulity at the look on the chipmunk's face, but she quickly recovered herself, and when she spoke, the old squirrel's voice was laced with surprising energy.

"Has it ever occurred to you," the black squirrel hissed to her, and Rin felt the knife graze her neck more deeply, due to the other's excitement, "that we could help each other?"

Rin stared blankly at her and the black squirrel moved the dagger away from her throat. The excitement in Rin's blood faded and they were left staring at one another.

"How do you know what I want?" Rin said carelessly.

"My name is Mercurie," said the black squirrel, already turning her back and starting away, though the winged squirrel with her remained in place, looking after her. "And I know much more than you think."

CHAPTER XIX

Night fell over the borderlands with a precision both frightening and deadly. In the dark, everyone was at a sore disadvantage, and those fighting needed to rest. Ritorren had spoken with the leader of the chipmunks, one character called Vogt, and reported back to Gerien and Venul with a smug smile, which he had paraded around the room before turning to his two advisors.

"They are waiting for the morning to continue battle," he said.

"I still don't understand why you've asked them about it," Venul had said. "It only makes us appear weaker. If you'd just waited, they might have retreated to sleep as well."

Ritorren turned a cold look on him, but he was ready for it and faced it without flinching.

Ever the peacemaker, Gerien had stepped in. "Either way," he said, "Chipmunks can see better than us at night, so it's a good thing they're not planning to attack. We should still keep sentries, of course."

"Of course," Ritorren had said, but from his voice it was hard for Venul to tell if he'd really thought of it. He had decided that if Ritorren didn't put a watch up, he and Gerien would go around assigning one. The king wasn't looking so good, pale and slow to speak even when it was to assert his power and authority, and now that Venul stood in the darkened hallway outside his quarters alone, the image of Ritorren's face and the uncharacteristic strain in it would not leave his head.

"Sleeping at all?" Gerien asked, and Venul turned around, stepping back to allow the gray room to pass. Gerien merely shook his head and stopped across from

Venul, leaning back against the wall and looking both ways before speaking.

"You noticed it, too, didn't you?"

Venul nodded slowly. Somewhere below, where their fighters slept, he heard a sound like someone stirring and disturbing a pile of weaponry. He paused before whatever it was he meant to say, letting the words settle in his mouth as he waited intently for any other sound. When none came, he turned back to Gerien.

"Do you know if he set lookouts?"

Gerien shook his head and groaned lightly. "I forgot. *He* can't have forgotten, can he?"

Venul didn't know how to answer that question; he didn't want to know, honestly.

"I think he's cracking," he said at last.

Gerien nodded. "I think it's that white squirrel."

Venul felt his neck crack, he turned so fast to look back at Gerien. "The white squirrel?" he asked, and Gerien frowned at his excitement.

"Hey, are you all right?"

Venul waved a paw, indicating that Gerien should continue.

"It's just—" Gerien began uncertainly, looking up at Venul, wary of another unwarranted reaction. "It's just that the white squirrel is so...random. Where did he come from? Why is Ritorren always hanging around him lately? Or why is *he* always hanging around Ritorren, for that matter? I just think it's suspicious. Right around the time the white squirrel appeared, he started acting weird. He's up in his chambers all the time, he doesn't want anyone to talk to him, and he won't even watch the battle. We're hurting and he knows it, but he seems to have stopped caring."

"It could just be the battle itself," Venul suggested. "Ritorren was never the paws-on type."

Gerien peered at him oddly, and he did his best to appear cool and unaware of the scrutiny.

"I only think," Gerien said, after a time, "that someone should ask the white squirrel what he's up to. It seems too perfect that he arrived right when the chipmunks did. How do we know he's not some strategy of theirs, softening Ritorren up and cracking his defenses, so that we become leaderless."

"Leaderless wouldn't be so different from now," Venul said, but softly, so that Gerien couldn't hear.

"What was that?" the gray squirrel asked, looking at him askance.

"The white squirrel is not a spy," Venul said, and turned to go into his room, unsure why he felt so strange, as though he'd just been personally attacked by his friend.

"Do you know him?"

Venul opened his door, giving himself time to think in the noise it created.

"No," he said at last. "I just don't get a bad vibe from him, that's all."

He walked into his room and shut the door, trying to figure why he felt as though he'd just told the biggest lie in a long time.

He didn't understand. The white squirrel had never explained anything to him. He'd never even *seen* Zirreo once since he saw the white squirrel with Ritorren, walking about on the balcony. The first time he'd spotted them together, he'd felt something outrageously like jealousy, a sense of being wronged by the white squirrel. There was no reason for the feeling; Zirreo had asked him where his leader was when first he'd come to the borderlands. But now Ritorren was rarely without the white squirrel whenever Venul saw them, as if there were some plot or machination between the two that he and Gerien, that *no one* else, as far as he knew, was privy to.

It *was* strange. For all he knew, Zirreo could be a spy, he could be making Ritorren ill and forgetful. All he knew was that every time he saw Zirreo at Ritorren's side, conferring with him or merely standing there, Zirreo seemed to refuse to look at him. Perhaps he wanted to disassociate himself from Venul.

I let you in, the young black squirrel said to Zirreo's image in his mind. He kicked his bed to relieve the tension he felt and collapsed atop its surface, letting the comfort of its warmth take him down. Somewhere in the back of his mind, some alarm was flaring, some signal telling him not all was right, but he pushed it aside and turned over, wrestling himself under the covers. It was too late for this; whatever he was forgetting could wait until the morning.

But the nagging continued. Taking up room in his mind, it became more of a presence, a sound, repeated over and over. *Tap, tap, tap.*

Bang.

Venul jerked out of sleep like he'd been stabbed and lay, listening in the dark of his room, trying to separate sleep from waking. He could hear no other sound, but his eyes would not shut. He traced his waking vision around the room, over the outline of his window and his single chair, the little table in the corner where he stored his private writings.

Nothing is the matter. There's nothing there. Nothing is the matter.

But there was. No matter how Venul tried to tell himself, staring around, that everything was as it should be, the nagging in the corners of his mind would not let up. He slid from his bed and took his dagger from the corner table, feeling its smooth, cold weight in his palm. Feeling only marginally comforted, he moved to the door, checking his room over before opening it. He knew there was nothing in here. He knew all along where he would find the source of his sleeplessness, though he wouldn't let himself admit it until he saw for sure.

Venul was halfway down the hallway and past Gerien's door when he paused and looked back, indecisive for a moment. He entertained the notion of barging up to the door, of knocking, of calling an alarm.

How stupid would you feel when you found it was only a dream?

Fine. That was it, then. It was only the fact that he could be wrong that kept him from waking Gerien. Or at least that was what Venul told himself as he approached the top of the darkened, downward racing stairs that signaled the entrance to the warrior's barracks.

Again he listened, and again there was no sound. There was too little sound, in fact.

Venul put his foot on the top step and went down from there, holding loosely to the wall in case he was startled into falling. Down the long series of steps Venul went, until he reached the floor below, turned the corner, and found himself staring out over the dirt floor that marked the lowest level of the great tree. He could see the sleeping lumps of the fighter squirrels spread out all across the floor to the other end of the long room.

There was nothing. No sentry either, he noticed, and as his eyes drifted among the sleeping bodies, he caught a glimpse of movement.

Just for a second. When Venul reverted his eyes back to where he'd seen the flitting movement and peered more closely at the spot, he could see nothing.

But something was down here. He would stake his life on it, and he intended to uncover it tonight.

Venul took a step forward, then another step, and then another, until he was standing between two sleeping squirrels, a gray and a black he thought, though it was hard to tell in this dimness. He needed more light to confirm what he knew. He needed—

The object that flew past his head obliterated his thoughts for good. Venul felt a stinging on his cheek and reached up cautiously, wiping the minimal wetness he found there away, letting his paw fall to his side and wondering why he still didn't call an alarm. Someone had obviously shot at him, and whoever that someone was wouldn't take long to figure out that his weapon of choice was poorly suited to the circumstances.

The room was still completely dark, the squirrels completely still. Keeping both eyes always trained in front of him, Venul hunkered down and touched one of the squirrels at his side. He didn't move. Frantic, Venul shook squirrel harder. No movement at all, though when Venul placed a trembling paw on his chest, he could still feel the other squirrel, a black, breathing. He trailed his paw down the other's chest once more just to make sure, feeling his eyes getting heavier as he did so.

That was when he found the dart sticking out like a bullet point from the other squirrel's stomach.

It was so small it almost went missed, but as he stared he began to understand. Venul climbed to his feet and rocked backwards unsteadily, righting himself as quickly as he could find his bearings and steering for the stairs. It was then that the enemy made itself known.

Venul heard a sound behind him and turned because he couldn't help it; he knew he would find someone this time, and sure enough, the small shadow of a chipmunk rose, uncoiled itself from the ground and the indistinguishable mass of bodies there.

Sleeping bodies, the lot of them. Drugged.

Among them rose several other smaller forms, some of whom were grasping the small bows from which the darts were shot; some held long, twisted daggers, and Venul knew it wasn't possible to assume those blades were clean. He turned and began to run in earnest, bolting up the stairs step by stumbling step, feeling as though his eyes were withering in their sockets the longer he tried to keep them open. A chipmunk came up beside him once, almost like he'd been waiting in ambush, and attempted to stick him with another dart. Venul turned around quick, disoriented for a moment, and made an educated try at stabbing where the enemy was standing. The solid body his own dagger met confirmed his powers of accuracy. For a moment, he stayed and tried madly, feeling half-blind as he did so, to pull the dagger from the chipmunk's body. Soon, however, he had to give it up for lost. He could hear more of them coming, perhaps only to see what the racket was, perhaps to give pursuit. Venul dropped the dagger, and the unlucky chipmunk with it, letting them both fall back down the stairs. He was losing control of his motor functions, and began to fall to the ground at the top. With one last burst of manic energy born of desperation, he was able to pull himself up again using the wall and stumble out.

Venul was in the hallway now, the quiet shadows the same as he had left them; running down the hall to Gerien's room, he knocked several times, pounding up a storm. He thought he heard other doors opening into the hallway, and he welcomed the idea. He felt too faint to turn and check.

Gerien opened the door on the third knock.

"What is it?" the gray asked, still in his nightclothes and looking distinctly puzzled. Venul tried to listen for the sounds of the chipmunks coming up the stairs, but he couldn't hear them over the pounding of the blood behind his eyes. He took a step towards Gerien and fell to the ground and into the welcoming blackness waiting for him there.

CHAPTER XX

Llewellyn was living a nightmare.

Ever since they'd left the fallen tree way back in Beechwood, Mercurie had refused to answer any of her questions, had refused to crack or give any information on what she was planning. She remembered Mercurie telling her Absoulim would meet them somewhere along the road, but now, as they lay in the dark staring down at a camp of what had to be a thousand chipmunks at least, they appeared to be at the end of their road and still there was no sign of Absoulim. Mercurie didn't seem the least bit concerned—quite the opposite, in fact—and this was what made Llewellyn anxious. Anything that made Mercurie so happy could not, by definition, be good.

The few conversations she'd gotten in with Mercurie were all typically unpleasant, and all came back to the same thing: Llewellyn's power. Every time Llewellyn made a comment, or asked Mercurie a question, Mercurie had not only refused to answer, but had turned the conversation around so that she was the one doing the asking.

Llewellyn hated it, and it made her nervous. She couldn't understand why Mercurie was so interested in her power, and half of the questions the old black squirrel asked her, she couldn't answer anyway. Could she tap into her power without the use of a crystal ball? Did she know what her power could be used for? What were its limits? Did it have uses other than prophecy? What did her power feel like?

The last question was the only one Llewellyn could honestly answer, and she had, because the black squirrel's gaze was piercing, and she understood that she would not be left alone until she came out with some sort of explanation.

"It burns," she said, and the black squirrel had nodded, like that was exactly what she'd expected.

"Do you need healing, then?" she'd asked, staring hungrily at Llewellyn under the canopy of brush they were taking refuge under. It had been raining on that particular night, and both squirrels were damp from the drizzle that came through their makeshift shelter.

"No," Llewellyn said, and she wondered then as she wondered now, why she had felt strangely triumphant in that moment, sitting in front of the sorceress and denying her her guess. "It burns *inside*."

It had been the last trivia Mercurie had given her; not long after that, they ran into the chipmunk.

To Llewellyn, she looked just like a small squirrel, perhaps a chickaree, with a thinner tail and strange markings, but every time Llewellyn called the creature a squirrel by mistake, her whole body would stiffen and she would become terse, her voice sounding like a tight lid on some inner violence.

"We're here now, then?" Llewellyn asked, just to break the silence and maybe a little to get on Mercurie's nerves. She'd figured out how to play on them by now, and she took full advantage of it; she'd learned some time ago that for whatever reason, Mercurie needed her and would not kill her no matter how she pushed the old sorceress's buttons.

And how could she resist? She wasn't, after all, a much different squirrel from the one who'd loved to flout the elders' authority as a novice or the one who'd messed continually with Horus back at Edgewood, just to see how far she could go. That squirrel hadn't been afraid to mess with the consequences; this squirrel truly didn't know what they were. There was little difference.

Mercurie glanced at her, and she could tell her remark had landed where it was meant to: the old squirrel's mouth was tight-set.

"Yes," the sorceress told her, "as you know already. We've come."

Llewellyn was about to supply a snappy comment back, but her attention drifted to where Mercurie and the chipmunk were looking. The chipmunk hadn't said anything for some time; it seemed as though she refused on principle to talk to either of them unless the moment absolutely required it.

They had come over a large rise in the land, covered with brush sprawled out in a wild mess, and were staring down at the hard, frozen ground below them, a stretch of land with only small, chilled patches of grass for nearly as far as the eye could see. Nearly.

Up against the sky on the horizon rose the forms of several giant trees, the beginnings of some gargantuan forest. Stretched out over the land between where they sat and where the forest began, there was an extraordinary number of chipmunks.

She'd heard from Mercurie about the borderlands being attacked, but the sheer number of the attackers made her feel weak. She watched them move about on the ground below them, settling into circles she guessed were campsites or conversations or simply milling about, sharpening their weapons. As she watched, a rather large chipmunk made his way through the multitude nearest them, leaning close and saying something to select members. Everyone began to straighten up, to face the direction of the trees on the horizon, and Llewellyn wondered what the large chipmunk was saying.

"We'll have to go down there," Mercurie said casually, through the rustling and clanking of the horde below.

The chipmunk with them was still staring down at the others of its kind. When she realized the statement was directed mainly at her, she turned and there was a horrifying sort of grin on her face.

"You want me to bring you safely through them."

Mercurie locked eyes with Rin she gave a little shrug.

"Of course I'll try. I can't make any promises though."

Mercurie continued to keep eye contact. "I would suggest you try your very best."

Rin smirked, and Llewellyn sensed no fear from the chipmunk. It was something she'd begun to notice from the first, right when Rin had run into them. She could have been killed by Mercurie then and there, but still Llewellyn had detected not the barest hint of fear.

Someone shouted something down below and Llewellyn jerked her head up to stare at the trees on the horizon.

"That's where he is."

"What?" Mercurie turned to her, but she ignored the other squirrel's question. She knew now why they had to get past the chipmunks—whatever Mercurie wanted was on the other side, in the trees there.

And so was Zirreo.

"I asked you what you said," Mercurie said dangerously, but Llewellyn still refused to meet her eyes.

"Zirreo's in there, that's what I said," Llewellyn told her at last. Another thought occurred to her, setting her heart to a queasy thudding pace. "Absoulim, too?"

Mercurie only smiled at her.

"Come lead us, chipmunk," she said to Rin, who came forward eagerly enough and began the descent down the steep side of the rise, Mercurie right behind. Llewellyn wondered if she should chance running now, find an alternate way to Zirreo to try and warn him before they even got to him. *Past Llewellyn would have done so without hesitation,* she thought, but she only turned and followed Mercurie's retreating back into the army below them.

I am not a coward, she thought with the smoke and the mangy scent of too much fur in one place and the cold sour night upon her. *I am not a coward.*

~~~

Kinder heard the army before he saw it, and he stopped, cocking an ear in the direction the noise was coming from. He and Mariyen had walked tirelessly until they reached this place, which should be as far west as the land was allowed to go, he thought grudgingly.

"Why are you grabbing your ear like that?" Mariyen asked, laughter in her voice despite all the worries of the moment.

"What?" Kinder said, turning to face her. His face was getting hot again. "I'm just—it makes it easier to hear."

"I've never heard of someone manually cocking an ear," she grinned. "Maybe I'll have to try it."

"It works," Kinder began, "except you become deaf from other angles. So you have to be sure that the thing you're trying to hear is the most important thing you could possibly hear at the moment."

Mariyen didn't answer. Kinder followed her sudden, blank stare, and saw what she was looking at.

Only a few yards from where they stood, there was a line of brush beyond which apparently lay a hill, for the ground dropped away soon after. Part of this brush was moving, as though it had recently been pushed aside.

"She came this way, d'you think?" Kinder asked. "What's all the noise below?"

One look at Mariyen's face told him that she was filling up with memories of every bad dream and every premonition she'd had since she'd come to this point.

"I think it's the dreadful army," she said in barely more than a whisper. "The one attacking the place where Zirreo is in all of my dreams. Which means... Zirreo is close to us."

Kinder nodded slowly. Mariyen had started to edge from the thin covering of trees they were hiding in to the spot where the brush had moved, and he followed. The wraiths hadn't made an appearance since they'd captured the chipmunk in the forest, and he didn't feel the signature cold of their presence now, but he knew they must be around. They hadn't got what they wanted yet, after all. Trying not to think too much about the wraiths and their demands, Kinder looked over the hill with Mariyen and immediately felt dizzy and a little faint.

"There are so...many of them, Mariyen," he whispered, but Mariyen put a paw to her mouth and pointed. Going down the slope in front of them towards the horde of chipmunks was the chipmunk they'd caught in the woods, but she wasn't alone.

"Who are *they?*" Kinder asked of the two squirrels he saw with her. He was confused; the last time they'd seen the chipmunk, she had most definitely appeared to be alone.

"Well," Mariyen whispered, staying low to the ground, "one of them is my mother."

Kinder started, and stared more closely at the forms moving off through the dark.

"How can you tell?"

"I just can. The other one I don't know, but I don't have such a good feeling about them."

"What do you think they're doing here?"

Mariyen shrugged. "I have no idea." She was still staring at the backs of the two squirrels and the chipmunk, but Kinder knew the focus of her gaze was for one of them alone. He didn't presume to know how Mariyen must feel at the moment.

"The last time I saw her, she was jumping off a balcony, and she had a child with her," Mariyen said incredulously. There was something else in her voice, a concentrated well of emotion, but he knew she was trying to keep it down, so he said nothing.

Nothing until a coldness as icy as death closed around his shoulder.

"Agh!" Kinder cried out, causing both himself and Mariyen to turn around. It was Engelwaithe.

So he hasn't left us after all, Kinder mourned privately. He knew what this was about. Engelwaithe's stare was not impatient, only cold and calculating.

He thinks we've just had him along. He thinks—

Someone down below yelled, perhaps an alarm at seeing the three figures moving towards them at last, and an idea occurred to Kinder. It might work. He didn't know whether he could be sure, and if it didn't work he was as good as dead, but he had little options otherwise. He could not talk to Mariyen about it, not with Engelwaithe standing—or floating, or whatever it was he did—right there.

Kinder cleared his throat, and Mariyen, immersed in watching whatever was going on below once more, turned to look at him.

"I know you've been waiting for a long time," Kinder began, doing his best to meet the wraith's staring eyes. "I couldn't feel any disturbance in the ground, so we brought you here. Those chipmunks down below, they're the ones who own the gorepedes. Even though the gorepedes killed your colony, the chipmunks are the ones who sent them to kill you all. I can't control whether a gorepede appears or not, but I can bring you to those who are really at fault."

He stopped talking and watched Engelwaithe, looking for some sign that the wraith believed him. He didn't know if he believed it himself, but they needed to take the risk. They needed to get to the trees that the chipmunks were attacking, and the only way they would have a chance of making it through the horde down below would be to have the wraiths with them.

"Protect us," Kinder said. We have to get to those trees on the other end of the field. Once we get there, you can let yourself loose upon them wherever, but we need you around us at first. Is it a deal?"

Engelwaithe stared out across the field and then nodded, once, breaking Kinder's held breath into shards of relief. His eyes said quite clearly that if Kinder were lying, he would be the one the wraiths took revenge on. He would, after all, be their last true option.

Kinder turned to Mariyen and saw that her eyes were fixed again on the place in the crowd where she'd last seen her mother with the chipmunk and the black squirrel. It was too dark and they were too far for her to see them now, and when she sensed Kinder looking at her, she turned to him with an embarrassed smile and pulled her dagger from its sheath.

"Now?" he asked her.

"When else?" Mariyen asked, and there was no quiver to her voice.

~~~

Rin pushed aside the first chipmunk who got in their way with disinterest. The squirrels she was with had told her they were on the same side of this war as she was. She didn't want to trust them, didn't truly trust them, but she had no options; the black squirrel's pull on her was just as powerful as it was invisible. The squirrel called Llewellyn didn't have a weapon of her own, so Mercurie and Rin had to defend her against several of the chipmunks who recognized the two squirrels as imposters and ran at them.

The first of these chipmunks, Rin recognized.

"Kuffner," she snapped at him, grabbing him by the paw and twisting it back.

Kuffner, a brilliant fighter but a very slow-minded fellow, had to look at her twice before recognizing her. When he did he fell back, dropping his weapon from nerveless paws.

"You're the one who killed—"

"Yes," she said, flinging him away from her and continuing onwards. The throng was never-ending, and Rin exulted in revealing herself to the others of her colony, whether it was in greeting someone or jabbing her dagger at them. Mercurie was on guard beside her, weapon out. Often, all the black squirrel seemed to need to do was to look at the chipmunks to convince them not to tangle with her. Llewellyn kept up the rear, her eyes in a daze; she didn't look as though she even remembered where they were.

Rin had a horrid thought. What if after all of this pushing and shoving and obeying the whims of the black squirrel, the black squirrel didn't let her go? She pondered this new unpleasant thought as the crowd continued to part around them.

Several of the other chipmunks began whispering as they moved aside, and some even pointed to her as they backed up to let her entourage through. She studied their shadowed faces, wondering what tales they might be telling of her in the cover of darkness. Would she be the subject of stories seasons later, when all of this was forgotten and the chipmunks were nestled, victorious, in richly decorated corridors far below where they stood now? She resolved that she would be; it was the only way she could see herself after the fighting was no more.

As they approached the trees that marked the border of Oakwood they were stopped by a dark figure stepping out at them, bumping them unexpectedly and causing Mercurie's pack to fall to the ground. Something round and glinting rolled out, and Mercurie was immediately on the ground, grappling with whatever it was. Llewellyn's eyes were fixed on the black squirrel with an expression that was almost hungry as she watched the other try to put whatever had fallen back where it belonged. Rin alone faced the intruding form and saw it for what it was.

"Yassar Pelf," she greeted him coolly.

Pelf cast an eye back to the trees, towering just beyond his back, and then back to Rin.

"The rumors are true," he said with a light smirk.

Rin raised a brow at him.

"Things travel fast in this crowd," he said, still smirking that strange smirk. "You're a bit of a legend in any case, as I don't think I need to remind you."

She shrugged it off and started to go around him; Pelf threw out a paw.

"Everyone here has wondered where you were."

"Well, no need to miss me any further," Rin said through gritted teeth, slapping his paw away with the flat of her blade. He recognized the danger in her voice, hesitated for a moment, and backed up a step.

"They don't miss you," he said to her back. "Much, at least. They're afraid of you."

"Well," Rin said, turning back to him, "They're wise."

Pelf considered her for a curious moment.

"You've turned traitor, haven't you?"

Rin's blade sliced out without warning and cut a dark slash across Pelf's belly. The Yassar stepped back and put a paw to his stomach with a gasp. His narrowed eyes followed Rin to the trees, but she didn't turn to pay him any mind—she'd given him his warning—until his voice drifted to her yet again.

"Look behind you, traitor," he said, "It seems that you've been betrayed as well."

Rin turned, taken by surprise, and found that the squirrels were nowhere to be found. Brushing it off—no time to think about that now—she looked back to the trees in front of her and kept going, right up to where a crowd of her fellow chipmunks were huddled around a particular section of root.

"What are we doing here?" she asked, ignoring the heat of the wounded Yassar's eyes at her back and trying not to think about the missing squirrels. Mercurie's spell was no longer exerting any force over her as far as she could tell, anyway. She'd kept her side of the deal, let the foolish Yassar and the others who doubted her deal with their doubts on their own time.

One of the chipmunks she'd spoken to looked up from where she crouched on all fours, staring at a point in the roots of the group's selected tree. Her face registered no recognition at the sight of Rin, and she answered simply.

"Overnight invasion," she grinned.

Rin smiled back. "Let me in."

"We can only really let in those on second shift right now. What's your wave?"

"Let me in," Rin repeated, and the other chipmunk looked back at her fellows uncertainly.

She made the right choice in the end.

~~~

The second Mariyen started down the slope she'd seen her mother disappear down, one of the chipmunks nearest the rise turned and looked at her. In the night she couldn't see his or her face, but she knew she was spotted. She stopped, digging her paws into the ground and causing some small rocks and sand to come sifting down in a small avalanche. One of the rocks rolled into Kinder and he stopped, too, realizing the danger.

The wraiths were nowhere to be seen, and herein lay the problem. Mariyen felt hopelessly naked before the threat of hundreds of chipmunks who considered them enemies, and she could not move for the life of her. Kinder looked back at her encouragingly, but his face registered fear as well and it took all of her nerve to take another step forward, towards the staring chipmunk.

"Intruders! More intruders!" someone yelled, and it took Mariyen a while to locate the shouter in the crowd. Another chipmunk spoke from somewhere in the midst of them, loudly.

"What if they're using a trickle-in effect? What if they have more squirrels behind us?"

"Quiet," said the original speaker. "We will take care of them as they come."

"Take care of me, then," Mariyen said, freezing in horror inside as she said it. She didn't give herself time to think or to change her mind; instead she stepped toward the chipmunks, dagger out. One of them shrugged and raised a bow.

"Engelwaithe!" Mariyen shouted, but there was no need to call; the wraith was already materializing between her and Kinder. One of the chipmunks noticed it and began to elbow the one with the bow, who shot wide of Mariyen as a result. He turned to give the other chipmunk a piece of his mind and saw what was unfolding before him.

"What...is that?" he said, voice trembling a little.

"It's magic!" another chipmunk yelped from nearby. "The magic of the squirrels!"

The chipmunks, busy backing away and talking among themselves, did not notice the translucent smoke rising like coiled ribbons among them. They didn't notice until it was too late. As the rest of the wraiths began to materialize in the middle of the group of chipmunks, Engelwaithe glided towards the one with the bow, who dropped his weapon and began to run.

Engelwaithe caught him easily, moving closer, closer, and then through the unfortunate chipmunk, who slumped to the ground, shivering like insanity and twitching. Engelwaithe turned to the two rather horrified squirrels on the hill and motioned for them to come closer. Mariyen looked at Kinder and Kinder looked at her. Together they slipped from the hill to stand as close beside Engelwaithe as they dared. No one reached for them as they passed, and the screams and scrambling composing the soundtrack all around them left them with no doubt that the chipmunks had greater problems at the moment.

Engelwaithe started off, indicating that they should stay close to him, and Mariyen happily complied. The ground before them was solid with the bodies of chipmunks, faces painted and weapons at the ready, but they moved across it with no obstructions. Mariyen and Kinder found themselves having to step over bodies that their security circle of wraiths had gone through up ahead of them.

"Are these the right victims?" Kinder dared to ask Engelwaithe, and Mariyen watched the wraith with baited breath to see what his answer would be.

Engelwaithe gave a little shrug and then nodded, eyes still blank and staring up ahead.

"I think he means he's not sure yet but he thinks so," Kinder confided to her.

Just then, a paw shot out and grabbed Mariyen's leg, causing her to trip. The wraiths behind her luckily stopped before they ploughed her through, but when Mariyen tried to get to her feet again, the grip on her leg tightened and a voice ground something out.

"Try to get free," it said. She turned to look over her shoulder, vision and body cramped from the unusual angle, and found that one of the shivering, mad-eyed chipmunks who'd been felled by the wraiths had managed to get a hold on her. His paw was as cold as ice, and she tried to pull away again to no avail. There was a sudden, sharp cracking sound, and the chipmunk's grip loosened slightly; Mariyen quickly jerked herself free and stared, horrified at the chipmunk who had nearly dragged her down. Next to him lay a carrot pie, cracked in half and falling out of its pan. She turned to Kinder, who shrugged.

"I've only got a few things left to use," he explained.

She kissed him.

For a moment, everything stopped; it actually seemed as though the sound around them had become muted. Then Kinder, face hot, opened his mouth as though to speak and Mariyen pointed behind him at Engelwaithe, who stood observing them blankly. When Kinder turned back around, she was already moving forward into the crowd again, a barely suppressed smile on her lips.

~~~

Yassar Krimpt was not happy. The inner invasion of the squirrels' domain was going extraordinarily well, according to the last report he'd received. A vast number of the squirrel army had been put into a deeper slumber when sleeping, with the use of sleeper darts, dipped in moth wing powder. Then they had been systematically killed. If someone hadn't come down and sounded the alarm, they might have eliminated the bulk of the fighting force earlier.

Now Krimpt was running low on the rare darts, and without a doubt all of the squirrels were alert and up now. Dozens of them were shooting their bows down into the wave of chipmunks closest to their doors, but the Yassar had placed himself slightly beyond this firing range, just inside of the woods where he could monitor the chipmunks slipping through the roots of the great tree. It was their entrance into the world of the squirrels, and Krimpt took it as a good sign that no one had yet managed to block this easy-in route. Other chipmunks were taking the more dangerous approach of climbing the trees to meet with the archer squirrels, but this method was risky: the chipmunks weren't accustomed to the trees, and usually came off worse for wear. The Yassar wasn't bothered. They had numbers on their side.

At least, he was not bothered until he chanced to look back over the rise and the sounds of discordant screams hit his ears.

"What is that?" he asked Yassar Pelf as soon as he located the other Yassar, who was staring off grumpily into the distance, clutching a wound on his stomach.

"What?" Pelf snapped, breaking himself from his reverie. Krimpt hit him hard on the shoulder and pointed off towards the far end of their army.

"*That*," he said.

Pelf looked, not without reluctance. "It looks like ghosts," he said.

"I know that's what it *looks* like," Krimpt ground out, "But ghosts aren't real. What *is* it?"

"Ghosts," Vogt said, coming up behind them, and both Yassars spun to face him, jaws agape.

"That's just how they appear though, surely?" Krimpt said, staring at Vogt with his calm eyes and his cool façade, begging the leader to agree with him.

"One rule of war, Krimpt," Vogt said. "Take everything as it appears. It's safer that way."

CHAPTER XXI

Venul raced among bodies, pushing some aside and excusing himself when he could. The hallway was blocked in this part of the great tree, and he had no doubts in his mind as to whose work it was.

The young black squirrel had awakened in Gerien's room feeling woozy but unharmed. His body had wanted to sleep some more, but he hadn't let it; instead, the memories of where he had been, what he had done, and what he had seen had come flooding back to him and he'd realized the reason for Gerien's absence.

There had been noise outside the door, and Venul wondered how long he'd been asleep for, how long the dart had put him under. He hoped it wasn't too late for him to do something, to be instrumental in some way.

When he'd come rushing out, he'd run into a whole group of squirrels swarming up from down the barracks. They were pressed so close to one another in the hallway that Venul couldn't get out. In the end, he'd had to usher a group of them into Gerien's room.

"Out the window," he told them, assessing the situation correctly: somehow, the chipmunks had managed to get ahead of these squirrels and were blocking them at the end of the hall. "Take your chances outside, it's the only way."

A number of the squirrels took him up on his offer, while some of the more battle-hardened bodies remained, persistently pushing forward. They were making progress, but it was slow going.

"Out of the way, I'm sorry, but there's no time! Out of the way!" Venul panted, as he rushed for the end of the hall and the stairs. When the squirrels recognized him as one of Ritorren's advisors, he did not get much resistance from them, though some of them were in too much of a panic to pay him any mind either way. Venul lost his footing once on what turned out to be some unfortunate's body. Whether it was a squirrel or a chipmunk, he never found out, as the movement of the crowd was finally beginning to thrust him forward rather than hold him back. Venul broke into the front of the crowd and found Gerien standing there around the bend, two daggers in his paws lowered at his sides. Below him were the bodies of several chipmunks, the ones who must have been holding the hall.

"Gerien!" Venul shouted, because the clamor of the others was too loud for him to be heard plainly, "Where is Ritorren?"

"In his quarters!" Gerien shouted in answer. Venul nodded and started past him up the winding stairs. Gerien grabbed his arm as he went past.

"Venul, we need to help those outside. Everyone counts now that we have so few."

"Few?" Venul was momentarily distracted. The squirrels stuck in the hall were clambering over the bodies in front of them and through a side arch into the wider hall that would ultimately lead them up to the balcony where they could disperse.

"What happened down there? Was it as bad as I thought?"

"They had sleeping darts," Gerien said, "and they attacked us unaware. We lost at least thirty down there. So yes, it was bad." He looked apologetically at Venul, but when the black squirrel tried to go up the stairs, he stopped him again.

"Forget about Ritorren."

"Gerien, we're losing. I need to talk to him, or nothing will change."

"What sort of change do you think could stop this?"

Venul only stared up the stairs and down again at the last of the fighter squirrels trickling out of the hall.

"Our only hope is to press on."

Venul started up the stairs again suddenly, before Gerien could pull him back.

"If that's true, then at least we'll do it with a leader," he muttered, more to himself than anyone else, for Gerien had already left the hall.

~~~

One rotation of the clock later found Venul out on the balcony, leaning over the edge and staring at all the tiny little dots that he knew were actually chipmunks. As he looked, they all blended together into one watery masterpiece of—

He snapped out of it, standing up straight and wiping his eyes.

"There are a lot of them, aren't there?"

The voice had coincided exactly with his straightening up, and Venul resisted the urge to turn around. It was the squirrel behind him he ought to be mad at for how things had gone, the squirrel who had perhaps urged Ritorren into the decision he'd made.

"Those ghost things are taking a toll on them," Venul said, bottling his accusing words.

"It looks hopeful," Zirreo agreed.

"Where did they come from?" The number of chipmunks the wraiths had depleted did seem to be turning the fight around. He wondered where Gerien was, if his partner in useless advising had seen what was going on below.

"They're a gift for us from a friend who has come to see me," Zirreo said, as always leaving Venul feeling like he hadn't truly been answered. "See, there are some benefits of my being here." Venul could hear the slightest bit of bitterness in the white squirrel's voice.

"I thought I saw one of those worms you told Ritorren about, once," he said, but he broke off prematurely. Saying Ritorren's name made the squirrel behind him a villain once more.

"Why'd you give him warded chambers? He's never going to want to leave. He hasn't left, since you gave him that little gift." Venul turned to look at the white squirrel at last, his face a barely contained minefield of emotion.

"I wanted to give him something," Zirreo shrugged, apparently unperturbed by Venul's sudden hostility. "And has it ever occurred to you that Ritorren might be better off closed away up there than anywhere else?"

"We need a leader."

"You are a leader. You and Gerien."

Venul was shocked into stunned silence for a moment. "I was knocked out half the time," he reminded the white squirrel. Zirreo shrugged.

"I have faith in you."

Venul turned away so Zirreo couldn't see how absurdly the notion had touched him. The distrust due to his family history that he'd faced from several of the squirrels, not only the grays, but even the blacks from his own native Oakwood, had perhaps had a bigger toll on him than he'd realized.

"Ritorren has a plan for ending it," he told Zirreo at last. "Did you know about it?"

"No," Zirreo answered him, and this time Venul did turn to look at the white squirrel, surprised.

"It's not fair," he said.

"For whom?"

He looked out over the balcony at all the small, red-brown dots below.

"For them."

Zirreo was silent a moment. When he next spoke, his voice sounded further away, as though he were walking out of the picture even now.

"Do you owe them anything, truly?"

Venul only stared at the ground far below him and let the watery masterpiece unfold again before his eyes, watching the colors blend until nothing was for certain.

CHAPTER XXII

Zirreo walked away from the balcony as though he were walking in slow motion, his mind in so many different directions at once that later he would blame it for not alerting him to what should have been obvious as soon as he left the open air.

The hall was too quiet.

There was a door ajar to his right, and he pushed it back absentmindedly as he began his descent down the sloping hallway.

A moment later he stopped, suspicion finally sinking in. The floor before him suddenly seemed strange. Was it always truly sloping down? Because now it seemed that it was sloping...up.

He turned around slowly, resisting the signals in his brain that recognized before he did what was going on, telling him that turning around was the worst thing he could do.

There was a blank wall right behind him.

"Ah," Zirreo breathed. He had long ago learned how to keep the fear out of his voice. "You're good."

~~~

Mercurie watched the white squirrel turn to face her, working hard to keep her jubilance from registering so visibly on her own visage. She'd caught the white squirrel, and it had been easier than she'd expected! She watched him turn about in the false room she'd created, staring at the walls that boxed him in and squinting in the artificial lighting.

"I like to be the best at what I do," Mercurie said, accepting his compliment. She didn't care how genuine it had been; it *was* a good mirage, and she would take praise in any form. Much as she would have loved to toy with the white squirrel for a while before handing him over to Absoulim, she knew she did not have much time. The protective illusion of such a room would only last for a number of minutes, she guessed a half hour at the very most. She couldn't afford to take risks, not with her goal so close at hand. Mercurie wanted to look around behind her for Llewellyn, but she didn't want to take her eyes off of the white squirrel for even a second. She wouldn't let the easiness of his capture make her cocky.

"You've been very elusive for a very long time," Mercurie said, hoping to make the conversation light enough so that she could turn around at least for a moment to get to her bag. She could still feel its weight on her shoulder, so she knew it had made the room; sometimes things were left behind in such illusions. She couldn't hear Llewellyn though, and it concerned her.

"How does it feel to know you've finally been caught?" she asked Zirreo, looking him in the face and searching for any sign that he saw Llewellyn. The white squirrel's eyes were carefully blank.

"Again, you are very good, but I cannot see the point of this," Zirreo said, gesturing around at the room. "It's very nice, but we have never met. Unless..." The white squirrel stared beyond Mercurie now, and the sorceress knew the flyer had made the transition. "Unless you have a partner?"

"Llewellyn, come forward," Mercurie demanded. Behind her, someone shifted, and Llewellyn came into view beside her. The flyer's eyes were trained on Zirreo the whole time, and she hardly spared a glance for Mercurie. The black squirrel didn't like it; it showed an irrational absence of fear.

"She cannot talk?" Zirreo asked, turning to Mercurie at last. The black squirrel smiled.

"I can create my own rules here," she said. "Or do you not fully understand the basics of creating one of these rooms?"

Zirreo nodded, again looking less awed than she would have liked.

"There is more to it than that," Mercurie pressed on, becoming desperate for him to understand just how deeply she'd prepared for this moment. "Over the years I've been able to improve on this one. And since I've had more years than most squirrels will ever have," she gave him a meaningful look, "I've improved on this and other spells far more than even you might think possible. Of course, I've added my own inborn skills to the mix." She laughed.

Zirreo looked at her for a moment, then his eyes narrowed and she was gratified at last to see the lofty white squirrel betray some emotion.

"How much control do you have over her now?" he asked her. His gaze somewhat unnerved her, but she returned it steadily.

"Enough," she said.

~~~

As Kinder and Mariyen reached the main door to the great tree on the borderlands, the wraiths around them began to thin out. Some had gone to attack others, leaving he and Mariyen partially unguarded. They'd come to this realization when one of the chipmunks went for them, actually scratching Kinder with his dagger in his rush-attack, so ill-prepared were the two squirrels. Mariyen, luckily, had quicker reflexes and her paw was out in a flash.

The screaming sounds the chipmunk had been making when he or she had attacked them were now reduced to screams of pain, but not for long. Mariyen gave a twist of her dagger and then attempted to pull it out of her defeated enemy. It was harder than it looked, and she ended up pulling the chipmunk's body towards her along with the dagger. Its head lolled grotesquely and she jumped back, dropping the hilt of her dagger like it was a rotten acorn she'd already half-eaten. She stared at the ground where the chipmunk lay and shook her head. The air around them was becoming less frigid, and Kinder could feel the wraiths pass him on one side as they went about their business, running through the bodies of whoever came too close.

"We've got to make a dash for inside," he said; he couldn't see Engelwaithe anywhere. Mariyen was unresponsive; she stood staring down at the fallen chipmunk, oblivious to the movement all around her. Kinder grabbed her paw and pulled to get her going. They needed to get to where they were partially sheltered by the trees, because the promise of a wraith protecting them every time they faced danger could no longer be expected. Engelwaithe obviously believed that he had fulfilled his end of the deal by bringing them up to the trees, which was true enough, Kinder thought with an inward sigh. He'd never exactly specified that they needed to get them inside.

From here on out, things were going to get a lot harder.

"Take your dagger," he told Mariyen, still clasping her paw. She looked at him and suddenly he was reminded of what had happened between them only half a field and a hundred chipmunks away. His face began to feel slightly hot, and he became conscious of his paw on hers.

"I can't take it," Mariyen said, turning from him to look at the body of the chipmunk again. "I killed him, Kinder. I killed him. When my paw was there, on the hilt, I felt the life kind of...go out. I don't think I can do that again."

"You may have to," Kinder said, surprised at how firm he sounded. He didn't know what it was like to be in Mariyen's position, not exactly, and he was afraid himself that he might have to face it. But now there was movement in front of them; they'd already waited too long and they'd been found, only halfway into the protective woods.

"Hello there, squirrelys."

A strangely bean-shaped chipmunk with a whip coiled at his side and a gash across his stomach leered up at them. His eyes were painted with spiky yellow rings; it was anything but a welcoming sight. As they watched, frozen in place, another chipmunk appeared to materialize behind the first. This second chipmunk was larger and built more compactly; his fierce black eyes took them in exultingly. He too carried a whip at his side, a whip which his left paw was currently stroking.

"Who are they?" the second chipmunk asked the first, and the bean-shaped one turned on him.

"How am I supposed to know? They just got here, Krimpt."

"You haven't questioned them yet? They're squirrels, but they're not blacks or grays. Where do you suppose they're from, Pelf?"

The first squirrel, instead of diving on Mariyen and Kinder, turned on his partner again.

"If you'd been around when the last strange squirrels appeared, you would know this isn't the first time this has happened here."

"First strange squirrels? What do you mean by that?" the one called Krimpt asked, narrowing his black eyes.

"Well," Pelf said, not seeming to sense the danger in the other's tone, "there was a black squirrel, who I thought might be from here, except she was coming the other direction...all the way from behind us. So I thought we were being attacked from behind, like those ghost things did," he cast a nervous glance over to where the nearest 'ghost things' were. Kinder followed it and caught a glimpse of Engelwaithe, rising above the crowd for a moment. It seemed in that instant that the wraith's face had some expression to it, one he couldn't name at first, until he realized: contentment.

"Oh," the bean-shaped chipmunk said, so loudly and suddenly that Kinder jumped. "By the way, Rin is back."

"What?" The fierce-eyed chipmunk turned at the news, and for once his darting eyes did not rest on Mariyen and Kinder; his full attention was on Pelf, whom he grabbed by the shoulders.

"Do you have proof of that?" he roared. Pelf pulled away and gestured towards his wounded belly.

"All the proof you need," he said dryly.

Kinder took the opportunity to gesture to Mariyen that they ought to go. He had just seen a chipmunk disappear into a hole in the roots of the great tree behind them, and thought that if only he and Mariyen could make it to those roots, they would be saved from everything out here.

There was no such guarantee they'd be safe from whatever waited inside.

"Where are you going?" the one called Pelf cried when he noticed belatedly where the two squirrels were headed. "Come back—"

His words were cut off permanently by the arrow that found him in the neck. Apparently, Pelf had lined himself up perfectly for one of the archers above him to take him by surprise. The chipmunk, immediately dead, fell over into Krimpt, who jerked away from him. The sudden kill had distracted Kinder, for the tapping on his shoulder from Mariyen made him realize that he was no longer running. He turned to go and that was when he felt it. That slow murmur in the ground, the feel of the unspeakable coming to the surface, closer, closer.

"The ground is wrong," he told Mariyen's excitable tapping. She frowned, pulling away from him.

"Kinder, what do you mean? We've got to—"

"Just what I said, Mariyen. The ground is wrong! Quick!" With that, he tore off towards the roots he'd seen the chipmunks disappear into. By the pounding he heard behind him, he knew he was not alone; Yassar Krimpt had decided to follow them. The crack of a whip on the hard ground behind them informed them that he was not far behind either. The world shook in Kinder's vision, the ground impossibly jostling under his feet. The whip cracked again, closer.

That's got to make an impact, Kinder thought as he leaped for the roots.

An impact that can be heard underground. Or felt.

He clawed at the ground in front of the roots, getting back to his feet much too slowly, his thoughts instilling a fear in him that did not come from the whip alone. Kinder knew what was coming.

"It's too small," Mariyen said beside him, and he realized she was right. The hole before them was not made for any squirrel to get in...or out. In that instant, a paw reached out and clasped him on the shoulder from behind. He slipped out from under it before it had time to close on him.

"Up!" Kinder cried to Mariyen, who was digging at the edges of the hole. "We don't have time! We need to go *up*!"

"But there's no door—"

"Trust me!"

She must have sensed the urgency in his tone at last, for the speed with which she leaped for the trunk of the great tree was astounding. It was all Kinder could do to stay close behind her as they bolted up the trunk in flashing circles, the only way they knew to confuse whoever was pursuing them. The whip cracked once more, and then there came another sound.

I'm high enough, Kinder thought to himself nervously, *I'm high enough.*

He looked down.

The beast that reared itself slimily from the ground, all muscle and green-tinted pale, eyeless and menacing, was swinging its head from side to side, searching. The tentacle-like feelers that served as its eyes searched the air in mad flailing gestures and then stopped, stock still in a way that neither Kinder nor Mariyen had seen before. The creature only stopped moving for an instant though, and with a jolt, Kinder realized why.

It was locating its prey.

Yassar Krimpt stood directly in the shadow of the beast, swinging his whip from side to side in front of him. He was facing the thing, Kinder realized. The creatures belonged to the chipmunks after all. Perhaps he was telling it to—

But his thought was broken off by a hissing sound from below. The creature had made its decision. The whip cracked out once, futilely slipping off of the gorepede's body as it hit. It left no mark. The gorepede reared back and then came closing in, plantlike feelers searching, searching. Krimpt's whip fell from his nerveless paw as he realized too late that he was done. The feelers found Krimpt's face, trailed up to his eyes, and then, as if by some strange power of suction, seemed to latch on. Kinder could only imagine the blindness that the chipmunk down below was experiencing as he gave a strangled scream which soon fell silent. Kinder turned away at the last moment, unable to watch.

After a moment, Mariyen tapped him, pale-faced, and he turned to find the creature gone once more. Krimpt, or what was left of the once-intimidating chipmunk, was laying sprawled on the ground, looking as though he'd had everything sucked from him, an assessment which Kinder now knew was completely spot-on.

"I didn't need to see that," Mariyen said.

"At least we know the gorepedes aren't biased," Kinder offered.

Mariyen choked on what sounded suspiciously like a laugh, though Kinder supposed there was an equal chance that it was a sob.

CHAPTER XXIII

There was a lot that Llewellyn couldn't remember, spaces in her mind that had simply been blanked out. She could remember entering the great tree of the squirrels of the borderlands, could remember going up several sets of stairs and up one long, sloping hallway. This last memory, though it was the most recent, was also the most foggy. Beyond that, she couldn't remember a thing. They'd reached the beginning of that slanted hall, and she remembered, faintly, that Mercurie had begun to talk to her, begun to tell her that they were in a room, even though they were blatantly not. She'd opened her mouth to tell the sorceress so, and she found she couldn't talk. Then there had been a moment where she could have sworn all she remembered was standing alone at the end of the hallway. *It's my last chance to speak*, she'd thought, but she hadn't, and the rest seemed like sleep to her mind, as though she'd just awoke from an uneasy dream.

And then Zirreo was there, in front of her. When she'd first seen him, she'd been afraid she would say something stupid, that she would confess to some feeling she didn't feel or didn't want to admit to feeling. But she'd forgotten that she couldn't speak, and even as she remembered this, she couldn't remember why.

Zirreo was talking to Mercurie, and then Mercurie was talking to Zirreo, and she heard what they were saying only faintly; she had to really listen to understand their words, and really listening hurt her, so she collapsed into the blank realm her mind had become, only watching. Zirreo's face was the same, she thought. He hadn't really changed in all of the years since he'd come to Edgewood, and she liked that. She found that if she focused on that, on how young his movements were and how assured his jaw sat on his face, though his eyes were older and his tail thinner, her nameless anxiety drained out of her bit by bit. So she kept looking, and she kept hearing the dulled vibrations of his voice mixed in with those of Mercurie. Mercurie's voice was louder to her ears, and she knew it was because the black squirrel was closer, but it bothered her. She needed to concentrate on Zirreo, and she couldn't with Mercurie so close.

"Come here, Llewellyn," Mercurie said, and her voice was unmistakably loud and clear in Llewellyn's head now. It was so loud, in fact, that she wanted to clap her paws over her ears. Her vision became keener for an instant, and she gained control of her feet and began to walk up to where Mercurie wanted her. Though the black squirrel hadn't specified a spot, she knew when to stop. It seemed obvious to her. As soon as she stepped into Mercurie's sight, in front of the black squirrel so that she could no longer see Mercurie but Mercurie could see her, the world around her became fuzzy again, and when Mercurie next spoke, her voice was no longer so loud and grating. She began to slip back into her pleasant daze again, but just then Zirreo caught her eye, and she began to feel uneasy against her will, against Mercurie's will.

There was something she desperately needed to remember, and it was *what was wrong with this situation.* Zirreo's face told her as much, or perhaps it was Zirreo's mind that told her so.

We used to have a mind link, after all. A dream link, that is.

Did we? she asked herself, unable to keep the surprise out of her inner voice. All of her memories were obscured by the strange fuzziness she felt covering her like a particularly stifling blanket.

"Take this, Llewellyn," Mercurie said, and her voice was again deafening in the flyer's ears. Llewellyn turned to the black squirrel, and in that instant, in the passing of the object Mercurie held out to her, she understood. She knew.

She tried not to let it register on her face as she recovered the crystal ball, feeling its cool weight in her paws, but she pushed the fuzz back from the corners of her mind and found that she was able to keep it at bay. Perhaps holding the crystal ball itself was keeping her from being lost in the dark again, or perhaps it was the contact of Zirreo's bright eyes across the room, but suddenly she was able to think a lot clearer. She still couldn't speak and she still couldn't hear what Zirreo and Mercurie were saying unless she listened very close.

But she could *think*. Something in being handed her own crystal ball back had given her a sense of clarity that reached beyond whatever spell Mercurie had placed on her.

What is wrong with this situation? She asked herself again, and at the same time she felt Mercurie's eyes fall upon her. Mercurie seemed to be waiting for her to do something, but she didn't pay it any mind; she'd figured out what was missing.

Absoulim was still not here.

She looked down at the crystal ball in her paws. It seemed more than passing strange: Mercurie had denied her the crystal ball the whole time they were travelling together, refusing her the right to even hold it, but now she had given Llewellyn the crystal ball as though it were nothing.

As if she wanted her to have it.

Llewellyn stood in a pocket of the deepest silence her brain had ever created for her to think, and think she did, putting two and two together at last.

She understood. It was the oddest and yet most fitting thing; the most impossible, and yet it must be true.

Absoulim was not here because he did not need to be. In a way, he already was. All of Mercurie's questions about her power, all of her probing, began to make a dreadful sort of sense to Llewellyn.

Llewellyn stared into the crystal depths of the dewy globe and ordered herself to focus. She could see nothing but swimming clearness, as though the orb was translucent, though she knew it was not; unlike an ordinary bead of dew, she could not see Zirreo's shape through it, only endless water drained of its blueness and gently undulating, lulling her in.

The image of a face flashed out at Llewellyn, taking her unaware; she stepped back and nearly dropped the crystal ball, breathing hard. She had been right. He was in there. Somehow, Absoulim had become a part of the crystal ball, of *her* crystal ball.

She turned to find Mercurie staring at her. The black squirrel's eyes were open wide, giving her a crazed appearance. She still couldn't figure out what Mercurie had to do with all of this. If she was right about what the sorceress was trying to make her do, she didn't quite understand. What did Mercurie stand to gain from it? She knew the black squirrel had made some deal with Absoulim; perhaps Zirreo knew Mercurie and Mercurie was yet another of the many squirrels who Zirreo seemed to have collected as enemies. It was perfectly possible; there was so much Zirreo had never told her, after all, so much Zirreo never told anyone.

"Isn't there something you're supposed to be doing?" Mercurie asked her, and Llewellyn suddenly felt a viselike sensation close over her neck and head. She felt herself turn, saw the imagery quickly flash by until she was looking back into the dreaded depths of the crystal ball again. Mercurie had somehow regained enough of a hold on her that she could not look any other way, but she could still think, and it was thinking that would have to save her. Save them both.

Zirreo stood still at the end of the room, exactly where he had been from the very beginning. *He's afraid to move,* she realized, *because if he moves, who knows what will happen.* His eyes didn't leave her, though. She could feel that.

Llewellyn steeled herself, and took the only option she had left, the option Mercurie had saved for this moment alone.

She looked into her own crystal ball for the second time in her life, and for only the second time, she connected with her power. She felt it rise up to meet her like a pet that had waited all this time with surreal obedience, and pleasantly surprised by the encounter, she followed it where it led her, through her arms and pawtips and into the depths of the orb of dew before her.

Tell me what you would have me know, she whispered into the crystal ball.

At first, the blank, undulating depths did not react to her request, and then up rose a flare, of color or of light, in front of her eyes, and a scene began to play in her mind. Mariyen rose before her, the daughter she'd left at Edgewood, the daughter she'd abandoned all of her life. But Mariyen was not at Edgewood in this vision. She was standing on a hill backlit by the light of a dawn sky, a burning stick held aloft in one paw. Behind her there was another, but his face was hidden in her shadow.

Next she saw a chipmunk, poised in the air over some great height before falling, falling for the depth of forever into a bottomless white. And the sound of rain, from somewhere, falling all around.

The flash of light that had prompted her vision and the intensity with which she'd witnessed it, began to fade, and there was something else now, something working its way into the perfect emptiness, a twinge of horror, the blank sheet of her projected visions being prodded, torn. She remembered why she'd been afraid in the first place. Something was trying to get through, and the more she resisted it, the more she feared it, the bigger it grew.

Finally, she could resist no longer, and the new, negative presence sifted through the tear and into her consciousness. She could see it in the crystal ball, could hear it in her head. Its gaunt face swam into her vision, its mouth curling up in a sick smile.

Hello, Llewellyn, the face of Absoulim said, and she felt him latch onto her, his pale eyes boring into her own. Nothing could prepare her for what came next, for how Absoulim leaned forward, how Llewellyn felt as though she'd been flung out of her body, how he grasped her with his long-clawed, bony paws and pulled her close. She could feel him on her for real, a sensation so terrifying it could not be true. Then he was kissing her, if she could call it a kiss, for it was sucking the life from her.

No. Not the life. The power. All of the seer's power that Llewellyn had never learned to direct in her younger years back at Edgewood, all of that boundless, abnormally strong power that had once backfired on her and nearly killed her. All of that power was flowing out of her and into Absoulim, and she could not pull away.

She could not, and she didn't want to either. Llewellyn leaned forward suddenly and returned the kiss with fervor, feeling her heavy, burdensome power leave her for once and for all. She was free. She was—

Llewellyn.

It was a different voice now that spoke to her, and though at first she brushed it off, it only grew louder with patient insistence.

Llewellyn.

Absoulim's grip on her changed, as though he recognized and understood the implications of this other voice. She felt the vice grow heavier on her, drop further, but at that moment, she pulled herself back with more might than she thought possible.

No.

The writhing beast in her mind tried to fight her, tried to twist that word around, to invert it, but she recognized its writhing as simple terror and with one mighty push, she pulled herself away.

In that one second, she had control again, she was really and truly free. In that instant, Llewellyn parted her paws and let all she was holding go.

She did not hear the impact of the crystal ball hitting the floor, but she did hear Mercurie's scream and she felt Absoulim's fury in the moment before her paws lost contact with him for good. She looked up across the room, and her eyes, clear of all possession, locked with Zirreo's, but only for an instant, for at that moment, all of the power that had been sucked from her came back to her in one rushing impact. The world went quiet first, and then dark, and Llewellyn Edgewood knew no more.

~~~

Mariyen watched Kinder fumble about in the dark hallway in front of her. They'd come in through an open door, hanging on its hinges near the top of the great tree, and the scene before them was oddly deserted. The sounds of battle raged on around them, but they had become muted upon their entrance and now played merely as background music to whatever titleless play was unfolding around them.

"Something's wrong with this," she said, mainly to herself, but Kinder nodded at her words, banging into a table as he did so. Mariyen didn't understand why he was moving around so desperately unless it was the aftershock of the gorepede's appearance, in which case she could relate. However, she couldn't afford to be too sympathetic. If Kinder continued to bang around up here, whoever was still in the tree would hear them.

"Can you contact him now do you th—" Kinder began, but stopped abruptly. Mariyen stared at him, for he was now sitting on the floor a yard or so from her, digging under the table he'd bumped into seconds before.

"Kinder, what are you—"she began, but he held up the object he was examining, answering her question for her.

It was a firefly lantern, broken and empty, the insects within having made good on their escape.

"Someone's knocked this out on purpose," Kinder said.

"Come on, now," Mariyen replied, nervously. "It was probably you."

"No," Kinder said, his tone still one of grave seriousness. "It's cold. Someone else knocked it off. Someone was down here, someone who wanted to keep those who live here from escaping. They've already reached the upper levels. Do you think that means—

"No," Mariyen said, not in answer to his question as much as to shut him up. "The squirrels here are still around. Just because this lantern is out, it doesn't mean anything. So the chipmunks could have been up here, but that doesn't mean the squirrels are all..." she trailed off.

"Dead?" Kinder supplied.

She nodded, blowing on her paws to warm them. She felt as though the air around her had suddenly dropped several degrees.

Kinder looked her over and nodded once, slowly. Then he winked one eye and then the other, got up and spun in a circle, putting his back to the ravaged entrance and standing there, paws out, for a count of three. She could hear him mutter the numbers under his breath. When he turned around again, she tried not to look too amused.

"Luck?"

"We're going to need it."

Mariyen couldn't argue with that.

For a while, the two squirrels made their way down the hall without speaking, keeping close to one another for security and for support in the darkness. All the noise they seemed to be hearing was coming from outside, though once they rounded a bend and had to step over the bodies of several squirrels, both black and gray, who Mariyen guessed had fallen when trying to escape. She prayed as she made her way among them that their pursuers were far away now. The silence was dreadful; after the noise of outside, this tree seemed a place near deserted and the stillness of it made her stomach turn.

"Where is he?" Kinder dared to whisper once. "Could you use your link to him?"

"I don't really know how," Mariyen confessed, but at that moment they turned a corner and felt a fresh gust of breeze hit them. Both squirrels surveyed the rising passageway open before them, and the three figures sprawled out over the ground there. Only one of them appeared to be moving, and Mariyen's heart skipped a beat. She reached for her dagger and remembered she hadn't brought it with her; it seemed a foolish move now, for she was sure that the creature raising its head to look at them would be the attacker of the two lifeless forms before it. Kinder, too, was tensed for a fight, but nothing could have prepared them for what they saw when they got closer.

It was Zirreo.

Unmistakably so, too. The white squirrel's fur glowed even here in the dim passage, making him stand out so boldly that Mariyen wondered how she ever could have mistaken him for someone else.

There passed a moment of silence between the three squirrels, and then Kinder stepped forward.

"Zirreo!" he called, and made his way for the white squirrel.

Zirreo did not acknowledge his greeting, though he had clearly seen them, nor did he rise from his position on the floor. Something was wrong, Mariyen knew it instinctually, but it was too late to call Kinder back so she came after him, paw still resting firmly on her knife.

When she arrived beside her friend, she saw the prone forms of the other two squirrels on the ground more clearly, and froze.

One of them was a black squirrel, no one she knew, but her attention focused not on this squirrel, but the one that Zirreo was leaning over.

It was her mother.

Mariyen watched from a frozen bubble of horror cased in a slick layer of numbness as the white squirrel, staring down at Llewellyn the whole time, put a paw atop her chest and held it there for what seemed like eternity. Even after he should have pulled away, Zirreo kept his paw there, as though by doing so he could stave off the obvious truth.

Llewellyn was not breathing.

CHAPTER XXIV

Venul faced the crowd below the balcony now as he had an hour ago, the only difference being that an hour ago everything had been different. There was still a number of chipmunks milling about below them, Venul would have guessed a couple hundred, but they were leaderless and frantic looking, and what was more, they were surrounded by a group of squirrels, what remained of the army the borderlands had brought to the battle. What they'd done was horrible and needless and Venul could find no explanation in his heart for it, for all the squirrels and chipmunks that now lay dead and dying, strewn about a place that had never seen such violence; a place that had been built on peace and cooperation.

They had won, and Venul knew that he should be triumphant, or at the very least relieved to be alive. All he felt now was hollow and conflicted.

Ritorren, decked out fully in crown and robe, joined him at last, Gerien at his side. Venul was relieved to see the gray squirrel alive and well, and flashed him a smile, pushing down the dismal sinking in his gut. Ritorren cleared his throat, and in a collective gesture, the army below, along with the chipmunks, who followed accord for their own safety, raised their heads to look above them.

"Chipmunks," Ritorren began, "You have attacked us without cause. We offered to negotiate with you, and all you did was dishonor us by accusing us of doing things we have never done, committing crimes we have not committed. This is what I say to you: do you expect that, after all of that on your part, we are going to let you go free? Back to your holes in the ground? Back to a world undisturbed by our kind? No. You asked for the disturbance, and you cannot take it back. You are to remain aboveground on our terms."

The chipmunks below shifted about, but no one voiced any protest. No one made a sound. Ritorren looked about him, then, apparently satisfied with what he saw, continued.

"We will not kill anyone who asks for mercy," Ritorren said, and the expression on his face was so classic Ritorren that for a second, Venul forgot his worry and was transported to the days when he and the gray king had hung around shady copses and rivers as children. That image vanished with the king's next words, the ones Venul had been afraid to hear all along. The ones he'd hoped against hope itself that Ritorren would find it in him not to say.

"If you wish to remain alive, you will remain alive in servitude to us here at the borderlands. We have lost many and your addition to our ranks in honest service would go part of the way to making up for our losses. If, on the other paw, you would deceive us or run from us to go back to your tunnels, we will find you and we will kill you."

The weighty silence that came after this briefest of speeches was laden with tension. Venul's stomach was tied in knots over what he knew Ritorren wasn't saying, the unspoken words that felt like betrayal. Ritorren broke the silence to issue one more instruction.

"Though you will be in service to us here, should you choose to accept our offer, you will not be armed. Everyone who agrees to these terms, hand over your weapons. Anyone who disagrees, say I."

There was another breath of silence, and in that time, Venul never thought to look behind them, never even turned around until Gerien lurched forward beside him. Venul reached over to steady his friend, and in doing so noticed the tip of the arrow shining at him from where it poked out of Gerien's chest. It had gone clean through.

Gerien pushed Venul away and, in so doing, fell to the floor, the life leaving him almost as soon as he hit the ground. Venul turned, feeling fury pump through his veins, and saw the offender, standing very still behind them, in full view of he and Ritorren. She did not make any move to escape when both squirrels noticed her.

"I," Rin said, speaking clearly and deliberately into the silence.

~~~

She didn't understand it. All of the chipmunks below her seemed to have given up already, but Rin no longer cared for them. It was unclear to her whether she ever had. She had lived the last hour in a state of bliss, ripping through anyone who got in her way as she made her way to the top of this tree, and she would be damned if she stopped now. Strapped along her waist were an assortment of daggers she'd found interesting; the bow she'd shot the foolish gray squirrel with was her most recent acquisition. Rin nocked another arrow on her bow and went to fire, this time aiming for the black squirrel. She figured she would save the, cowering, crowned one for last.

The black squirrel dodged towards her suddenly, and the arrow she'd meant for him flew off course, over the balcony a few feet from where he'd been standing only moments before. Rin moved backwards as he came forwards, pulling out one of her daggers and trying to disentangle herself from her bow as she did so. Her heart beat faster as the adrenaline coursed through her body and she bared herself for the blade or the dart or whatever it was he would come for her with. She decided to give him one good shot; she welcomed it, standing in wait, but soon she realized that the black squirrel had a very different idea.

Before she could steady herself against him, Venul was bowling into her and she had nowhere to go but backwards. Rin scrabbled at the edge of the balcony, trying to maintain a good grip on the worn wood. The black squirrel caught up to her and slashed at her paws with his own claws, not bothering to use a weapon. Rin let go reflexively and fell.

Even as she fell she fought, twisting in the air even as it tore back her eyelids and forced tears from her eyes, trying, for the few seconds she was in the air, to position herself so that she would land on her feet once more. When she hit, it was different than she expected. She heard something loud and crunching in her ears and felt a certain amount of pain, though nowhere near as much, she thought, as she would have liked. For a last scene it was disappointing, and as Rin felt herself fading out, her mind became her own no longer. Scenery flashed behind her eyes, visions of a part of her life she'd lived so long ago she'd nearly forgotten. Somewhere in a well-lit room, someone held a book out to her, turning the page before her eyes, and she observed a picture of a tree, its branches fanning out over a body of water, and of leaves falling, ever so constantly, so real that she could reach out and touch them. And then she heard a voice, achingly familiar, deep and calming, talking to her steadily, fondly.

"It's your turn to turn the page, Rain," the voice said. She hadn't allowed herself to remember the sound of that voice for years. "The next page is about your namesake, Rain. The water from the sky. Someday I will show you." Even as the voice spoke, it faded into nothing, and Rin felt something soft and wet fall onto her fur.

"I feel it," she said, and she went to turn the page.

~ ~ ~

Venul couldn't stop staring down at the body of Gerien, though he knew no amount of staring was going to make his friend suddenly better, make him come back alive and talk again, help Venul temper his decisions in a warm dose of reason.

He was on his own. Feeling the tears begin to prick his eyes for not the first time that day, Venul felt Ritorren's gaze on him. For once, the king wasn't focused on the crowd of captured chipmunks below, even when, as Venul listened, the sound of several knives, daggers, and bows hit the ground with a finality that made him weak. Ritorren held his gaze, his face showing the first real compassion Venul remembered since they were young. He tried to hold the gaze, but it made him nearly break down and he looked away. When he looked back, Ritorren had turned away.

"I'm glad you all seem to have made the right decision," Ritorren told the chipmunks below them, and the dread at what was coming filled Venul once more, keeping him from his grief and from any peace he might still have salvaged.

Ritorren turned back to Venul. "Get the burning party ready," he said. Down below, the sounds of their comrades leading the chipmunks toward the great tree resounded in his head.

"No," he said.

Ritorren blinked at him. "Come on, Venul. I know you're upset by Gerien's death, but—"

"Don't bring him into this," Venul snapped. Ritorren shut up for once, and Venul could hardly believe it. He spoke quickly, punctuating each word with a gravity that he knew the king could not escape.

"You know I disagreed with you on this before any of this ever happened. Nothing has changed. They aren't all like that one."

He meant the chipmunk who shot Gerien, and Ritorren seemed to understand.

"Accidents happen," the king said coolly. "And the chipmunks themselves aren't the only problem. Would you like to explain to me how you would deal with their giant worm creatures? We must kill off any chance that anything still lives down there, for our own safety and sanity. If you have a better idea, why don't you voice it?"

Venul was surprised at the venom in Ritorren's voice, even now, after years of disagreements.

"It's just not something I can get behind," he said calmly, and turned to go. Where he would go, he wasn't certain, but it was not going to be to find a burning party. Ritorren could do that himself, as Venul didn't doubt he would.

"Stop," Ritorren said, but Venul did not. The next time the young king spoke, there was unmistakable desperation in his voice. "Stop. For crying out loud, Venul, it's a bunch of chipmunks. *They* attacked *us*, if you don't remember."

Venul turned back to Ritorren, and couldn't find any of his friend in what he saw. Where was the squirrel he'd played near shaded brooks with as a child? He couldn't remember; he must have misplaced him. He found his lack of caring to be his new strong suit, and he donned it against his former friend without fear.

"What are you going to do to me if I don't listen to you?" he asked, genuinely curious now. By the sound of it, the warrior squirrels had all entered the great tree now and it wouldn't be long now until some of them came up to meet Ritorren for further instructions, but Venul felt like he had all the time in the world. He waited on Ritorren's answer with a persistence that he could see was, second by second, getting on the gray squirrel's nerves.

"I have been very patient up until now," Ritorren said, and Venul snorted. He couldn't help it. Ritorren's eyes flitted over him, and this time there was no warmth left in them.

"If you disagree with me at this point, Venul," he said calmly, tight-lipped and glaring, "you can leave. Go all the way back home to Oakwood, I don't care. Start a new kingdom, I dare you. You'll find it's not as easy as you seem to think it is when you lecture *me*."

Venul sensed Ritorren's insecurity as the base of all he said, and wondered how he hadn't seen it all along. It was the cause for everything, of course, and if he could only break past that barrier...

But he wouldn't. Venul's mouth began to move before he could really think anything through, and the words that came spilling from his mouth were irrevocable.

"Maybe I will start my own kingdom," he said, and he was surprised but for once not a bit ashamed of his courage. "There are those who would join me."

"Are there?" Ritorren looked at Venul and his look this time was a challenge.

"You no longer recognize me," he observed.

"Should I?" Ritorren spat.

Venul only shrugged. "I'll be gone by morning," he said. His anger was gone, and in its place he only felt sad and tired.

"Venul," Ritorren said, catching him by surprise. He turned, feeling a faint surge of hope in his breast, but the king's face was stony and unforgiving.

"If you leave right now," Ritorren said, "You will be exiled. Whether others choose to go with you or not is beside the point. *You* will never be able to come back."

Venul stared at him, astounded, and then turned on his heel and left.

"The choice is made then," Ritorren whispered to the empty air, just before the crowd of squirrels he'd previously labeled as his burning party turned the corner.

"Ah, my friends," he said, a little too enthusiastically. "I'm glad you've come. Down to business, as always."

~~~

Kinder and Mariyen heard the ruckus outside, but neither of them deigned to move, even as several squirrels passed them in the sloping hallway they squatted in, several at a time.

"It's over, I think," Kinder said once, awkwardly, and then subsided into quiet when he realized that the other two squirrels occupying the hall with him weren't up for any talking. He felt awkward and overlarge, as he had most of his life, and no matter how he tried to scrunch up in his mind, he couldn't curl away from the weight of sadness that surrounded them.

"I'm sorry," he said to Mariyen, not knowing why he said it, knowing that he should *shut up* if he knew what was good for him.

Mariyen smiled at him, though, and it blew him away. He hadn't expected this. He smiled back uncertainly, and she took his paw and stood up.

"Zirreo," she began, staring down at the white squirrel, who was still kneeling over Llewellyn. "What is it that you've been doing?"

Zirreo looked up at them, and Kinder had never seen anyone look more tired.

"I can't tell you now," he said, "Now is not the time."

"Then when?" Mariyen demanded. "She was my mother. If I can talk, so can you. You didn't truly love her, after all."

There followed a silence as thick as ice and Kinder thought Mariyen had surely gone too far, but at long last, the white squirrel actually smiled.

"What do you want to know?" he asked. Though he looked up at them, ready for questions, he remained hunkered low to the floor, on level with Llewellyn's prone form, and Mariyen took a while before she puckered up the courage to speak again. When she did, her tone was softer.

"Sorry."

"Don't be," Zirreo said, still kneeling and looking up at them. "You are right, perhaps I did not. How would I know?"

The two squirrels looked askance at each other, but Zirreo, unperturbed, continued to stare at them.

"What do you want to ask me?"

"Who are you?" Kinder finally said, getting over the shock, the strangeness of the situation as best he could.

Zirreo rocked back on his heels and studied them. A patrol of squirrels about a mile long chose that moment to file past them. Kinder tried to smile at them to indicate that everything was normal, but Mariyen punched him hard and he desisted.

"I am," Zirreo said, speaking only once the crowd had passed. "The messenger of Astrippa."

There was a pause in which Kinder merely stared at him, and then at Mariyen. The look on her face was equally stricken.

He'd known. Of course he'd known. As far back as Edgewood, he could remember the rumors about Zirreo, and the stories Mariyen had told him of the prophecy her mother had once given. Even before that, he'd sat with Lute in the rotting tree Absoulim called home as the seer explained who Zirreo was and how they should attempt to find him. He'd never thought he'd have it confirmed, but now here Zirreo was sitting in front of them, vulnerable, as though the admission had taken something out of him.

"What else?" Kinder said, feeling like he was drunk on some very strong dew. Zirreo turned to him, and he didn't know whether he would be rebuked or answered, but the white squirrel only smiled.

"I have hidden much over the years, from all of the squirrels I have ever known. I know by talking to the both of you it won't make much of a difference, but I need to be honest. As honest as I can be. As honest as you have been with me." He looked at Mariyen as he said this last statement, and Mariyen colored.

"I didn't mean—"she began, but Zirreo cut her off.

"No, you did," he said, "and I accept it. I was originally sent here as a messenger of Astrippa. I can't tell you much about that, I can't get into detail. I'm not sure if I even *could*, if you know what I mean."

Kinder nodded even though he wasn't sure he did know.

"I came here with a purpose, though. I didn't go along with that purpose, and, as Absoulim no doubt told Kinder, I ignored that purpose and I went a little wild. I wasn't prepared for the wonder of being mortal, you know?" He paused and rubbed his eyes. "Rot it all, I wish I had some pipe reed. You know, I don't remember what it was like to be immortal. All I know is that I have this running fear of ever being so again. Here, the place you are, you are very...free. You may not see it, but I do."

Zirreo looked around at them, and must have observed their lack of understanding, because he chuckled embarrassedly.

"Don't worry. All I mean to say is that you are very lucky, even if you don't feel it now. I was made with a purpose, and that is all there is to me. Even if once, I liked to believe there could be more. Curse Astrippa, really."

He muttered this last so softly that Kinder thought he must have misheard the shocking blasphemy. But when Zirreo continued, his face was set.

"I didn't complete my purpose. I wasn't on track. I am on track now. I promise. That is really all you can and should know."

"What happened *here*?" Mariyen asked, and from her tone Kinder could tell she'd been waiting for more than a while to ask this particular question.

"Here," Zirreo said, following her lead and then pausing for an inordinate amount of time. The troupe of squirrels that had passed them moments earlier went past them again, talking and laughing amongst themselves. He waited for them to file by again.

"Llewellyn came to me accompanied by a sorceress. A black squirrel who, incidentally, is related to one of the top squirrels here. This sorceress asked me at first what I know you both must have wondered as well. Where is the child?"

Mariyen flinched back and Kinder nearly did the same. It was one of the questions he'd been waiting to ask, but with Zirreo's track record, he never expected that the white squirrel would answer it of his own volition.

A moment later, he was almost relieved when Zirreo dodged the question, answering it without really doing so.

"I did not have our child with me, any of the time I was travelling." He paused, staring at a point beyond Mariyen or Kinder.

"Why did she think you had the child, then?" Mariyen asked critically.

Zirreo shrugged. "Because she found Llewellyn and Llewellyn didn't?" he asked. "There is a missing piece of this that even I don't have. I believe it died with Llewellyn. There was another third party involved in this, someone who wanted me dead, and—

"Absoulim?" Mariyen asked. Kinder thought about it; it made perfect sense.

"Yes," Zirreo said after a moment. "That might fit. But Absoulim—

"Didn't die back there," Mariyen finished, in full flow now. "I tried to tell you, through the dream link. He somehow survived and escaped Edgewood. I've no idea how he managed it, but he could have been involved with my mother and this sorceress, I suppose. Unless anyone else...?"

"Hated me?" Zirreo laughed. "Unfortunately, yes. But what you say makes sense. Absoulim positively lusted for my secrets...he asked me for them once, long ago, you know, when I was at Edgewood. I did try to explain to him that I couldn't give him what he wanted, but he took it very badly. He already hated me, you see; where Llewellyn was concerned he was always...well, let's just say I think your suggestion has merit. He wanted power for all the wrong reasons. I felt sorry for him, a bit. I think he knew it and that only made him hate me more."

Zirreo peered at them for a second under his brows and then said, "I'll tell you a secret too. He'd never have believed it, but I never really had what he was looking for."

"Why then," Mariyen asked, "did you have to come here?"

"It is part of my plan to do so. Or rather," he said, smiling wryly, with a bitterness that did not sit well on his normally serene face, "I am here because it is my purpose to be so. I am back on track and we will see in time what unfolds."

It was rather unsatisfying as an answer. Both Mariyen and Kinder knew it, but neither of them wanted to be the one to tell Zirreo so, and the white squirrel was getting up at last. His paw fell from Llewellyn's chest, and he seemed to make an effort not to look at her the whole time he rose from where he crouched. Once he was up, he turned away from them.

"I must do what I came here to do," he said, "and then I will go. I suggest that you two do the same."

Kinder opened his mouth to protest, but found he didn't know what to say. All the questions he'd wanted to ask Zirreo had been answered, however unsatisfactorily, and there was nothing to do really, other than walk home.

He wouldn't do it, though.

"Come with us," he said to Zirreo, "I'm sure you can achieve your purpose that way as well."

"I prefer to work alone," Zirreo said to him, and something in the white squirrel's tone was suddenly unkind. Kinder could tell that the conversation was over and they had overstayed their welcome; all that was left for he and Mariyen to do was to walk out politely.

Kinder turned, but Mariyen remained facing Zirreo. There was anger in the set of her jaw and the tilt of her ears.

"We've journeyed all this way, risked all we have to find you, despite your wishes—"

"I always intended you to find me," Zirreo said, but Mariyen shook it off and continued doggedly.

"Whether you meant us to find you or not, we have, and I at least deserve an answer to the question of my mother. What happened to her?"

Zirreo was quiet a moment, as though collecting his thoughts, and for a while, Kinder thought he might just turn as he'd been about to do and leave them there, but in the end he merely sighed.

"Your mother appears to have been used by Absoulim. He seems to have had the help of the sorceress Mercurie in being bound to the crystal ball that was meant for your mother in her potential career as a seer. She was never attributed the crystal ball and her power was destructive because she never learned to channel it. Absoulim, bound to the crystal ball, was able to take Llewellyn's power and channel it towards whatever he wished. Rather predictably, he chose to channel her power towards me, and in doing so, he would have killed me, and then Mercurie could have proceeded to unbind him from the ball, freeing both of them at once. I don't know what Mercurie thought she'd get out of it—she's no old enemy of mine— but I doubt Absoulim planned on keeping whatever promise he must have made her. In any case, their plan almost succeeded, but Llewellyn—your mother," he nodded to Mariyen, "resisted at the last possible moment, when I wouldn't have believed she could. She died a hero, Mariyen."

Mariyen stared at the white squirrel for a moment, at his earnest pink-tinged eyes and his set mouth, and she began to cry.

It was the beginning of many things Kinder had never seen.

CHAPTER XXV

When the two young squirrels had gone and only then, could Zirreo breathe again. Eventually, he left the place he'd occupied by the body of Llewellyn, accepting at last that it was only a body and would never speak to him again, would perhaps never have done so anyway, in the way that he wanted, that he so selfishly needed.

Zirreo pocketed himself away for the next day, for more than a day, even when Venul came by for the last time.

He knew Venul was leaving. He knew why, too, and he approved. Venul couldn't accept the burning of the chipmunks' prior home, he could not compute the idea of so utterly robbing another kind's pride. Zirreo envied that kind of drive, an idealism he'd lost himself long ago. Ritorren would treat the chipmunks all right, he did not doubt it. He was not a bad squirrel, if overly pompous, and Zirreo couldn't afford to be too worried for the chipmunks now. They had seemed so fierce to him, so ready for anything. Was any creature's slavery forever? He hoped there was some positive answer to that question, but for now he let it drop. It wasn't his business.

Venul, however... there had been something in the young black squirrel's eyes when he'd left, south for Firwood. A strange place to start a new life, especially for a black squirrel. Zirreo had the oddest feeling then that he wasn't seeing Venul for the last time; it was not an unpleasant sensation. He expected their paths would cross again in due time, but for now he felt there was some waiting he had to do. His mission, as he'd told Mariyen and Kinder, was now underway, but the thing he'd never told either one of them was that he himself wasn't so sure what it would entail.

How embarrassing it was, he thought. He'd been running so long that he'd forgotten exactly what it was he'd been running from.

Zirreo pulled the package he'd carried with him all the way from his home in the Aspen Forest out from under the bed they'd given him here at the borderlands. Taking the thing into his arms, he cradled it, judging its worth. From any viewer's perspective, it would appear just a plain leather-bound something, curiously round but otherwise simple and uninteresting. Zirreo smiled as he untied the simple packaging.

A glint of gold sparkled up at him as soon as he completed the movement. Zirreo remained staring at the shining facsimile of a chestnut, wishing he could share it with someone and knowing he could not. The time would come, perhaps, but not now. It had been hard to keep such a treasure, so rare and so beautiful, from the eyes and paws of others along his way, but he had; it was the one thing he'd managed to stay true to all this time. After long seasons of running, Zirreo was ready to be what he needed to be. He only hoped it was not too late.

Someone will come, or something, he thought, staring out of the window to his guest room, at the lightly sprinkling rain and the bright dawn light, just now breaking through the cold winter sky.

Someone will come or something will happen, and I will know what to do. Until then, there is only waiting.

Waiting, the white squirrel thought, as he stared out the window at the peaceful dawn, might not be so bad after all.

EPILOGUE

"Where do we go next?" Kinder asked, dropping the still-warm stick he carried to the ground and turning to Mariyen.

The flying squirrel's sable fur ruffled slightly in the breeze coming in from the hills to the north of them. She shrugged, giving him a look that said, *relax.* He knew. He knew and he tried. Every day now, he'd been trying to cancel any routines, any superstitious patterns, from his day. It was easier said than done, though.

Kinder tossed the second of his sticks, unused, to the ground and faced Mariyen, who was staring into the distance, chewing something that sounded suspiciously like the raspberry tarts she'd warned him away from earlier.

"What are you thinking?" he asked, squatting down beside her and shivering in the cold of another morning's early dawn.

"Oh," Mariyen sighed after a time. "I don't know. How much longer do you think we'll have to do this?"

By 'this', Kinder knew that she meant finding the holes, the many holes spread over the countryside for which they fastidiously lit matches and let them drop, down to a world they would never see. Kinder sighed. The days previous had left him with many questions, all in the vague form of a tugging in his chest. A tugging for more. What was magic when you didn't know from whence it came? Who was the goddess you named and then blundered for in the dark?

He didn't know the answer to anything lately, but he didn't much mind because for the countless days since they'd left the borderlands, he hadn't felt once that the earth was unsafe to walk upon. Being able to place one foot before the other without the fear that at any moment he could be eaten up was so pleasant that Kinder had vowed his hardest never to take it for granted again. When he had gone to share his thoughts with Mariyen, she'd only surprise kissed him and run away. She liked to do that a lot lately. Kinder thought it unfair because he was never ready for it, and each time, he turned red as a late-blooming poppy over it.

"I think," he said, in answer to Mariyen's question, "that we don't need to do this for any longer than we want to. We've travelled far enough from the borderlands that they'll never find out if we quit. There are plenty others doing the job, too, so I don't see the point of you and I sticking around after all."

Mariyen gave him the look she typically gave when she was trying very hard not to laugh.

"That sounds like a deal," she said, "but we're both so far from home. Whatever shall we do afterwards? Is there some sort of superstitious formula you've got to carry us through?"

Kinder pretended to think about it, staring off into the sunrise and rubbing his chin.

"I think," he said finally, turning on her and watching the anticipation slowly come to life in her eyes, "that we'll just make it up as we go."

Before she could do or say a thing, he had kissed her, and faster than she could say "unfair", he was off across the field before them, running into the new day.

Mariyen held her breath, then opened her mouth and let out a surprised squeak meant to be indignant, when all she really meant was, *At last.*

Then she gave chase.

www.ingramcontent.com/pod-product-compliance
Lightning Source LLC
Chambersburg PA
CBHW071052250626
47159CB00002B/455